Revelle

Revelle

Lyssa Mia Smith

BALZER + BRAY
An Imprint of HarperCollins*Publishers*

Balzer + Bray is an imprint of HarperCollins Publishers.

Revelle
Text copyright © 2023 by Lyssa Mia Smith
Broadside and hand lettering copyright © 2023 by Nina Hunter

Library of Congress Control Number: 2022940804
ISBN 978-0-06-323926-5

Typography by Chris Kwon
22 23 24 25 26 LBC 5 4 3 2 1
First Edition

For my cousins:
A million books couldn't capture the magic of growing up with you.

Sponsored by
DEWEY CHRONOS:

PER PASSENGER
10 C

Charmant's Favorite
TIME TRAVELER

CHARMANT

— IS ONLY —

A FERRY RIDE AWAY

GIVE A

FOR A CHANCE
★ ★ ★

TO FEEL ECSTASY
★ ★ ★

REVELLE A JEWEL

*L*ET AN *Effigen* COCKTAIL CARRY YOU AWAY

*H*EAR THE *Truth* FROM AN EDWARDIAN *Mind* READER

*F*IND AN *Elusive Strattori Healer* TO REMOVE YOUR PAIN*

*INJURIES MUST BE TRANSFERRED TO A WILLING VOLUNTEER

 ONE

LUXE REVELLE

It was our first show of the summer, and if fate had its way, it might also be our last.

The energy in the theater crackled with anticipation. While Nana stacked the champagne flutes into our signature *R*, I held the back of her chair, suppressing a smile as she grumbled about her decades of tightrope walking without a spotter. My uncles cast bemused glances our way as they swept windblown sand between the floorboards, the scratching of their brooms drowned out by giggles from the mezzanine, where the littlest Revelles huddled, plucking cockroaches from the torn velvet upholstery. A few years and a lifetime ago, that had been my job.

Nana positioned the final glass and stood taller on the chair, pride shining in her topaz eyes as she scanned the pit. After a bit of booze, and plenty of magic, the tourists might mistake the Big Tent for a classy establishment.

With a *pop*, I uncorked the champagne and handed it to Nana, but instead of shimmering gold, a clear, dull liquid dribbled out.

Watered down. Again.

She took a swig and grimaced. "This tastes like piss."

"How do you know what piss tastes like?"

Her eyes narrowed. "Don't sass me, child. Is this the last of it?"

"I'm sure there's more somewhere," I lied. As if Uncle Wolffe hadn't spent all winter trying to scrape together enough liquor to get us through opening night.

In a rare concession, Nana allowed me to help her off the chair. Although time had curved her shoulders, she still moved with the grace of a woman who'd spent years in the spotlight. A grace I should have inherited but didn't, along with the cleavage she flaunted in her skintight crimson sequined gown.

"Let's make it a cider fountain," I suggested, leading her away. "The tourists will be too drunk to notice the difference."

"Cider in our *champagne* fountain? We're Revelles! We can't be as dry as a nun's—"

"Easy, Nana." Fixing my smile, I stole a glance at the others. "Uncle Wolffe and I have a plan."

More like a Hail Mary.

I started to turn away, but she grabbed my wrist, her voluminous bracelets cool against my skin. "Wolffe told me all about this plan of yours. Your magic may be strong, Luxe, but even you can't charm a bloody Chronos. There's no way he'll give you a jewel."

True. The Chronos family raised their young on tall tales of my family's magic. Give a Revelle a jewel, and they'll charm you into drowning yourself in the Atlantic. Give a Revelle a jewel, and they'll shred your mind and keep your body as their own. Dewey Chronos would have to be a fool to give me the very thing I needed to manipulate his emotions.

Good thing I had a source of magic other than jewels. Not that Nana knew.

I squeezed her hand and checked my lipstick in the mirrored wall beyond the bar. Bloodred. Perfect.

With my head high, I crossed the theater, narrowly missing a burst of fire. My flame-throwing cousins snickered, and I flashed them a faux glare.

The familiar scent of buttered popcorn greeted me backstage. I maneuvered through a rowdy game of tag, averting my eyes from the tigers' vacant cages. When our pantries had emptied this past winter, it was either eat them or sell them, and Nana had refused to serve her pets for supper.

Stepping between the costumes strewn across the worn wooden floor, I nearly knocked into my aunts wrestling themselves into their cancan dresses. Layers of colorful tulle pooled at their ankles as they paused to watch me pass. "Are you joining us in the Fun House tonight for once?" Aunt Caroline teased.

Always the same joke about the Fun House, the private rooms behind the Big Tent where customers went after the show. I flashed the haughty smile they'd come to expect. "The star shouldn't get her hands dirty."

"You're supposed to use your magic, not your hands, silly." She leaned closer, her breath sharp with the champagne they must've pilfered from our last case. "Is that what you're afraid of?"

Like the rest of my family, when I was given a jewel, I could charm the gem's giver into believing their fantasies were coming true. No desire was off-limits in the Fun House: bloody revenge on a rival, an intimate meal with a beloved celebrity, or the tourists' favorite, bedroom delusions of grandeur. As long as they paid us in jewels, the customers' emotions were ours to bend as we pleased. We didn't even need to touch them. The fantasies were as fake as the enormous diamonds dangling from Nana's ears, but the customers didn't mind as long as they enjoyed themselves.

"I'm not afraid of the Fun House," I assured my aunt. "I just need my beauty sleep after the show."

Aunt Caroline's grin widened as I patted her cheek and walked away.

"You have to join us before too long!" she called after me. "The customers don't like 'em wrinkly!"

"And yet you do just fine!"

Uncle Wolffe peered up from his paperwork as I closed his office door, muting my aunts' laughter. Little streaks of silver wove their way through his slicked-back dark hair, and I thought of my mother, his sister, frozen in time. Forever black-haired and twenty-nine.

"What's wrong?"

My mask of calm must have faltered. Uncle Wolffe and I worked together, uncle and niece, showrunner and star, but we didn't lean on each other. Uncle Wolffe leaned on no one, as far as I could tell.

I sank into an armchair. "We're out of champagne. Whiskey's low, too."

"Already?" He grabbed a worn notebook and flipped through the pages. "I thought we hid some backstage."

"Your thirsty siblings found it." Champagne on opening night was tradition, one Uncle Wolffe didn't have the heart to forbid. He never liked the rest of the family to worry. "Did you invite the bootlegger?"

His outlandish clown smile tightened to an eerie red line. More than once, I'd seen grown men tremble at the sight of Uncle Wolffe in full makeup. "I don't like this plan of yours."

"Do you have a better idea?"

"No," he admitted. "If we don't secure a liquor contract tonight, then tomorrow, we'll either open bone-dry or not at all."

Stunned, I sat back in the rickety chair. When hurricanes pounded our illustrious island, he'd kept our doors open. When puritanical protesters took the ferry from New York to picket us in droves, he'd kept our doors open. When the best among us drowned, and the Big Tent had been shrouded by grief so dark that my vain grandmother didn't change out of her nightgown for months . . . Uncle Wolffe had kept our doors open.

But now my fierce uncle was afraid. Of Prohibition.

I'd imagined the new law to be a distant problem for main-landers, not for our little isle of Charmant. Yet here it was.

"So, tonight." The words squeezed past the knot in my throat. I lifted my head higher, lest he think me nervous.

Uncle Wolffe shook his head. "You're too young for such responsibility. You're still a child—"

"I'm eighteen. Most mainland girls are popping out their second baby by now."

"Your mother wouldn't have wanted you to debut with a bloody Chronos." His dark eyes flitted to the framed photograph on his desk: Nana's eight children in full showtime regalia. All of them laughing, as always. That had been the soundtrack to my childhood: belly laughs and clinking glasses and the *rat-a-tat-tat* of the Revelle drums.

And then grief. Nana's sobs so raw, they hardly sounded human. A hole in our family so wide, we couldn't fathom a way forward. But the Revelle show went on. It always did.

I rose from my chair. "My mother wouldn't want us homeless,

either. Don't make this into a big deal, Uncle Wolffe. We both know my plan's a good one. Is he coming or not?"

Nana claimed we Revelles had giants' blood that made itself known every few generations. As Uncle Wolffe stood, towering a good two feet over me, it was easy to believe her. "The kid bootlegger's on his way. I'll seat him in the executive suite and serve him what remains of our best brandy, not the watered-down junk in the pit."

"Can't have him thinking we're desperate," I added drily. As if we could obtain alcohol from anyone but him. The bloody battle over Charmant's liquor industry had been fought, and the island's youngest bootlegger was the last one standing. The last one *alive*, if the rumors were true. "Nana said he bought that old warehouse by the docks."

A tight nod. "My sources say he's turning it into a theater. A big one."

Like he could find an act to compete with ours. "How will I know it's him?"

As the mayor's oldest son, Dewey Chronos had been in the public eye when we were children, but for the past few years, he was rarely seen outside his harborside mansion. Perhaps he'd grown even sicklier than he'd been as a pallid little boy clinging to his mother's skirts. Or perhaps he, too, had secrets he wished to keep from the mind readers.

"White boy," Uncle Wolffe grumbled. "Dark hair, brown eyes."

I gave him a look. He'd just described the majority of our audience.

"He wears his company's emblem on the lapel of his suit jacket. It's a—"

"Diamond-shaped clock," I finished. As if I could forget the black symbol cropping up all over the Night District, a taunting reminder of the Chronoses' familial power: time travel.

We might be the heart and soul of Charmant's tourism, but the Chronoses were the landlords and politicians. They ruled over our small island, and they kept it that way by turning back the clocks to sabotage the other magical families, especially mine. We Revelles were allowed to exist, to entice the tourists to flock to our shores, but the Chronoses were wary of our ability to influence voters' minds. If we dared inch too far above poverty, tragedy always seemed to strike. Like the time my great-grandfather attempted to open a much-anticipated family-friendly show, but met his bloody end in a supposed robbery gone wrong before opening night. Or three years ago, when the Chronoses failed to tell us a massive hurricane was barreling toward Charmant, though they evacuated in secret. We lost four of our own in that storm.

Just thinking of cozying up to one of those time-traveling goons made my stomach twist something awful. And I needed to convince him to do business with us. For cheap.

Uncle Wolffe nodded toward the door. "Go tell the others you're joining them in the Fun House. I'm sure Colette and Millie will be glad."

Doubtful. A few years ago, they would have been thrilled, but these days, we hardly spoke to each other outside rehearsals.

"Having second thoughts?" His booming voice remained casual, but concern flickered in his dark eyes.

I flashed him my most confident stage smile. "By tomorrow, we'll be swimming in the world's finest booze."

"At a steeply discounted price, I hope," he muttered. "With how much he's charging the hoteliers, the whole island is going to be either indebted to him or out of business soon."

"Not us."

"Never us." He turned to his paperwork, my cue to leave.

Careful to keep my head high and my smile self-assured, I returned backstage.

"Looking for your cousins?" Nana, seemingly recovered from her bout with the champagne, stood in front of the rusty backstage mirror draping strings of faux jewels around her neck. "I saw Colette and Millie climbing the rafters with those boys from the lighting crew."

Millie loved to flirt with the few non-Revelles she could find in the Big Tent. Colette, however, was more likely to challenge them to a wrestling match, then plant a knee in their most sensitive places to ensure victory.

"It's almost showtime." I glanced around the backstage mess. "Is everything ready?"

"You should be canoodling in the rafters, too! A pretty girl like you should have plenty of beaux."

I rolled my eyes. "You were the star once. You know they only want to boast to their friends about what's underneath this leotard."

She winked. "That's half the fun. Now go. Find your cousins."

As if they wanted an intruder. Instead, I did a final sweep of the theater. Someone had already lit the candles, their long shadows hiding the cobwebs. With their soft luminance, the thick purple and black stripes of the outer canvas painted the pit in mystical shades of plum. My mother used to say the Big Tent reminded her of the inner chambers of a beating heart. An enormous, unbreakable Revelle heart, fit to hold everyone we loved safe inside it. But she hadn't been safe. None of us were, not with the Chronoses in charge.

And tonight I was going to make one of their fantasies come true.

In a flash of skinny limbs and faded hand-me-downs, my youngest cousins burst from the mezzanine stairwell. Little Clara led the way, the others at her heels. She skidded to a halt in front of me. "I won!"

I lowered myself to them. "Did you miss any?"

"'Course not." She knocked her too-big newsboy cap away from her eyes. "I checked each seat three times. There's no roaches left."

"Nice work." Roaches crawling into the bootlegger's lap wouldn't exactly be seductive.

"Caught one the size of my fist," she added, holding out her hand. She was just as competitive as Colette, if not worse.

With eyes as round as their distended bellies, the children watched as I reached into the pocket of my backstage robe for the prize I'd promised the winner. Sensing my Revelle blood, the jewel prickled my fingertips, hot and insistent. I'd missed the ease of gems, the way my Revelle magic kissed the nape of my neck. There was nothing sweet about my other magic.

The emerald was a tiny flake that could barely buy sodas, but Clara cradled it as if it were priceless.

I fixed her cap and rubbed her brother's head. "Go to bed, all of you. And nice work."

Clara blinked up at me with her big chocolate eyes. "How about a demonstration?"

She was a Revelle, all right. "A fast one, okay?"

They squealed, and for a moment, it was Colette, Millie, and me, begging our older cousins for magic lessons backstage. How I'd lived for those moments.

Clara offered me her minuscule emerald, but I produced a few more shards from my pocket and laid them in the palm of my hand. The candlelight refracted off the sharp edges.

"Everyone take one. Careful, Clara."

It was a risk, giving Revelles jewels. They could turn around and charm *me* if they pleased.

"Now give them back. Remember, our magic only works on gemstones freely given."

The children dropped the emeralds in my waiting hand and leaned forward, their smiles taking shape before I began. The power of anticipation.

"Now what should I focus on?"

Clara rocked on her heels impatiently. Every Revelle knew the basics. "The emerald. Trying to make it last."

"And what happens if I use it all up?"

"It'll turn to dust, and you won't be able to spend it on anything else."

"Exactly." My mother had drilled this lesson into me countless times. "Magic always has a cost, and ours is the jewels themselves. They crumble under our power, and if we're not careful, we won't have anything left over for food, or costumes, or any of the things we need."

"Aw, c'mon, Luxe! Do it already!"

I closed my fingers around the emeralds. The magic called to me like the sea to a sailor, and I let myself drown in it. The rush was exquisite. *This* magic felt right.

You are happy, I whispered in my mind. *Perfectly happy, like you're being tickled.*

They roared with laughter, collapsing on the ground in a heap of skinny, sun-kissed limbs. The jewels shrank, leaving glittery green dust in my palm.

Everything is funny. The air, the ground, the clothes you wear.

As the children rolled and hooted, Colette glided down the ladder, pausing at the bottom to watch. The ghost of a smile graced her lips, as if she, too, remembered how we used to laugh until our sides ached, tickled by our family's magic.

Our eyes met, and she looked away.

You feel the love of all ninety-six Revelles wrapped around you. You are on top of Charmant, on top of the world, and you're never, ever alone.

Their smiles grew dreamier, their faces softer. And even though, at their age, I would have given anything to be old enough to perform, part of me longed to be seven years old again, when summer shows meant magic and sweets and falling asleep backstage with Colette and Millie, our limbs as tangled as our unbrushed hair. No Prohibition. No Chronoses to charm. Just the three of us playing until we woke to the gentle sway of our mothers carrying us to bed.

I kissed my little cousins' foreheads, letting the jewel magic slip away.

They groaned in protest. "One more time?" Clara begged.

"You always have to leave some left over for profit. See?"

Even the older children leaned close to glimpse the emerald remnants in my palm. My family believed I was the most powerful among us, making jewels last longer than anyone else. In their eyes, it was the only plausible explanation for Uncle Wolffe naming me the star instead of Colette, who was twice as talented and even harder-working. We couldn't tell them the truth, not when the island was crawling with mind readers.

Uncle Wolffe strode to the center of the stage and clapped his hands, any sign of distress replaced by his unflappable focus. "Places, everyone! It's time to open the doors."

Revelles sprang into action. The children darted for the costume racks, hoping to catch the first act before they were chased to bed. A familiar pang of longing snuck up on me as their parents caught their hands and planted kisses on their little foreheads.

The lights dimmed. My uncles drew the enormous velvet curtains in front of the stage, cloaking the theater in familiar lilac and candlelight.

The air stilled. I'd performed in countless shows, but never before had my heartbeat thrashed the way it did now.

What would happen to us if Dewey Chronos didn't fall under my spell?

We'd lose it all—the theater, the Fun House, the ramshackle bedrooms we crammed into beside the sea.

I couldn't think such things. Seduction required confidence. Besides, any hint of unease from me, the unflappable ice princess, would lead to questions Uncle Wolffe couldn't answer. Not until we secured booze.

With her head high and her sagging cleavage jutting forward, Nana strutted toward the foyer like a sparkling peacock. She'd greet customers, collect admissions gems, and send word back about whose pockets were the heaviest.

"Did you find Millie and Colette?" she asked. "You should celebrate your first night in the Fun House!"

Our mothers had raised us together, hoping we'd be as insep-arable as they were.

They'd died together, too.

"I'll find them now," I demurred.

The cancan dancers took their places behind the curtain, ready for the opening number.

Alone, I waited.

Nana opened the doors, and the crowd roared as they rushed into the pit, vying for coveted positions beside the stage, pink-faced and sweaty, like pigs in colorful top hats. Somewhere among them was Dewey Chronos, with that garish diamond-shaped clock sewn to his lapel. He was destined for the executive suite. Center mezzanine, roach-free.

The band began plucking a punchy melody. Nana's hips swayed at the entrance, and through the haze of cigar smoke, she looked young and beautiful and so much like my mother, I had to turn away.

The drums went *rat-a-tat-tat*. Anticipation whipped the tourists into a frenzy.

Within my pocket, the jewels sang.

Rat-a-tat-tat. Rat-a-tat-tat.

Showtime.

TWO

JAMISON PORT

"Well?" Roger pressed his flask into my palm. "What do you think?"

I leaned over the railing for my first glimpse of Charmant. The guy hawking ferry tickets had called it "Coney Island, but with enchanted booze that'll kick ya and magical girls that'll trick ya." Growing up, the friars called it "the devil's toilet." Roger simply called it "home."

"It's incredible," I breathed. The mist parted like curtains, revealing golden beaches glittering like jewels in the final breaths of daylight. Sharp, looming cliffs dripping with lush emerald greenery cut into the darkening sky. In the center of it all, the setting sun silhouetted a vast triangular peak. The Big Tent.

A strange sense of déjà vu trickled through my veins. Foolish, I knew. Roger would tease me until eternity if I admitted it.

"Don't be deceived." Roger hoisted himself onto the slick railing. "If we're not careful, we'll leave here years from now, wallets emptied and sins too plentiful for penance."

"Lucky for me, my wallet is always empty," I quipped. "And the friars' rods taught me how to repent."

His smile darkened. "One day we're going to burn that damn orphanage to the ground." Roger whistled. "Well, hello. Look who's dressed all spiffy."

Trysta wove through the mob of tourists, three lowball glasses balanced in one hand. Because of a childhood foot fracture that had never healed properly, she strutted with a limp, but her cane only helped her to bulldoze a path through the drunkards. She handed us our drinks and smoothed the black beaded gown hanging from her pale shoulders. "Glad you managed to put on suits. No ties?"

I shuddered. "Ugh, ties. They're so . . . restrictive."

"Like dog collars," Roger agreed. "You don't want to collar us, do you, Trys?"

"And pull you around on leashes? No, thank you."

Roger and I grinned over her head. After three years of traveling together, Trys still couldn't admit how much she loved us.

I took a curious sniff of my drink. "You found Scotch? Should we hide it?"

"See that man with the whiskey?" She nodded at a portly gentleman in an expensive fedora. "Artie Woods, former New York City police commissioner. The one with the mustache is Senator Calder. He voted for Prohibition."

"Yet they're all getting tanked. Bunch of hypocrites. Hello!" Roger threw them a dazzling smile as they looked our way. "See? They might pretend Charmant is governed by New York laws, but these rich bastards would lose millions if they actually enforced them."

"The Eighteenth Amendment doesn't get enforced on Charmant," Trys said firmly. "My family makes sure of it."

Trysta had been born and raised in Charmant, too, the

excommunicated daughter of Mayor Chronos himself. When I'd asked if she was allowed to return, she'd just smiled that lethal smile of hers and purred, "Let them try to stop me."

"Let's toast." To the dismay of our fellow passengers, Roger leaped onto the top rail, wobbling precariously for a moment before finding his balance.

Trys rolled her eyes. "Here we go again."

"To Jamison's first trip to Charmant." Roger's rich voice drew everyone's attention. I used to think people stared because of the scars etched in his golden-brown skin, stretching the length of his left cheek and stopping just before his chin. And people did stare at the scars, of course, but that wasn't why they watched Roger. It was part of his magic, he'd told me. Revelles drew people to them like moths to a flame. "As a Night District native, it's my holy duty to be the patron saint of your debauchery. Do I sound like a real priest, Jame-o?"

I dipped my head reverently. "It's like I'm back at St. Douglas's."

"Excellent. My first commandment: don't drink anything made by someone with horns."

As if he and Trys hadn't already warned me about Effigen cocktails. The Effigen family possessed the power of potency: they could create the world's most delicious blueberry by concentrating the flavor of a dozen into one. Or they could concoct a shot of gin as strong as six shots. Magic always has a cost, however, so the other five gins turned to dust. A bit wasteful under Prohibition, but Charmant was about pleasure, not practicality.

"No horned bartenders," I repeated. "Got it."

"Rule number two," Roger continued. "Don't give a jewel to anyone."

"Easy. I don't have any jewels."

"See?" Trys patted me on the back. "Destitution works in our favor yet again."

Roger nodded at my jacket. "My family will sense your mother's brooch a mile away."

I laid a protective hand over my pocket. My parents had only left me two possessions: a bejeweled crescent moon pin and a photograph of the three of us standing in front of an old beachside dock, its planks carved into a strange rectangular pattern. My mother wore the pin in the photo, just above her heart. "You know I wouldn't part with it."

"Good. My family's magic doesn't work on stolen jewels, but be careful. Magic is more potent on Charmant. I can't wait to be at full strength again." He patted his pocket, jingling the minuscule gems, Charmant's official currency.

Trys steadied herself on the railing. "This is the longest toast ever. Let's drink already."

"Fine." Roger's eyes glittered. "To not wasting a drop of our beautiful lives together."

"Amen to that." Trys drained her cup, and Roger and I followed suit.

My pulse quickened as the ferry was sucked into the vortex tides circling the island. Charmant was made of myths, stories whispered by the older boys at St. Douglas's. The friars had crossed out the fleck in the Atlantic with a thick X on every map. Yet here it was.

I turned to my friends, but their gazes remained fixed on the island. They hadn't wanted to return, but Prohibition was drying up all our favorite haunts. The thrill of opening weekend on

Charmant was worth the risk of seeing their disapproving parents, they claimed. But maybe that was just an excuse to come home.

Home.

A familiar pang of longing struck deep in my chest. Once I turned sixteen and left, I never missed St. Douglas's, especially after I met my friends and realized just how vast and vibrant life could be. For three years, we'd been hopping from one adventure to the next. Would that end once they tasted home again?

And if it did, where would that leave me?

Roger stared at Charmant like a starving man gazed at poisoned fruit. "Before we disembark, make sure I'm seeing double."

Trys's long exhale blew her bangs from her face. "Me too."

By the time we stepped onto the gangplank, my vision was spinning.

"Welcome to the Island of Sin!" an enormous man hooted. The crowd cheered, propelling us forward as the savory scent of fried dough overcame the briny ocean breeze.

A raucous band played at the end of the dock, the cymbals clashing violently. I threw one arm around Roger and the other around Trys. Together, we stumbled down the pier.

"What do you think?" Trys shouted in my ear as she ducked underneath a stilt walker.

"Amazing," I breathed. "I've never seen so many people!"

"They're here for opening night." Roger pointed to a dozen posters of a stunning girl with milky white skin and dark curls cascading down her skintight plum dress. *LUXE REVELLE PERFORMS TONIGHT*, they read. Her gaze followed us down the pier.

Unable to take my eyes off those cherry lips, I tripped on a loose board. "Are we going?"

Roger laughed darkly. "Another rule for you, Jame-o: no falling for Revelles."

"I am perfectly capable of enjoying the company of a beautiful girl *without* getting attached, thank you very much."

Trys quirked a brow. "What about Betty?"

The name nearly ruined my buzz. After twelve years in an all-boys' orphanage, Betty had been the first girl I'd kissed. Naturally, I'd assumed we were getting married. "Betty was . . ."

"A mistake?" Trys steadied herself on Roger's arm. "Your biggest regret?"

"A learning experience?" Roger suggested. "A lesson in what *not* to do?"

A *harsh* lesson at that. I'd made a fool out of myself following her around. "Well, I'm fully committed to the bachelor life now."

"Sure you are," Trys teased.

Night fell as we stumbled along the waterfront promenade, the music drowning out the faint splash of waves. Lanky boys with shiny cheeks and newsboy caps carried crates of apples, sacks of flour, and other goods from New York down the docked ships' ramps.

Roger paused to haggle with several women wearing nothing but stacks of colorful top hats, and I busied myself studying the fireworks reflecting off the water. It wasn't that I hadn't seen breasts before; I'd just never seen so *many*.

With our newly acquired tourist hats, we continued along the promenade. Roger pointed to a man in a ritzy black suit standing with two police officers. "Is that a Chronos?"

Trys froze. "It's my brother."

Roger and I exchanged a look. Trys rarely spoke about her brothers, but I remembered the basics: at twenty-one, Dewey was the oldest, while George was younger and a bit of a jerk. Which, of course, meant he was their father's pick to follow in his footsteps as Charmant's next mayor. As a family of time travelers, dynasties were easy to establish: they had plenty of do-overs to win elections.

"George!" she called, waving her hands.

Whirling at the sound of her voice, he regarded Trysta coolly, as if she were merely another constituent, not the exiled sister she hadn't seen in three years.

He turned his back to us, and Trys's smile shattered.

Roger pounded his fist into his palm. "Never too early in the evening for a fight."

"Happy to oblige." I rolled my neck. "You okay, Trys?"

"I'm fine. Perfectly fine. And we're here to get jazzed, not fight my miserable family."

She pulled our hands, but Roger didn't budge. "Why is he with those bulls?"

I craned my neck. In front of George, an elderly man knelt on the promenade, protesting as the police sifted through his things. George barked something I couldn't hear over the music.

The officers raised their batons and slammed them on the old man's head.

Someone shrieked, and the crowd surged backward, abandoning the man as he collapsed onto the dock. For a selfish moment, it was me on the ground as the friars searched *my* belongings, confiscating the banned books I'd rescued from the church basement, their pages my only escape to the outside world. The other boys didn't stand up to the friars. And who could blame them? They were powerless. We all were.

But I wasn't a scared little boy anymore.

"Hey!" I marched up to the officers fumbling with the camera. "What's going on, fellas?"

"This man was taking pictures of our VIP guests drinking," an officer growled.

The old man gripped his bleeding head. "I didn't take a damn photo here! These are from my granddaughter's wedding. They're the only photos she has, and I promised her—"

"Silence," George said calmly, "or these good men will silence you."

The officers banged on the camera, flipping it upside down.

"No need to break the thing." Stepping forward, I motioned for them to hand it to me. "I used the same one to take Easter portraits at my church. Here, let me remove the film spool."

The officers hesitated, but I gave them my best choirboy smile. Before they could change their minds, I took the camera from them and twisted it around, patting a few random spots. "Aha! Here it is—oh no, I dropped it."

"No!" The old man lunged for the film as it rolled off the dock and into the Atlantic.

"I am so sorry, sir." Doing my best to look contrite, I handed him back his camera.

George Chronos grabbed me by the shirt collar. "Who do you think you are?"

I smiled with all my teeth. "A friend of your sister's. Remember her?"

He tightened his grip on my one good dress shirt. This close, he looked a decade older than Trys, though he was born only two years before her.

With a shove, he released me. "Get the hell out of here. Now."

"Pleasure to meet you, too!" I shouted over my shoulder as Trys pulled my arm.

Roger lifted his middle finger as we sauntered away. "Did you really ruin the pictures?"

"Of course not." I patted their backs. "But I hope you weren't too attached to those ridiculous portraits we took in Philadelphia."

Trys grinned. "You left the film in the old man's camera."

"Attaboy, Jame-o." Roger tousled my hair as he jumped ahead. "C'mon."

We continued down the promenade, weaving through scores of dancing tourists.

Beautiful, beautiful Charmant. Tilting my head to the obsidian sky, I breathed in this magical place. The stars seemed to spin around me, faster and faster. Maybe Charmant was spinning. Maybe *I* was spinning.

I took another step forward and—

Trysta barreled into me, flattening us both on the ground.

Something smashed behind us, the sound deafening. I turned to stare at a mess of wooden splinters, painted porcelain, and amber liquid. An enormous crate had fallen off the ship and landed where I had just been standing. The exact spot.

It would have killed me.

The crowd screamed, hands raised to protect themselves. George Chronos slipped between them, smirking over his shoulder as he sauntered away.

"Are you okay?"

Bits of debris floated in the water. Porcelain angel wings. Broken ones. The friars would've been absolutely thrilled to tell the other boys how God had punished me for my sins. Death by cherubs. In Charmant, of all places.

"Jamison? Are you all right?"

Roger hovered above me. Numbly, I nodded.

"He's alive!" Ever the entertainer, Roger lifted his arms, and the crowd cheered.

Beside me, Trys grew paler. "It—It *crushed* you. You were dead."

Dead?

She retched over the water's edge, and Roger and I grabbed her shoulders. Even vomit was colorful in Charmant.

Roger gaped at her. "You *traveled?*"

A small nod. "It's a lot harder when I'm positively zozzled." She backed away from us, panting against a mooring pole.

You were dead.

I'd always known Trysta could time travel, but I'd never seen her do it. She hated it. She hated the dizzying, disorienting feeling of landing in the past. She hated that she couldn't jump forward again. Most of all, she hated the cost of her magic: however far back a Chronos traveled, they aged a hundred times that, shortening their lives and adding premature wrinkles. One day relived meant one hundred days aged. One year meant aging one hundred years: instant death.

Trys held her trembling hands in front of her. "Do I look older?"

"More like you've been up all night." Roger helped her to her feet. "How far back did you go?"

"Only a minute, I think." She let out a shaky breath, her skin still as white as a sheet. "Jesus. One wrong move, and I could've shaved years off my life."

If Trysta had just relived one minute in order to save me, that was one hundred minutes she wouldn't breathe, wouldn't laugh, wouldn't love—because of me.

"Thank you." I pulled her in for a hug, and for once, she didn't roll her eyes.

"Your jacket's all torn up now." Her voice was muffled against my shoulder.

"A small price to pay for not being flattened like a pancake."

Roger flipped a broken cherub statue, holding it up so we could see. "Recognize this?"

Ducking out of my embrace, Trys took it. A black diamond was painted on the bottom. Inside, elegant clock hands pointed to nine and twelve. "That's Dewey's company. It's his logo."

"Are we picking fights with both of your brothers tonight?"

"I saw George." I rubbed my head. "Not sure if he did this, but he looked pretty pleased."

"He knew I'd have to travel. Fucking George." Trys traced the diamond-shaped clock. "Dewey's a lot nicer. He's one of the good ones. The *only* good one, maybe."

Roger dipped his finger in the dark pool seeping from the broken crate. "He must be hiding booze in these statues to get it past the mainland authorities."

Trys picked up her cane and nodded at the police making their way toward us. "Let's scram."

"What happens to the old you, when you travel?" I asked as we slipped through the crowd, leaving the mess behind.

She frowned. "There is no 'old' me. It's the same me. I just replace myself."

"And what about the old timeline?" I continued. "Is there some alternate universe out there where I'm now dead, courtesy of a crate of cherub statues full of booze?"

Roger groaned. "I really hate time travel."

"How should I know?" Trys nudged me. "If I'd realized you were going to overthink this, I would have let the crate have you."

"Shoot," Roger muttered under his breath. "George's cronies are flagging an Edwardian."

"A mind reader?" I asked, glancing over my shoulder.

"Exactly." Roger grabbed three bright yellow drinks from the cart of a man with silvery antlers, dropping three jewels on his tray. "Chug this."

"But you just said—"

He handed me the drink. "They can't hear our thoughts if we're absolutely ossified."

"Bottoms up, boys." Trys raised her glass and we downed the saccharine drinks.

The lemony flavor ignited my veins with honey-colored fire, and the world swayed, taking on a strange, sunny hue.

Whoa. Bees buzzed in my head, singing a sweet song. Why hadn't I noticed them before?

"Bees." I giggled.

Trysta shot me a strange look. "Bees?"

I opened my mouth to explain, and a swarm of bumblebees flew out. *"Beeeees."*

Roger snickered. Trys rolled her eyes, but her shoulders trembled.

Tears of laughter rolled down my cheeks. I tried to ask if they heard the bees, too, but words were heavy things. I couldn't lift them.

"*Beeeeees*," I whispered. My whole life, I'd seen bees, but I'd never really *seen* them, you know?

Roger collapsed, dragging me to the ground with him. My best friend, my magical, worldly buddy, laughing so hard he couldn't stand.

The music swept me above my friends. I flew with the bees, spinning among the stars—

And then I saw it. The diamond-shaped clock, sewn to the lapel of a young man's suit jacket, glowing as if the bees had enchanted it. They wanted me to see it, my bees. They wanted me to follow the symbol that had almost ended me. I tried to tell Trys and Roger, but words were still uncooperative. So I pointed—and followed.

My vision whirled around the young man as I trailed him to the grandest tent I'd ever seen: at least ten stories high, covered in swirling purple and black stripes with an oval ceiling left open to the night sky. Music poured from the entrance, a siren's call luring me closer.

Beside me, Roger laughed darkly about a family reunion, but I could hardly hear him over the buzzing in my mind, my bones. *You've seen this tent before*, the bees whispered to me.

Had my parents taken me to Charmant, of all places?

The diamond-shaped clock disappeared into the crowded tent, entering beneath a life-sized poster of that enchanting girl. I stumbled after it, but deft hands yanked me backward and reached into the pockets of my ruined jacket. My mother's brooch. I covered it, and an elderly woman in a fire-red sequined dress screamed at me, the music and bees drowning out her words.

Roger threw his arm over my shoulder and she released me, gripping his face. He melted underneath her touch, morphing into a giddy little boy, his tawny skin smooth and scar-free. I blinked, and he was Roger again. The bees sang, urging me deeper into the tent. *You've been here before*, they whispered. *Follow us.*

Otherworldly music pulsed through the theater. My heart raced with the drums, with the dizzying pace of the riotous piano. Glitter whirled through the humid air, mimicking the stars above. Bodies raked against one another, eyes unfocused in a feverish trance.

So much skin—soft, supple skin.

Beautiful girls slid long nails down my neck before pirouetting away. Bare-chested boys winked as I passed, their heated gazes trailing the length of me. Smiles became infectious things, and soon my cheeks ached from the joy of it all.

On the stage, a human pyramid climbed toward the sky. Women in jeweled bikinis spun in unison, hypnotizing me. With my feet glued to the sticky ground, I absorbed it for seconds, minutes, hours. I'd never felt so alive.

"Dance with me!" A girl pulled me close, spinning me onto the dance floor.

A blink later, Trys pinned me against a wall, yelling something about finding seats, about Roger, but the bees flew up toward the aristocratic boxes, circling the man with the diamond-shaped clock. Good little bees.

Another blink, and Roger was shaking my shoulders. "You all right?"

That stupendous honey still heated my veins, but I managed to point toward the clock.

Crushed velvet stairs, a quick exchange between Roger and the guard posted atop them. Joyful recognition. An embrace. We ducked under a curtain, entering an ornate box suspended over the action. The bees quieted, their buzzing fading. I was exactly where they wanted.

The man with the diamond-shaped clock stared at my muddied clothes. He was white, with jet-black hair and curious brown eyes. About our age, but with impeccable posture and a smile that oozed confidence. His ritzy black suit—a double-breasted jacket with faint silver pinstripes—hadn't a single crease.

I blinked, and his face morphed. Blood dripped from his monstrous jaws. I yelled, backing away.

He frowned. "Are you okay?" No blood now. No fangs.

I pressed my hands against my racing heart, still unable to speak.

"Hey, Dewey." Trys waved casually, but her grin betrayed her.

Dewey—Trys's *other* brother.

"Trysta?" He gaped at her. "You're back?"

"For the weekend." They stared at each other before he strode toward her, scooping her into a hug. Her eyes squeezed shut, thinly veiled emotions playing over her face. For all her "damn the Chronoses" and "better on my own" talk, she'd clearly missed him.

He pulled away to examine her. "You haven't aged a bit."

"Neither have you." She pinched his cheek. "I was expecting an old man. When I heard you were bootlegging, I figured you were using your magic."

"I travel here and there, but only when *I* want to, not Father."

Trysta did a double take. "You left home, too?"

"It wasn't any fun without you," he teased, though his smile betrayed his sadness.

The Chronoses pooled their magic, taking turns traveling back in time to advance the family's wealth—and ensure other magical families didn't become too influential. When Trys refused to help, she was disowned. "And Father lets you stay in Charmant?"

"He has no choice." Dewey straightened. "My booze fills every cup on this island."

"So you're the hooch guy." Nudging Trys out of his way, Roger offered a hand. "Roger Revelle."

Trysta's brother shook it eagerly. "Dewey Chronos. I hadn't realized you'd returned."

"And I hadn't realized we were acquainted."

"I've done my research on your family's show. Your reputation precedes you."

Roger's smile faltered. He missed performing terribly. Whenever he had too much to drink, he tried to goad us into betting him to swing from some absurdly tall branch. He was proud of his acrobatics, but after the ordeal that had given him those scars, he'd left it all behind.

Roger waved me closer. "Our esteemed friend, Jamison Port. He seems to have lost the ability to speak, thanks to an Effigen Bee Sting."

"I'm impressed you found enchanted booze. Very expensive these days." Dewey squeezed my hand as if my pain threshold was a measure of my worthiness as Trys's friend. "Next time you need a stiff drink, come and find me."

"Thank you," I managed to say, pulling my hand away. Finally, words were cooperating.

With a smile, Dewey lifted his glass. "Look at us: the Revelles and the Chronoses, getting along. Our ancestors must be rolling in their graves."

Roger perched on the edge of the railing, daring gravity as always. "One of your crates nearly sent Jamison to *his* grave earlier. It fell off your ship and would have crushed him to death, had Trys not worked her magic. Literally."

As he pointed to the diamond-shaped clock sewn to Dewey's suit jacket, Dewey's face fell. "My apologies, Jamison."

"I'm fine," I assured him. "Not a scratch on me, thanks to your sister."

"But your jacket's ruined." He shrugged his off, revealing a dark vest and pearl-white shirt. "Here. Take mine."

I took a step back before he could hand his to me. "That's not necessary."

"I insist. It's the least I can do." Before I could refuse again, the lights flashed and cheers erupted below. Dewey draped it over my arms. "I'll get it back tomorrow."

"I really don't want—"

Ignoring me, he strode toward the curtains. "It's time for Luxe Revelle's act. I want to watch from the pit, for the customers' perspective. Trys, meet me afterward?"

Trys waved, and he was gone.

"Is Luxe the girl from the posters?" I asked Roger, removing my mother's brooch from the breast pocket of my ruined jacket.

"The one and only." He helped me slip on Dewey's coat. "Black is definitely your color."

"My coat was black, too."

"Okay, fine. *Expensive* is your color."

It was, by far, the richest thing I'd ever worn. "I feel like I'm going to burst out of it."

A spotlight illuminated center stage. Roger slunk into his seat. "Here comes my father. Just wear it, Jame-o. If he realizes his guest of honor left, he'll blame me."

An enormous man sauntered across the stage. His pin-striped suit hugged the barrel of his chest, the sleeves belling into the mouths of hungry wolves, poised to devour his thick hands. White powder caked his pale face, and his lips and cheeks were scarlet. Half clown, half monster.

"Welcome, you insufferable creatures!" Wolffe Revelle's rich voice boomed.

"Or should I say," Roger murmured in unison with his father, "welcome *back*."

THREE

LUXE

My manicure sparkled against the crude rope ladder as I climbed to the rafters. Uncle Wolffe's taunting of the crowd had already begun. Mere minutes now.

"There goes our star!" Aunt Caroline yelled. The rest of the performers gathered around the bottom of the ladder.

"Time for your daily hour of work, Luxie girl?"

"She makes more in an hour than you do in a whole night!"

If they'd known about our champagne crisis, they wouldn't be laughing. Perhaps Nana had managed to keep a secret to herself for once. Good.

"Look at that *behind*!" Aunt Caroline catcalled. "A money-maker, if I've ever seen one."

"Is that a gray hair I see?"

"On her head or her cookie?"

For Pete's sake. My family was incapable of being serious.

"Shame you won't join us in the Fun House," Aunt Caroline continued. "A night with the ice princess would earn us plenty of jewels."

They'd called me that for years, assuming I was too uppity to earn my keep in the Fun House like everyone else. Uncle Wolffe told them it was his idea—that he liked to keep his "most precious jewel" a rare sighting for the customers—but that hadn't stopped the family from teasing me relentlessly about going to bed while they went to work.

But not tonight. "Actually," I called down, "I'll be taking a customer."

My aunt's smile was an enormous, devilish thing. "No way."

I shrugged. "Can't let you have all the Fun House glory."

Their cheers and jeers drowned out Uncle Wolffe's booming voice. If my mother were still alive, she would have been right there beside her sisters, brimming with pride. Or maybe she'd be waiting in the rafters to repeat the advice she'd given me my whole life. *Pull just enough magic from the jewel to make it believable. Slow and steady. And never lay a finger on a customer—no matter how sweet their face, use your magic, not your body.*

When I neared the top, I turned to face them. Dancers and clowns, flamethrowers and tightrope walkers, beast tamers and contortionists. There wasn't a family on the planet that could compete with ours. Nothing—absolutely nothing—beat being a Revelle.

Nana pressed her hands over her heart and lifted them to me. "Go get those jewels, my darling girl."

"Just like you taught me." I blew her a kiss. For her, I'd seduce a hundred Chronoses.

By the time I stepped on the trapeze platform, my heart had swelled to twice its size.

For the final act, the spotlight belonged to Colette, Millie, and me: the Trapeze Three. We'd given ourselves that lofty title as little girls daydreaming in bed. No space between us. No boundaries, no secrets.

That was before Uncle Wolffe named me the star, four years ago. Aunt Adeline had been the show's first Black star, and Colette was poised to follow in her mother's footsteps. She'd prepared for it her whole life, always a step ahead of Millie and me. And when our mothers died, she'd taken over our training. She deserved the position. If I hadn't discovered my strange, secondary magic, if Uncle Wolffe hadn't helped me hone it into a secret weapon, she'd be the star. Not me.

As devastated as Colette had been when her father picked me, that wasn't why we'd grown apart. No, that was my doing, courtesy of years of hiding in Wolffe's office while my cousins gallivanted about the Night District. I couldn't risk an Edwardian learning what I could do. So I declined my cousins' invites, becoming the lazy, brown-nosing star. Their ice princess.

Eventually, they stopped asking.

When I appeared atop the ladder, Millie was laughing at something Colette had said, and I couldn't help but admire the way her abundant figure filled out her leotard while my flat chest could double as an ironing board. Along with Nana's curves, she'd inherited Nana's perennially amused smile, too. My mother used to tell me to copy Millie's smile during dance lessons. *The audience loves a happy girl.*

When she spotted me, Millie lifted a perfectly arched brow. "Are you really working in the Fun House tonight?"

"I am." I dipped my hands into the chalk bag and clapped away the excess.

"Well, that's just the bee's knees! Isn't it, Col?"

"Thrilling." Colette continued to fix her lipstick without looking away from the small mirror. "Three minutes until our first leap."

An all-too-familiar silence fell over us. Once upon a time we'd never run out of things to say to each other. Now we were experts at polite conversation.

"I like the new leotards," I offered. Our measly budget only allowed for a new costume for me, but Colette had recycled bits of the gymnasts' apparel for her and Millie, too.

Millie smoothed the sparkling silver fabric. "Light colors wash me out, but you know Colette always has to look the best."

The light fabric didn't wash out Millie's fair complexion, but it shimmered like starlight against Colette's warm brown skin. Her braided updo accented the sharpness of her cheekbones, and the faux jewels she'd applied to the corners of her wide eyes made them pop.

Millie reached into her leotard to scoop her ridiculous cleavage. "Did Uncle Wolffe give you a mark for your first time? Or will you go with the highest bidder?"

"I have a mark." I straightened my legs in front of me and bowed into a deep stretch.

"Let me guess. Another rich tourist."

Colette rolled her eyes. "It's *always* a rich tourist."

Uncle Wolffe's jeers filled the silence as I braced myself. By the end of the night, the whole family would know my mark. Chronoses never set foot in the Fun House. They never so much as *held* a jewel within ten yards of a Revelle.

There was no point dodging the question. "Actually, it's Dewey Chronos."

Their jaws snapped open.

"You're debuting with a *Chronos*?" Colette hissed.

"I can't believe Uncle Wolffe would do that!" Millie exclaimed. "Who knows what sorts of fantasies a Chronos will want you to conjure for him?"

I couldn't let my mind go there, not when we were moments away from jumping.

Colette crossed her arms. "No way a Chronos forks over a jewel. Not even for you."

"Is he the one who's always with the mayor?" Millie asked. "Or the other brother?"

"The other one's the bootlegger." Colette's frown deepened. "We're not buying booze from a Chronos, are we?"

As if we had any other choice.

Millie's sweet smile faded. "Is this why Nana was crying earlier?"

Oh, Nana. The last thing we needed were rumors that we'd gone dry on opening night.

It wasn't fair. If our mothers were still alive, *they* would have dealt with the liquor crisis. They still would have been the family's primary breadwinners, and as Nana's daughters, they'd be best at consoling her. I wouldn't have to magically seduce a damn Chronos. And I wouldn't have to lie to my cousins about it.

But life wasn't fair. Whining about it wouldn't bring them back to life.

With my chin high, I flashed them my most confident smile. "Don't worry. Everything's hotsy-totsy."

Millie seemed to relax, but Colette watched me as I finished my stretches. Millie and I used to joke that someone on Aunt

Adeline's side must have had Edwardian blood, because Colette almost always could see through our lies. Even when we were little, she was the rule follower, while Millie and I had no qualms about picking the lock on Nana's candy drawer.

The crowd laughed as Uncle Wolffe teased a customer about overcompensating with the size of his top hat. Any moment now.

Millie grabbed the bifocals and leaned over the edge. "Which one is he?"

"Executive suite, I bet." Colette peered at the crowd below. "I hear he always wears a black jacket with that ridiculous diamond-shaped clock on the lapel."

Millie stiffened. "I see him. Look."

Colette squinted into the crowd below. "Wait . . . is he sitting with my *brother*?"

"Roger's back?" I nearly lost my balance. Three long years, he'd been gone.

"Omigosh!" Millie squealed. "There he is!"

Colette pressed her fingers to her lips as she struggled to regain her composure. Roger's abrupt exit from Charmant had been hardest for her. Uncle Wolffe did his best to be a good father, but with Aunt Adeline gone, and ninety-six Revelles looking to him to keep them afloat, Colette had been mostly on her own. "Of course he *has* to make an entrance. He couldn't just come backstage. He has to sit in the executive suite acting chummy with the bootlegger."

I couldn't help but smile. "That sounds exactly like Roger."

"The bootlegger looks different. *Good* different." Millie's eyes sparkled mischievously. "Maybe you'll fall in love! You could have charming, time-traveling babies together."

Colette arched her brow. "You want her to marry into a family of rotten politicians?"

"Fair point."

"Love?" I had to laugh. Falling in love was the silliest thing a Revelle could do. "I don't need love; I need *rich*."

Millie's grin widened. "You're going to *love* the Fun House. I just know it."

Far below us, the drummers began their slow, torturous tempo. Our cue.

"Here goes nothing." Colette and Millie grabbed their bars and lined up their toes at the edge of the board.

Here goes everything. I braced myself. Time to call on my other magic.

"Are you ready for the dazzling Daughter of the Night?" Uncle Wolffe boomed.

The rafters rumbled and shook as the crowd stomped their feet. I closed my eyes and squeezed my hands together. Now or never.

"Are you ready for the irresistible, the exquisite, the Radiant Ruby of Revelle?"

My mind was a knife, and it cut down my throat, through my ribs, into my core. Sweat beaded at the top of my forehead. It felt wrong, like swallowing a flame that burned me from the inside out. Every instinct urged me to withdraw, but I let my magic cut deeper.

Magic always has a cost, and mine was pain. Deathly, mind-numbing pain. As soon as I envisioned charming someone without jewels, a headache cleaved open my skull with the force of a thousand axes. But if I could withstand it, I could charm anyone. Even a Chronos.

I held on, trembling, while Colette and Millie exchanged looks. They thought I panicked right before every performance. As I struggled to keep my composure, I bit my tongue so hard, I tasted iron.

Strings of light blinked into existence—stunning, ethereal things of varying colors and illuminance. Jewel magic was invisible, but these luminous wisps of color whipped around me like untied hair on a windy day. Each lightstring led to an audience member, a vibrant manifestation of their emotions so I could mold them as I pleased.

This was why my show was the most popular, why Uncle Wolffe had made me the star. Millie was the prettiest, and Colette the most talented, but *I* gave the tourists a taste of heaven.

Nana was going to bathe in champagne tonight.

I grabbed hold of the nearest lightstrings, my throbbing head protesting as my mind gripped another.

And another. And another.

The bursts of color swirled, too many to catch individual emotions. Red was always lust. Green, jealousy. Blue, sadness. And a smoky darkness for simmering anger.

I would seduce them.

I would charm them.

They would empty their pockets, claw diamonds from their settings and throw them into my waiting hands. Dewey Chronos would be so impressed with me, he'd fork over ships full of liquor. We wouldn't just survive Prohibition; we'd *thrive*. We'd be a boozy sanctuary for all the world's sinners.

Most important, we'd keep our business. Our home.

Colette tugged on my arm. "Are you ready?"

I nodded, my body acclimating to the pain.

She signaled to Uncle Wolffe far below. Fighting a burst of dizziness, I located the lightstring leading to the young man with the diamond-shaped clock on his lapel. Fortunately, there was no sign of Trevor Edwardes, Dewey's mind-reading assistant, who, according to Uncle Wolffe, was present for nearly all his deals. Instead, Roger lounged beside the bootlegger, wearing a neon green touristy top hat and his usual mischievous grin.

Dewey Chronos leaned forward, and a surprising surge of pleasure threatened my focus as a stray spotlight passed over his face. He wasn't just handsome; he was *gorgeous*. Unruly dark hair, broad shoulders, and a strangely earnest lightstring. A far cry from the sickly little boy I remembered.

I searched his whorl of emotions for something I could use to our advantage. He was excited, of course, and rather drunk. Good. Also a twinge homesick. Apparently, the rumors about his estrangement from his family were true.

"I don't think she can hear you!" my uncle taunted.

You belong here, I whispered down his lightstring. Hope surged, blindingly golden. Jackpot.

Pain shot into my skull hard enough for me to cry out, but no one heard, not over the thousand hungry mouths shouting my name. With his lightstring firmly in my control, I gripped my trapeze swing and inched closer to Colette. The humid air over the pit greeted me, thick with cigar smoke and cheap beer.

Millie swung out over the crowd. They went wild, a frenzy of colorful top hats. The spotlight flashed toward the sky once more, and Colette swung from the rafters in a graceful dive. The crowd shouted impossibly louder, their voices shaking my wooden platform.

My turn to fly. Despite the pain of my magic, I was ready for the coolness of the night to rush over my bare skin, the roar of the audience quieted by the sheer concentration required to perform trapeze. For a few blissful minutes, it would be only me, my cousins, and the unbreakable trust that still tethered us together. They'd catch me. They always did.

I caressed Dewey Chronos's lightstring. *You're about to see the most beautiful girl in the world.*

The audience screamed for me, for Luxe Revelle, Daughter of the Night. Gripping the trapeze, I allowed myself one final breath—

—and I leaped from the ledge.

FOUR

JAMISON

Bodies flew through the tent, tumbling in graceful twists in sync with the band's dark, seductive melody. The spotlight flashed upward, and I craned my neck to see where it led.

And then I saw her. The most beautiful girl in the world—falling from the stars.

She swung from the trapeze, her long legs caught by a curvy acrobat. The crowd was deafening as she flipped through the air toward the next swing, and the next, again and again until she finally landed on a cloud-shaped crystal platform. She draped herself over the ledge, the spotlight blinding against her sequins. The cloud lowered her until her face was even with mine, though a sea of bodies still stretched between us.

Our eyes met. A desire I'd never before experienced gripped me.

Home. She's my home.

She couldn't be looking at me—she was the most sublime being in the entire world, and I was a nobody. Yet it was as if her heart was beating in rhythm with mine. I could practically smell her perfume, feel the softness of her lips. A thousand pictures fluttered before my eyes, a life we'd never lived together, but we could—we could. She blinked at me from beneath thick lashes, wild curls barely kept tame by the ribbon circling her head like a crown. The mere act of breathing was too much in her presence.

She turned away, her gaze sweeping over more worthy admirers. I cried out, begging her to look at me again. But the crowd was packed with New York's best, and she was going to have her pick.

I could hardly make out a single word of her angelic song, not over the thrashing of my heart and the commotion of the crowd. If only I could get closer to honor the connection glowing between us. I climbed over the railing—

Strong hands pulled me back into my chair. Roger.

"He must have given her a gem!" Trys yelled.

"But he's broke!"

I felt their hands on my back, heard their concern, but she was all that mattered.

Her flips and jumps on the trapeze swing were sweet torture. To see her finely tuned muscles in action lifted my spirits to dizzying heights, but I gasped with relief each time she made it safely to a platform. My whole heart, my whole world, was hanging from those precarious swings with no safety net beneath her.

Minutes passed like fragments of seconds. Her siren's song continued as she swung her hips on the stage. *Look at me*, I begged her. I would have given her anything, all the jewels I'd ever touched, the clothes off my back, anything at all—

Roger's hands pressed against my shoulders, pushing me back into my seat.

Trys stomped on my foot to hold it in place. "Should we get him out of here?"

"It's almost done. See?"

The other acrobats caught her and lowered her onto the cloud again. Men flung fists full of precious gems onto the stage, and women pried the jewels from their rings. She deserved them all. If only I had something to show her how much she meant to me—

My mother's brooch.

I didn't have time to claw the gems from it; I'd toss her the whole thing—

"No!" Trys tackled me on the dirty carpet. I swung my arms wildly, but she yanked the brooch from my grasp and rolled away.

"Give it back!" I shouted, but I couldn't look away from Luxe long enough to grab it.

As I scrambled to my feet, Luxe's gaze found mine again. Roger and Trys disappeared. The scores of intruders melted into oblivion.

We were alone, floating to the moon. To the stars.

Her crystal cloud kept lifting her higher, too high for me to reach. Her lips curled into a secret smile only for me.

Then she turned away, blowing kisses to her fervent fans.

Utterly drained, I collapsed into my seat.

Roger patted me on the cheek. "And now you've met my cousin."

"Poor Jame-o." Trys gripped my shoulders. "You understand Revelle magic now?"

I couldn't look away from Luxe. "She's my *home*."

Trys shot Roger a look. "Now, that's just cruel."

"That's show business." Roger fixed my crooked hat. "You paid the admission fee, didn't you? That's how she charmed you."

I didn't pay a damn thing. Sure, she possessed magic like all Revelles. But without jewels, it *had* to be real.

"Hang in there, Jame-o. We'll be here when it wears off."

It wouldn't. My friends could not begin to understand what I knew with absolute certainty: Luxe Revelle was my destiny. Everything tonight had led me to this moment. The déjà vu. The crate. The bees.

For the first time in my nineteen years, I was exactly where I belonged.

She perched on the edge of the cloud and waved to her many suitors. Children darted across the stage, sweeping the jewels into the wings. Sapphires, emeralds, topazes, even diamonds soared through the air, but I kept my sights on the girl high above them all. Her smile strained at the corners. She was exhausted.

Our eyes met once more and—

Her hands flew to her stomach. Her feet slipped.

Fear flashed in those perfect eyes.

Roger screamed her name.

And she tumbled

from

the

sky.

FIVE

LUXE

"Luxe? Can you hear me?"

Pain exploded through my chest. I cried out, hands searching for whatever knife was stabbing my stomach, but my leotard was too tight.

The show.

Dewey Chronos.

I *fell*.

"Lie down!" Nana barked. "Where does it hurt?"

"Everywhere," I grunted. The pain was blinding, worse than the magic, because I couldn't make it stop—

"Fetch Dr. Strattori." Footsteps scurried away. "Someone help me cut open this leotard!"

They rolled me onto my side, and I shrieked as darkness overtook me.

"Luxe?" Nana tugged at my faux lashes.

I forced my eyes open. Still in the tent. Still alive somehow.

She pressed her cool, dry hand to my head. "Dr. Strattori is here. She needs your consent to proceed."

I tried to sit again, but my arms gave out beneath me.

Uncle Wolffe patted my shoulder. "Don't try to move. Just give your consent."

I glared at them. The Strattoris could remove any ailment— but only by transferring it to someone else. Both participants had to be willing.

"Don't be stubborn," Uncle Wolffe warned.

My family had sacrificed enough for me, from the food they didn't eat so I could save my strength to the extra shifts they worked in the Fun House so I didn't have to. "Not a chance."

His gaze flickered toward the theater. "I need to be out there. Make sure she agrees."

"*No.*"

"Do it, Luxe. That's an order."

He was gone before I could protest further.

I sunk against the pillow as Helen Strattori suspended her hands over me. Not touching but *sensing* my injuries. The Strattoris' strange religious morality made them wary of our lifestyle, so most didn't come near the Big Tent. Fortunately for my family, Helen Strattori was a lush.

"You're not dying," she slurred, her breath spiced with gin. "Though from that height, you should have."

So consenting to her magic wasn't *murder*, just torture for another Revelle.

"You have two broken ribs and a frightening bruise forming on your left side. And there's some strange internal damage, too, maybe an older injury you aggravated tonight." Dr. Strattori looked troubled, but there wasn't a Revelle alive without their fair share of half-healed injuries.

"We won't be requiring your services."

Her frown deepened. "You won't be able to perform for several weeks."

Weeks? I didn't have *minutes*, let alone weeks.

It had been going so well! I couldn't even count how many lightstrings I'd held. The audience had rained jewels on us quicker than my little cousins could sweep them away. Most important, Dewey Chronos had literally attempted to climb out of his seat to reach me. He would have given us anything I desired. Booze. Jewels. A unicorn named Woodrow Wilson.

I had to finish what I'd started before he realized I'd been charming him—and left the Big Tent for good.

Shifting my weight onto my elbows, I bit my cheeks to keep from yelling out again. "Help me up. I'm going back out there."

"Hush," Nana hissed. "No one can see you like this."

Of course not. The Radiant Ruby of Revelle had to be perfect. All the time.

Even when she ruined *everything*.

Closing my eyes, I sucked in a deep breath. "How in seven hells am I alive?"

"The tourists broke your fall. Thank God we were at full capacity tonight, or . . . damnit, Luxe"—Nana's voice broke—"we almost lost you."

"I'm okay. Really."

She clasped my hand, shifting her fingers over and over again. Nana could never stay still, not even when she held hands. "You scared your Nana," she whispered.

Her face was as ghostly as it'd been seven years earlier, when Edwardian police officers had tiptoed into the Big Tent during our vigil for my missing mother and aunts. Nana's face growing whiter with each nightmarish word. *Found. Drowned. Condolences.*

Dr. Strattori stood, leaning on the cot to steady herself. "Will you be requiring my services, or can I get back to my night?"

"No," I replied firmly.

At the same time, Nana said, "Yes."

With a sigh, Nana lowered herself so her face was inches from mine. "You heard your uncle. We can't afford to sideline our star for weeks."

Letting go of Nana's hand, I covered my face and tried to slow my breathing. The orphans usually volunteered for Strattori magic, always trying to make themselves useful. Feisty little Clara could have her ribs broken because of me.

No matter what I did, my family suffered.

"I'll do it."

I turned toward that silky voice, deeper than I'd last heard it. "Roger?"

There he was, touristy top hat and all. He stood in the doorway, painfully familiar and yet changed. Still as skinny as a string bean, but he'd grown taller, almost as tall as Uncle Wolffe. His hair was shorter, too, combed into the conk style the Black tourists favored. Colette's glittering eyes, Aunt Adeline's easy smile, and those scars. Those damn scars he'd gotten before he left.

"You're back?" It was emotion, not pain, that stole the strength from my voice.

"Just visiting." He hopped onto the cot beside me. "Look at you, bleeding all dramatically. Aren't you afraid I'll use your blood to summon magic-sucking shadows?"

"I'm not seven anymore. I know shadow magic isn't real."

He chuckled. "When I left, you were a mousy fifteen-year-old with hair twice as big as your hips. Now look at you. Here." He tossed me a copper mainland penny.

I turned over the dirty coin. "Why are you giving me this?"

"The mainlanders think they're good luck. Besides, I know how much you loved mainland money when you were younger. Remember those pictures you cut from newspapers and magazines? All those places you wanted to visit—"

"And then I grew up." *And stayed, unlike you.*

He squeezed my shoulder. "C'mon, cousin. Let's get this over with."

A few minutes home, and he was already resuming his role as the family martyr. During the long winters, Roger had always been the quickest to share his plate. Or to charm the worst customers, never complaining about their terrible fantasies. He never let the others call me "ice princess," never stopped asking me to join them in their Night District escapades.

"You've been back for a full minute!" I exclaimed, my ribs smarting. "Do you really expect me to hurt you right away?"

His smug smirk somehow made me miss him more. "Nana, if I take Luxe's injuries, will you make sure my father provides room and board for my friends and me while we're here?"

Roger had friends now? He had fifty-three cousins within spitting distance, yet he'd still left Charmant. To make *friends.*

I could practically see Nana's wheels turning: Roger was no longer a performer, so there was no loss of income. The only challenge was Uncle Wolffe. He'd practically disowned Roger when he left. Members of the other magical families sometimes lived on the mainland, but we Revelles stuck together. That three-hour ferry to New York might as well be to a different planet.

"I'll make sure," she finally said.

"See? Now we both get something out of it." Roger swung himself onto the sick cot beside me. "You have my consent, Dr. Strattori."

The doctor winced as he turned to face her. She'd been there the terrible day he'd gotten those scars. "I need her consent, too."

Nana pressed both her hands on her hips. "Give it. Now."

I couldn't let him do it. *Wouldn't* let him do it. "No."

He lay down beside me, turning his head to whisper, "Don't let my father kick me out."

"Absolutely not."

"You know I love the attention I get when I'm a martyr."

"Being Margaret's martyr is why you left in the first place."

Pain swept over his handsome face, strong enough for me to immediately regret my words. Of course he wasn't over Margaret, over everything that had happened. "I'm sorry——"

"Don't." Hurt still lingered behind his eyes. "Just do this, okay?"

I blinked back pathetic tears. I'd pushed myself too hard, gotten too greedy with my magic. And now Roger——Roger, who was finally home, who always took everyone else's pain as his own—— would suffer the consequences.

But I *had* to get back to Dewey. No more booze meant no more shows.

No shows, and we'd be on the streets.

I couldn't even look at my cousin as I uttered the hateful words that gave my consent. "Just the new injuries. Leave the old ones."

Before I could change my mind, Nana pushed me down with surprising strength. Aunt Caroline stepped forward to grab

Roger. Dr. Strattori laid one hand on my side, and the other circled his wrist.

Roger cried out. I yelled for him, "I'm sorry, I'm sorry . . ."

"Luxe? Deluxe? Delores Catherine Revelle!"

I blinked wildly, Millie slowly coming into focus. Judging by the chipped ceiling paint, we were in one of the Fun House rooms behind the Big Tent. The open windows carried a much better breeze than our bedroom windows a floor below. Always the best for our customers.

"What happened?" I rasped.

"You fell at the end of the act. Uncle Wolffe pretended it was all part of the show."

Roger's screams, the regret I'd glimpsed on his face at the onset of the pain . . .

Colette stood by a framed photograph of three beautiful women in matching striped bathing suits. Our mothers, the infamous ABCs: Aunt Adeline, Aunt Bonnie, and my mother, Catherine. "My father asked us to stay until you woke up. If you don't need anything . . ."

"Colette!" Millie threw her a look.

"What? I want to check on Roger before the customers arrive."

Roger, who was hurt, because of me. Uncle Wolffe gave me one person to charm, but no—I'd had to charm them all.

My uncle also made sure I woke in the Fun House. Our nicest room, no less.

I shot out of bed, the world tilting on its axis so hard, it nearly knocked me off my feet. Stumbling to the closet, I flung open the doors. My Fun House attire hung on the only hanger.

Uncle Wolffe still believed I could do this.

Colette watched me remove the lacy garb. "What are you doing?"

"I need to find my mark." I couldn't get out of my ruined leotard quickly enough. If Dewey Chronos was already gone, we were cooked—

No. I'd hunt him down and charm him into a lovesick puddle, if that's what it took.

Colette looked at me as if I'd grown Effigen horns. "You can't go back out there looking like that."

"That's why I'm changing." My bloodied leotard slipped to the floor. Not a mark on me.

Poor Roger.

"Even with my father's cover-up, the Strattoris will be furious if you flaunt your health. You know how private they are about their magic."

Damnit, she was right. Some tourists placed Charmantian magic in the same category as palm reading: entertaining but inauthentic. In our Fun House, Revelle customers tasted the truth, but rumors of hallucinogens and other tricks still circulated. Disbelief worked in the Strattoris' favor. They hid their healing abilities from the rest of the world, providing their services only to other magical families. If the mainlanders realized their ailments could be transferred, the Strattoris would be in high demand. Helen Strattori would steal our gin and run for the hills.

Pulling the lacy straps over my shoulders, I threw Colette a small smile. "Can you escort the bootlegger here?"

"No way."

"Pretty please?"

"You need to rest! You overdid it tonight."

"I'm fine, I just—"

"You got cocky. You pushed yourself too far."

"I know." All those jewels they'd thrown onstage, and still I'd wanted more.

She opened and closed her mouth, but we both heard the words she bit back: *If I were the star, this never would have happened.*

Colette wouldn't help me. In fact, she liked refusing me. Millie, on the other hand, avoided confrontation at all costs. "Please, Mills. Fetch him for me?"

Her teeth scraped her bottom lip. "I don't know . . . You kind of look like hell."

I checked myself in the mirror. My curls were a frizzy mess, and dark thumbprints bruised the skin under my eyes. Not a problem; I'd charm Dewey into finding me beautiful.

Gripping the bedpost, I closed my eyes and called to my magic. The pain sparked from my skull, a claw of lightning, blinding, blackening—

I let it go before it knocked me out again.

My secondary magic wasn't limitless. I'd always pictured it as a little inkwell buried deep in my mind. If I drained it with overuse, the ink crusted to flakes, and I'd pass out from the pain. If I left it alone, it replenished.

Right now, it was bone-dry.

Seven hells. Our survival was a delicate untied string of pearls, and I'd already let them slip between my fingers.

Magic or not, I still had to try. If I had to seduce him the old-fashioned way, so be it.

I scooped my meager breasts over the top of my plunging neckline like I'd seen my mother do countless times. "Uncle Wolffe had you bring me here. This is his plan."

Millie sashayed toward the door, but Colette blocked her path. "Tell us the truth, Luxe: Why are you doing this?"

"I already told you—"

"Oh, c'mon!" Colette lifted her chin. "You hate the Chronoses as much as any of us. And there's no way he brought jewels with him. Something's up."

Colette never left any stone unturned. I didn't want her to worry, but I didn't have time to fight with her. "Okay, fine. We need booze."

Their eyes widened. Whether out of surprise that I'd been honest for once, or that our liquor supply was low, I wasn't sure.

Millie blinked rapidly. "We're desperate enough to buy from a Chronos?"

"He's the only bootlegger left." It was hardly a secret. Ever since the Eighteenth Amendment had passed, one at a time, Dewey's competition had disappeared.

Colette studied me. "So you're going to try to get him to give you a jewel, then convince him to sell to us."

"That's the plan."

"And if he doesn't?"

Then our doors won't open tomorrow. "Look, I'm not going to throw myself at him. I'll just flirt a little so he'll sell to Wolffe at a price we can afford."

"Ooh!" Millie clapped her hands together. "Let me do it."

"That's not necessary—"

"Did you see that beautiful face? The cat's meow, if you ask me."

"No." My voice was sharper than I intended. "I mean, no," I said more evenly. "I should see it through."

"Aww, Luxie, look at you blushing!" Millie pressed her hands over her heart. "You're going to make sweet, time-traveling babies together, just like I said."

Colette glanced at the framed picture of our mothers. "If they could only hear us now."

"Does this mean you're going to help?" I asked.

"I'll check the Fun House lobby. Millie, you check the Big Tent. Do not seduce him."

Millie pouted. "But—"

"Luxe is the star." Colette's words dripped with disdain. "We all have to do our part."

That was all the encouragement Millie needed. She slipped through the door, throwing me a wink over her shoulder.

Colette lingered in the doorframe. "You still look sickly."

"I'll use extra blush."

She hesitated, perhaps considering yet another lecture on all the missteps I'd made tonight. Bracing myself, I turned back to the mirror, but the door clicked shut softly behind her.

If my mother were watching me, she'd be proud, wouldn't she? For being the star, for putting the family first. No matter the customer. No matter the cost.

Unable to help myself, I rose and walked to the framed picture. My mother stood between my aunts, their arms tangled in an embrace. Over Aunt Adeline's shoulder was an old wooden dock, the planks carved to resemble the Manhattan skyline that hid beyond the mist on the horizon. The sun was setting, illuminating their laughing faces.

I turned away, but grief had already snuck into my bones, making me tired, sluggish.

No more thinking about them. Not tonight.

SIX

JAMISON

Glittering cocktail servers flooded the pit. Perfect smiles adorned their painted faces, revealing nothing of Luxe's fate. Was she alive? Were her graceful limbs as broken as those cherub statues on the promenade?

And where the hell was Roger?

Trys stuck a curious finger into the champagne fountain. "This tastes like piss."

"Are you really thinking about that right now?"

"C'mon, Jame-o, you don't even know her. We just need to be here for Roger, in case it's bad." She glanced around. "Is it me or is everybody staring?"

Though most tourists were still pressed against the stage, waiting for Luxe to reappear, the bartenders were whispering and pointing to Trys. "I guess it's not every day they see a Chronos in the Big Tent."

"Two Chronoses tonight." She smirked at the bartenders, who wisely looked away. "I'm going to check on Dewey. Tell Roger I'll be right back, okay?"

Tucking her cane to her side, she slipped into the crowd before I could protest. Trys had a way of blending in when it suited her. Though it rarely suited her.

As I waited for Roger to return, I slid my mother's brooch out of my pocket. Good, it was still here, along with the photograph of my parents standing on a beautiful beach, a worn wooden dock behind them, the boards carved in that intricate rectangular pattern. And me, as a baby, nestled in the thick blankets my mother held.

I slipped the brooch into the jacket and the photograph into my wallet, where it'd be safe.

"Well, hello there, gorgeous."

A stunning white girl with soft curves spilling out of her gown ran a finger down my arm, flashing me a smile I'd seen Roger use countless times. Definitely a Revelle. I checked behind me to see who she was talking to.

She giggled. "I've been looking for you."

"Me?"

"Come with me." Taking my hand, she pulled me into the crowd.

I stumbled behind her. "Did Roger send you?"

"How do you know Roger?"

"We're friends. We came here together."

"That's a story I'd love to hear. Another time, handsome. Just follow me."

She moved with a practiced grace. I tried to keep up, but paths opened for her and eclipsed for me. "Where are we going exactly?"

"It's your lucky night. Luxe Revelle has requested a private meeting with you."

The party blinked from existence.

So I hadn't imagined the connection between us. She was alive. And she was asking for *me*. "She's—She's okay?"

The girl giggled. "She's fine. Come see for yourself."

She led me through crushed velvet curtains. Performers draped in colorful costumes crossed paths with organized chaos. A pack of children wielding broken hangers smacked my legs, collateral damage in their battle as they swept past us. My unfazed guide turned a corner, slowing only to wave to a woman breastfeeding a sleeping baby, her sequined cocktail uniform pushed off her bare shoulder.

Up narrow stairs next. The walls were no longer stripes of plum and black, but dark, aged wood. With the quiet came the onslaught of reality: there was no way Luxe Revelle wanted to see me. "Are you sure about this?"

She gave me a funny look. "Of course, gorgeous!"

We passed a door left slightly ajar. Inside, an elderly man with silver hair giggled gleefully, his fingers poking the air around him. "Bubbles!" he sang.

The girl snorted. "That's Mr. Lee. He lives in the Day District, but every Saturday evening he walks to the Night to ask for the same fantasy: to frolic in a room full of bubbles."

"That's . . . Wow."

"I know, right? We can make him experience anything he desires, yet every time he chooses bubbles. Harmless, at least."

A scream sounded from behind the next door. "Are some of the fantasies *not* harmless?"

My guide didn't even flinch as the screams grew louder. "Nothing we can't handle."

We came to a stop in front of a wooden door at the end of a long hallway, the face of which was carved in a series of dizzying diamonds. Luxe Revelle was behind this door.

"She, ah, probably needs her rest after that fall," I stammered. "I could come back."

The girl winked. "All part of the show. But if you'd prefer, I can take you to *my* room instead. All it'll cost are a few teensy, tiny gems."

"I'm afraid I don't have any money," I admitted. She at least deserved a tip or something.

Her laughter came out in a snort. What a strange sense of humor.

My hand hovered over the doorknob. "And you're certain she asked for *me*?"

"A word of advice." The girl leaned closer. "When the Radiant Ruby summons you, don't ask questions. Just count your lucky stars." She thrust open the door, pushing me inside.

As the door clicked shut, the softest giggle rang out behind me. Slowly, I turned.

Luxe Revelle leaned against the bedpost wearing little more than a skimpy robe of raven black. Pale curves peeked out between dark lace appliqués. Straightening herself, she uncrossed her ankles and the delicate fabric shifted, revealing the lush skin of her thighs.

I spun to face the wall. "I'm sorry, I didn't mean to barge in like this."

"From where I'm sitting, it looked like Millie dragged you here."

Her voice. That airy, ethereal voice was even sweeter here

than it had been onstage because it was real—and it was tinged with exhaustion.

I'd ask after her. That was all. "I . . . I, uh, just wanted to make sure that you're okay."

"So that's why you're here. To make sure I'm . . . *okay.*" She ran her hands over the lacy robe, her eyes sparkling.

"You gave me quite a scare earlier. Not just me, of course. I mean, all of us watching."

Curls tumbled over her shoulders as she glided toward me. And those pouty lips, the flush in her cheeks, the delicate smattering of freckles over her nose—

I stepped backward. "I should, ah . . ."

"You were saying?" A wicked smile settled on her lips. She knew the effect she had on me—and she was enjoying it.

Was Luxe Revelle *flirting* with me?

The realization sent a thrill right to my core, and my body responded in ways that, according to the friars, should have had me struck by lightning on the spot.

The sense of rightness when we'd locked eyes, the rest of the world disappearing as she'd sang to me—*she'd felt it, too.* I wasn't one to believe in fate, but maybe, just maybe . . .

She stepped close enough to intoxicate me with her sweet perfume, but this time, I didn't retreat. Onstage, she was a fully grown woman, but up close she was my age or a little younger.

And she'd fallen.

Only then did I notice the shadows under her eyes, the faint tension in the corners of her mouth each time she moved her head. "Are you hurt?"

She pressed her palm to her chest. "Worried about my

well-being? How *touching*." Her hand slid downward, shifting the robe ever so slightly to reveal those perfect—

"I'm sorry!" I blurted again, turning away.

"For what, exactly?" She tugged gently on my arm, turning me back to her. Everything about her was inviting, flirtatious, dizzying, and yet there were fleeting glimpses of her waning strength. A waver in her step, tension in her smile, all gone as quickly as they appeared.

The friars had never liked us to advertise our injuries to the parishioners in church on Sundays. When their heavy rods left dark bruises, they were always in places we could hide, like our backs and stomachs. To reveal your suffering was a surefire way to get beaten again. We learned to conceal our misfortunes. And I learned to read the subtle signs of masked pain.

She caressed my shoulders, loosening Dewey's tight jacket. Maybe I was wrong.

"Why don't you take off your coat and stay awhile?"

"Me? I, ah . . . yes, I suppose." I shook off the too-small coat. Christ, I was tripping over my words like I was fresh out of St. Douglas's. A few hours ago, I had stumbled off a ferry and admired her posters. Then I'd watched her fall at least six stories. Yet here she was, in one piece, curling her hands around my suspenders. Maybe I had given a Revelle a jewel after all, and this was but a magic-infused dream.

Her lips curving, she rested her hands on my shoulders. Such soft hands. So warm. And, if I wasn't mistaken, they were trembling.

Not a dream, then. In any dream of mine, she'd never be in pain.

Gently, I removed her hands.

She blinked at me. "Is something wrong?"

Time to say something intelligent. Gentlemanly.

"I, uh, I'm sorry," I stammered. "I didn't wish to disturb you, just to make sure . . . because you fell . . ."

"All part of the act, I assure you." There was that kaleidoscope smile again. Beautiful, ever-shifting, as if trying to find the right permutation to please me.

I didn't want her to *try*; I just wanted her to talk to me—and to sit before she collapsed again. "Maybe you should rest," I tried to say, but her proximity rendered my mouth useless.

"You can see I'm quite unharmed." She motioned over her body, and I squeezed my hands into fists at my sides. As if sensing her effect on me, she inched closer. "There must be something else I can do for you."

"Do for *me*?" A laugh escaped me.

Her smile slipped, a rare glimpse underneath the mask. "Why is that funny?"

I was tempted to laugh again so I could see another flash of her authentic self, but I couldn't upset her, not even for a moment. "You must be exhausted. Why would I ask you to do anything for me?"

She arched her brow. "You accepted my invitation for a reason."

To see you again, to be near you, to see if you felt what I felt.

"If you'd like me to go—"

"No!"

"You want me to stay?"

A single nod. Somewhere in the distance, an accordion picked up a lively tune.

She wanted me to stay. *Me.*

"Why?" I found myself asking.

"You'll think me silly."

"I assure you, I won't."

She looked down at her feet. "It *is* silly, especially given your family, and my family, and, well . . . you know."

Our families? She was holding back because of concerns about our *families*? "I don't have any family." Never before had I been so happy to utter those words.

"I'm glad you see it that way." She drew a deep breath. "I noticed you in the crowd, and I . . . well, I was just telling my cousins that I'd like to get to know you better. And here you are."

"And here I am." By some miracle, I managed to keep standing. "Your cousin came and found me."

She scraped her white teeth over her pouting lip. "Millie can be a little forward. I'm sorry if we disturbed your night."

"Not at all!" I squeaked. *Keep it together, Jamison.* Roger used to tell me to stop acting surprised when someone showed interest in me. But this wasn't just anyone, and her interest in me certainly wasn't another fleeting flirtation. She'd invited *me* here when she could have had anyone in the crowd.

I steadied myself. "To be honest, your performance was absolutely hypnotizing. I was in awe. And then you fell, and I couldn't bear the thought of something happening to you. I know it sounds like complete nonsense, especially because I don't know you, but—"

"It's not nonsense," she breathed.

My heart ballooned to twice its size. "You don't think so?"

"No." She looked up at me with the sweetest smile. "It might be the most noble reason anyone has entered the Revelle Fun House."

I glanced around the room, at the ornate gold-painted bed, the crushed velvet curtains, and her negligée. "I'm in the *Fun House?*"

She stiffened. "You don't intend to use that jewel?"

"My mother's brooch? No! I mean, I would be honored, but . . ." How could I have been so thick? I'd been so desperate to see her, I hadn't even paid attention to where her cousin took me.

"Are you *laughing?*" Frustration tightened her sweet voice.

"I'm sorry." I tried to hide my amusement behind my hand. I was never going to live this down with Roger and Trys. *Remember the time Jamison stumbled into the Fun House and didn't even know it?* "Do you mind if we have a seat? My head is spinning a bit."

She looked relieved. She refused to sit when it was for her sake, but for someone else's, she would. I tucked away that little detail about her.

There were no chairs in this room. Just the bed.

She patted a spot beside her, but I stood a safe distance away. "If, ah, you're looking to make money . . ."

She waved a hand. "You and I are becoming such good friends, aren't we? Let's not ruin that by talking about money."

Relief swept over me, a balm to my misgivings. "I couldn't agree more."

"So now that we've established that we are, in fact, in the Fun House, and I am, in fact, a Revelle, perhaps you could tell me what your fantasy *would* be, if you gave me that jewel." She wore the mask of the seductress once more, flirtation dripping from each word.

A rush of heat coursed through my veins. "I'm sorry?"

She patted the bed beside her. "Tell me what you want to experience more than anything in the world, and we can see about making it come true."

My mind went blank. Not a single coherent thought rose to the surface.

She watched me carefully. Waiting.

"I, uh, I don't know."

From beneath those thick lashes, her eyes smoldered. "Not all fantasies require magic, you know."

My mouth went dry.

The seconds ticked away as she pinned me under the heat of her gaze. "Surely there must be something."

"I'm trying to think."

She smoothed the comforter, waiting.

And waiting.

". . . Anything?" Frustration tinged her sweet voice. "What would make tonight absolutely incredible for you?"

"You may not believe this, but meeting you has already made tonight incredible."

There. I'd said it.

Surprise loosened her mouth into a delicate *O*. My heart squeezed. "And all we've done thus far is talk."

"That's more than enough," I said honestly. "To talk with you, to learn everything I can about you. That's all I want to do."

The silence stretched for a heartbeat. Then another.

If I wasn't mistaken, the formidable edge to her gaze softened. "You're a bit of a puzzle."

"You're the real puzzle. You—You remind me of a kaleidoscope."

That Effigen drink had robbed me of all sense of self-preservation. Apparently, any blasted thought running through my head was fair game.

"What?"

No smooth way out of this came to mind, so I resorted to the truth. "You flash these pretty, distracting versions of yourself, and you seem to know just how to adjust them to fit whatever fancy you believe me to have. As I shift, they shift, too, distracting me from . . . well, distracting me from the girl at the center."

She sat up straight. "The girl at the center?"

"She's even more beautiful." I waited until she looked at me so she could see how much I meant my words. "She hides her pain. And she's . . . sad. I'd do anything in my power to take away her sadness."

My pulse thudded in my ears, the only reprieve from the silence as she gawked at me.

I'd said too much. Any moment now, and she'd laugh in my face.

"Do you really want to know what makes me sad?" No longer was she the star of the Revelle show, not with her shoulders caving underneath the weight of the world.

"Tell me." I leaned closer. "Please."

Kicking off her shoes, she hugged her legs to her chest. "My family. Even after nights like tonight, after we've accounted for all the expenses, the profit margin is thin. And with black-market liquor prices what they are . . ." Her sweet voice trailed off.

When the older orphans had whispered stories about the Revelles, I'd pictured their luxurious tent draped in gemstones and riches. But Roger had explained his family's awful conundrum plenty of times: jewels crumbled under their magic, making it difficult for all but the strongest Revelles to turn a good profit. Lowering customers' inhibitions helped—through booze, risqué costumes, and, of course, the acrobatic spectacles that welcomed the tourists every night. The less magic required, the more profit for the Revelles. But there were too many mouths to feed and not enough gems left over. Their brand was built on decadence, but the Revelles were broke.

Before I could respond, Luxe's mask snapped back into place. "It's not easy to explain."

She didn't like to be vulnerable. Another precious tidbit I tucked away. "You don't need to. Roger told me all about your family's financial woes."

That got her attention. "Roger already asked for your help?"

"I don't think he realized there was a way I *could* help. But I'd be glad to. Anything for Roger's family. For you."

She sat perfectly still, as if frozen in shock. "Really?"

Emboldened, I laid my hand over hers. God himself might have smote me down in that moment, but I didn't care. Her skin was soft, the bones of her wrist delicate. "I know I've just met you, but . . . I'd do anything to keep you happy."

That was certainly on Roger's list of things I should never say to a girl.

"I think you know what I want." The vulnerability in her voice pierced my heart.

"Anything for you."

She leaned closer, her lips grazing the tip of my ear as she whispered, "Even liquor?"

For all that was holy. If she asked me to sell my soul to the devil, I'd ask where to sign.

"I'd give you all the liquor in the world, if I could," I murmured, "and my heart, if you'll have it."

A storm of emotions washed over her graceful features, relief among them. As if there were any doubt about how I felt.

Before I could utter another word, she closed the space between us. Those same lips that had sung to me, had twisted into a dozen permutations of her dazzling smile—those lips found mine. A thousand fireworks sparked over my skin, engulfing me in sweet flames.

I forgot how to breathe.

I forgot how to move my arms, my legs, anything but my lips.

I forgot my own name as I melted against her.

SEVEN

LUXE

I'd had my fair share of kisses, checked them off the list of experiences my mother would have wanted for me. A Night District boy whose family worked the docks. An Effigen who broke the kiss to blurt out math problems to make sure I hadn't obliterated his mind. An overconfident tourist so determined to seduce the star of the Revelle show that he'd dipped me backward like he was auditioning for a motion picture. Those kisses had been fine. Exciting, even.

But no kiss had come close to this one.

For a heartbeat, Dewey froze in surprise. Then he leaned forward, brushing his lips to mine with a tenderness that warmed me deep in my chest. His mouth moved slowly, dotingly, stealing my breath. As he pressed a steady hand to my cheek, his thumb brushed against the spot where my pulse beat erratically at my throat. He kissed me delicately, every pass of his lips brimming with possibility, but there was nothing delicate about the dizzying rush of adrenaline coursing through me, more thrilling than letting go of the trapeze and somersaulting through the air, those electrifying moments where sky and ground swirled together, daring me to fall.

The Big Tent's music faded to oblivion. The chattering of distant voices disappeared. We'd stumbled upon something incredible, something startlingly potent, and it was only us.

He broke the kiss, sucking in air as if he, too, had forgotten how to breathe. With our foreheads pressed together, neither of us spoke. Silent in quiet reverence to this perfect, fragile moment. His shoulders rose and fell with each ragged breath, but his awe-struck gaze never wavered from me. Waiting. Savoring.

I wrapped my arms around his neck and kissed him again. His skin was feverish through his tuxedo shirt, but he shivered as I buried my hands in his hair, dark locks cool between my fingers. He inhaled softly against my mouth as I melted into him, his arms cradling me as if I were something precious. Our lips grew bolder, and my heart raced so fast it might burst—

Someone knocked.

We froze, our mouths millimeters apart. He cupped my face as if he couldn't believe I was real. A Chronos who was kind and inquisitive and kissed like *that*? The feeling was mutual.

And he was going to give me all the liquor in the world.

Another knock.

I groaned. "Go away!"

Laughter relaxed his face. I couldn't help myself; I ran my thumb along his jawline. It could have cut diamonds. And his thick hair, the way my hands had ruined whatever he'd used to slick it back, sending it tumbling over his forehead—

That damn knocking again, this time more insistent.

I untangled myself from his arms. "Don't move an inch."

Whoever was at the door was fired. Immediately.

Colette stood there with a handsome guy with dark hair and porcelain skin. Rich, too, judging by the expensive-looking vest and tie he wore. Good for her.

"This room's taken." She should have known better than to interrupt.

She grabbed the door before it shut again, her eyes flashing in warning. "Luxe, this is *Dewey Chronos*."

I narrowed my eyes at the imposter, ready to give him a piece of my mind, but he held out his hand, his wristwatch unmistakable. One of a kind. He *was* Dewey Chronos.

Oh no.

No, no, *NO*.

Every black opal on his watch sang to my Revelle blood as he kissed my hand.

I couldn't think. Couldn't breathe. Couldn't believe I was such a fool.

"Your cousin said you wished to meet with me?" He arched a brow over his dark eyes. Brown, like Uncle Wolffe had said.

"Yes, of course. I, ah, noticed you in the crowd, and . . . my sincerest apologies, but give me just one teensy moment?"

Colette looked ready to throttle me, and Dewey opened his mouth to say more, but I closed the door. "Don't go anywhere!" I called.

Bloody hell. I just slammed the door on the guy who held our future in his rich hands.

"Who was that?" the beautiful imposter asked. The one who had promised me *all the liquor in the world*.

"Get. Out." I pointed to the window.

His eyes widened, their sapphire shade so lovely I wanted to gouge them out.

I grabbed a discarded high heel and aimed it at him. "Get out, or I'll stab you in the neck and feed you to the tigers."

"Luxe?" Colette fumbled with the keys. "We're coming in."

I was a dead girl. I'd had *one* job to do—

"Under the bed. Quick!" I lifted the shoe over the imposter, and he stumbled off the bed.

The door burst open just as the damn trickster crouched at my feet, barely out of sight.

"Welcome!" I dropped the shoe behind my back, and the stranger hissed in pain. I stomped my foot to drown out the sound.

Colette gave me a funny look. "I'll leave you to it."

The real Dewey Chronos removed his hat as he surveyed the room. Gone was the pale child I'd seen hugging his mother's skirts all those years ago, replaced by this young man who, with his pristine haircut and sharp suit, looked as though he'd walked right off the page of a fashion magazine. The *other* one had messy hair in desperate need of a trim. He hadn't even worn a tie. And I'd kissed him. Like a fool, I'd lost myself in that kiss.

I pressed a hand to my swollen lips and flashed Dewey a coquettish smile.

He handed me a bouquet of purple calla lilies. "Oh!" I exclaimed. "They're—"

"Your favorite?" He smiled, revealing a faint dimple on his left cheek.

"Actually, yes." He'd done his research. Who could have told him my favorite flower?

I nudged the imposter by my feet. He was much too big to fit under the bed, but he was going to have to try. "Thank you for meeting with me," I began again. "I hope my cousin didn't disturb your evening."

He waved a dismissive hand. "When the star of the Revelle show summons you, it's a good night indeed. Though I'd like to be clear up front: I won't be giving you a jewel."

My heart sank. I could practically hear the imposter chuckling.

"How about we get some fresh air?" I suggested. Loudly.

"So you don't think me rude, then?" He was testing me. If only I could tap into my other magic to see what response would win him over.

Young and rich. Newly successful. He wanted to be admired.

Stepping around the bed, I looped my arm in his. "For not giving me a jewel? That makes you smart."

He flashed two rows of brilliant white teeth. He was handsome, all right, and he knew it.

I led him toward the door, kicking the suit jacket with the diamond-shaped clock out of our way. "Allow me a moment to put on something a little, ah, warmer."

"I'll wait here." He turned in the hallway, letting his eyes roam the length of me. He liked what he saw. Hopefully well enough to give us seriously discounted booze.

I held my smile while he pulled the door closed slowly. Very slowly.

As soon as it clicked shut, the other boy rose to his feet. So tall. If the real Dewey were this big, my uncle would have mentioned it. He strode right past me, stopping in front of the framed photograph of my mother and aunts on the beach.

"Where was this taken?" His voice was breathless, almost reverent.

Was he really asking me about a beach right now? "You need to leave. Now."

He traced the intricate carvings on the dock. "Is this dock here, in Charmant?"

"I have no idea," I lied, trying—and failing—to pull him toward the window.

He tore his gaze from the picture, eyes stormy. "Do you ever tell the truth?"

"*You're* the liar!" I exclaimed. "You're the one who talked your way into the Fun House pretending to be someone else. And then you promised me liquor!"

"You made me believe you felt something for me." He shook his head in disgust.

Even worse, I *had* felt something. Like a lonely, lovesick sap, I'd taken one look at those pretty blue eyes and abandoned a lifetime of lessons about handling customers.

"And *you* made me believe you were worth my time." I pointed to the window. "Now leave before you do more damage."

"I'm not breaking my neck climbing out a second-story window. And I'm taking this." He removed the picture from the wall, tucked it under his arm, and headed toward the door.

"Have you lost your mind?" I grabbed him, ignoring the hard muscle of the arms that had just held me close. "Out the window. And the picture stays."

He ripped his arm away. "You want it? Then tell me where I can find this dock."

"Do I look like a tour guide?" I ripped the frame from his hands, surprise working in my favor. "I don't have time for this. Now go! Before I call the police."

He narrowed his eyes. "Dewey's a nice guy. I should warn him about your little games."

He wouldn't dare. "Dewey's a businessman. He knows exactly what this is."

"Then he won't be surprised that you kissed me a few minutes ago."

My cheeks burned. How dare he try to *shame* me. A high heel to the jugular was what he deserved, but I didn't have time to hide a corpse. "It's a small beach just west of the promenade. The dock's gone—"

His face fell. "Then how will I know it's the right beach?"

"*Still* not a tour guide." I motioned toward the window.

He crossed his arms. "*Still* not leaving."

"Fine," I growled. "I'll show you tomorrow—as long as you leave right now and never utter a word of this to anyone."

He hesitated, clearly not trusting a word I said. Smart boy. There wasn't a chance in hell I was going anywhere with him.

"Please," I hissed. "Go."

"Like I'd want to stay." He climbed out the window, eyes shooting daggers at me the whole time. As if *I* were to blame for his deceit.

No time to lick my wounds. Or to scream. I threw on a long silk skirt I found in the bottom of a drawer, squeezed my tired feet back into my heels, and checked my little inkwell. A small fleck of magic had returned, hardly enough to magnify a naturally occurring feeling.

I'd use it to read Dewey's emotions. Nothing more.

As I called to my magic, sharp talons dragged down my skull. I bit my knuckle to keep the pain at bay, but my overused magic dug deeper, sharper—

His lightstring appeared through the door. Excited. Cautious. A bit wary.

I'd worked with less.

Swallowing the pain, I grabbed the lilies, threw open the door, and batted my lashes at him. "Ready?"

In silence, I led him down the side stairwell to avoid the influx of customers—and Revelles—through the main doors. He held the bottom door for me, and warm, salty air rushed into the hall, so humid I could practically feel my hair frizzing.

To the left, the stone walkway wove between the Fun House and the ocean, disappearing into the fog. If we walked that way, we'd have privacy from the tourists, but any curious Revelle child could eavesdrop from the first-floor windows. The path to the right led back to the front of the Big Tent, where music and shouting blared through the crowded streets, and the dark cliffs of the slumbering Day District blotted out the stars—far from private, but perhaps he'd feel more comfortable in view of the Chronoses' ritzy neighborhood.

He took my arm as we started down the path to the right. "Miss Revelle—"

"Please. Call me Luxe."

The corners of his mouth twitched. "All right, Luxe. I know we've only just met, and there's a bit of—bad blood, shall we say?—between our families. But I'd like us to be honest with each other."

If he truly desired honesty, he would have brought Trevor Edwardes, his mind-reading assistant. But he hadn't. He wanted me to trust him.

"I'd like that, too."

"Now tell me the truth: you fell by accident, and a Strattori fixed you up."

I shouldn't have been surprised; it was clear from how young he looked that he rarely used his magic, which meant he had talents other than time traveling. Perhaps he was clever. A pity. Simpler men were far easier to win over.

"Helen Strattori. She's a friend of my family."

He slowed his step to study me. "Using Strattori magic makes you uncomfortable."

Perceptive, too. "I don't like when other people make sacrifices for me."

"I used to feel the same. In my line of work, it's important that I'm at full capacity at all times. If I spend a week recovering, I lose money, and the people who work for me do, too. Money they depend on to feed their families. It's better to let them endure my ailments for me so I can better provide for them. I reward them generously, of course. Don't get me wrong," he added quickly. "I still don't like.it. I'm just . . . I do think it's for the best."

We can't afford to sideline our star for weeks, Nana had said. "Well, Mr. Chronos, I daresay we have that in common."

He chuckled, his lightstring flashing with a spark of affection. "Call me Dewey. Now, entertain me for a moment. Our families' views on our, ah, feud, are probably quite different."

That was an understatement.

"My family, for example, taught me we came here first. My ancestors felt the pull of magic as they sailed to Ellis Island. They returned by canoe a few days later, and the vortex tides brought them to shore. Does this sound right so far?"

"More or less." I had no idea what he was trying to accomplish.

"Rumors of the island's amplification of magic spread, leading other families with magic to immigrate here, too, including yours.

As the world grew more wary of magic, this island was one of the few places left where we could live in peace." An amused smile darkened his features. "I suppose this is where our versions of history differ."

I kept my face a mask of calm. Sure, my family had arrived after the Chroneses, but we'd won the first election—and several after that. Under my ancestors' leadership, Charmant's tourism boomed. Any entrepreneur could find work here, with or without magic. But not everyone loved the bawdy good time the island had become. The Strattoris retreated to the eastern hills, their sacred magic little more than a legend to the tourists. The Chroneses took the seaside cliffs in the north, making careful investments that increased their wealth while hardly setting foot on our beaches. Their candles were snuffed shortly after nightfall while the Big Tent's parties continued until dawn. Hence, the Day and Night Districts were born.

"To spread the Revelles' influence, your family changed Charmant's currency from US dollars to gemstones," he continued. "But politicians who could manipulate public opinion were practically unstoppable. So my family began pooling their magic together. It's no secret how we thrive: like a colony of ants, all the workers run themselves ragged in service of their *chosen one*." Bitterness punctuated his words. "My great-grandfather was the first Chronos mayor of Charmant. You know the rest."

What did he expect me to say: The Chroneses had gained power nearly seventy years ago, and they'd never let it go since? They'd sabotaged my family over and over again, each disaster robbing us of our status, our wealth, our security? I nodded. "I know the rest."

He studied me for a long moment. I held my breath and stared right back.

"You're not like the Revelle stars of the past," he finally said. "You're . . . different."

Dangerous territory. "What makes you say that?"

"Pockets were being emptied for you tonight. Diamonds were pried from their settings and tossed in your direction." He stopped walking, the music of Main Street still a good distance away. "You're more powerful than the others."

He was edging too close to the truth. "I can make the gems last a little longer, yes."

"That wasn't what I said." His tone remained curious, even amused.

I leaned closer, inhaling the rich spices of his cologne. "Would you like to trade secrets, Mr. Chronos? I'll tell you mine if you tell me yours."

"I would like that very much, Miss Revelle." His smile made him even younger. The kid bootlegger, Uncle Wolffe had called him. Rich and successful without time traveling often enough to wrinkle. "How about the fainting? Does that happen often?"

I'd risk overusing my dwindling magic before I let him think of me as weak. "Fortunately, no. I hadn't had enough to eat earlier. First-night jitters."

A strange disappointment seeped into his lightstring, gone as quickly as it had appeared. "You know, I had to seek the services of a Strattori tonight, too."

"Oh? What happened?"

"I tried to catch a falling star."

Catch a falling—a gasp escaped me. "I landed on *you*?"

The dim light of distant Main Street revealed his faint blush.

"Technically, I caught you, and we crashed into a portly gentleman. He's fine, by the way. I paid for his healing as well."

Seven hells. I hadn't even considered the tourists I'd hurt. And I'd fallen on Dewey Chronos—my mark, of all people. What were the odds?

Next to none.

"Did you *travel* for me?" I could hardly believe the words I uttered.

With a cryptic smile, he nodded.

Chronoses didn't use their magic to help others, and they certainly didn't use it to help *us*. "I don't know what to say. If you hadn't been there—"

He winced, which was all the answer I needed. However I'd first fallen, before Dewey traveled . . . I owed him my life.

"I didn't come here for your gratitude. I came here to make a deal."

My heart thumped within my chest. It was now or never. "A liquor deal?"

He fixed his silk tie. "Perhaps. If you agree to my terms."

I leaned into his lightstring, my pitiful magic protesting with a sharp bite of pain in my skull, so abrupt and so brutal, I nearly cried out. *You're feeling generous*, I whispered down his lightstring, *extremely generous*.

"You're a talented young woman, Miss Revelle, but you need to dream bigger. Picture this." He spread his arms wide, moonlight capturing the excitement in his eyes. "A new leader of Charmant, one who can stop my family from meddling in *your* family's business so everyone on the island has the opportunity to prosper. What do you think?"

"Sounds like you've had one too many Effigen cocktails."

He laughed, a deep, throaty sound. "My family has gone too far in their quest to keep your family weak. Revelle children wither away all winter long, while Chronos children throw away more food than they eat. It's time for a regime change, don't you think?"

But there was no beating a Chronos, not when they controlled the police, the banks, even time itself. "Pray, tell me: Who is this mystery candidate willing to take on your family?"

He leaned closer, his lips spreading in that devilish smile again. "Me."

The little bit of hope I'd foolishly mustered blew away like glitter on a breeze. Of course. A Chronos replaced by another Chronos. "Aren't you a little young to be mayor?"

"I'm twenty-one." He tugged on the lapels of his vest. "It's unconventional, yes, but won't people be more likely to trust a Chronos without wrinkles? One who doesn't abuse his magic?"

"To be perfectly honest, I'm not sure Night citizens can tell one Chronos from another."

He frowned. "I'm different from my family. I've lived in the Night District for two years now. It's my home. Everyone who works for me receives a fare wage, and I only travel to protect my investments. Even that's rare, as you can see." He flashed that youthful smile again, holding it until I cracked one of my own.

"With Prohibition," he continued, "we still need a time traveler in charge to prevent any surprises from the mainland police. Now, I'm no fool; I know most of the Night hates my family. But my liquor keeps the tourists happy and businesses open. My company employs more than a third of Night District citizens. If I had more time, I could win them all over, but my father just announced a special election in August, four weeks from now. He's stepping down and has endorsed my brother to take his place. George's candidacy is uncontested, of course."

There was that anger again, gathering in his lightstring like shadows at dusk. Jealousy, too. So the rumors were true: his father had skipped over Dewey and chosen George as his successor. And now Dewey wanted to take them all down.

"And let me guess," I said slowly. "You want my family to endorse you."

"I want *you* to endorse me."

The lilies in my hands suddenly felt too heavy, their sweet aroma too pungent. "I see."

"You're the most celebrated face in the Night. If you supported me publicly, we'd have a real chance at beating my brother."

"Which your family would never allow," I reminded him. "Like you said, they pool their magic together. What's one time traveler versus dozens?" Dewey would have to travel so much to keep them in check, he'd be old and feeble before the election ever happened.

"There are more Chronoses sympathetic to our cause than you think. My sister, for example, has spent the last three years traveling the country with your cousin Roger."

Roger had been traveling with a Chronos?

He fiddled with the rim of his hat. "These are my terms, Miss Revelle: You endorse me for mayor, and I'll sell your uncle all the liquor the Big Tent needs. For cheap."

There it was. Exactly what we needed, dangling right in front of me like a heavy diamond pendant. All I needed to do was reach out and grab it.

But I'd already been fooled by a handsome face tonight. Already heard empty promises of *all the liquor in the world*.

"If I helped you," I said carefully, "I'd be painting a big sparkling bull's-eye on my back. Your family would make sure I suffered some fatal 'accident' long before the election."

His face darkened. "I'd never let anything happen to you. Even if I have to become old and gray long before my time, I promise: no one will lay a finger on you."

More promises, though his lightstring shone with surprising loyalty. He'd already saved my life once. But even if he could keep me safe, he couldn't keep *all* of us safe. And once the election was over, what was to stop him from raising his prices again?

"So I risk your family's wrath, not to mention *my* family's wrath, and we get discounted booze. But you get to become mayor? Hardly seems fair."

"You'll have a mayor of Charmant indebted to you. Your family will prosper again."

Such pretty words. I was so tired of pretty words.

"I'm sorry, Mr. Chronos." I held out the lilies for him to take. "As badly as we need hooch, I won't put my family at risk for a coupon."

He didn't take the lilies, but he let me walk away, though his lightstring brimmed with frustration. He needed me just as much as I needed him.

Two steps. Three. Four. Uncle Wolffe would have my head if I actually walked away.

"Name your price," Dewey called.

The night hid my smile.

Slowly, I turned, letting the slit of the long skirt ride up my leg.

His eyes grazed over me. Beneath the caution in his lightstring, red began to take root. Lust.

"The old warehouse by the docks. You bought it."

The strangeness of his new theater had prickled the back of my mind since Uncle Wolffe had spoken of it earlier. Dewey was too clever to try to outdo us. The tourists would accept nothing less than our magic-infused spectacles and the Fun House fantasies that followed, and he knew it.

Sure enough, no surprise flashed in his lightstring, only excitement. "What about it?"

"I want it."

His lips quirked. "Why?"

Because Dewey was right; too many Revelle children went hungry all winter. The Big Tent's dilapidated canvas was no match for the frigid autumn winds, and the ferries were too blisteringly cold for the tourists to trek here only to freeze at our show. By mid-September, tourism slowed to a crawl. To survive the long winters, we had to stretch our summer gems.

But if we had a place to perform with thick walls and a roaring fire . . .

Decadent winter leotards draped with fur. Snow-kissed wreaths. My family with meat on their bones all year long. The Big Tent would always be the heart of the Night, but an additional winter theater, where Prohibition was a faraway nuisance? Freezing ferry or not, the customers would come in droves.

"In addition to liquor at half price, we could use another place to perform in the winters."

He arched a brow. "I've already started to turn it into a performance center of my own."

What good was a theater to a bootlegger? His fleet of ferries made sense; they helped transport liquor as well as tourists to drink it. And another warehouse could store his booze, sure. But a theater, especially one without Revelles? Maybe this was what he'd wanted all along.

"That should make this easy," I said lightly, studying him from beneath my lashes.

He laughed. "I knew we were going to get along splendidly."

"So we have a deal?" The pitch in my voice betrayed my desperation. *You wish to make a deal*, I whispered down his lightstring. Pain radiated down my head, my ears buzzing loud enough for me to wobble on my feet.

He stepped closer. "I give you an expensive piece of prime real estate, plus liquor—for half price—and you say a few words lending me your support? I think we've swung too far in your favor, don't you?"

"I quite like where we've landed."

"I bet you do." He stepped even closer, his chest nearly grazing mine. "I'll lease it for a share of the profits, but you need to do more than endorse me."

My pulse quickened. For the second time tonight, I was inches from an attractive young man offering me everything my family needed. But this time, I would keep my wits about me. This time, I'd get it. "What do you have in mind?"

"If I'm going to be king of the Night District," he said quietly, "then I need a queen."

I didn't dare move, not as he lifted his hand to my cheek, angling my face toward his.

"I want you by my side during all my public appearances.

Shake hands, kiss babies, everything. Let everyone believe the Revelle star has fallen in love with the bootlegger. And if anyone happens to give you a jewel, I want you to charm them into voting for me." His thumb caressed my chin. "Once the election is over, we can stage a breakup, if you'd like."

A ruse. A prolonged performance. "Interesting proposition."

"Do we have a deal?" He kept his hand on my chin, so close to where the *other* Dewey had so reverently touched my cheek— *No.* No thinking about that disaster yet, not when I was so close to getting everything we needed.

Liquor. A winter theater. The chance of a mayor sympathetic to the Revelles—still a Chronos, but better than George and his vicious temper. Maybe, just maybe, we stood a chance.

"No Revelles get hurt." I kept my gaze trained on those clever brown eyes. "If something happens to anyone in my family, the deal's off."

"No Revelle gets hurt," he agreed. "I'll make sure of it."

He could, too. With his magic, he could literally rewind time to prevent disaster. He'd done it tonight. For me.

"So we have a deal?"

Nana might murder me for making a deal with the devil, but Uncle Wolffe would understand. "If my uncle approves, I'm in."

"I have it on good authority he'll agree."

"It's settled, then."

"Excellent." He stepped back, clasping his hands together. "Four weeks isn't much time to win an election, so we'll need to start campaigning immediately. To announce my bid, I'm throwing an enormous party for celebrities, politicians, and all my donors. Every magical family will be invited. Except mine, of course, though they'll wish they were." He laughed darkly, two rows of straight teeth glistening in the moonlight.

"Sounds divine." I was tempted to dig into my magic, to carve away the hurt that flashed whenever he mentioned his family, but the pounding in my head was a jackhammer, and I had little left to keep me upright.

He took my hand and pressed a kiss to it, letting his lips linger there. "We're going to be unstoppable, the two of us. You'll see."

With a tip of his hat, he walked away, whistling to himself as he strutted toward the bright lights of Main Street. How bold he must feel all the time, never looking over his shoulder, knowing he could turn back time if someone came for him. How bold indeed.

I turned back toward home, but— *Whoa.* My legs wobbled as the world tilted, the night's heat suddenly burning me up. Gripping my head, I released his lightstring as slowly as I could, the pain easing until he turned the corner and I let it go completely.

The pain faded as I stumbled off the walkway, kicked off my shoes, and let myself fall into the soft sand. A warm, wet drop slid from my nostril—a bloody nose. My magic's tax for the possibilities now dangling before me.

Liquor. A heated theater. A partnership with a Chronos. Protection from his family.

Year-round income. No more starving winters.

All I had to do was be his queen.

EIGHT

JAMISON

I circled the narrow alley around the Big Tent, yanking yet another thorn from my pants. The bush had *looked* soft enough from the window, but its sharp leaves had greeted me with a hundred little tears in the only nice trousers I owned.

Everything about tonight was a damn illusion.

A young man guarded the entrance to the Big Tent, his welcoming smile fading as he took in my torn clothes. "Three sapphires."

"I was just inside—"

"Three. Sapphires." He held out his hand expectantly.

I craned my neck around him, but he blocked my view. "Get outta here."

"I'm a friend of Roger Revelle. He'll tell you—"

"No jewels, no entry. Shoo!" He shoved my shoulders.

I stumbled backward, my protest dying on my lips. There was no way they were letting me in. Not without a—

Wait a second.

I patted my chest furiously, but my jacket was gone. *Dewey's* jacket, with my mother's brooch inside it.

"Damnit!" Even though Trys had stopped me from flinging the brooch onto the stage, I'd still managed to lose it. It wasn't freely given, so Luxe couldn't use it against me, though that hadn't stopped her earlier.

I'd get it back. Even if it meant scaling the Fun House walls, I'd get it back.

Music blared from the after-party. All of Charmant flooded through those double doors, pausing only to deposit gems in the waiting hands of the Revelle man. I sat on the curb, the wind blowing sand in my face as I waited for my friends.

This damn island. The devil's toilet, indeed.

Roger had warned me. Trys had, too. Yet I'd still managed to fool myself into thinking a Revelle performer—no, *the* Revelle performer—liked me. Her kiss had felt so right, so perfect—and it'd taken her all of two seconds to find a richer guy and throw me out with the trash.

At least the trash left through a door.

After Betty, I thought I'd learned. Yet here I was, as gullible as ever, convincing myself I'd struck gold when all I held was a fistful of dirt.

Giggling ladies rushed past me, their beaded flapper gowns rustling over the music. "Are you coming inside?"

"I'm broke," I replied gruffly.

They hurried away.

Whenever I was stuck waiting somewhere, my mind liked to torture me with one of the few memories I had of life before the orphanage: waiting for my parents. Time made most of the details hazy, but I'd sat on a soft, worn couch in an unfamiliar living room, playing with a loose tufting button. Strangers had fussed over me. I'd waited, staring out a window, holding my breath every time someone appeared. I'd waited and waited, fighting anyone who kept me from that window. But my parents had never returned.

I'd get my mother's brooch back. Find that dock, the one in my parents' photograph. And once I did, I was going to get the hell off this damn island and never look back. Keep the past in the past, just like Roger always said.

By the time I stood again, dawn glowed just beyond the horizon. An elderly woman sat by the Big Tent's entrance, the same one who had greeted Roger so warmly earlier. With stiff legs, I waited in the dwindling line until it was my turn. "Do you remember me?"

With a sly smile, she looked me up and down. "You'll have to be more specific, sweet cheeks."

"I'm a friend of Roger's. We came here together, but I can't find him."

Her smile slipped. "James, is it?"

"Jamison." I could have collapsed with relief.

She whispered something to the woman beside her, then pulled me to the side, her grip surprisingly strong. "Behind the tent, there's a dirt path in the beach grass. Follow it and you'll come to an old barn beside the beach. Roger's inside."

Finally, some luck. "Thank you."

"Make sure he rests!" she called after me.

There was no escaping the Revelles' music. It echoed off the water as I trudged through the beach grass, dodging the broken glass and sand crabs hardly visible in the hazy light. To the north, the first lamps blinked to life. The Day District, waking up just as the Night went to sleep.

The barn wasn't much to look at: peeled paint, grayed after years in the sun, and heavy wooden doors. Big enough for four horses, at most.

Inside was more storage than barn, with discarded instruments blocking one of the two windows, and lit candles scattered on top of crooked boxes and empty milk crates. Silver moonlight poured through the remaining window, illuminating Trys lounging on a haystack. Beside her, Roger lay on a small cot, his night scarf already tied over his hair, along with crisscrossing bandages over his bare chest.

"What happened?" I exclaimed.

He smirked without lifting his head. "You first."

"I jumped out of the Fun House and landed in a thorn bush. You?"

"I traded my cousin's injuries for free rent at this glorious barn. What a deal, right?"

Luxe. No wonder she was strutting around like she didn't have a care in the world. I slumped into a pile of hay beside the cot. "It has a roof and four walls. We've slept in worse."

"It's the best I could do. Unless Trysta dear wants to pay a visit to her parents?"

"I'm not setting one foot in the Day District." She handed me a tin cup full of water. "What were you doing in the Fun House?"

I told them everything: Millie bringing me there, Luxe playing me like a fool, my graceful exit out a two-story window. I left out the kiss—the mind-blowing, worlds-colliding, absolute rightness of that kiss. Damn Luxe and her magic.

When I was finished, Roger gave me a look. "There's no shame in falling for Revelle magic, you know. There's no way to stop it."

"Except, I don't know, listening to us and not *giving* a Revelle a jewel," Trys muttered.

"I didn't give her a jewel," I insisted. "I don't have any jewels!"

Roger lifted a brow. "Where's your mother's brooch?"

His Revelle blood could tell it wasn't on me. "I left it there, but I didn't *give* it to her."

They exchanged knowing looks.

"I swear, I didn't give her anything. She just . . . tricked me somehow."

A cunning actress. A cruel liar.

Roger sighed. "I know Revelle magic when I see it. Here. Let me show you."

With a grunt, he sat up and pulled out the velvet sack he'd carried as long as I'd known him. Trys leaned closer. "You have a Jamison jewel in your little revenge stash?"

"It's not a *revenge* stash." He dumped the colorful gems into the palm of his hand. "It's more like a just-in-case stash. Anytime I meet someone, I get a jewel from them, just in case."

She examined the colorful jewels. "Still have the one from me?"

"Sure do."

"Before I knew you were Roger Revelle." She shook her head.

"And here I thought I had a famous face. See this one, Jame-o?" He held a canary-yellow gem in the palm of his hand.

"You asked me to hold on to that for you." I had been touched that my new friend trusted me with something so precious.

He smiled guiltily. "I gave it to you. And then you gave it back to me."

Roger. I stared at my friend, getting lost in those glittering

Revelle eyes. He was the most enchanting person I'd ever seen. My heart soared for him, to touch him, to taste his mouth—

As if I'd been doused with a bucket of ice water, all the warmth coursing through me froze, then shattered. I blinked. Trysta was doing a terrible job of hiding her laughter.

Roger couldn't have looked more pleased. "Well? Did you fall in love with me?"

I gaped at my friend. "For a moment there, I thought you were perfect."

"I *am* perfect."

I pressed my hand over my heart, trying to slow its racing. "It felt so real."

"They're still your feelings," he explained. "My magic triggered a genuine emotional response in you. Emotions don't care if they're inspired by the sight of my beautiful face or a little magical cajoling. Feelings are feelings."

It wasn't the first time he'd explained Revelle magic. As much as I hated to admit it, part of me had known all along. That kiss had been too incredible to be real. And magic made far more sense than Luxe Revelle falling for me. "Even without a jewel?"

"You must have given her one. Magic always has a cost, and for my family, it's jewels."

Trys rubbed her hands together. "Well, I'm going to give her a piece of my mind."

"Trys," Roger warned.

"Or maybe I'll travel back to the moment she decided to make her injuries *your* problem and tell her to get lost."

"How would that work, exactly?" I asked. "I mean, what

would happen to this moment right now? Would we disappear? Would this timeline just—cease to exist?"

She shrugged. "There's only one timeline as far as I'm concerned. When I travel, I'm just editing it. Like erasing part of a straight line, then redrawing it in a new direction."

"You'd shave hundreds of hours off your life for me, Trysta dear?" With a smile, Roger closed his eyes. "I knew you loved us."

Trys pulled her blanket close to her chin as she settled into the hay. "The cost of my magic is unfair. Even traveling back a few seconds is rarely worth the risk. If an earlier memory crosses my mind, I could end up accidentally going too far back. And I can never go forward. Other than cheating at cards, there are very few perks."

I sat up straight. "You cheat at cards?"

"Of course not."

We stared at her.

She rolled her eyes. "Okay, fine, occasionally I have a look at your hands."

"So there are unfinished timelines out there," I mused, "where you owe us money."

"And at least one where you're crushed by a crate of booze."

"I can't believe you cheat at cards!" Roger exclaimed. "There truly is no such thing as a trustworthy Chronos."

Trys shot him a look. "And yet a Revelle made a fool out of Jamison tonight."

"It's fine. Truly." I tried to sound convincing. "I'm *really* glad I went to the Fun House because now I have a lead on my parents' photo. Maybe I can track down a record of them visiting here. An old hotel bill, or an address. Who knows, maybe I have a wealthy uncle somewhere who wants to bankroll our debauchery."

"You've said you were close before," Trys said gently.

"This is different. Charmant feels familiar."

"You've said that before, too."

I tried to find the words to wipe the doubt from their faces, to convince them this time wasn't like the other times, when I'd let hope cloud my judgment. "The picture of your mother and your aunts, Rog—it had the same carved dock in the background."

"I wish I remembered the dock. Or the picture." He stifled a yawn. "Once I get back on my feet, we'll walk every beach until we find it."

I settled into the hay, curling underneath the blanket Trys offered me. "Luxe is taking me there later today. Then I'll gladly avoid her for eternity."

Roger's brows lifted. "Are you sure she's helping you?"

"Positive. I made it *very* clear I'd tell Dewey about her scheming if she didn't cooperate."

Trys bit back a smile. "No offense, Jame-o, but you're not exactly intimidating."

"I'm six foot four!"

"With that baby face, you could be as tall as Wolffe and still look like a choirboy."

Ignoring Roger's chuckles, I pulled the blanket closer. "She's coming today. First thing in the morning, I bet. Trust me."

"I can't believe she never came," I muttered.

Five days had passed. Five days, and Luxe never showed up.

Five sleepless nights, too. I'd lain awake, studying every detail on my photograph, comparing it with my memory of the one in the Fun House. Had I imagined the similarities?

I'd walked on every beach in Charmant, but without the intricately carved pier, they all looked the same. At Roger's request, Colette and Millie had tried to find the framed photo for a side-by-side comparison, but it was gone. Luxe didn't want anyone helping me, apparently.

Tonight I would give her no choice.

"And I can't believe I'm going to a Chronos party." Roger lifted his cane—he'd insisted on bringing one as black and sleek as the one Trys always carried, no matter how many times she pointed out that he'd broken ribs, not legs—toward the mansion at the end of the quiet street. Tall hedges cut as straight as a razor lined the perimeter of the property, interrupted by the long brick driveway. In the center of the lawn was an elaborate statue of a diamond-shaped clock.

"And *I* can't believe you talked us into matching tuxedos." Trys pulled on her bow tie. "We look like a tap-dancing brigade."

"A tap-dancing *company*," Roger drawled. "A brigade goes to war, not to a party."

Black and gold, Dewey's invitation had said, which was all the encouragement Roger had needed to raid the Revelle closets. Black tuxedos, golden suspenders, black bow ties, and wide golden ribbons around our top hats. He'd procured golden glitter, too, but Trys had threatened mutiny.

Armed guards patrolled Dewey's roof, the shadows of their guns rising like spires in the moonlight. Despite the humid night, a chill swept the back of my neck. "Sure looks like war."

Trys squinted at the guards. "What is my brother up to?"

"Going somewhere, Trysta?"

We turned as a figure stepped out from a driveway we'd just

passed. Black suit, black suspenders, black dress shirt. He looked a little younger than us, but with a Chronos, one could never be sure.

With a loud sigh, Trysta crossed her arms. "What do you want, Freddy?"

"So you *do* remember your family," the boy sneered.

"Dewey didn't invite you," she said firmly. "So go."

"I have a message from your folks: if you stand by Dewey, there will be consequences."

"I see you've been promoted to errand boy. Tell me, Freddy: Any gray hairs yet?"

"Better than shacking up with Revelle scum." He spat, the glob grazing Roger's shoe.

"Do that again, and I'll charm you into skinny-dipping at Sapphire Cove so all the tourists can have a good laugh at your little Chronos." Roger crooked his pinkie finger for demonstration.

"A swim?" Freddy snickered. "Maybe I'll see your mother on the ocean floor."

I hardly heard their distant music, hardly heard anything except the rush of blood to my head. I surged forward, but Roger grabbed my arm.

"Frederick Claus Chronos," he said evenly, "son of Frank and Lacey Chronos. Nephew to the mayor himself, and cousin to dear Trysta over here." Roger retrieved the velvet jewel sack from his pocket and dumped a few into his hand. "Four years ago, you changed out of your gaudy black suit, put on a sky-blue touristy top hat, and came to the Big Tent. I collected your admission at the door: a tiny black pearl." Roger held the smooth stone up to the streetlight.

All the color drained from Freddy's face.

"You have five seconds to get out of my sight, or you *will* go swimming with my mother tonight." Gone was the usual cadence of Roger's singsong voice. "Four."

Freddy glared at Trys. "Traitor."

"One."

"You said *five* seconds!"

Roger simpered at him. "We Revelle scum never learned to count."

Freddy tripped as he ran away, cursing under his breath.

I stared down the street as he retreated. "Is everyone in your family that awful?"

"Yes," Roger said.

"No," Trys said at the same time. "At least there's Dewey."

"No wonder he left the family right after you."

"He wanted to be mayor. My father said no." Trys twirled her cane as we turned away. "The eldest is usually groomed for the position, so it was Dewey's for the taking, but he suffered from fainting spells. My father decided we couldn't have a 'sickly' leader, so he chose George instead. Dewey was devastated. Fortunately, bootlegging has worked out well for him."

"How fortunate indeed," Roger murmured, staring at the enormous mansion.

The roof guards kept their guns trained on us as we walked up the long driveway. Rows of golden torches lit our path, their fires sparkling like liquid gold. Roger wiggled his fingers over one. "Effigen flames. They combine the flames of several fires to make these burn brighter and longer. Dangerous, but beautiful."

Roger waved to the guards on the roof as we slipped into the yard.

In every direction, crowds of people stretched over the green lawn, their voices a jubilant cacophony on top of the fourteen-piece band playing on the patio. Waiters wove through the crowd, their coattails fluttering in their wake as they offered golden drinks to radiant guests. At the edge of the lawn, elegant couples danced on a sandy beach, their quick feet illuminated by the moonlight sparkling over the harbor.

For most of my life, I'd slept on one of twenty cots stuffed in a room behind an abbey. And in every city I'd visited since I left, there were children on the streets, hawking goods for a bit of money to bring home. If they were lucky enough to have one.

Yet Dewey lived alone. In a house that could swallow ten homes, easily.

Roger froze. "There's Lucy Effigen, the matriarch of that bloodline. See her with Nana?"

Trys watched him carefully. "Do you think Margaret's here?"

Margaret Effigen, Roger's former flame, the girl who'd broken his heart right before he left Charmant. When he'd gotten those scars.

"And risk running into me? Not a chance." He turned away, his smile fading.

"The Strattoris came." Trys pointed to a cluster of people standing awkwardly by the bay, their plain white robes in stark contrast to the dazzling black-and-gold finery surrounding them. A reclusive bunch, I'd only heard of them from Trys and Roger, and even they knew little.

Roger clapped me on the back. "Let's find something stronger than champagne."

We wove our way through the crowd. "Do all these people have magic?" I asked.

"Most don't." Roger grabbed an hors d'oeuvre from a passing waiter's tray and popped it into his mouth. "Plenty of folks without magic live here. Shopkeepers and their employees, merchants who sell goods from the mainland, tourists who find odd jobs so they can stay. Plenty of New York playboys have summer homes in the Day District, though the harbor's becoming more popular."

"Rumor has it a US senator bought the place next door," Trys added. "He publicly denies it, of course."

"What in the world is your brother up to, bringing all these people together?"

"Let's ask him. Look."

There he was, the youngest man in a circle of black suits. And on his arm was Luxe.

A golden dress overlaid with intricate black beading clung to her curves. The shimmering slip ended at her thighs, though the beaded fringe kissed her knees. Her dark curls were swept upward, held in place by an embroidered gold headband with black feathers.

My mouth dried as remnants of her magic surged through my veins. She was beautiful, all right. Like the sky before a hurricane.

I slammed my champagne flute on a nearby cocktail table. "Here goes nothing."

Dewey gestured wildly, regaling his sycophants with tall tales as Luxe stood dutifully by his side, her smile painted like a portrait of merriment, though her eyes dimmed with boredom.

She spotted me approaching, whispered in Dewey's ear, and slipped away.

Damnit. I couldn't exactly chase after her.

"Trysta!" Dewey lifted Trys off the ground and swung her in a big hug, which almost coaxed a smile from me.

"Everything's beautiful," she gushed. "I can't believe you live here."

"I needed a big space to fit all my friends. Did you see Mayor Hylan from Manhattan? And the Fitzgeralds are here, too, by the champagne fountain." He winced. "Let's hope Zelda doesn't fall in again. And you just missed the Radiant Ruby, of course." He elbowed Roger. "She's a looker, isn't she?"

"Cousin," Roger reminded him.

"Right. Of course." Dewey shook my hand, once again applying more pressure than necessary. "Your tie's a bit loose."

"I know." I tugged at the damn thing. "I hate ties."

"Some people just don't belong in a suit." He clapped my shoulder and turned back to Trys.

Wonderful. I'd been here only a few minutes, and I already stood out.

As Dewey began introducing Trys and Roger to the nearest rich men in richer suits, I spotted Luxe beside a thick wooden bar. Roger gave me a small nod as I walked away. Dewey watched me, too, his brow furrowing in a scowl that was so much like Trys's, I nearly laughed.

Keep her, Dewey. Be my guest.

She poured champagne into golden glasses, taking a covert look around before stealing a sip straight from the bottle.

"I saw that," I announced.

Her head whipped toward me, fizzy bubbles mingling on her crimson mouth.

That kiss was going to be the death of me.

I blocked her path. "No show tonight, right? The first summer night off in years?"

"Don't talk like you know anything about my family," she spat.

"I've spent the last three years with Roger, the most talkative person on the planet." I took a swig from the champagne bottle. "Trust me, I know all about your family."

Her eyes flashed with irritation. "Why are you here?"

"I was invited. Besides, you and I had a deal." I leaned closer, lowering my voice. "I haven't mentioned our . . . encounter to Dewey."

She blinked those thick lashes in feigned innocence. "Did we rendezvous? I can't recall. I've been *so* busy with Dewey this week—"

"Just show me the beach." I tried to keep my voice even, to hide my frustration. "At the very least, tell me exactly where it is."

She stole a look toward Dewey. "Would you just let it go already?"

"I can still tell him everything, you know."

"Why do you even care about the beach?"

My parents' sun-kissed, smiling faces burned in my mind. "None of your business."

"It's west of the pine barrens, but east of the tourists' beach."

West of . . . "I tried that already!"

A dismissive shrug. "Then you've seen it."

I reached for her arm as she attempted to step past me again. She shook herself free. "Stop," she hissed. "Before someone gets the wrong idea."

As if anyone would believe the gold-digging Revelle star would waste her time on me. "Trust me, you're the last person I want

103

to talk to tonight, but I need your help. No one else knows which beach it— Hey, where are you going? I'll tell Dewey!"

"Be my guest."

I remained motionless as she sauntered away, her head high, her pristine smile plastered on her face. She slipped her hand in Dewey's and glided through the crowd, the sight of them met with equal parts awe and disapproval. And what a sight they were: young and beautiful and so very affectionate with each other. She leaned closer to him, whispering something with her feather-soft lips.

Lies. Every memory of that mouth was a magic-infused lie.

I forced myself to unclench my teeth, but I couldn't look away as Dewey snaked an arm around her waist. Together they climbed the stairs to a small stage erected in the corner of the patio. Once they reached the center, he brushed a kiss along her temple. So intimate, as if he'd done it countless times.

Damn this party, and damn Luxe. I'd find the beach myself.

Trys caught me by the arm. "Where are you going? Dewey's about to make an announcement."

"I don't care. I came here for—"

"Look."

The band stopped. The crowd quieted to a murmur as everyone stared at the dazzling couple onstage. A Revelle and a Chronos, arm in arm—Charmant's very own Romeo and Juliet.

Dewey clapped, and the molten gold torches blinked off, enveloping us in darkness.

Nine

LUXE

Dewey pulled me closer as I bit back a scream. He'd warned me about the lights, but between the armed guards, the handsome imposter, and my family glaring at me all night, my nerves were frayed.

With an ominous, high-pitched whistle, the sky erupted as a riot of fireworks exploded overhead, painting the crowd's shocked faces in red, white, and blue. Dewey chuckled beside me. How I longed to tap into my secondary magic, to see what he was hiding behind that calm, confident exterior. But I couldn't risk it, not with so many Edwardians here.

I glanced at the crowd again, easily spotting the tall imposter, the only person staring at the stage instead of the sky. His face seemed so honest. So hauntingly familiar. Dewey caressed my bare shoulder, and the handsome imposter's jaw tightened. As if twenty minutes together were enough for him to give a damn who touched me.

Twenty minutes of sugar-coated lies. *All the liquor in the world.*

Dewey released a shaky breath. "Here goes nothing."

In a fury of explosions, the fireworks crescendoed, and the crowd gasped as enormous golden letters pierced the dark sky over the harbor, bold and bright enough to be seen all the way in the Day District.

Dewey Chronos for Mayor

A reluctant round of applause spread through the crowd. Mainlanders, mostly, and several of the wealthy business owners. A few Edwardians clapped politely, their stony faces betraying no emotion. Most of them were staunch supporters of Dewey's father, but some had come tonight anyway. The Effigens whispered furiously behind their hands while the Strattoris glanced at each other warily. Only a few had accepted Dewey's invitation, and they hadn't touched the food or the drinks, nor left their small huddle.

And the Revelles? They laughed, none louder than Nana.

Dewey bristled. It would be so easy to charm him into overlooking my family's blatant contempt—if I could use my magic. Uncle Wolffe had agreed to Dewey's proposition, but no one else knew how close we were to collapsing, how desperately we needed an alliance with the kid bootlegger. The prospect of a winter theater had piqued their interest, but Dewey's lawyers made the lease contingent on his winning the election. Judging by the muted response to his campaign announcement, it'd never be ours.

"I'll keep this brief." Dewey's eloquent voice turned every head back to the stage, his youthfulness lending him an eager quality not often seen in politicians. "A few hours ago, my father announced that he is stepping down as mayor. A special election will take place on August first, twenty-five days from now. He's endorsed my brother, George, to take his place."

Not a soul flinched. The mayor had been grooming George for the position for years. He was young for public office—even younger than Dewey, though George *looked* a decade older.

"For far too long, my family has put their own interests before everyone else's. Night District children starve while Chronos children eat from silver spoons. Night District businesses are the backbone of Charmant's economy, yet Day District pockets grow fat from your taxes." He paused, letting the crowd absorb his words. "That all changes when you elect me mayor. I promise to use my wealth, my connections in New York and beyond, even my magic, to better *all* of Charmant. Not just the wealthy. I promise we will never be surprised by any misfortune, from a hurricane to a visit from the Prohibition police."

"Have your balls even dropped?" someone heckled.

Dewey leaned into the microphone. "You're welcome to come up here and check."

That earned a laugh. My family, though, remained unimpressed.

"I have no interest in growing old before my time, but I'll do it, if it means Charmant will prosper." He tilted the microphone toward him. "As a show of good faith, the unused refreshments from tonight's festivities will be delivered to needy Night District families. Eat up, my friends. There's plenty for all."

Murmurs of approval rose from the crowd.

With a snap of his fingers, waiters began passing out champagne. Dewey motioned for me to join him at center stage. *Back straight, chin up.* This was a performance like any other.

He handed me a flute of bubbly, his diamond-shaped clock painted on the golden glass.

"To new beginnings." Though he spoke into the microphone, his gaze fixed on mine, unwavering, as heat rose to my cheeks.

"And to Charmant!" He turned to the crowd and lifted his glass as the band belted out a celebratory tune. The resounding cheers were much more enthusiastic, especially as Dewey raised our clasped hands. Plenty of Big Tent regulars were in the audience.

His assistant, Trevor Edwardes, escorted us down the stairs. Dewey accepted a towel and patted his forehead. "Well?"

"You did great," I said, surprised that I meant it. "Truly inspirational."

"And the crowd? What did they think?"

"Hard to tell." I stole a glance at the dispersing audience. "I'll do some digging."

"Thank you, my sweet." He lowered his voice. "If you use any jewels, be discreet. I don't want anyone to accuse me of cheating."

As if everyone here hadn't taken one look at us onstage—a charmer and a time traveler—and wondered how we'd use our combined magic to our advantage. "I recognize a few Big Tent regulars. I'll do my best."

I slipped into the crowd, Fake Dewey's gaze burning into my back as I made my rounds among the rich tourists and the Big Tent regulars. If he tried to ask me about that beach again, I was going to lose my cool, and I couldn't afford to be anything less than perfect tonight.

Fortunately, the imposter stood by the bar with Colette and Millie—my cousins had hardly said a word to me tonight, but they had all time in the world for the blue-eyed fraud—though his stare followed me like a spotlight in a dark theater.

Nana lounged at a glass table by the beach with Lucy Effigen, their silvery heads bowed in their usual gossip. I draped my arms over the back of Nana's chair. "Well? What do you think?"

She patted my arm. "The house is gaudy. And the band's bland."

The band was far from bland. Dewey had hired the best jazz musicians from Harlem so no Revelles had to work tonight—our only night off all summer. "I meant about Dewey's speech."

"A Chronos running for mayor?" She dropped her jaw in exaggerated surprise, earning snickers from the nearby Effigens, who were accustomed to Nana's antics. Their Night District restaurants and nightclubs were major tourist attractions, eclipsed only by the Big Tent. Over the years, deep friendships had formed between our families. A few romances, too, including Roger and Margaret's. But that had ended in literal flames, shattering Lucy's and Nana's dreams of sharing great-grandchildren with the power of potency *and* emotional manipulation.

Lucy leaned closer. "The mayor's two sons running against each other is new, though. Do you trust him, Luxe?"

"I like him," I said honestly, meeting Lucy's discerning gaze. "He means well. And he's our best chance at getting out from underneath the thumb of the current mayor."

"With another one of his sons." Nana stifled her yawn. "How clever."

"Don't be a spoilsport." I hugged her over the back of her chair, nestling against her upswept hair. "You're in such a mood tonight! Have you eaten yet?"

"Are you trying to kill me, child?"

"For the last time, he didn't poison the food," I hissed, flashing a practiced smile at a nearby server. "Can you at least *pretend* to be enjoying yourself?"

"I stopped faking pleasure once your grandfather passed." Her face brightened. "Look! Roger!"

My cousin waved to Nana and Lucy as he trotted down the grassy hill, his tall friend beside him. They had already rebelled against their tuxedos: jackets discarded, bow ties dangling precariously around their necks. The handsome imposter had undone three shirt buttons, hinting at the smooth muscle underneath. Skinny-boy muscles, Millie had called them, licking her lips.

With a quick squeeze of Nana's shoulder, I slipped away, not daring to look back. Dewey was my focus tonight—*real* Dewey, not tall, fake Dewey.

I found him with the Strattoris, who glanced warily in my direction as I approached. The holier-than-thou healers disapproved of our lifestyle, but there was no real bad blood between us. As I took my place at Dewey's side, they said their goodbyes.

Dewey sighed as we watched them leave, their crisp white tunics out of place in the sea of black and gold. "The Edwardians left right after my speech. It's not even midnight, and I've lost two magical families."

"They still came," I reminded him. "That's more than I ever imagined possible."

"Right again. What would I do without you?" He took my arm, wheeling me back toward the crowd of waiting sycophants. "Have you met my sister yet?"

Trysta Chronos had been trying to murder me with her eyes all night. "Why don't you grab her, and I'll grab drinks?"

He squeezed my arm in gratitude.

Once he slipped away, I gripped the chair in front of me. The Edwardians were gone, except Trevor, who would expect me to use my magic to ensure the party was a smashing success. My *jewel* magic, of course. But Dewey was too smart to give me any gems.

I could do this. I'd done it countless times before.

With my eyes squeezed shut, I imagined Dewey's lightstring— and mentally slammed my head into a wall of pain, as cold and hard as ice. That was new. Apparently, my little inkwell didn't like working overtime these days. I hurled my mind against it, digging deeper into the pain. Blinding lights flashed behind my eyes. Not lightstrings, but warnings, *warnings*—

The cold wall crumbled, and I was flooded by a stabbing headache. Brutal, but familiar.

The soft glow of lightstrings drifted toward me. Bright pinks and yellows. Three hundred people having a grand old time, Dewey included, though his lightstring was veiled by tremendous caution. He was wise, not getting his hopes up. Twenty-five days was hardly enough time to win an election.

You're having an excellent time, I whispered down his lightstring. *Everyone loves you.*

Cool drinks in hand, I cut across the lawn to— *Whoa.*

The world swayed, the music suddenly off-key, the grass off-kilter . . .

Let go, my magic urged. *Let go, let go, let go*—

Leaning against a lawn chair, I tried to breathe, to give my body a moment to acclimate to the pain. Now was not the time for a magical hissy fit.

Like sand settling in the ocean, my vision cleared.

"Well, well." Roger stood in front of me, his lips twisted in perpetual amusement. "If it isn't the Radiant Rainbow Ra-Ra of Revelle, or whatever you're going by these days."

He had a way of exonerating himself with a single grin. My irritation with his absence all week, with his new habit of surrounding himself with outsiders—it was all melting away.

He held out his arms, and I sank into them, the stinging sensation behind my eyes surprising me. When was the last time I'd hugged someone?

"Colette's looking for you."

"For *me*?" I stood taller, glancing around.

"Of course. She still loves you, you know." Even though his easy smile betrayed nothing, his lightstring shone with concern. But that was Roger's way. Underneath all the jokes, all the mischief, he had an enormous heart that bled for his family.

Sure enough, Colette was looking at us as she cut through the crowd, Millie by her side. They both looked beautiful in evening finery, but Colette looked particularly stunning tonight, with her hair elegantly coiffed atop her head and the cut of her beaded gown accentuating her toned shoulders. Her eyes met mine as she announced, "This party's missing something."

"A fire-breathing tequila contest?" Millie suggested. "Effigen drinks?"

Colette's lips curved in an all-too-familiar challenge. When we were little, she'd look at me like that before daring me to jump off the docks in my knickers. "There are newcomers with us tonight and we haven't done the Swap Trot."

Oh no.

Millie clapped excitedly.

"What's the Swap Trot?" Dewey asked, sidling up beside me. Trysta followed close behind.

Colette took his arm. "It's a beloved Revelle tradition. A dance to welcome new friends."

More like a hazing. Revelles despised outsiders.

Trysta had the wherewithal to appear skeptical. "You want *us* to dance?"

"It's a partner dance-off," Roger explained. "We Revelles pair with a newcomer, and we do most of the work. All you have to do is stay on your feet, and you win."

"That sounds easy enough. Especially since my partner's the star." Dewey wrapped an arm around me. Sweet, ignorant fool.

"She's the star, all right. Hey, Pops!" Colette called, though her glittering eyes found mine. "How about a Swap Trot?"

"Excellent!" Uncle Wolffe boomed. My family never turned down a dance competition—or any competition, really. As they cleared a space on the beach, Revelle musicians grabbed the band's instruments. "Partner up, kids!"

Roger rested his arm atop Trysta's head. "You up for this?"

She tossed her cane onto the sand. "Worry about yourself."

"Are you sure *you're* up for this?" I asked. Trysta was right; he still had my broken ribs.

"You just don't want me to beat you," he teased. "Who wants to dance with Jamison?"

So the imposter had a name. A good one—not that it mattered.

Millie looped an arm through Jamison's. "I will!"

At the same time, Colette said, "I will!"

They grinned at each other. Jamison's cheeks turned as red as they had when he'd realized he was in the Fun House.

"Share him like the French do!" Nana called.

Colette took Jamison by his other elbow. "You know I can't let my brother win. He'll be insufferable, especially because he's still injured."

Except she wasn't out to prove she was better than Roger.

Releasing Jamison, Millie scanned the crowd. The rich mainland men stepped forward, puffing out their chests, but Millie looked right past them. "Ooh! I'll take the Edwardian!"

Heads swiveled toward Trevor, who froze by the refreshments, midbite.

We took positions: Dewey and me, Roger and Trysta, Colette and Jamison, and Millie and Trevor. Four Revelles, two Chronoses, an Edwardian, and a mainlander. Every round, we'd switch partners. Unless Jamison was eliminated early, I wouldn't be able to avoid dancing with him.

"Are you okay?" Dewey asked. "You look a bit peaky."

I flashed him a serene smile. "I just don't like losing."

"When you're with me, you'll never lose." He caressed my bare shoulder. "I promise."

If only it were that simple.

The band played the first few notes. I draped an arm around Dewey's neck and clasped his other hand.

"Any advice?" He leaned closer, his lightstring glowing with desire. So our relationship wasn't entirely a ruse for him. Interesting.

"Let me lead," I said.

"A girl leading?" He tipped his head back and laughed. "My dance instructor would roll over in her grave."

"Trust me." The tune was mournful, but the saxophone was about to change that. "Just try to stay on your feet. When we switch partners, they're going to spin you faster than—"

"Begin!"

I could almost hear my mother's training. *Back straight. Chin up.* With a firm hand between Dewey's shoulder blades, I guided him through the steps. Once he ceased trying to lead, he caught on quickly. Somewhere behind us, Colette giggled with Jamison. If he fell in the next two rounds, I wouldn't have to lay a finger on him.

The music quickened. "And spin!" Uncle Wolffe called.

Here goes nothing. Crossing our arms, I took Dewey's hands, leaned back, and spun us. Dewey laughed, his lightstring flaring with excitement. The golden torches, the silver moonlight— everything blurred as we turned and turned.

When we were too little to perform, we used to Swap Trot backstage during shows. Millie used to spin me so fast, I'd have to sit in my mother's lap with my head between my knees afterward. Even then, we rarely beat Colette and Roger.

"And switch!"

If I fumbled the timing, Dewey would go flying into the audience. Or the surf. Or to the wrong partner. As long as he stayed on his feet, we'd survive the round.

I let go of his hands. Colette high-kicked over his head, flashing me a wicked grin before pulling him closer. Show-off. I hardly had time to register the strangeness of that duo before Trevor barreled into me.

I caught him by the back of the shirt, gave him a little whirl, and led him through the steps. His eyes were dizzy, unfocused, but he was smiling.

"You're enjoying yourself?"

"Yes. Your cousin Millie is . . . Wow."

I stole a glance at her and Trysta, their cheeks red from laughing. "She's great."

"Her thoughts are like cotton candy. So sweet and fluffy. Such a refreshing mind."

That familiar longing tugged deep in my chest. God, how I missed Millie. Even though the chasm between us was my fault, she'd never snapped at me. Not even once.

"I could put in a good word for you." An honest guy like Trevor would be an upgrade from the tourists usually competing for my cousin's affection.

His smile faded as he glanced at her. "Courtship with a mind reader is far from appealing. No secrets. No mystery."

What an incredible power, to hear all conscious thoughts. But it came with an incredible cost: Edwardians had to speak the truth, no matter how much it pained them. They couldn't even keep their mouths shut. Whenever an Edwardian was directly asked a question, they had to respond honestly. The Chronoses were smart to hire them.

"No lying, either," I pointed out. "That's a perk."

Just as he was beginning to get the hang of the footwork, the music shifted again.

"And *spin!*"

I crossed my arms and gripped his hands, spinning us both so fast, he turned green. This was a competition, after all, and I was a Revelle. I *hated* losing.

"And switch!"

I angled him just left of Colette, then let go.

Trysta Chronos barreled into me a moment later, nearly knocking us both over. If she wasn't Dewey's sister, I might have let her fall. Next round, I would.

Next round . . . with Jamison.

Trysta glared at me as I took her hand and her waist.

"It's lovely to meet you," I said. "Dewey has told me so much about you."

"Don't talk to me."

"What? I was just—"

"I see the games you're playing. First with my friend and now with my brother. So save your affectations for someone else. I don't like you." She gifted me a fake smile of her own.

Seven hells, she was blunt.

Cheers erupted as Colette helped Trevor off the ground. His lightstring beamed with happiness as Millie pulled him off the makeshift dance floor, laughing. Roger scrambled to replace Millie as Jamison's partner while Colette grabbed Dewey again.

"And spin!" Wolffe boomed.

Trysta groaned. The spinning was hard on both partners, but I'd had much more practice. To her credit, she remained firmly on her feet, even as we spun and spun.

The music sped up, a frenzy of trumpets and clarinets and racing drums. "And switch!"

Colette spun into a dramatic pirouette as Trys arrived, catching her with ease.

Jamison nearly spun by me. I should have let him whirl into the foamy surf.

But I wanted to win.

My hand caught one of his firm biceps, and traitorous sparks flitted over my skin. All week, I'd been trying to forget about him. Kissing him had been like mistaking a stick of dynamite for an ordinary candle. I'd nearly blown up all my careful plans.

As if reading my mind, he stepped closer, daring me to back away. Jerk. I draped my arm around his neck, not giving him the satisfaction of seeing me squirm. He was just another dance partner, no different from a customer. Or a stranger. Really, it was like dancing with a statue.

"I've walked every beach in the Night District. Twice." His hair fell over his forehead as he leaned even closer.

"Then you've seen the one you're looking for."

From this close, his blue eyes were startlingly bright. "I need you to show me, Luxe. No one else seems to know where it is."

My name on his lips sent a thrill down my spine. If only Dewey had the same effect. No, better that he didn't. With Dewey, my mind needed to be sharp and focused.

"*Please*," Jamison pleaded.

"Why does it matter to you?"

"It's hard to explain." A whirl of purple swept into his lightstring, as dark as a bruise. The blues of sadness and the maroons of love, woven together. Grief, as familiar to me as my shadow.

Who had he lost?

The music grew faster and faster. He kept his warm hand on my waist, his feet not missing a single step. Roger must have taught him.

"Fine," I found myself saying.

"Really?" His lightstring was so earnest, his relief instantaneous.

"Come by tomorrow, after rehearsals," I muttered. "Then we'll never speak of it again."

"And *spin!*"

Crossing my wrists, I took his hands and leaned back. Bloody hell, this was dangerous, especially with a stranger. All he'd have to do was let go, and I'd break my neck.

His strong hands tightened their grip on mine, the world blurring as we spun faster.

One trip to the beach. Nothing more.

Our audience roared. Someone else had been eliminated. Dewey or Trysta?

"And *switch!*"

The world continued to spin, even as I dug my heels into the sand. Aiming Jamison was impossible. I let go and tried not to tip backward.

Dewey bumped into me a moment later, and I threw my arms around him. No heady rush, no sparks where his skin met mine. Good riddance to that feeling.

"Don't fall on me!" He laughed.

"I'm a Revelle," I reminded him. "We never fall."

Roger helped Trysta to her feet. Only Colette and Jamison remained. Our feet blurred—

Someone let out a bloodcurdling scream.

I halted and let go of Dewey, the beach tilting dangerously as I looked around. Colette lay on the sand, clutching her foot. Revelles crowded around her, Roger among them.

Oh no.

Dewey threw out his arms to catch his balance. "Does this mean we win?"

"It's her ankle," Roger said grimly. "She's twisted it."

Colette covered her head. No tears marred her pretty face. "I wasn't even dizzy yet!"

Roger and Millie helped her stand. As Colette put pressure on her foot, her face twisted.

One week into the season, and our best performer couldn't walk.

Uncle Wolffe clapped his hands. "Everything's fine, ladies and gents! If you head to the bar, a special treat will be waiting for you."

Once the audience dispersed, Colette tried her ankle again and groaned.

"How did this happen?" Uncle Wolffe demanded.

"There was a ditch in the sand! I stepped right into it."

"Did no one think to smooth out the ground before our headliners danced?"

Colette's face squeezed with pain. "I checked the ground. Twice! It wasn't there before."

He rubbed his temples. "Let's get you to Dr. Strattori."

"Absolutely not."

"You can't walk," he said gently. "And tomorrow, you must *fly*."

Colette's face crumpled. Her solution to every setback was always to work harder, to train longer, just like her mother had done. And she never, ever showed weakness.

Aunt Caroline scooped her up before the first tear spilled.

The crowd cheered as she carried her toward Dewey's mansion. Colette waved to them from her aunt's strong arms, smiling as radiantly as ever. Injured or not, she was still a performer.

"Terrible," Dewey muttered beside me.

Uncle Wolffe was already scanning the family for a volunteer. The children froze. Only Clara dared move, stepping in front of her little brother. Brave, headstrong Clara. My stomach performed its own acrobatics as I imagined her bony little ankle, twisted and bruised.

Roger stepped forward, but Jamison blocked his path. "I'll do it."

"Jamison!" Trysta hissed, grabbing his arm. "You don't mean that."

"I do." He straightened, wiping off the sand from where he'd knelt beside Colette.

I gaped at him. Outsiders usually didn't know about Strattori magic. And they certainly didn't take pain *away* from the Revelles. What was his angle?

"You're volunteering?" Uncle Wolffe exchanged a glance with me. I'd told him about the mix-up in the Fun House. All week, he'd been keeping tabs on Roger's friend.

"I can do it, sir. Unless Strattori healing requires me to have magic of my own?"

"I'll do it." Dewey stepped forward, clearing his throat.

Dewey, take Colette's injury? Before I could protest, he clapped Jamison on the back. "I've got this, Mr. Port. You have enough to worry about already."

Jamison shrugged. "I can be poor and injured at the same time, I assure you."

That earned him some chuckles. Dewey's lightstring—wait, when had I dropped it?

Without my magic, his excitement had evaporated. There was dread and uncertainty, along with that pervasive caution that seemed to be his default. He never let loose, especially not around my family. I smoothed his discomfort while my uncle appraised him.

"I don't think that's necessary, Mr. Chronos."

"I insist. Have your Strattori meet me inside with her healing kit."

Helen Strattori never bothered with the incense, candles, and prayers the rest of her family used, but Uncle Wolffe didn't correct him. I widened my eyes in warning, but my uncle shook his head slightly. Were we really going to let Dewey sacrifice himself for Colette?

I pulled Dewey to the side. "You don't have to do this."

His gaze fell to where my hand still gripped his arm. "No Revelle harmed on my watch, remember?"

Our deal. Without using his magic, he was still keeping up his end of the deal.

"Don't look so surprised! Your cousin is important to you, so she's important to me."

I'd never even mentioned Colette to him, nor the fact that we'd been close. He'd done his research.

"Thank you," I said honestly. "You don't understand how much this means to me."

"I'll always keep your family safe. And you." His arms circled my waist, pulling me to him. This close, his confident facade cracked, revealing the uncertain boy in the politician's suit.

His forehead met mine. His eyes fluttered shut, the moment stretching longer.

Dewey Chronos was going to kiss me. Here. In front of my family.

You wish to go inside, I whispered down his lightstring. *You don't want Colette to wait.*

He pulled away, searching my face. "Time to have my ankle sprained. Meet me inside?"

"In a moment." *You feel happy. Desired. And you wish to go without me.*

He tugged on his lapels, checked his watch, and sauntered away.

Someone cleared their throat behind me. Trevor Edwardes.

Bewildered, he stared at me.

He *knew.*

"Were you listening to my thoughts?" I managed to ask.

Trevor's throat bobbed. "Yes."

No! What a fool I'd been, using my magic tonight.

"He gave me a jewel." My voice remained even, despite my growing panic.

He looked down at his feet. "I can hear the truth in your head."

Bloody hell. He knew what I could do.

Worst-case scenario, he'd reveal my secondary magic to Dewey, who'd never trust me again. No, *worse* was the Chronoses discovering what I could do. If pain allowed me to avoid the cost of my magic, they wouldn't rest until they found a way to avoid the cost of *their* magic. If they couldn't, they'd kill me rather than risk me charming them. And if they could, then they'd travel whenever they pleased, without aging—

"Are you going to tell Dewey?" I asked quietly, my heart pounding in my chest.

Trevor's face paled. "Not unless he asks. Then I won't have a choice."

Interesting. He couldn't lie . . . but he wasn't jumping to reveal the truth, either. Was Dewey's dutiful assistant not as loyal as he seemed?

"Is he suspicious?" I pressed.

"Not at all."

Sweet relief coursed through me. Trevor stepped closer, keeping his hands raised as if I were a feral animal about to sprint away.

"Mr. Chronos is a good man," he murmured, "but your . . . talent can never get out. If the Chronoses find out what you can do, it'll be bad for all of us. Magic *needs* checks and balances."

I could have cried from relief.

"I can teach you how to control your thoughts," he continued. "It's not foolproof, but it's better than nothing."

"That's possible?" Uncle Wolffe had never mentioned it.

"The Chronoses train their children. Dewey's quite good at it, but I can still hear how often you're on his mind. He likes you, you know."

And now I was receiving dating advice from an Edwardian. "The feeling is mutual."

Trevor didn't look convinced. "It can't be easy for you to trust a Chronos. But Dewey is different. There's nothing he wouldn't do for the people he cares about."

It didn't matter if he was a good Chronos. If he found out about my magic . . .

No more mistakes. I wouldn't let it happen.

TEN

JAMISON

In the unforgiving light of day, the Big Tent was far less enchanting. Trash and windblown sand littered the street in front of it, and the breeze carried the sharp scent of spilled beer and seaweed. This close, mismatched patches marred the tent's swirling purple and black stripes. Still, Roger swung open the double doors like a king returning to his palace. "Home sweet home."

Without the tourists, the pit seemed strangely empty. A few men mopped the sticky floors while younger Revelles dragged crates bearing Dewey's logo backstage. Behind the bar, Roger's aunts polished glasses, laughing uproariously until the contortionists onstage shouted for them to pipe down. Luxe, as usual, was nowhere to be seen. She wasn't going to make this easy for me.

Trys sighed as she lowered herself into a folding chair. She rarely complained about foot pain, but the dancing last night had worsened her limp today.

Nana smacked Roger with a towel as he sank into the chair beside her. "When you're here, you work. You too, Jamison. And . . . Chronos girl."

"It's Trysta, ma'am."

Roger rolled his eyes. "She knows your name. Nana, have you seen our lovely star?"

"She's getting changed." Nana pointed to the bar. "Help your aunts while you wait."

The Revelle women greeted us with enthusiasm. Most of them had come by the barn to fuss over Roger while he was recovering from Luxe's injuries—and to tease me relentlessly. Apparently, my attempts to climb over the executive suite balcony had not gone unnoticed.

Caroline Revelle handed me a glass. "Stick your nose in this. What does it smell like?"

I did as she asked. "I'm not sure. Dust?"

"Tell me the truth, boy."

"All right." I took another whiff. "It smells like piss."

She dropped the glass back on the bar. "No matter how many times we wash 'em, they still smell like piss."

"The whole tent smells like piss," Trys pointed out.

The Revelle women blinked at her. Once Roger had told them of my orphan roots, they'd welcomed me into their fold, insisting I call them aunts. Trys, however, they'd mostly ignored.

"She's right," Nana said. "The boozed-up fools always find a way to piss in the corner."

"Have you tried lemon? It's excellent for getting rid of the smell." Seeing their blank stares, I added, "I, ah, had to clean up after the little boys at the orphanage." Not just the little boys. The friars made me clean my own bedsheets—naked, in the blistering cold courtyard, so homesick I couldn't speak—after those nightmare-fueled accidents during my first year there.

Nana arched a brow. "Lemons are imported from the mainland. Not cheap."

"What about these?" I grabbed a lemon garnish from a dirty glass on the bar. "If you scrape the rinds, add vinegar, and drain it through a cheesecloth, then voilà. Lemon cleaner."

Roger clapped me on the back. "See? I leave and return with a bona fide genius."

"Ah yes, this makes up for the years of chores you missed." Nana grabbed another glass. "How did you all meet, anyways?"

Roger placed a hand on my chest. "Let *me* tell it, Jamison. You see, we were on a transatlantic voyage."

Aunt Caroline frowned. "You told me you were all arrested for public indecency."

The truth was far less interesting than either. Roger and I had both discovered that the Library of Congress Building in Washington, DC, had the best bathrooms—and the staff didn't check the stalls before locking up for the night. Imagine my surprise when one rainy night, while searching for something new to read, I stumbled upon Roger Revelle eating a sandwich he'd charmed from one of the librarians. I'd been out of St. Douglas's for a few weeks, failing miserably in my foolish quest to either find my family or settle down and find work. Enigmatic Roger was like no one I'd ever met. All night, he spoke of Charmant, of the parties and the magic, but most of all, he spoke of the Revelles. He'd lived so much in sixteen years while all I'd done was clean, pray, and study. And he was intrigued by my solitary, sheltered life. By morning, we'd mapped out a cross-country adventure on a stolen atlas.

A few days later, we stumbled upon an elegantly dressed

teenage girl at the train station, beating a bunch of unsuspecting men at cards. Recognizing the mayor's daughter, Roger hadn't been able to resist the chance to toss a gem into a game. Once he'd won it back from Trys, we boarded the train. To our surprise, Trys followed us to berate Roger for tricking her. When the train started, she was stuck, but after a whole night of Roger's relentless teasing, she agreed to join us for another day or two. The rest was history.

"You're all wrong," Roger drawled. "We were on a sparkling beach in Miami. Trys got stung by a jellyfish, and Jamison and I volunteered to piss on her."

Trys rolled her eyes. "He's lying. I'd never let them piss on me."

"Not even me, Trys?" I teased.

"You, maybe. But Roger Revelle? I'd never be clean again."

That earned a laugh. Trys smiled shyly, tucking her hair behind her ears.

"What'd we miss?" Colette glided through the pit with Millie, their cheeks shiny from rehearsal. The entire family was unfairly good-looking, even when they were sweaty.

"Come to steal our booze, Roger?" Colette teased.

"You've got plenty to spare." Roger kissed his sister on the cheek. "Ankle's all better?"

"As if it never happened." She flexed her foot. "Worried about me, big brother?"

"Always." Roger leaned against the bar. "We're here for Luxe, actually."

"The ice princess?" Colette didn't try to hide her surprise.

"C'mon, Col, don't call her that."

"Okay, fine. Why are you looking for our dearly beloved star?"

Roger's gaze slid to mine. "She's taking Jamison to the beach."

That earned me more than a few curious stares. "She's not taking me anywhere," I said quickly. "She's helping me find one specific beach."

"As much as I'd love to see this for myself, we were about to get doughnuts." Colette tipped her chin to Roger. "Care to join us at Sweet Buns?"

"You still go to Margaret's bakery?" Roger pretended to look affronted, though the flash of sadness across his face seemed genuine.

Millie smiled guiltily. "We've tried to stop, but the Effigens make the best doughnuts."

"Traitors, all of you." He slid off the bar. "Let's go to Studebaker's instead."

"I'll come." Trys tucked her cane under her arm.

Roger quirked a brow. "Weren't you meeting your brother?"

"Dewey can wait." Catching my eye, she shrugged. "What? I'm hungry."

As they walked away, Colette whispered something in Trys's ear, and Trys snickered.

"It looks like I warned the wrong friend away from Revelle ladies," Roger mused. He clapped me on the back. "Meet us after?"

"Wouldn't miss it."

As I sorted lemons and waited for Luxe, the Revelle aunts peppered me with questions about everything from life at the orphanage to Betty. That one, at least, was a quick story to tell: an orphan boy so desperate for a family of his own that he thought he'd marry the first girl to give him attention. The Revelles listened intently, shaking their heads as I told them how she'd dumped me by letter, and cackling when I described how Roger and Trys had crashed her parents' dinner party in retaliation.

I reached for another lemon rind—and found Luxe standing behind me. For God knows how long.

One day, I'd be able to look at her without my heart leaping into my throat. But not today. Without her evening makeup, freckles dusted her button nose, and her eyes seemed wider. Younger. Dark curls sprang free from beneath the wide brim of her hat.

Magical hangover indeed.

"Luxie girl," Aunt Caroline cooed, pinching Luxe's cheek. "I didn't see you at breakfast. Did you stay at Dewey's mansion last night?"

Luxe twisted her lips into a haughty smile—not as fake as the one she flashed around Dewey, but guarded nonetheless. "Of course not. You know I need my beauty rest."

"Good." Aunt Caroline's teasing tone faded as she leaned closer. "It's never a good idea to let the customers get too close. They tend to get a little obsessed."

"Good thing Dewey's not a customer." With a reluctant nod in my direction, Luxe sauntered outside.

"Make sure she eats something!" Aunt Caroline called after me.

As if she'd listen to me. I gave them a little wave before I trailed behind Luxe.

Daylight blinded me as I stepped outside the Big Tent. Luxe stuck out her hand, something sparkling in her palm. My mother's brooch.

I moved to snatch it but stopped myself. A Revelle and a jewel? Dangerous combination.

She shoved it into my hand. "My magic only works if you give *me* the jewel."

So everyone kept saying. "I didn't give you a jewel last week, yet I almost broke my neck climbing out of the mezzanine."

She batted her lashes in feigned innocence. "That was just my natural charm."

Without another word, she began walking, leaving me a half step in her wake. Tourists spilled out of bars, their brunch drinks sloshing on sidewalks as they halted to watch the Radiant Ruby pass. Each of her steps fell rhythmically with the street band's song, her head remaining high without a glance toward her awestruck admirers.

Her pace was so brisk, I found myself breaking a sweat just to keep up with her, but I wasn't about to let her lose me.

She paused at the corner. "Do you need to rest?"

"I'm fine."

"Do you ever tell the truth?"

I met her stormy eyes. "I've never lied to you. Not even that first night."

"And yet you said you'd give me 'all the liquor in the world.'"

Christ. What a fool I'd been. "I was bewitched, to say the least."

At least she didn't deny it.

"How is the liquor man?" I asked. "His ankle must be in bad shape this morning."

"He's fine." Something I couldn't read passed over her face.

"'He's fine' as in resting up?"

She twirled a loose curl, tucking it behind her ear.

"Or is his ankle someone else's problem now?"

Her gaze cut to mine. Jackpot.

"Interesting."

Her eyes narrowed. "He's got twenty-four days to win the election. It's better for everyone if he's on his feet. Don't look at me like that."

"I wasn't looking at you."

Loosing a breath, she turned down a narrow alley. Gnarled weeping willows blocked the end of the street, but Luxe paused only to push back the thick branches, revealing a foot-trodden path. I followed her through the thicket, the earthen scent of dirt and leaves replacing the stale stench of Main Street. After a few minutes, she ducked under a branch and pushed away the leaves, revealing sparkling ocean.

"We're here."

With each step, my feet sank into the golden sand. Thick groves of weeping willows sheltered the beach from either side. No wonder I hadn't found it on my own; I would have had to swim out past them to even see this stretch of sand.

"See where the waves swirl a little strangely?"

I blocked my eyes from the relentless summer sun. In the lull between waves, a mooring pole jutted out of the water. Half-broken, covered in barnacles. "The dock's still there?"

"Barely."

There it was, between the waves—a dock. The same shape and size as the one in my photo.

Hope squeezed my rib cage so tightly, I couldn't breathe.

She settled onto the sand, curling her legs to her chest. "Why do you care so much about seeing this dirty old beach?"

My photo beckoned from my pocket. I longed to take it out, to map out every similarity, but I couldn't stand it if Luxe were to be cruel about it. "My parents visited here." A truthful answer, just not a full one.

"So you're a mama's boy, then? Desperate to follow in your tourist parents' footsteps?"

"Actually, I'm an orphan."

That wiped the haughty mask right off her face. "Oh. I didn't know."

Clearly, she hadn't asked anyone about me. "You don't have to stay."

"And be accused of abandoning Roger's best friend, the one everyone seems to like *oh so much*, on a seedy Night District beach? Not a chance."

"I can find my way back."

"I don't mind. Really."

There it was again: pity.

Luxe or no Luxe, I'd waited too long for this beach to not make sure it was the same one.

Her eyes widened as I removed my shoes. My shirt next.

She shielded her eyes from my bare chest. "What are you doing?"

"Swimming." I considered removing my trousers, just to watch her run off the beach in horror. "Want to come?"

"I don't swim."

"Can't ruin your hair before a show, I suppose."

Her eyes narrowed. "Since my mother drowned, I've lost my taste for it."

If I could have eaten my words, I would have. I'd known Roger's mother had drowned with two of his aunts. Or more accurately, had *been* drowned. Roger still blamed the Chronoses, though there was no proof they had any connection to the magic-less people who'd taken the women out on a boat, then fixed cinder blocks to their ankles and pushed them overboard. A hate crime, the police had called it. Even on Charmant, some people thought magic was an abomination. "I'm sorry."

"Don't be." She leaned against the dunes and lifted her face to the sun. "I'll wait here."

Resisting the urge to study her unguarded face, I made my way to the waves.

Swimming near a wrecked pier was a lot more difficult than I'd imagined, so I half floated, half hopped out to the mooring poles. I couldn't risk the waves knocking me against the ruins, but I waded as close as I dared, then ducked my head under the surface.

The water was freezing, despite the heat of the day. And cloudy, too, the salt burning my eyes. Still, I squinted into the abyss, desperate for any sign of the dock.

The waves settled, and there it was: dark wooden poles jutting into the sand below, rickety old boards covered in rectangular grooves. Intricate carvings of a cityscape, like the Manhattan skyline. The algae covering the faded artwork swayed in the waves as I swam closer. This really was the dock.

In Charmant, of all places—the home of my two best friends. What were the odds?

A pair of sunbathers were kind enough to lend me a towel when I emerged. I dried myself hastily, turning back to the ocean over and over for more glimpses of the dock. With the tide rising, it was hard to see, but it was here.

I'd actually done it. I'd found one definitive place that my parents had once stood. If the hotels kept records, I might be able to find out exactly where we'd stayed. Or even better, their home address.

Home. I might be able to track down my real home. And maybe my family.

With my heart in my throat, I watched the sunken dock appear and disappear in the sea. I had the photograph memorized by now. The carved dock to the right, over my mother's shoulder. My father's heels sunk in the sand. His arm around my mother's waist, like it belonged there. My beautiful mother, leaning into him while gazing down upon an infant wrapped in linens that billowed in the ocean breeze. Me.

I located the exact spot the photo had been taken, where none of the surrounding overgrowth could be seen. I stood where my family had once stood and breathed the salty air they'd once breathed. The upward angle of the camera wasn't the result of an incline, but a very short photographer. Someone kneeling, perhaps?

Or a child.

Goose bumps formed on my forearm as a breeze swept over the beach.

"Well?" Luxe kept her eyes trained on the horizon as I pulled my shirt over my head.

"It's the right beach. The dock's still there, underwater."

"Like I said." Her dress rode up her thighs as she stood and stretched her hands over her head. I looked away. The last remnants of her magic still lingered in my system, stirring up a longing I didn't dare acknowledge.

In silence, we wove our way back through the maze of branches and leaves. Once we emerged in the alley again, she leaned against the wall while I retied my shoes. "So your parents visited here before they died?"

"I don't know if they're dead or not," I admitted. It was foolish, telling her. Betty had outright laughed when I suggested my parents still could be alive. Roger and Trys were kinder about it, but even they thought I was making too much of my fragmented memories.

Luxe, at least, didn't laugh.

I reached into my pocket. "Here, let me show you their picture."

"It's okay." She examined her manicure. "When you swam, I went through your things."

Of course she did. "The price I pay for leaving my belongings with you."

During the walk back, she didn't speak again, but she also didn't walk ahead of me. Once we reached the doughnut shop, she pointed to where Roger, Trys, Colette, and Millie sat inside, their backs to us. For a moment, she looked as though she'd join us, but then started to walk away. Before I'd even reached for the door, she pivoted, her face uncertain. "I've been thinking . . . tourists almost never go to that beach. They don't usually know it exists."

That explained the rare peace and quiet. "So my parents were trespassing?"

She hesitated. "Or they weren't tourists."

"Oh." I rested my head against the brick wall. "*Oh.*"

My parents left me with two things: a photograph of a

Charmantian beach and a jewel-encrusted brooch. Gems. Common possessions for citizens of Charmant.

"What were their names?"

"The Ports." The plural of my last name sounded strange to my ears. For so long, I had been the only Port. "I don't know their first names."

She chewed her bottom lip. "Nana knows just about everyone who's ever lived around here. Perhaps if you show her that photograph—"

"She may recognize them." Even as the plan formed in my mind, I couldn't shake the absurdity of it. I couldn't be from Charmant. Jubilant Roger? Of course he was raised here. Trys, with her pristine style and unflappable confidence? Absolutely. But I was mere rocks to their glittering jewels. This wonderful, mystical island couldn't be my home, too.

Could it? Plenty of magic-less families lived here.

"If you'd like, I can bring you to her now."

"I couldn't take up more of your time—"

"It's fine. Unless you'd rather have a doughnut." She blinked up at me with those whiskey eyes, waiting.

My foolish heart quickened. "If you truly don't mind."

"It's back this way." She headed down the empty alley beside the doughnut shop.

Not empty.

A man was lying across the cobblestones. A bit early for drinking, but this was Charmant. Another man shook him by the collar, his face contorted.

That's when I saw the blood: a riot of red dripping from the prone man's temple, staining the white shirt underneath his suit.

"Do you need help?" I called.

Luxe gripped my arm, sending a wave of pinpricks rushing over my body. But she wasn't looking at me.

She was looking at the unconscious man, and the diamond-shaped clock sewn to his lapel.

ELEVEN

LUXE

"Dewey!" I grabbed his wrists, feeling for a pulse. He needed to be alive, needed to be okay.

Jamison yelled, and I turned in time to see him slam into the cobblestones. Hard.

I gaped at the man who had shoved him, his chest as wide as a refrigerator. Jamison struggled to his feet as the man pulled back his fist, his gold watch glittering in the sunlight—

"No!" I screamed.

He pummeled Jamison's beautiful face, smacking the back of his head into the street with a sickening *crack*. Jamison got his hands in front of him quick enough to block the next shot, but the man was all over him, kicking his stomach, his ribs—

"Help!" People were close. Main Street was only twenty yards away, and my cousins were on the other side of this brick wall. At the end of the alley, a man in a dark suit peered from behind a nearby building but quickly disappeared in the shadows. The damn coward.

The attacker swiveled at the sound of my voice. Had he . . .

gotten older? His hair looked thinner now, and his face appeared older than it'd been mere seconds ago. But that was impossible.

Not impossible—a goddamn Chronos. One who'd traveled really bloody far.

I grabbed a stray rock and hurled it at him, but it bounced off his barrel chest. With an irritated look my way, he stalked back to where Jamison was scrambling to his feet.

Jamison's eyes were dazed, his legs swaying as he stepped in front of Dewey and me. He lifted his fists, his face already swelling. Taller than the attacker, but half his weight. The Chronos barreled toward Jamison, his expression almost remorseful for what he was about to do.

"Please help us!" I begged the crowd forming at the head of the alley, but they backed away. No one risked taking on a Chronos.

With hair graying and thinning by the second, the man slammed Jamison against the wall. He pressed his forearm to his throat, not even flinching as Jamison clawed at his arm, fists flying to no avail.

My screams died in my throat. He was going to kill Jamison.

I threw myself at the man, leaping onto his back, driving my fists into his head. Letting go of Jamison, he spun around, trying to shake me off. He made it one step, two—

His knees cracked under my weight, and we crashed onto the ground.

The Chronos squirmed beneath me, his skin ancient and papery, hardly human anymore. I scrambled backward. Jamison pulled me farther away, not stopping until his back hit the wall. I pressed into him, still not far enough from our attacker.

The man stopped moving. His hair silvered and disappeared,

and his skin hung longer and longer off his cheekbones. Deep wrinkles marred what had only moments ago been a broad, healthy face, and his eyes shrank until they were little black orbs.

He gasped for air with his rotting mouth—and breathed his last breath.

His thick body shriveled. Gray skin curled off his arms like bark off a sycamore tree. And underneath the skin, bones as white as pearls.

I squeezed my eyes shut, nausea pooling in my stomach. Beneath my ear, Jamison's heart raced. "What the hell is happening?"

Speechless, I shook my head.

"Luxe?" Across the alley, Dewey lifted his head, blinking as if the world was just coming back into focus. As he struggled to sit, he assessed the scene before us: the body, the near-empty alley, and Jamison and me clinging to each other like lovers.

His eyes narrowed.

"Dewey!" I untangled myself from Jamison and ran to him.

He rubbed the side of his head, his fingers coming away red. "What happened?"

"You were attacked."

The crowd pressed into the alley now, eager for a peek. Trysta pushed her way through the tourists, my cousins close on her heels. She skidded to a halt in front of Jamison, who was slumped against the alley wall, his face bloody. "What's going on?"

"Someone attacked Dewey." Jamison's words bled into each other.

"Then why do you look like you lost a fight?"

His split lip jutted forward with his feeble attempt at a smile. "Got in the way."

"Are you hurt?" Dewey pressed his hand to my cheek.

I shook my head. "He didn't lay a finger on me. Only you and Jamison."

Trys crouched beside Jamison. "You're bleeding." Ignoring his efforts to squirm away, she separated the back of his thick hair, then shot Roger an alarmed look. "He's bleeding. A lot."

Colette poked the rotting man with the tip of her shoe. "You were attacked by a corpse?"

Jamison's eyes found mine. No one could possibly understand what we'd seen.

"He didn't look like that at first," I said, my voice hoarse. That wouldn't do, not with so many onlookers listening. I cleared my throat. "At first, he was in his forties, but he was aging quickly."

Trysta narrowed her eyes as if I were personally responsible for the scene before us. "When we travel, we arrive at our new age. No one sees the change, not even us."

Ignoring her accusatory tone, I met her glare. "I saw it with my own eyes. By the time he hit the ground, he was twice as old."

"He's still aging now." Colette nudged the body with her foot. "See?"

Sure enough, it was decomposing at an alarming rate. More patches of skin melted away, and underneath, pink muscles shriveled and grayed. My stomach churned.

Apparently immune to disgust, Trysta poked the body with the tip of her cane. "He's a Chronos, all right. He's got the watch to prove it."

Dewey tensed beside me. "Who?"

"Uncle Frank. Freddy's pops." Trys backed away, her expression unreadable.

"Freddy, who found us before the party?" Roger asked. "This is his father?"

Trys nodded. "Far from my favorite uncle."

"Not my favorite, either, but I never thought he'd try to kill me." Betrayal swept over Dewey's face. I squeezed his arm, but he didn't register my touch, not even when I slipped my hand into his. A week of earning his trust, ruined by his family in an instant. If their scare tactics worked, he might abandon his plan for mayor—and his deal with us. No more crates full of hooch. No winter theater.

We wouldn't last the summer, let alone another winter.

As Dewey stood and examined the still-rotting body, I squeezed my eyes shut and called to my magic. The pain accosted me, a dizzying sense of being swallowed by relentless fire, burning hotter than ever. I could hardly hold on while my magic exacted its payment . . .

"Are you okay?" Jamison was beside me now. Of course he'd seen me. His left eye was nearly swollen shut, and his lightstring was hazy, as if his grip on consciousness was fading.

"You need to get to a doctor." On unsteady legs, I pushed myself to my feet.

A storm of emotions brewed in Dewey's lightstring, dark and thick like aged syrup. There was his perpetual cautiousness, the politician careful with every word, every emotion. Beneath it, hues of sadness swirled with betrayal, frustration, and, worst of all, regret.

That wouldn't do.

I gripped his chin and turned his face to mine. "You know why your family did this, don't you?"

His eyes narrowed, and even though I was no Edwardian, I could practically hear the words he considered spewing: *Because I'm helping the Revelles.*

His lightstring fought against my mind, only relenting as I began to infuse a calm down it. *You trust me. You know I speak the truth.* "Because you're going to win."

"What?"

You feel the truth of my words. "Think about it. For a Chronos to age this much, how far did he have to travel back? Six months? A year?"

Trys frowned. "That's suicide."

"An attempted *murder*-suicide," I corrected her. The sheer power of the Chronoses, to be able to travel back an entire year in order to change the course of history, even if it killed them. "And why would he do that?"

"It would have to be a sacrifice the family deemed absolutely necessary," Dewey said slowly. "Like stopping me from becoming mayor."

"That's right." And keeping him from releasing my family from underneath the Chronoses' thumb. I straightened my back, my gaze fixed on him. "In twenty-four days, you're going to win. And after that, you're going to change Charmant for the better, just like you said."

Dewey dusted off his jacket. "My God, you're right. I'm the key to all this."

"Exactly." *You are the most important person in Charmant.*

Hubris surged through his lightstring. "Well, they certainly judged us wrong. We can't be scared into submission, can we, my sweet?"

Easy for a time traveler to say. Without him, they could have me shot on Main Street in broad daylight, and there was nothing my family could do about it. "Not one bit."

You see the threat your family poses. You wish to keep the Revelles safe.

"Rest assured, citizens of the Night," Dewey continued, letting his voice carry to the bystanders. "We're going to put an end to my family's tyranny once and for all."

I turned to Colette and Millie, but both looked skeptical. They'd see. Once the first snow fell and we were still making money, they'd be his biggest fans.

Trys pulled on Dewey's arm. "Let's not jump to conclusions, okay? Luxe is far from an expert on our family. She's hardly an expert on her own family."

I kept my face a mask of calm, not giving her the satisfaction of seeing how her words stung. "If you have a better explanation, I'm all ears."

She frowned. "Uncle Frank was a jerk, but he loved his wife and son. He'd never willingly leave them behind. And he's far too selfish to sacrifice himself to help George win. Maybe Dewey fainted again, and—"

"Maybe I *fainted*?" Dewey's ears pinkened.

Trysta leaned closer and dropped her voice. "You have that pale sheen you always get when you wake up from a fainting spell."

"Because I was knocked out cold!" Dewey exclaimed, turning away from her.

Roger gripped Jamison's shoulders, steadying him. "You okay, buddy? You're swaying like a sailor."

Jamison managed a nod, but his lightstring was fading by

the second. Trys and Roger needed to get him to a physician, and fast.

Dewey looked back and forth between us, tendrils of pea-green jealousy snaking their way into his lightstring. "Why were the two of you together?"

"We weren't. We stumbled upon you at the same time." *He means nothing to me.*

Ignoring my lie, Jamison leaned his head against the wall. "Should we call the police?"

The last of the bystanders scurried away. Trysta shook her head. "We don't even have a body anymore. Look."

Sure enough, no skin remained beneath the man's clothes. Only bones and dust.

Dewey held his arm out to me. "Let's go. I need to see Trevor immediately, and I'm not letting you out of my sight."

All I wanted was to crawl into bed and forget this nightmare. Or at least talk to Uncle Wolffe and figure out what the hell we were going to do. Time travelers didn't simply give up. Another would take his place. Soon.

I looped my arm in Dewey's. "I won't leave your side."

From my periphery, Trys rolled her eyes.

"Wait a second." Colette handed me her handkerchief. "You're bleeding."

As I pressed it to my nose, she murmured, "Maybe you should come home."

If only I could. "I'm fine. Really."

Her mouth tightened to a thin line. She didn't approve of whatever I was doing with Dewey. No one did, though I didn't hear them complaining about our stocked liquor closet.

She looked as though she wanted to say more, but Dewey beckoned me. Fixing my smile, I tucked her handkerchief into my cleavage. "Jamison needs a Strattori," I whispered. "I'll find you all later, if I can."

With one last appraising look, she nodded and let me go.

TWELVE

LUXE

Dewey wasted no time. At eight the next morning—an ungodly hour by Revelle standards—he called a meeting with my family in the repurposed warehouse by the docks. Our soon-to-be winter theater.

Per Dewey's request, Trevor stayed glued to my side as we walked over together. At least the Edwardian was good company. He'd even stayed late after last night's show to teach me the first of his mind control techniques.

As we wove through the eerily quiet streets, I scanned for any threats, but at this hour few tourists were awake, let alone plotting against us. No, to find the true culprits, I'd have to walk the Day District, and Dewey had forbidden me to set foot there. But if I used my magic—

"Too dangerous. If another Edwardian heard you . . ." Trevor shuddered. "Let me do the investigating for now. If anyone's planning something, I'll hear it first, okay?"

"Do *you* ever rest?"

He laughed outright, a high-pitched sound that made me smile. "Mr. Chronos gives me every Sunday off so I can bring my grandmother to church, mostly so she doesn't get herself in trouble. She's a bit like your nana, I suppose. She says what's on her mind."

An old Edwardian lady with a mouth—what a combination. "Is she your only family?"

"I have plenty of family. Two sisters, a brother, a nosy mother, and a quiet father. A few cousins, too, though not as many as you. But I like taking my grandmother to church."

"Why?"

He winced. I shouldn't have posed it as a question; he had no choice but to respond.

"It's quiet, I suppose. People's thoughts are much more peaceful during Mass."

I hadn't given much thought to Edwardian magic, and how they couldn't simply turn it off. "Well, I'm glad you work for Dewey."

"I'm glad you work for him, too."

"I don't." I turned the corner, Trevor right beside me. "I work *with* him."

Trevor smiled but said nothing.

This early, the waterside promenade was a ghost town. No music, no tourists, only the skittering of litter over the cobblestones and the occasional clamor of metal chains against a ship's hull. I glanced around, unable to shake the feeling that someone was hiding in the gray mist, waiting to strike.

Trevor cast a wary look toward the Day District, their lantern lights cutting through the morning fog. We both knew where the enemy lived.

I pulled my shawl closer. "Any leads on yesterday's attack?"

"I've personally spoken to every Edwardian who works in the

Day District. No one has heard anything about a plan to take out Mr. Chronos. The only thing out of the ordinary are the Strattoris. Apparently, a few boys have gone missing."

"Missing?" I asked. "Or ran away?" Once they were old enough to board the ferry on their own, plenty of Strattoris abandoned their family's strict religious lifestyle.

"That's on my list of things to find out. With my family's magic, few secrets remain uncovered in Charmant. All it takes is one of us hearing the right thought, then anyone who hears that person's thoughts is also aware of it. Anyone who hears either of *those* people's thoughts also knows, and so forth. If the secret is interesting enough, it spreads like wildfire. An attempt to take out the Night District's bootlegger and mayoral candidate is certainly newsworthy."

He was right; the Night relied on Dewey. From the brothels to the hotels, our customers expected a bawdy good time, and that meant booze.

"Is it possible for an Edwardian to keep a secret?" As soon as I uttered the question, a ball of panic twisted my stomach. Trevor knew *my* secret.

He smiled knowingly. "With enough training, yes. In order to reveal a secret, they have to be directly asked about it. Speaking of which, have you been practicing those exercises?"

"A little." Uncle Wolffe and I had reviewed Trevor's mind control techniques after he'd left last night. "Is it really as easy as singing in my head?"

"For beginners, yes. Just practice with the same song. Once you get good at it, we can move on to more subtle techniques."

And then I'd be able to slip into the Day and see which lightstrings looked the guiltiest.

"Your cousins are behind us."

Sure enough, Colette and Millie were crossing the street a ways down, their gait purposefully slow, as if they were trying to keep their distance from me.

"No, they're not," Trevor said quietly. "They're actually hoping you'll wait for them."

"Really?" I slowed my step as I glanced over my shoulder again. They still wore their stage makeup, and their eyelids were heavy with exhaustion. Another long night in the Fun House while I slept soundly.

I wouldn't blame them for walking right by me.

He tapped the side of his head. "Can't lie, remember?"

I squeezed his arm. "One of your best traits."

Millie stifled a yawn as they approached. "Morning, Luxie girl. Mr. Edwardes."

"Miss Revelle," Trevor breathed. "You look absolutely radiant today."

She grinned, her tired eyes glittering. "I love that you can't lie."

"Are you Luxe's bodyguard now?" Colette asked.

"Yes. Until the election." Twenty-three days away.

Colette leaned closer. "And what will you do if someone is thinking about harming her?"

With his narrow frame and modest height, Trevor wasn't exactly formidable. "My instructions are to yell and make a lot of noise."

The corners of Colette's mouth quirked. "That could work."

Once we reached the warehouse, Trevor held the door. Colette entered first—and gasped.

The warehouse had already been transformed into a theater. An absolutely gorgeous one.

It wasn't as tall as the Big Tent, and it didn't open to the night sky, but a sparkling mural of a celestial starscape graced the domed ceiling. The stage was wider than the one at home, and the pit floors were dark, scuff-free oak. Rows of seats climbed in sweeping arcs, the velvet such a deep black, it soaked up the little light from the open doors. There was no piss smell, only the faint aroma of fresh paint and new wood.

"He did all this already?" I asked Trevor breathlessly.

"Yes. He started months ago."

Quite a gamble. What would he have done if we hadn't agreed to his proposition?

Dewey stood at the back of the stage, looking as dashing as ever in his closely tailored black suit with the infamous diamond-shaped clock. As he bent to show Aunt Caroline the pulley ropes controlling the curtain, the maroon bump on his temple caught the light. He hadn't sought a Strattori for yesterday's injuries, instead wearing his bruises like badges of honor.

As Colette and Millie checked out the box seats, someone disappeared through the curtains, their large frame unmistakable. Uncle Wolffe. We'd hardly had a chance to speak since the attack.

I slipped backstage after him, weaving through the maze of empty rooms. The lights back here had yet to be installed, cloaking the dressing rooms in a quiet, eerie darkness.

"Uncle Wolffe?" I called.

Sniffling echoed from a few doors down.

I followed the noise, all too aware of how easy it'd be for someone to hide back here and grab me. But Trevor likely tracked my every thought, and my family was only a scream away.

"Uncle Wolffe?"

"In here," Uncle Wolffe's voice boomed.

I found him in a dressing room with Nana, who sat on the floor, her eyes wet. Uncle Wolffe crouched beside her. He was a wonderful showrunner—organized, fair, and absolutely brilliant at finding ways to keep us afloat—but emotional support was not his forte.

"What's wrong?" I wrapped my arms around her, resisting the urge to magically smooth away all her pain. Other than the occasional prank, we never charmed our own.

"She's been back here for an hour." Uncle Wolffe rubbed the bits of white powder that still clung to his temples, remnants of last night's show. I was, perhaps, the only Revelle who'd managed to get a few hours of sleep.

"I've got this," I told him, rubbing her back.

Relieved, he straightened. Dark circles stained the skin under his eyes. "You good?"

With yesterday's attack, with cozying up to Dewey, or with the fact that the Chronoses are gunning for us? But I only smiled. Uncle Wolffe had enough to worry about. "I'm good."

Once his footsteps faded, I stroked Nana's soft white hair. "What's wrong?"

"This is a mistake," she rasped. "We shouldn't be meddling in the election. And we can't work for one of them!"

"We don't work for him; it's a partnership. And with Dewey, we're protected from any Chronos attacks. He can always just go back and warn us. Even if he only travels a few minutes, it's enough to stop the worst from happening."

"The worst has already happened. They already took my sweet girls!" As she uttered the words, she shattered against me, a fragile doll deflating.

Her raw grief was a serrated knife, and it tugged on the stitches holding my heart together.

"They were my daughters." Nana's voice trembled. "Adeline, too. I couldn't have picked a better wife for Wolffe, but Bonnie and Catherine were my babies."

She covered her head in her hands as she tried to contain her sobs. In the year after they drowned, Nana had gotten so lost in her grief, she couldn't find her way out of it. She'd been a ghost of herself: a white-haired, frail woman who never wore makeup, never left her room. The family had nursed her back to life, but whenever grief struck again, it struck hard.

No wonder Uncle Wolffe had left; he never spoke of Aunt Adeline, never even spoke of Roger after he left Charmant. As far as I could tell, he had yet to acknowledge his return.

A selfish part of me wanted to leave, too, but my mother had always been the best at soothing Nana, at keeping the family calm. With her gone, Nana needed me.

As I crouched in front of her, she uncovered her face, her bangles sliding down her too-slim forearms. "They blamed those magic haters, but the Chronoses were behind it somehow."

"I know, Nana." The family who owned the boat rentals despised people with magic. They blamed them for the disappearance of their daughter years earlier. But that didn't explain why, after years of living peacefully in the Night, they'd decided to drown three Revelles. It didn't matter. The Chronoses strapped them to the electric chair and fried them for it.

"My girls were destined for greatness, and they never got to achieve it. The Edwardians hardly even investigated, and the mainland coppers couldn't be bothered. Easier to let a couple of nobodies take the blame."

Our mothers, the infamous ABCs. How the mainlanders had

loved them. The *New York Times* even did a full-page write-up about their trapeze act. My mother had been so proud, she'd kept it pinned on the mirror in the bedroom we shared.

I squeezed her hands. "Things are going to change around here. If Dewey wins——"

"What if he loses? We're putting out our necks for him."

"He's going to protect us, Nana. Either way." I'd make sure of it.

She held my gaze. "I don't trust him. I don't trust any of them."

"Do you trust *me*?" I gave her my most innocent smile.

She almost laughed. I took her hands and helped her to her feet. "C'mon. Let's see why he got us up at this awful hour."

I kept my arm over her shoulders as we wove through the maze of dressing rooms. Once we reemerged on the stage, Aunt Caroline spotted us.

"Not bad, Luxie girl," she whispered, throwing me a grateful smile as she wrapped her arms around Nana and led her to the front row.

Uncle Wolffe clapped. "Everyone take a good look around. Because in twenty-three days, we're having our first show here."

"I thought this was going to be our *winter* theater," Uncle Thomas called.

Despite the cool morning air, beads of sweat glistened on Uncle Wolffe's forehead. "Mr. Chronos here has asked us to perform at his election night party. Press from as far as the mainland will be here. It'll be great publicity for us, and a way to celebrate Dewey's victory with a bang, as only the Revelles can do."

And it would drive a knife into the heart of the Chronoses—the Revelles performing in honor of the current mayor's excommunicated son.

Dewey stepped forward. "If yesterday's attack taught us anything, it's that the Revelles are about to enter a new era of prosperity." He made eye contact with each skeptical face. "My family sent a time traveler on a suicide mission to assassinate me. If it were as simple as them sabotaging my victory, my uncle would have only had to travel from election night—about three weeks from now—to stop me. But he aged so much, it killed him within minutes, which means they were trying to prevent something further down the road: the Revelles rising up."

My family watched him, their careful expressions not betraying any emotion.

"You see, my family fears your magic. Your influence. But with a time traveler on your side, not a single Revelle will be harmed. You have my word."

I couldn't help myself; I had to know if my family heard the truth of his words, of how much we had to gain in a partnership with Dewey. Turning away from the stage, I squeezed my eyes shut and braced myself for whatever punishment my magic solicited today.

The pain swarmed me like one thousand knives through my skull, the need to cry out all-consuming, and still no lightstrings, nothing but black, black, as I dug deeper—

They blinked into existence. Revelle lightstrings were a little different than typical ones: more iridescent, shimmering like wet paint. Nervous but listening intently as Dewey described the increased security, the rehearsal schedule for the election night extravaganza.

Like fireflies gathering at dusk, the first sparks of hope spread through my family. For once, success was within our grasp. Almost.

But Dewey's lightstring was fraught with his perpetual caution.

He was so careful to keep his every emotion in check, so afraid that my family might view him negatively. I knew better than anyone how exhausting the spotlight could be.

They believe you, I whispered down his lightstring. *They're beginning to think of you like family.*

His eyes found mine, his genuine smile so boyish that a pang of guilt tugged at me. But I had to keep him close to us. Too many people were depending on it.

Dewey handed Uncle Wolffe a bottle of champagne. My uncle popped it with a long knife and sprayed it in sweeping arcs over the pit. Uncle Thomas yanked the bottle from him and poured some over Uncle Wolffe's head. Naturally, Uncle Wolffe tackled him in retaliation. As they rolled across the stage, Aunt Caroline jumped on top. Aunt Marie wasn't far behind.

From the first row, Nana relaxed into her seat. "It's not a party without at least one wrestling match."

Dewey motioned for me to join him, a deep scarlet tinging his lightstring as I crossed the stage. Not just desire. Something a little more . . . amorous. The line between business arrangement and genuine feelings was becoming blurred.

Would that be so terrible? Charmant needed to believe we were in love. And there were far worse people to date than Dewey Chronos.

His dark eyes glittered as he slipped an arm around me, caressing my lower back.

"Uncle Wolffe!" Millie called. "Any ideas for the show?"

Detangling himself from his siblings, Uncle Wolffe settled onto the edge of the stage. "It's a lot to piece together in twenty-three days, but picture this: an enormous American flag, each star replaced with a sparkling crystal."

An excited murmur passed through my family.

"The flamethrowers will battle with fiery muskets. The cancan dancers will wear curly white wigs, like bawdy founding fathers, and their bloomers will be stars and stripes. Of course, the Trapeze Three will star."

Millie clapped excitedly, her eyes finding mine. Even Colette grinned.

"*Luxe* will star," Dewey interrupted, "alone."

Like a storm cloud over the sun, my family's lightstrings dimmed. If I could have crawled backstage, I would have.

"And I was thinking black and gold, like fire and night. Those are my colors, after all. And diamond-shaped clocks everywhere. A jewel and a clock: Fitting, isn't it?"

Wolffe's mouth formed a tight line. "I thought the creative would be up to me."

Dewey rubbed my shoulders. "Luxe is the face of the Night District. And if my sources are correct, the Big Tent's profits have increased threefold since she began starring."

"How did you—"

"Luxe will star," Dewey interrupted. "She is unparalleled."

"So she'll just catch herself?" Disdain dripped from Colette's words. Even Millie's perennial smile failed her.

Dewey slid an arm around my waist. "She'll share the spotlight with no one."

"That *does* sound like Luxe," someone muttered, followed by snickers.

It took effort not to wince, especially as their lightstrings darkened with disapproval. Charming Dewey to abruptly change his mind might raise suspicions. I'd try later. For now, I sharpened my smile and shrugged, the haughty star they knew so well.

Dewey lifted his champagne. "To Luxe, whose hard work made this all possible."

Back straight, head high. My family raised their glasses, but their subdued applause wasn't loud enough to mask the theater doors clicking shut behind Colette and Millie.

Uncle Wolffe clapped his enormous hands. "All right, everyone, go home and sleep. We still have a show tonight."

I squeezed Dewey's arm. "I need to get ready." My act was hours away, but if I left quickly, I might be able to catch my cousins.

He glanced at his watch, but I leaned into his lightstring. *You want me to rest.*

"You'll take Trevor with you?"

"Of course," I murmured from beneath my lashes. *Your generosity is appreciated.*

Before I could ease up on his lightstring, he leaned down, his lips parting.

Oh. He wanted to kiss me.

Revelle eyes burned into my back as I leaned in, too.

His lips moved with practiced skill over mine, his hand resting on the back of my head, anchoring me in place with surprising gentleness. It might have been a great kiss, albeit brief, had my aunts not been standing a few feet away.

I wish we didn't have to stop, I whispered down his lightstring as I pulled away. The perpetual throbbing in my head worsened.

Dewey caressed my back. "Was that okay?"

"Of course." Not a lie, exactly, but my emotions were too jumbled to sort through. *You wish to let me leave now.*

As I walked to the exit, blackness obscured the doorway, and as soon as Trevor and I stepped outside, darkness cloaked the bright sun, the tourists . . .

"Miss Revelle, are you all right?"

With my eyes squeezed shut, I massaged my temples and eased my grip on Dewey's lightstring, eventually letting it go.

Trevor handed me a handkerchief. "Your nose."

I dabbed at my nosebleed, my magic's petty punishment for working overtime lately. As if I had a choice. "Did you happen to hear Colette's or Millie's thoughts when they left?"

Trevor winced. "Yes, but please don't ask me to repeat them."

Wonderful. They hated me. "Where were they headed?"

"To Roger's barn." He offered his arm as we stepped off the curb.

I'd make this right. With a little more magic, Dewey would understand that I couldn't perform without them. Twenty-three days was plenty of time to convince him to let us have the show Uncle Wolffe envisioned for us.

I'd make this right.

Trevor watched me from his periphery. "Do the nosebleeds happen often?"

Usually, I told people I was sensitive to the heat, but Trevor was always honest with me. "Only when I push myself too hard. It's the cost of my . . . other magic. Pain."

"I must admit, that's a relief. When I first realized what you could do, I thought it might be shadow magic."

Shadow magic was the sort of thing our older cousins used to threaten when we wouldn't stop pestering them. It gave me nightmares as a child, their taunts about slitting our throats or using a life-sucking kiss to turn us into magic-less wraiths who did their bidding. "My lightstrings are the opposite of shadows." I paused, turning to face him. "Shadow magic isn't real, is it?"

He smiled. "No."

Like my mother had told me countless times.

When we reached the barn, Trevor tipped his hat. "I'll wait here."

He was doing me a favor by staying out of my head. I squeezed his arm in gratitude.

As I pulled open the heavy barn door, Roger pressed his fingers to his lips. "You just missed Col and Millie," he said in a low voice.

My heart sank. "I'm sure they're glad of it."

"Can you blame them?"

Not one bit.

Jamison's cot was too small for him, and he let out a little sigh as he shifted in his sleep. After spending so much time with Dewey, everything about Jamison seemed large. His long legs, his broad hands relaxed at his sides. It was hard to be around him without remembering his body pressed against mine in the alley. Or that incredible kiss.

"How is he?" I asked, examining a few books stacked on the windowsill.

"Concussed. His ribs are bruised, not broken. Same with his cheekbone." Roger adjusted the silk square he'd tied over his head, his latest attempt to protect his relaxed hair from the humidity. "It could have been much worse if you hadn't stopped Frank Chronos."

Frank Chronos, the biggest prick in a family of pricks, according to Dewey. The only nice thing anyone ever said about him was that he loved his son and spoiled him rotten. "His face looks better than yesterday, at least. Less swollen."

He produced a small block of ice from the hay. "Effigen ice. Colette got it for him."

I pressed my finger to the little square, surprised by the sudden chill on my fingertip. Regular ice was a rare enough commodity in Charmant. "Did he tell you about the beach?"

"I can't believe he finally found it. The guy deserves closure." He produced a half-eaten croissant from a cloth napkin and took a bite.

"From Sweet Buns?" I asked casually.

He sighed. "Trys got it for me."

"You really don't want to see Margaret?"

"No." His tone shut down further questions. "Does Dewey have any leads?"

I shook my head. "The only man who knows why he did this traveled back so far, he's now a pile of bones. We may never know."

Someone was making knots in our timeline, trying to trip us before we had a chance to succeed.

Jamison shifted, and his damp hair fell into his eyes. I nearly reached out and brushed it away. Nana never let the Revelle boys' hair get that long. The moment it neared their eyes, she chased them, shears in hand. A mean crescent bruise surrounded Jamison's right eye, his dark lashes fluttering against it as he stirred. To think I'd once mistaken him for a Chronos.

Better that he wasn't Dewey. With Dewey, *I* was in control. And judging by today's kiss, he wasn't going to walk away anytime soon.

"We're going to get to the bottom of this." It felt good to utter those words with the confidence they required. "We're so close, Roger. Now that Dewey's leasing us the new theater, we'll have an income year-round, even in the winter. All I have to do is keep him—"

"Completely and utterly wrapped around your finger?"

"I was going to say 'alive,' but yes. That helps."

"You know I've been in your shoes." Roger fiddled with a straw of hay. "It's never a good idea to have the same customer, night after night. They tend to get . . . obsessed."

The man who'd caused his scars had certainly been obsessed. "I'm not using magic. Not yet, anyways."

"Jewels aren't the only way to charm a guy." He flicked the piece of hay at me. "If our mothers were still alive, they'd throw you on the next ferry and keep you hidden away on the mainland until the mayor's son fell out of love with you."

It was growing harder to picture them here. Alive. They would have been world-famous by now, and affording Dewey's outlandish prices would have been no trouble. Aunt Adeline would have passed the star's baton to Colette, and I would have been happy by her side. We'd still be as close as sisters.

"He's not in love with me," I finally said, "and my mother hated the mainland."

"But *you* don't. You really should get outta here one day. It's incredible out there."

"Is it, though?" I ran my finger along the spine of the book beside Jamison's cot.

"After I left, the first place I went was Harlem, to visit my mom's family. My gran took me to my first jazz club." He paused, his smile growing, eyes distant. "That's when I knew: Charmant may be a big party, but the mainland is coming around. There's art. Culture. Jazz."

"The mainland passed Prohibition," I countered. "They only recently discovered that women are smart enough to vote. And if I'm not mistaken, your parents' marriage would have been outlawed in most states."

He arched a brow. "So I should stay in Charmant, where talented Black acrobats are replaced by their less qualified white cousins?"

My cheeks burned. "Touché."

"There's more to that story, and we both know it." He studied me carefully. "You and my father are hiding something. Ready to tell me what it is?"

"Forget all about the mainland, and maybe I will."

"Says the girl who keeps the mainland penny I gave her underneath her pillow."

Before I could chastise him for going through my things, Jamison stirred, and Roger sprang into action, hovering over his sleeping friend. The intimacy of their friendship struck me yet again. How lucky Roger was to have someone he could talk to about anything, both the mundane and the big hurts.

Some of us had to manage those sorts of things alone.

THIRTEEN

JAMISON

Per Dr. Strattori's orders, and Roger's insistence on following them, I was bedridden for an entire week with nothing to do but read. Visits from Roger's family helped, but most of the week they raced between rehearsals for the election night extravaganza and their nightly shows. By the time Luxe offered to bring me to her grandmother to show her my photo, I'd dulled my knife carving caricatures of Roger and Trys on the soft barn wood.

A midsummer rain kept the tourists indoors as we made our way down Main Street. "You can share my umbrella," Luxe offered.

"I don't mind getting wet." I paused to look down each street of the intersection. "Besides, I want to see if I recognize anything."

"Do you?"

Nothing. Everything.

Roger and Trys were worried I was reading into things, but Luxe simply seemed curious.

"The cobblestones," I admitted. "The way they crisscross."

She peered over the curb. "If it's still raining at high tide, these streets will be covered in seawater, and you won't be able to see a thing."

Even that image was familiar. I offered her my arm to help her over the puddle, but her smirk was all Roger as she leaped gracefully to the other side. "What do you remember about your family?"

"Very little." I sidestepped broken glass. "I was raised in a religious orphanage from around four years old to sixteen. The friars said my parents were still alive, that they surrendered me willingly because I was too much trouble for them."

She halted. "Who would say such a thing to a child?"

"Bad people. That's why I don't believe them."

The rain beat down harder as we turned south, and Luxe lifted her umbrella to share. I took it and made sure she was fully covered.

She stole a look upward. "What about before the orphanage?"

I had plenty of fragmented memories, like a warm blanket tucked to my chin, or a soft kiss on my forehead, but only one clear recollection. "I remember waiting for them. For years, I was convinced they were looking for me but couldn't find me because I wasn't where I was supposed to be. Once I ran away from the orphanage to try to get back to them."

That punishment was the worst: months of isolation in a locked, windowless room. No visitors. No books. No nothing. *If you want to be alone, we'll leave you alone.*

Luxe remained silent, the rain pelting the umbrella.

I forced myself to swallow the knot in my throat. "I know how clichéd that sounds, an orphan pining for his parents. It's ridiculous—"

"It's not. It's just—"

"Sad?"

"A little." She danced around another puddle, pausing so I could catch up with the umbrella. "I suppose I'm an orphan, too."

"What about your father?"

"A mainlander. He left before I was born." She pranced to the next curb, each little leap in sync with the music from a nearby hotel. "Why does that surprise you?"

She was even better than Roger at reading emotions. I followed her, my gait long enough to step over the deep puddles without making a fool of myself trying to jump. "Your family just seems so perfect. It's hard to picture someone walking away from all this."

"I couldn't agree more. I mean, sure, there's a whole world out there, but Charmant is home. I'd never leave." She nodded down the next street. "Anything familiar here?"

"Nothing solid." I fell into step beside her. "So you have no interest in traveling?"

"Traveling is for people without families depending on them. Or people with money."

"I don't have a dollar to my name, and I've traveled quite a bit."

"Ugh. Dollars." She scrunched her face. "Why would I want anything to do with ugly mainland money?"

Revelles and their jewels. "So even if you could leave, you wouldn't want to?"

"Of course not. I mean, a long time ago, I wanted to go everywhere." She paused, balancing on the edge of a curb. "When I was little, I found a magazine in the pit filled with all these pictures from around the world. Jungles, pyramids, cities that looked nothing like Charmant. Like New Orleans, with its old-world charm." Her smile softened, just like it did when she was around Colette and Millie. A rare glimpse behind her poised, indifferent mask.

"New Orleans is incredible," I told her. "You'd love it."

"You've been there?" As if remembering herself, she shook her head. "It doesn't matter. I was just a little girl who was avoiding dance lessons."

The rain came down in sheets as we turned down the narrow alley. I slowed, unable to shake the strange sense that we were being watched.

"If I really am from the Night District, is it possible that I have a tiny bit of magic in me?" I'd considered asking Roger or Trys, but they had their doubts about my history with Charmant.

"Probably not. One of your parents would need to be a member of one of the five magical families here. A few people have magic from more than one bloodline, but even that's rare. Most people on Charmant have no magic at all."

Like I suspected. Odds were, I was absolutely ordinary.

Under the persistent downpour, I could just make out another man walking ahead of us, a dark umbrella protecting his sleek black coat.

Luxe's step faltered. She threw out her arm to stop me.

"Who is it?"

"George Chronos," she whispered.

Trysta's other brother. The one who'd tried to drop a crate on me.

As if hearing my thoughts, his head whipped toward us. Luxe pushed me against the brick wall and tugged on the umbrella, blocking our faces from his view. "Don't look at him."

As if I could tear my gaze from her.

Rain hummed over her skin, sliding down the soft lines of her face, inches away. Her clever eyes remained on mine, but her attention was fixed on the arrogant man whose footsteps splashed closer and closer. Not afraid, but listening. Waiting. She was always planning, always thinking ahead.

Not yet, she mouthed. That perfect mouth—if only I could forget how soft it had felt on mine.

"And here I thought you were my brother's girl." A deep voice chuckled.

I pushed off the wall, stretching to my full height as I looked down at George Chronos.

He examined us from beneath his black umbrella, raindrops gliding down his long trench coat. "Silly of me to assume a Revelle would be faithful."

"What fun would that be?" Luxe simpered at him. "Here to try to kill your brother again?"

"Such vicious rumors you've been spreading. Trying to turn brother against brother?"

"You do a good enough job of that on your own."

"I had nothing to do with his attack. Yet." He tilted his head, a bird examining its prey. "You know, if I ever do eliminate someone from the Night, I don't think it'll be my brother. Watch your back, 'Radiant Ruby.'"

I hardly heard Luxe's tart response, hardly felt the rain as I dropped the umbrella. "Did you just threaten her?"

George pressed forward, his face inches from mine. "Let me tell you what comes next. I call her a whore, and you throw a punch, which is a stupid thing to do, because I'm a Chronos. You can't win a fight against me."

Can't win. All my life, I couldn't hit a friar, couldn't fight back whenever they lifted their staffs to me, couldn't do a damn thing when they went after the little ones.

Men in power. Fucking bastards, all of them.

I'd hardly formed a fist before George's slammed into my cheek, right into my bruise.

"I told you, kid. We always win."

Pain radiated from where he'd struck, drowning out his laughter as he walked away.

"Damnit." I pressed my fingers against my cheek. "He sucker punched me."

"I thought you were supposed to be smart!" Luxe yanked my wrist before I could go after him. "Were you really going to fight a time traveler?"

I watched as he disappeared around the corner. "Somewhere, in some unfinished timeline, I got him good."

"Well, in this timeline, you didn't. Because he's a dirty cheater!" she yelled down the empty street. "One who's going to *lose* in two weeks!"

I checked my jaw. Didn't hurt. If he hadn't hit the same spot as Frank Chronos did last week, it wouldn't have stung much at all.

"Why did you do that?" Her soft fingers prodded my hot skin, the bruise forming just beneath the surface. "'Whore' isn't even an insult. It's a profession as old as this world."

"I know, I just hated *how* he said it." I cleared my throat, looking away as she touched my cheek gently. "Let's keep going."

She hesitated.

"He barely got me. Really. And I've waited long enough for this."

With a nod, she meandered down the alley, her fingers grazing the brick wall. "My uncle's going to be furious that I left Trevor behind."

She glimpsed over her shoulder—still no sign of the Chronos—before she turned down a residential block. Identical houses lined both sides of the wide street, with chain-link fences around some of their front yards.

My feet slowed. I *knew* this street.

"What was he even doing in the Night District?" Groaning, she shook her head. "Dewey will want even more security now. I'm going to have an army following me everywhere."

The roar of memories drowned out the rest of her words. Neat little brownstones, each with a cement stoop. Each startlingly familiar.

Luxe stopped. "What is it?"

Behind her was an unassuming house: a few yards of green lawn, a tiny front porch with two wrought iron chairs, and a rusty playground behind the chain-link fence. The backyard was out of view from the street, but a tire swing hung from the thickest branch of an old oak tree.

"I've been here before," I managed to say.

"You mean with Roger?"

"No. A long time ago." My heart raced as I pointed to the slide, the royal-blue paint grayed by years in the sun. "You can see the ocean from the top of that slide."

Her eyes widened. "The beach is only a block away."

All the blood in my body rushed to my head. Before I could fall, I staggered to the curb.

She stood in front of me. "You're absolutely certain that you recognize *this* house."

Blurred images flooded me. Unfamiliar adults exchanging worried glances. My mother's voice. Eyes blue, like mine, wide with fear. *Stay here, my love. We'll find you when it's safe.*

"Jamison?"

I blinked at her, at the house behind her. "There's a living room when you enter, with a fireplace."

"Jamison."

"Stairs in front of the door, and a little kitchen behind it."

"*Jamison—*"

"And there's a tire swing in the back."

She crouched in front of me, her eyes wide. "Jamison, this is an orphanage."

"*What?*" Her words were distant, impossible.

"It's an orphanage," she repeated slowly, "but it's only for Night District children."

FOURTEEN

LUXE

Gathering the crinoline of my skirt, I lowered myself to the curb beside Jamison, who grew paler by the second. "What do you remember?"

"I don't know. My mother, frightened . . ." He shook his head. "I don't know."

Sitting this close, it was hard not to offer some sort of comfort as he struggled with the stream of emotions flooding his face. He might not remember his family, but he loved them with his whole heart, just like he did Roger. And Trysta. Brave, to love like that, when he knew all too well how quickly loved ones could be snatched away.

"I brought you here because Nana's watching the children while my cousin who runs the orphanage is out," I said. "If there are any records . . ."

He pushed back damp tendrils of dark hair, the ends falling into his bright eyes. "Okay."

The chain-link gate creaked as we opened it. Even though the orphanage was sorely in need of a handyman, Jamison was awestruck, each step unhurried.

Nana answered the door after the first knock. She slid a hand up the doorjamb, the fabric of her lace-and-satin nightgown riding to her thighs. At least she'd put on a brassiere—or two, judging by the unusually high cleavage proudly displayed by her plunging neckline.

She batted her lashes at Jamison. "I wasn't expecting company."

And yet she was in a full face of makeup. I kissed her on the cheek as I pushed past her. "I told you this morning."

"Did you? It must have slipped my mind."

White-faced, Jamison accepted Nana's invitation to sit on the couch. As Nana shut the door, he fidgeted with a loose tufting button.

"Where are the children?" I asked.

She waved a dismissive hand. "Jumping in puddles somewhere. Once the rain stopped, I couldn't keep them inside."

Five Revelle children lived in the orphanage. Until my birthday last month, I should have been among them. Nana had certainly threatened it many times, usually after she caught Millie and me sneaking out through our window. Colette always begged us not to disobey Nana. We were so afraid of being separated, even by a few blocks.

I walked toward the bucket catching raindrops near the fireplace. "Leaky roof?"

"Nothing new. Now, where's this photograph my granddaughter speaks of?"

"Right here, ma'am." Jamison removed it from a worn leather wallet as if it were as delicate as a rose petal. "Their last name is Port."

Nana held it with equal reverence, carefully balancing it in her palm as she slipped on her glasses. She squinted at the photograph—and froze.

All the blood rushed from her face.

Jamison and I reached her at the same time, easing her to a sitting position on the couch.

"What is it?" Hope clung to each of his words.

Nana pinned her smile with the practice of someone who'd spent years in the spotlight. "Oh, it was nothing, darling; I stood too quickly when I answered the door."

Liar.

"Your mother was beautiful. And your father . . ." She smiled knowingly at Jamison. "I see where you get your looks."

Jamison still held his breath. "So you don't recognize them?"

"Can't say that I do." She handed him the photo. "I wish I could be more helpful."

I watched her carefully as she adjusted her many rings. She knew something.

"Jamison's an orphan," I said, "And he recognizes *this* orphanage. He knew there was a tire swing out back."

Only a Revelle could have seen the brief flash of remorse across Nana's face. "I'll dig around for any old records. Would that help?"

"Thank you. You have no idea how much this means to me." He kissed the hand she offered. "If you'd like, I can take a look at that leak."

"Don't bother. Every time we fix it, the damn squirrels just find a new place to rip up the shingles."

"Still, I'll give it a try. It's the least I can do."

"That would be so very kind." Her smile was a genuine thing, but it was tinged with sadness. I was tempted to tap into my other magic, to see if I could piece together what she was hiding, but I knew I wouldn't need to—Nana was always forthcoming with me.

Jamison lingered by the door, but I lifted a hand. "I'll catch up with you in a minute."

With a hopeful smile that made my chest squeeze a little too much, he headed outside.

Nana rubbed the hand he kissed. "Sweet boy, that one."

"Mm-hmm." We watched him take the porch steps two at a time.

"And a looker, too."

I examined a loose brick on the mantel. "I hadn't noticed."

"Sure. And I didn't have cake for breakfast." Nana sat back on the couch, closing tired eyes as she sank into the worn cushion. "If you care about that boy at all, wait a few days and tell him I found no records. Or tell him his parents loved him very much but died on the mainland."

"Who are they?" I leaned closer. "And why won't you tell him?"

"Because sometimes the past needs to stay buried." She looked away, eyes watering.

I sat beside her and waited until she looked at me. "He's Roger's best friend, Nana. He's been looking for answers for a long time. Surely he has a right to know the truth, whatever it is."

"Is it really a good idea for you to be walking around with a handsome boy, so close to the election?" She arched a painted brow. "Dewey doesn't seem like the sharing type."

"Jamison is a friend." But that wasn't exactly true, not when I knew the taste of his lips, the softness of his kiss. "He's more like Roger's friend. And besides, Revelles are never exclusive to their customers." It was discouraged, in fact, after what had happened to Roger.

"But Dewey's not a customer, is he? Not unless he gives you a jewel."

There it was again: what separated me from the rest of the family. They cozied up to customers for jewels; I cozied up to Dewey for booze—and for that gorgeous winter theater.

I kissed my grandmother on the cheek. "I'll see you tonight at the show?"

"As if I had anywhere else to be." She settled back on the couch, still a bit pale. That photograph had truly unsettled her.

She'd do the right thing. In a day or two, I'd ask her about it again.

From the roof, Jamison stopped hammering once I appeared on the porch. "There's a ladder in the back. Just be careful, it's—"

In a single jump, I hopped atop the railing, then leaped onto the roof.

"Slippery," he finished.

"Perhaps for you." I lowered myself atop the wet tiles. "Why does it smell like dinner?"

"I tied some garlic from the back garden to the eaves. Squirrels hate garlic."

"Just like vampires." I rubbed my finger along a clove.

He froze. "Don't tell me vampires are real."

"Of course not. But Roger used to give us nightmares with stories of a Chronos Dracula who wanted to suck our magical blood." How Roger loved to make us squirm. Every time we got a paper cut, he'd tease us about hiding it, or else we'd be hunted down for shadow magic. "Need a hand?"

"Just finished." He clapped the top of the toolbox. "I found this next to the tire swing."

"You really have been here."

"Incredible, isn't it?" He offered an arm. "Should we go? I don't want anyone to panic that their star is missing."

"Trust me, Roger and Trysta are more likely to notice you being gone. You're closer to them than I am to anyone."

The foolish words slipped from my mouth, and Jamison turned to look at me, surprise etched across his features. If only I could erase those words. Not that they weren't true—they were painfully, brutally true—but I sounded ridiculous. Poor Luxe Revelle, complaining to an orphan about not feeling close enough with her fifty-three first cousins, fourteen aunts and uncles, grandmother, countless second cousins, once-removed cousins, and stepcousins.

Those blue eyes pinned me in place. "What about Colette and Millie?"

"I thought we were talking about you, for once," I said lightly. "You're very good at getting me to talk about myself." Maybe that was his trick to winning over my family.

"And you're very good at getting people not to ask."

There was a rare curiosity in his questions. He was clever enough not to badger me for answers. Not telling felt like letting him down, somehow.

"I love my cousins like sisters, but we're all busy these days."

"You miss them."

I forced a laugh. "We've shared a bedroom for seven years." It had been my mother's room, but Millie and Colette didn't want to share with their fathers, and we couldn't stand being apart.

"And yet you miss them," he repeated, this time softer.

The pressure to speak was a quiet ache in my chest. I couldn't confide in anyone about it. Not Nana, who couldn't bear to face that we'd grown apart. And certainly not Uncle Wolffe. But there were no words to describe what had gone wrong, not without talking about my magic. "We don't eat together anymore."

As if that alone could explain the chasm between us.

"What do you mean?"

I fiddled with a wet leaf on the roof. "After our mothers died, we became obsessed with sitting at a certain mess hall table. It was close to the kitchen, but also far from the aunts and uncles, which made us *very* adult. I don't know why I'm talking about this. It's silly."

He leaned back, resting against his hands. "There is nothing silly about the superiority of some mess hall tables to others. Trust me, I understand."

His orphanage must have had communal dining, too. "Those first few months without our mothers, we schemed endlessly about how to get to that table before Roger and the boys did. I know how ridiculous it sounds, to have cared about something like seating arrangements when our mothers had just died. But we were obsessed."

"You were eleven, right?"

I managed a nod.

"What changed with your cousins?"

"How are you so sure something changed?"

He hesitated. "When you're with them, you have a guarded

smile. You're glad to be with them, and you care about them, but . . . you're holding back."

I gave him a look. "You can tell all that from a smile?"

"I could be wrong," he admitted. "But I'm particularly sensitive to your smiles."

My heart skipped a beat. "Oh?"

"At St. Douglas's, some friars had tempers." He looked away. "I learned to read faces."

Bright eyes, dimpled smile . . . Jamison had masks of his own. "Did they hurt you?"

He chuckled. "It's fine. They gave me drinking stories for years to come."

I waited until he looked at me again. "Did they hurt you?"

Silence. I didn't need my secondary magic to see how deep those scars ran. What sort of religious men struck children, let alone one as inquisitive and kind as Jamison must have been?

"Let's just say," he finally said, "my orphanage was nothing like this one." With a quick shake of his head, he forced a smile. "Anyway, what was I saying?"

He didn't like to feel pitied. I leaned closer, lifting my brows in challenge. "I believe you were comparing my smile to a mean old priest's."

His laughter lit his face. Despite my rain-soaked dress, my entire body warmed at the deep, throaty sound. Nana was right. This felt a bit like playing with fire.

"Well, it's not my fault you have a dozen fake smiles," he teased.

"Fake smiles?" The warm feeling slipped away.

"Mm-hmm." He twisted his lips and batted his lashes. "This is your stage smile, see?"

He looked so ridiculous, I couldn't help but laugh. "I'd better not look like that onstage."

"Of course it's terrible when *I* do it, but when you do it, the tourists fall to their knees."

I rolled my eyes. "Okay, so I have a stage smile. That's not unusual."

He ticked off on his fingers. "You have a particular smile around Roger. That one's real, but it's still hesitant. An entirely different one when Trys is around. Very forced. Let me see . . . there's the one when you're being polite, another when you're clearly tired but trying to look awake. When you're charming Dewey, of course."

I almost fell off the roof. "Excuse me?"

He didn't seem as though he was *trying* to upset me. But he'd just casually mentioned the secret that could ruin everything. "You have a specific smile for when you're charming Dewey."

"What makes you think I'm charming him?"

There was that scrunch of his brows again—his concentration face. "You sometimes look like you're focusing really hard when you're around him. Like it hurts."

"I'm not in pain. I just . . . What makes you think I'm doing that?" If Jamison could tell, then *anyone* could tell.

He brushed his pointer finger on one side of my mouth. Then the other. "Your muscles here tighten when you're in pain. I saw it after your accident, too. The, ah, first time we met."

The heat of his fingers lingered on my lips, stealing away whatever point I was about to make. That gentle touch—it was the same as it'd been that first night, when my mouth had captured his, surprise freezing him for a blissful moment.

I stood, turning my back on him. "I get migraines. That's all."

"The point is, something changed between you and your cousins."

That was an understatement. "We all wanted to be the star. I was never even in the running until . . . well, until I was, I suppose."

"So they're jealous?"

Sometimes I pretended it was as simple as jealousy. But Colette wasn't jealous; she was bursting with righteous indignation. Through sheer talent and determination, she'd earned the right to be the star, but I'd robbed her of it. No one had even given her a plausible explanation.

No, it wasn't jealousy that had come between us. It was my secrets. My magic.

I scooted down the roof, toward the ladder in the back. "Everything changed. For instance, Uncle Wolffe wanted me to eat double portions so I didn't look meek to our audience. I couldn't stuff my face in front of them, especially not *that* winter. So I started eating alone."

How I missed those shared meals, the absurdly complex plans we created to slip away unnoticed and save our favorite table. In a world without our mothers, that was everything.

"Can you still have fun with them?"

"Fun?"

"Surely there's no rule against the star having fun."

There was an accusation buried there. "I have *fun*."

He leaned over the top of the ladder, a challenge sparking in those bright eyes. "I've never seen your 'fun' smile."

"I have many 'fun' smiles! You just don't see them because you haven't come to a show since . . ."

His cheeks flushed. Ducking his head, he climbed down the ladder. "Roger and Trys didn't think it was wise. With a concussion, I mean."

He was a terrible liar. His friends didn't want a repeat of his attempts to leap over the balcony. "I have plenty of fun at the shows," I called down to him. "Saturday, for instance, is a big one. It's Millie's birthday, and it's going to be a *lot* of *fun*."

"Well, I guess I'll have to see for myself."

"I suppose you will. Being that you've appointed yourself the Smile Police."

He laughed as he stepped off the last rung. "Are you going to use the ladder or do one of those fancy Revelle jumps?"

I stood at the edge of the roof. "Is this some sort of test?"

"It's just a question." He slid his hands into his back pockets. "Go ahead. Have *fun*."

How ridiculous. Fun wasn't jumping off the roof while Nana was watching our every move from the kitchen. Fun was a sold-out election night show at our brand-new winter theater. Fifteen days away.

I climbed down the ladder like the responsible person I needed to be, one who didn't slip and break her neck to make a point.

I had fun, didn't I?

It didn't matter. As the star, my job was to ensure everyone else was safe and cared for, so *they'd* have fun.

With a family of time travelers gunning for us, fun was not a priority.

FIFTEEN

JAMISON

Trys adjusted her black fringed gown one final time in the mirror. "Ready?"

"How do you manage to stuff so many dresses into a single suitcase?" I was wearing my only suit, the same one I'd worn my first night in Charmant. Roger had snuck our shirts into the Revelles' laundry, so they were white and starched. But Trys seemed to have a dozen black gowns.

Using her pinkie, she scraped at the edges of her red lipstick. "I get them from other girls."

Roger arched a brow. "You borrow? From my cousins?"

"I don't borrow; I *trade*." Trys kept her gaze trained on her reflection as she fixed her dark bob. "At the end of the night, when another girl compliments my gown, I offer to trade. We go into the bathroom and—voilà. New dresses for us both."

"So complete strangers just—take their clothes off for you?"

"Don't be jealous. We've been in Charmant so long, it's either that or repeat outfits. Speaking of which, are we ever going to leave?"

Ah, our eventual departure. We'd avoided talking about it for two weeks. Given Roger's broken ribs, it'd made sense to stay put, but now that he was back on his feet, we had no excuse.

"You want to leave, Trys?" Roger asked.

"I'm not quite done with this place," she said evenly. "I like being around Dewey."

"Dewey?" He wiggled his brows. "Or my sister?"

Trys ran a comb through her hair, pointedly ignoring his question. "How about you? Ready to leave your family already?"

"Being back hasn't been terrible," he said carefully. "I've successfully avoided Wolffe."

"And Margaret," I pointed out.

He flicked a piece of hay at me. "I could be convinced to stay a little longer. I forgot how fun it is to be a local celebrity. And it's been nice not dealing with the bigots."

His smile didn't falter, but Trys and I exchanged a glance. Even though we were careful about our destinations, the three of us had gotten plenty of strange looks as we traveled together. Roger, with his golden-brown skin, had borne the brunt of it. "We'll stay in Charmant as long as you'd like," I said.

Roger sighed. "The longer we stay, the harder it is to leave."

"How about we stay until the election?" Trys suggested. "That way, we're here to support Dewey, but if we leave the day after, we'll get to Michigan in time for the apple harvest."

For the past two summers, the seasonal work at the orchards had been one of our best-paying jobs. Last year, we'd made enough to fund months of traveling.

Roger shrugged. "Works for me. How about you, Jame-o?"

That gave me and Luxe two weeks to find out everything

we could about my parents. "We leave after the election," I agreed.

Trys checked her diamond-encrusted watch. "The Big Tent's waiting. C'mon, boys."

After sleeping in the barn for more than two weeks, the thunderous Revelle drums had become my nightly lullaby, and Wolffe's taunting voice infiltrated my dreams. Still, nothing could prepare me for the thrill of entering the Big Tent on a Saturday night.

The curtains parted, releasing silvery wisps that curled like fingers around our waists, luring us deeper into the darkness. Colorful lights cut through the black, their flashes capturing the gorgeous faces that surrounded me before they disappeared again. Under the haze of cigar smoke and flashing lights, I couldn't recognize a single Revelle in costume—though I could tell that Luxe wasn't among them. Wolffe liked to keep the crowd starving for glimpses of the Radiant Ruby.

Magic wove its way into every sip. Each moment felt wonderfully exaggerated. I could hardly keep my wits about me as Roger waltzed us around the pit, laughing with his family. *He* could recognize them, at least. And his family treated us like royalty. More than once, I found myself caressed by amused dancers, Trys and Roger egging them on as I grew more flustered. When we finally made our way to Dewey's seats, my cheeks already ached from laughing.

On the stage below, the flamethrowers caught torches while marching to a feverish drumbeat. With each fire hurtling toward them, I gasped, but their sultry smiles never faltered.

"Enjoying yourself, Jamison?" Dewey signaled for Trevor to

bring us another round. Before I could refuse, the Edwardian slipped behind the row of personal guards Dewey had brought with him.

I nodded toward the pit. "They're hardly paying attention down there."

He chuckled. "They're here for a different sort of entertainment."

The flamethrowers caught their torches in unison and the crowd erupted in applause. "Is the show at the winter theater going to be this risqué every night?" I asked. "With a few tweaks, there could be a family-friendly version."

"My great-grandfather tried that." Roger hopped onto the railing. "He was murdered."

Dewey winced. "That does seem like the sort of thing my family would have arranged. If I'm elected——"

"*When* you're elected," Trys interrupted.

"When I'm elected, I'll put a Revelle in charge of the police. Want the job, Roger?"

"Handouts for your unqualified friends?" Roger tipped his hat to Dewey. "You're going to make an excellent politician."

"What are friends for, if not to spoil you with their riches?"

"If that's the case, then I'm a crap friend." I lifted my empty glass to the three of them.

As Roger and Dewey laughed, Trys positively beamed. For the last two weeks, she'd been trying to bring us all together.

Trevor returned with our drinks as the flamethrowers took their bow. Hopping off the railing, Roger slung an arm over his shoulder. "Would you like to have one with us?"

Trevor winced. "No, thank you."

"You really mean that." Roger pretended to look wounded.

"Why can't Edwardians ignore questions?" I asked, careful not to direct my question at Trevor. It didn't seem fair that he couldn't choose not to answer.

"Why does Revelle magic only work with precious gemstones and not common rocks?" Dewey countered. "Why do Effigens have horns?"

"That, I've always wondered." Roger leaned against the railing and swirled his drink. "Nana says it's because their ancestors were European farmers who needed to look fierce so they could keep peasants from burning down their magical crops."

"What did the friars teach you again, Jame-o?" Trys nudged Dewey. "You'll love this."

"They said Effigens were descendants of the devil himself. They said that about all of you, actually."

"Amen to that." Trys lifted her glass to her lips.

Roger smacked her arm, nearly knocking her drink to the ground. "That's not a proper toast! In all this time, have you learned nothing from me?"

Trys groaned. "To Roger, for finally shaving that pathetic attempt at a beard."

"No snarky toasts, Trysta dear. You know the rules."

"Fine. To family." Trys paused to look at each of us. "Blood and otherwise."

I clinked my glass to hers. "To family." And to finding mine.

Bourbon again. I'd consumed more bourbon in the last two weeks than I had before Prohibition.

The band switched to a fast-paced crowd favorite. In the pit, Revelles paired off with tourists, leading them in a furious dance of sorts, like a less ruthless Swap Trot.

188

Dewey set his glass down on the cocktail table. "I'm serious, though. If any of you decide to stay, you have a position in my new government. Even you, Jamison."

Even magic-less, mainlander me. Except I wasn't exactly a mainlander. Trys and Roger knew about the orphanage, but I doubted Trys had told her brother. He had far more important things to worry about than my lineage.

Trys pushed her bangs out of her eyes. "Any update on your investigation?"

His face darkened. "If Trevor's magic is to be believed, no one had a damn thing to do with my attack. At least not yet. But tonight's about letting loose, not worrying about our family. I even booked Wolffe's nicest Fun House room after the show, for Luxe and me."

For a long second, his words were just syllables. Pseudowords.

Roger looked impressed. "Finally, a Chronos who's willing to try Revelle magic. I've been trying to get Trys to give it a shot all summer."

"You're going to give her a jewel, Dewey?" Trys asked.

Dewey shrugged, the diamond-shaped clock on his jacket rising and falling. "I'm thinking about it. It's probably a good idea to get the customer's experience."

The customer's experience. Of Luxe. In the Fun House, wielding that smoldering smile like a shield.

I took a long swig of bourbon, relishing its bite.

"See, Trys? You should have Colette give you the 'customer's experience.'"

"Will you shut up already?"

As they bickered, Dewey leaned closer to me. "As if I need to pay Luxe. We both know she owes me."

Stunned, I stared at him, which only made him laugh harder. "You should have seen your face!" He patted me on the back as he tried—and failed—to stop laughing.

There weren't many guys like Dewey at St. Douglas's. For better or for worse, the friars beat any bravado out of us. But I'd met plenty of his type after the orphanage. Guys with big pockets and even bigger egos. Trys loved him all the same, and Roger didn't seem to mind his constant bragging, but I was getting sick of the bootlegger and his "generosity."

A dozen barbed retorts flew to my mouth—as if I had any right to defend Luxe. She was perfectly capable of refusing him.

Wasn't she?

Dewey's liquor filled the glass of every patron here. That's what she'd been after that first night, when she'd pressed against me, asking me for what her family needed most.

And he'd given it to her. *All the liquor in the world.*

"Revelles don't actually touch their customers," I said carefully.

"I'm not exactly a customer, am I?" He picked up his crystal lowball glass and took a sip. "Luxe and I might have started courting as a way to drum up publicity, but the chemistry between us is real. To be perfectly frank, I think I'm falling in love with her."

I nearly choked on the bourbon.

Such monumental words, yet he spoke them as if he were ordering a meal. He studied my reaction, his eyes not leaving my face, even as he took another sip.

I glanced back at Trys and Roger, who were laughing with Trevor by the executive suite curtains. "Do you think she feels the same?"

"I'm sure of it."

I was going to rip that self-aggrandizing smirk right off his face. "But with the liquor and the winter theater—"

"Luxe and I understand each other." Dewey smoothed the diamond-shaped clock on his lapel. "I can provide for her. I can keep her family safe and their coffers overflowing with jewels. With me, Luxe will become a truly respectable woman in Charmant."

My jaws gnashed together. Her family meant more to her than anything. With their success in Dewey's hands, there was no way to know how she truly felt about him.

Better that she did love him. Because if she didn't, she'd fake it for the rest of her life. And with that pristine smile of hers, no one would know, especially not Dewey.

"I appreciate your candor, Jamison." He sipped his drink, then patted his mouth with a folded handkerchief. "You know, until I made a name for myself bootlegging, girls practically knocked me over as they pushed me aside to chase after the jerks. Hell, my own parents want nothing to do with me, but they worshipped my brother, George, because he was as healthy as an ox. You see, I had fainting spells, which my father saw as a sign of weakness. But Luxe makes me feel like a million bucks." He exhaled slowly, the sharp bite of gin lingering in the air. "She takes care of so many people, but I want to be the one who takes care of her."

He really did care for her. And he needed to believe her feelings were real, not just part of the strange arrangement they'd made. Maybe I was wrong, and they were deeply in love. Maybe my judgment was clouded by my magical hangover, by that lingering pull to be near her.

But her smiles were as cryptic as ancient texts, and I was becoming a scholar. She was pretending with him, at least in part. I could feel it in my bones. He was going to test the limits of how far she was willing to take her act.

And there was nothing I could do about it.

The lights winked out. In the cloak of blackness, the crowd roared to life, my ears ringing as they reached a fever pitch.

Trys draped her arms around both of us. "C'mon, boys. Get on your feet."

I tried to shake away the lingering sense of wrongness as Wolffe sauntered onto the stage. My second time at Luxe's show. Once again in the executive box. In the exact same company.

In Charmant, history loved to repeat itself.

"Ladies and gentleman, monsters and misfits!" Wolffe bellowed. "We have a Revelle birthday tonight."

A sizable chunk of the crowd cheered.

"She's one in a *milli*-on," he drawled. The crowd stomped their feet.

"You'll only see a beauty like hers once a *mill*ennium."

Terrible puns, even for Wolffe, but I could almost picture Millie beaming in the rafters.

"Call to her, you monsters of the night! She's *milli*ng around backstage, waiting for you."

"Mill-ie! Mill-ie!"

"Please wish a very happy birthday to the luscious, the irresistible, the one and only Miss Mildred Revelle!"

Millie swung over the crowd, her buxom figure dangling over the pit. We were on our feet, calling her name with the rest of them. The Revelle band somehow made "Happy Birthday" sound like a striptease. Millie swung from one side to the next, twisting upside down as she shimmied at her adoring fans. My ears rang as men and women alike screamed for her. There was going to be stiff competition for Millie in the Fun House tonight.

The thunderous applause rattled on until Wolffe silenced the crowd with a swing of his arm. "And you know who is with Millie tonight," Wolffe drawled into the mic. "Coquettish Colette, and . . . Her Radiance Herself."

The crowd's response shook the ground beneath us, and my heart thundered along with it. Fools, all of us.

"It's showtime!"

The band sprang into action, fighting to be heard over the Luxe-addicted audience.

By now I knew where to look.

She swooped from the sky, a single spotlight tracking her arc over the audience. Her costume was the most elaborate, of course: a snakeskin leotard of midnight black, hugging her lean muscles. And those lips, a tantalizing crimson, relaxed into a smile that drove the crowd wild. She was so beautiful it hurt to see her, knowing I'd never touch her again. But Dewey would.

Damnit. My magical hangover was particularly potent tonight.

She let go of the swing and I white-knuckled the railing—

She made it safely to Colette's waiting arms, and air filled my lungs once more.

My God, this was more dangerous than I remembered. The urge to scream each time any of them let go of their bars . . .

"You okay, Jame-o?" Roger shouted in my ear.

I pressed my palm over my erratically beating heart. "Why isn't there a safety net?"

"People spend more money when we perform without one. Here." He pushed a drink into my hand. "Never watch sober."

The crowd was ravenous as Luxe flipped through the air, landing on the stage. After spending time with her outside the Big Tent, I'd forgotten she could move like that.

Millie landed by Luxe's side, and Luxe began to sing, accompanying the band as Colette twisted and twirled in a solo of sorts, contorting herself with mind-boggling grace.

There was something different about Luxe tonight. Her back was still straight with the star's perfect posture, but her shoulders were less stiff. As she sang a particularly naughty lyric, she peeked at Millie, whose suggestive smile grew as if they'd just exchanged a joke.

Luxe was having *fun*.

I leaned forward. The possibility, however slight, that our conversation had somehow inspired her to try to enjoy herself tonight—it was intoxicating.

From the seat beside me, Dewey threw his hands in front of him, as if trying to steady himself. "I have to go." He burst from his seat and disappeared through the curtains, a shocked Trevor trailing in his wake.

"Is he all right?" I shouted over the music. With any luck, he'd drunk too much and was vomiting on the curb, and Luxe would be all by herself in the Fun House.

Who was I kidding? He was handsome, rich, and possibly the future mayor. Luxe knew what she was doing. She probably *wanted* a night with him.

Before Trys could answer, the center of the stage rumbled and shook. From beneath Luxe and her cousins' feet, a diamond-shaped platform broke free.

The crowd went wild as the three acrobats were lifted into the air. Luxe stood in the center, shoulder to shoulder with her cousins. There were still slight creases at the corners of her eyes, a nearly imperceptible strain—her magic, though she'd deny it.

The platform carried them right to Dewey's seats, stopping so close, I could see the sweat glistening on their foreheads. Millie grinned at me, her cheeks shiny in the flashing silver lights. Colette winked at Trys, who tilted her head back and laughed uproariously.

And there was Luxe, a mere arm's length away. She swung her legs over the ledge as if she were relaxing poolside, not floating above a sea of colorful, overeager top hats. Her siren's song was the only thing I heard, each sweet note landing in my chest.

As those whiskey eyes met mine, the Big Tent faded away, until it was just the two of us again. Her smile softened, and if I didn't know better, I could have sworn she felt it, too.

The crowd roared, snapping me out of my reverie.

Millie and Colette had leaped from the platform and grabbed Roger, to his utter delight. Luxe steadied his hands as Millie and Colette dragged him onto the floating stage. Roger tipped his hat and bowed to the pit, and the audience went wild. They remembered him, all right.

The band broke into a dazzling, dizzying tune and the cousins linked their arms, Roger included. Their feet kicked and twisted in a dance that was half kick line, half tap. It wasn't particularly sexy, but their audience ate it up. Was this spontaneous, or had Wolffe approved?

With her arms entwined with her cousins', Luxe glanced down at their feet and laughed—truly laughed. Colette said something in her ear, and Luxe's face stretched into a pure, open-mouthed grin.

It was a genuine Luxe Revelle smile. No kaleidoscope. No mask. I couldn't breathe.

Spotting me staring at her, her eyes sparked. She stuck out her tongue, as if saying, *See? A smile you've never seen.*

A bark of laughter escaped me, and she held my gaze a heartbeat longer.

And another.

This was worse than the first time. I wasn't leaping over the railing to touch her, but my insides were as warm and mushy as ice cream on a hot summer day.

The song ended in a flurry, and Roger did a forward flip onto the railing of our box seats. Balancing there, to the thrill of the crowd, he bowed again, tossing his hat to his admirers below. The diamond stage carried the acrobats back to the trapeze swings, where their performance continued.

Still I stood there, my melted ice cream of a rib cage rendering me useless. Motionless.

I'd do a hundred idiotic things if it meant seeing her smile like that again.

Magical hangover be damned. I was never going to get over her. But it didn't matter how I felt about her; Luxe was with Dewey. No matter how many times she stole my heart, once the curtain closed, the ending would always be the same.

She'd always choose him.

Sixteen

Luxe

With a squeal, Millie wrapped her arms around Colette and me. Laughing, we struggled to stay upright as the applause shook the stage.

We'd absolutely crushed it.

Every leap was perfectly executed, every twist both graceful and tantalizingly dangerous. Our Revelle blood had thrummed with the music, the magic crackling in the air. During that last song, I'd grabbed more, more, more lightstrings, not stopping until I glimpsed the bottom of my inkwell. Only then did I rein in my power.

The crowd had pelted the stage with gems as they whistled and cheered. Each piece was an offering to the Revelle coffers, security against whatever the Chroneses were planning next.

Nana greeted us with towels and water. "You were amazing, my darlings!"

Colette chugged her water and wiped her mouth with the back of her hand. "I still think that third sequence needs three rotations, not two. You almost had it this time."

From Colette, that was a compliment. She was constantly try-ing to squeeze more advanced routines out of me and Millie, but neither of us could keep up with her. "Maybe next time."

The corners of Colette's mouth twitched. "Other than that, we were the cat's meow."

Millie had been begging to pull Roger up onstage for weeks. She'd even gotten Colette on board, but I always stuck to the rou-tine. Tonight, I'd been spontaneous. *Fun*, some might say.

Jamison knew, and he hadn't looked smug. He'd just grinned and grinned.

"Go change, ladies. The reception is in five minutes." Nana shooed us toward the dressing rooms.

With a grimace, Colette tightened her bun. "Sometimes I hate this part."

Millie looped her arm around Colette's. "I'll give you first choice tonight, if you like."

"What makes you think you'll get your choice?"

"I always do. Besides, it's my birthday. Cake in the dressing room to celebrate? Luxe?"

I dabbed at my face with a damp towel. "Sounds great."

"Really?"

They hadn't invited me in a while, and I hadn't accepted in even longer. "Of course."

Millie's excited squeal could have broken my heart.

Uncle Wolffe barreled down the narrow hallway. "Luxe, get changed and head to the Fun House. Colette, help her. You know which outfit."

"The Fun House?" I stole a glance at my cousins. "Why?"

"Dewey reserved the Diamond Room." Uncle Wolffe dabbed

at the white powder on his brow. "Looks like he's ready to try Revelle magic for himself."

The backstage racket hummed to a stop.

Dewey was going to give me a jewel. The could-be future mayor of Charmant trusted *me* to enchant him. "How many carats?"

My uncle grinned. "Remember to pace yourself. Make a show of using the whole thing in one sitting, but pocket the rest. We need to hold on to that influence as long as we can."

He knew I didn't need the jewel to charm Dewey, but it helped. Besides, Colette and Millie were listening. "Got it."

"The reception's starting in a few. Better get going. And Luxe?" Uncle Wolffe squeezed my shoulder. "Nice work."

I'd done it. I'd earned the trust—and influence—we needed over Charmant's bootlegger.

"Sorry, Mills," I said as he disappeared around the bend.

She shrugged. "Charm Dewey into gifting me a case of his best bubbly, and we're even."

"At least you don't have to pretend to like him anymore," Colette added.

"I *do* like him."

Colette studied me but said nothing.

Didn't I? He was kind and generous, and he'd been nothing but a gentleman. Regardless, it was going to be a relief not having to dip into my little inkwell to keep him happy all the time. "I won't mind letting the jewel do the work," I admitted.

"So you are human, after all." She took my arm. "Let's get you ready."

The dress was imported from New York: violet beads with a

crisscrossing black inlay that hugged me tighter than a glove, dipping low over my chest in a sweetheart neckline. Millie squeezed me into a lilac brassiere that gave me the illusion of cleavage, though it made it hard to breathe. Black fishnet stockings—popular in the Big Tent long before the flappers copied us—and an amethyst necklace finished the look. Colette applied dark eyeshadow to give me glittering smoky eyes and scarlet lipstick that made my lips startlingly full.

She stepped back to admire her work. "You may not be able to walk in that dress, but it sure does the trick."

I took a few steps, but the fabric rode up my thighs. "I'll just sit the whole time."

From her perch on the bed, Millie opened her mouth then closed it again. Our eyes met in the mirror. "What is it?"

"You look like Aunt Catherine," she said softly.

My mother. I glanced in the mirror, and for the briefest of moments, my wide-eyed, curly-haired mother stared back at me. The dress squeezed the air from my lungs until I turned away.

Millie scraped her teeth over her bottom lip. "If Dewey's fantasy is particularly dark . . . don't be afraid to use the whole jewel and not turn a profit."

"It's okay to just get it over with." Colette smiled guiltily. "We've all done it. Even me."

If the gem was large enough, I could use it for weeks, maybe even months, to give me a break from the constant headaches and nosebleeds.

My cousins walked me to the Diamond Room. Trevor Edwardes waited outside, fidgeting in his three-piece suit. His eyes widened as we approached. "Miss Revelle, you look . . . Wow."

"Why, thank you, Trevor." I pulled the dress down my thighs a bit.

He blushed. "I, ah, meant Millie."

Colette snorted. I elbowed her in the ribs while Millie stepped closer to the Edwardian, batting her lashes. "Care to join me in the Fun House?"

He looked stricken. "There is absolutely nothing I'd like to do more right now, but Mr. Chronos needs me to guard the door."

"At least I know you mean it." With a little wave, Millie took Colette's elbow and pulled her down the hall.

As their voices faded, I smoothed my dress. "He's ready for me?"

"Yes. He's waiting inside."

Chin up. Shoulders back, just as my mother always said. She'd prepared me for the Fun House from that very first magic lesson.

As I reached for the door, Trevor touched my arm. "Use your inkwell."

He knew of my inkwell. Just how many of my thoughts had he read?

"Too many. You really need to practice those techniques I showed you." Remorse flashed over his face as he pushed open the door.

A man rose from the bed, his movements sharp, uncomfortable. Not Dewey.

I flashed him my stage smile. "Oopsie! Wrong room."

The doorknob wouldn't move. Trevor had locked me inside. With a stranger.

"Wait." The man removed his hat, twisting it nervously between his hands. When he lifted his eyes to mine, I gasped.

A Chronos. Dark hair, an even darker suit jacket folded on the bed. Midthirties. The spitting image of George, except he wasn't glaring at me.

"I think there's been a mistake." Risking my back to him, I banged on the door as loudly as I dared, but Trevor didn't open it.

I was going to murder him.

"Luxe?" The man stepped closer, his fingers squeezing the rim of his hat hard enough to break it. There was a jewel in his pocket—a big one. My Revelle blood warmed at its proximity, even as warning bells sounded in my head.

I kept my voice calm, my back to him as I replied, "Dewey's waiting for me."

"You don't recognize me."

That voice. I had heard a version of it every day for weeks, though never dripping with such bitterness.

I turned around slowly, my pulse thudding through my ears. "Dewey?"

His hands curled into fists, and tears filled his eyes—yes, his eyes were the same. Everything else about him was familiar, too, only warped, like a painting left out to soak in the rain.

He'd aged *years*. More than a decade, if not two.

I tried to keep my wits about me, but I couldn't stop staring at his strange face, both familiar and foreign and just *wrong*. "You—traveled?"

"You can't even stand to look at me," he spat.

Use your inkwell, Trevor had said. He knew I'd be shocked, and that my shock would rattle Dewey. He could have at least warned me.

I tapped into my secondary power, the usual stabbing pain

greeting me with renewed fervor, like metal scraping against metal inside my skull. Turning away from Dewey, I bit the insides of my cheeks, swallowing my dread, swallowing the bitter taste of iron, swallowing the excruciating pain until his lightstring flickered into sight.

His emotions swirled over his head in a torrent of anger and regret. There had to be a reason he'd traveled back so far. All I had to do was get him comfortable and he'd explain.

My God. He'd lost his twenties. Part of his thirties, too.

I took those strange hands and forced myself to look into his familiar eyes. "You caught me off guard," I cooed. A little bit of lust warmed his lightstring, though it was quickly eclipsed by frustration. I dug in deeper. Thanks to the show, my inkwell was fairly low, but I couldn't afford to be stingy with it. *You trust me. You wish to share this burden with me.*

He nodded tersely to himself. "It's a bit of a shock, of course. When I saw myself in the mirror . . ." Disgust exploded in his lightstring.

You are still attractive to me. You're happy with me.

"You don't look that different! Truly. I just wasn't expecting you to be, ah, matured." I led him toward the bed. Damn this room and its lack of chairs. "How far back did you travel?"

"Far enough to look older than my goddamn brother, even though he's abused his magic our whole lives." He kicked at a nearby table, sending the pitcher of water atop it crashing to the floor.

With a yelp, I backed away, losing my grasp on his lightstring.

His gaze flitted to me. There was no warmth in his eyes. No surprise, either, only disappointment, as if my being frightened was letting him down. I picked up his lightstring and infused so much trust and calm into it, my vision blackened at the edges. This was still the same Dewey. "Talk to me. Tell me what happened."

His will relented in my grasp before his face relaxed. "The last time you saw me was at breakfast this morning, yes?"

"I saw you in the executive suite, too. Right before my act." He'd looked just like his usual self as he was talking to Jamison about God knows what.

"I remember." He nodded to himself, his eyes distant. "For you, an hour has passed, but for me, tonight was weeks ago. I've already lived through this entire summer. For me, tonight was the inauguration. We were *just* there together before I had to travel backward."

The election was nine days away, and the inauguration was more than a month after that, in mid-September. The math failed me. I couldn't even think straight.

He watched me intently. "A lot has happened in the last seven weeks. We've grown close. But you're looking at me like I'm a stranger."

Seven weeks, he'd traveled. Which meant he'd shaved *seven hundred weeks* off his life, which, in years, was . . . ten years? Fifteen?

Focus. He'd lived seven weeks with me that I couldn't remember, and now he was back here. The same Dewey, but with all these experiences only *he* could recall.

His lightstring was sad, but it brightened a smidge when I pressed my hands into his. *I can handle the truth. I am with you.* "So we won the election."

His smile was the same, at least, though faint cracks framed his mouth like curtains. "I won indeed."

"Then why did you travel?" I asked, careful to keep my tone light.

A storm of black darkened his emotions, swift and thick. "George," he snarled. "He tried to kill me. My own brother shot me before the inauguration ceremony."

He fell to his knees with a desperate sound. I pressed into his lightstring so hard, I had to bite my tongue to keep from yelling out. Inkwell be damned, I *had* to know.

"You won," I whispered. "Which means you can win again. And you're safe now."

"He went after us both. I found you . . ." His voice broke, his anger flailing against my infusion of calm. "I found you on the ground backstage, covered in blood. He killed you because he knew you were the key to our success. And then he aimed the gun at me because he knew I'd travel to save you. But I traveled too damn far!"

Emotions exploded like fireworks through his lightstring. Horror. Rage. Despair. Still I held on, repeating the same calming words: *You're safe with me. You wish to tell me everything.*

"The only reason I'm alive is because of my magic. I should have just traveled back a few minutes, but I had a split second to react and—I panicked. The next thing I knew, I was in the executive suite, reliving the same blasted show I'd already seen. Only now I look like *this*." The reds of his lightstring faded to blue as his remorse took center stage.

First his uncle, now his brother. No wonder he was beside himself. The Chronoses were desperate to stop him from winning. To stop *us* from winning. And even though they'd failed, his escape had cost him over a decade.

"You survived. That's what you needed to do, and you did it."
I rubbed his hand with my thumb. He was still an attractive man,
just in his thirties instead of twenty-one. I'd get used to it. "There's
no preparing yourself for that sort of betrayal. Besides, you *won*."

For now. They would come after him again.

But would Dewey risk traveling again? After losing all this
time, would he still be willing to use his magic to stop them from
coming after me? Or my family?

Beneath the mess of his regret, genuine feelings for me lingered. I grabbed hold before they were eclipsed by his anger, my
magic multiplying them.

He took my other hand, pulling me closer. "In all the timelines
I've seen, that was the first time I've won. It was damn near perfect. *We* were perfect."

Timelines, as in multiple? He said he'd traveled once, not over
and over. "How many timelines have you seen?" I asked warily.

"It's no accident I traveled back to this moment, you know. I
mean, I didn't *plan* to travel this far, but . . . maybe some part of
me wanted to experience tonight again."

Revelle magic made an impression, apparently. I leaned closer.
"Was it a good night?"

His hand cupped my face. "It will be. But first there's something I need to ask you."

His lightstring, though excited, was tinged yellow. Nervous.

Dewey dropped to the floor. He dropped to the floor and *got
down on one knee.*

Oh God. Oh God, oh God, oh God . . .

"You are my most valuable asset, Luxe. From now on, *you* are
my family. The Revelles will never want for anything. All you
need to do is marry me." He reached into his pocket.

My heart beat a terrified rhythm against my ribs as he opened a black velvet box, revealing a thick platinum band. Twists of metal rose like jaws to hold an enormous jewel. One that wasn't there. No, whatever fat diamond had sat in that setting was still in his pocket. He'd clawed it out.

Dewey didn't trust me. Not enough to give me a jewel.

"You control the hearts of Charmant, and I control time itself. Together, we're unstoppable. We're a perfect match: the Night District's most dazzling jewel and the future mayor. Charmant's new beginning starts right here, right now. All you need to do is say yes, and our hearts will be joined forever."

I gripped his lightstring tighter to buy myself a minute. I couldn't marry Dewey. I didn't want to marry *anyone*. This was never part of the plan. He was supposed to become the mayor, not my husband. My family would be safe, I would be free, and we'd all be rich.

"We can be wed right away. I'll have Trevor fetch a priest."

"I—I'm only eighteen."

His lightstring warmed with affection. "And I'm only twenty-one."

Twenty-one, going on forty.

"Half the girls in New York are married by your age," he continued.

"But not on Charmant."

His face betrayed nothing, but darkness gathered in his lightstring. Anger. "I know this started as a business arrangement, but you care for me, Luxe. I can feel it when we're together."

My magic had been too convincing. "You've had seven weeks to date me. I'm still catching up."

He leaned closer. "I've been nothing but a perfect gentleman, have I not?"

"You have——"

"I brought you your favorite flowers. I let a Strattori sprain my ankle to spare your cousin. I made nice with your bitchy grandmother even though she spits at me like a feral animal every time I walk by. I even used my magic to save your life when you fell on opening night." He stared at me, genuinely confused. "But still you refuse me?"

I gaped at the man in front of me. These things were chores to him, tasks to accomplish on his path to some goal. Had he been pretending to be kind the whole time? Was *that* the carefulness that was always present in his lightstring?

"Even now, I just sacrificed an entire decade off my life to save yours—and that's not enough to impress the Radiant Ruby." He folded his arms tightly, his cold gaze pinning me in place. "You truly are heartless. The ice princess, indeed."

Gone was the eager-to-please politician, and worse, the emotions in his lightstring were more genuine than ever. No filters of caution, only raw, honest feelings. I tried to calm him down, but his emotions swirled so quickly, it was hard to know which to grab. "I didn't say no; I just need a moment to *think*."

His dark eyes narrowed. "There's someone else, isn't there?"

"What? No!" My magic scraped against the insides of my skull as I searched for the right combination to calm him. Trust. Contentment. Lust. Anything to get him to stop trying to marry me long enough that I could find a way out of this mess.

His face relaxed as my magic took root. Pulling me closer, he rested his hands around my waist. "Marry me, and the winter theater is yours. I'll give it to you as a wedding present."

Even if I married him, it wouldn't matter if he put the deed in my name; it'd still be considered his property. Like me.

Luxe *Chronos*.

"Think of how unstoppable we'll be. You'll sway public opinion in our favor, and I'll control time so everything goes our way. We'll start a new dynasty. Our children will charm history on a whim."

Children. With him.

"Was this your intention since the beginning?" I managed to ask.

"Of course, my sweet." He traced a slow circle on my lower back, sending a chill down my spine. "If all I wanted was to have you, I would have had you already."

I recoiled inside, but I buried my disgust. Every instinct urged me to get out of this room, but I couldn't leave. Not until I understood who he truly was.

You trust me, I whispered. *You don't need to hold back. Say what you truly think.*

He chuckled softly. "You know the best part of being a Chronos? Even if you say no, I can just rewind the clock and ask again. I have all the time in the world."

Seven hells, I was trapped. One wrong move, and he'd turn back time, redoing this conversation until it went exactly how he wanted. Adrenaline shot through my veins, every instinct preparing me to run. But there was no escaping a time traveler. Only charming him.

Leaning forward, I buried my disgust and pressed a kiss to each of his cheeks—the cheeks of a grown man now. "When you put a big fat diamond in that setting, I'll marry you."

He laughed, his lightstring swirling with desire. "You're perfect, you know. The crown jewel of my investments. And you're mine."

An investment. A possession.

He lifted my chin. "Are you ready to make my dreams come true?"

"Are you ready to give me a jewel?"

"You truly expect me to pay for you?"

"This is the Fun House." I kept my tone light, not betraying the cold trickle down my spine. That diamond was still in his pocket. "Don't you want to experience Revelle magic?"

"But I'm the boss, aren't I?"

My heart hammered in my chest. "You own the winter theater. Not the Big Tent."

Not *me*.

He twisted the strap of my gown hard enough to snap it. I yelped, which only made his smile grow. "You're a smart girl. You'll marry me."

"Will I, now?" I stepped backward, my knees hitting the back of the bed. The door was six paces away, but I couldn't run, couldn't risk him traveling for a do-over. Fear coiled in my belly, and it took everything I had to keep my head high, my focus on his lightstring. I had to keep him calm, but I also had to know what the hell was going through his mind.

You trust me. You wish to be honest with me.

"You will. Because as my wife, your family will have true power in Charmant once again. I can appoint them to whatever position pleases you. The rest of the Chronoses will leave you alone because I can undo anything they do. Going after the Revelles would be a waste of their magic. So you'll marry me. I may have to waste even more time redoing this conversation so you don't absolutely despise me, but in the end, you will be mine."

I gaped at him, at the cruel smile and laughing eyes, and for the first time, I saw him, truly saw him.

Worst of all, he was right. If I married him, the Revelles would prosper. And if I didn't . . . what would he do?

He controlled the liquor, the winter theater, and, with the targets on our backs for publicly supporting him, he controlled our safety, too. He had us completely and utterly in his grasp.

He chuckled. "Well, my sweet, as fun as this has been, I have worked far too hard for you to look at me like *that*."

No. Before he could travel, I poured an enormous whopping of arousal over him. He cried out, falling back onto the bed. I kept exaggerating his desire, talons clawing against my dwindling magic as I leaned over him. "You said tonight was going to be memorable."

You're having the time of your life.

He rose abruptly, hands gripping my wrist. "You know what I want? I want you to beg for me, on your knees."

"What?"

His smile morphed into a dark, cruel thing. "Tell me you want me. Tell me you're nothing without me."

Of course. A humiliation fantasy. "You need a jewel for that." And then I'd conjure him to believe I was doing as he asked while I remained firmly on my feet.

"Do I?" He arched a dark brow. Testing me.

He was trying to break me, to push me far enough to prove just how much I needed him. "I'm the star," I reminded him. "Better make it a big one."

He ran a long finger down my jaw, the slope of my neck. "You think you'd be the star without me? Think the Big Tent would still be standing without me? Without my liquor?"

My eyes snapped to his, and his smile grew. He knew he had me. Knew we needed him.

No part of me wanted to kneel in front of a Chronos, but I lowered myself to the floor.

"I want you," I said, my voice mechanical, my head high.

"You're nothing without me. Say it." I hardly recognized his rough voice.

"Absolutely not," I hissed.

But my refusal only excited him. He circled me like a tiger stalking its prey. "Say you need me, or I'll have Colette fall in a much larger hole next time."

I gaped at him, at the predatory glean in his eyes. "That was you?"

"Of course it was me. Nothing happens unless I want it to."

My God. He'd hurt my family so he could play savior. And now he wanted to humiliate me because *it turned him on.*

"Now say it."

Angry tears sprang into my eyes, but there was no way I was letting them fall. "I'm nothing without you."

My voice was broken. Desperate. Not at all the Radiant Ruby I'd been earlier tonight.

Who was I kidding? For weeks, I'd been desperate enough to overlook the rumors circling him. Like the other bootleggers who'd disappeared, or the way he jacked up prices for the hoteliers, making them completely dependent on him. The winter theater, the acts of kindness, the careful watching of his every word—it was all a pretty trap, and I'd waltzed right into it.

Worse, I'd brought my family with me.

Unable to stand it another moment, I threw everything I had into my magic, crying out from the icy pain. He fell backward on the bed.

Jewel or no jewel, I'd make him think he'd had the night of his life, so he wouldn't reset the clocks, robbing me of what I'd just learned: he was a wolf masquerading as a sheep.

You're having the best night of your life. This is ecstasy.

Careful not to touch him, I doused him in desire. The space between my eyebrows throbbed in protest, wetness dripping from my nostrils as I emptied my strange magic. He closed his eyes, his hungry smile making my stomach twist. Before he could reach for me again, I threw as much exhaustion as I dared down his lightstring. *You're feeling completely satisfied—and very sleepy.*

His body slackened. Stilled.

I forced myself to check his pulse. Still there.

Wife, he'd said. *Forever.*

Slipping into the sheets beside him, I leaned as far away from him as I could.

In all the timelines I've seen, that was the first time I've won.

How many timelines *had* he seen? He could have been jumping back a few seconds here, a few minutes there, to curate my impression of him. To make me like him. Trust him. *Kiss* him.

And, in nine days, with my help, he might become the most powerful man in Charmant.

Those damn tears still threatened, but I didn't let them fall. If he woke up and saw me upset, he'd erase the whole night, and I'd forget what lurked under that pleasant mask, that perpetually cautious lightstring. From now on, I'd have to charm him every second of every day.

I was trapped. Completely and utterly trapped.

My whole life, I'd believed we held the magic, the power. We made dreams come true.

Just never our own.

SEVENTEEN

JAMISON

The air was as thick and humid as stew, and it carried the Big Tent's merriment to the barn. Everyone else on Charmant was having a grand time. Maybe even Luxe herself.

In the Diamond Room. With Dewey.

If it would help her family, Luxe would stay by Dewey's side forever. Hell, she'd lie in front of a freight train, smiling all the while as if she'd just gotten her way. So thorough was her act, no one realized how deeply she held herself responsible for the entire family's success. Not her cousins, who believed she was too busy for them. Or her aunts and uncles, whose diffuse sense of responsibility for their orphan niece rarely went past jolly teasing. Maybe her mother would have protected her, but she was gone.

Or maybe that was wishful thinking. Dewey could be the man of her dreams.

I tossed my book into the hay. It might as well have been written in Greek.

The barn had to be a hundred degrees. I could go to the beach, but then I'd have to look at the Fun House. Too close to Luxe. And Dewey.

A hasty knock. Then another.

I leaped to my feet and, with my heart in my throat, pulled open the barn doors.

Luxe stood there, a delicate smattering of blood marring her nostrils, her chin. "What happened?" I exclaimed. "Are you hurt?"

If he had touched her, if he'd laid one finger on her without her permission—

Absently wiping her face, she marched past me to rummage through the crates by the window, her beaded dress swishing with each step. "Where does Roger keep the gin?"

"Luxe?" I pressed. "Are you okay?"

She paced the floor on bare feet, her soles dirty. She'd left in a rush. "It doesn't have to be gin. Anything will do."

I grabbed a dark green bottle from the shelf and handed it to her. "It's water."

She uncorked it with her teeth and took a long drink. The skin around her mouth tightened in her telltale sign of pain, and her gaze darted around the room, refusing to meet mine.

I was going to murder the bastard.

"Here." I dusted off an upside-down bucket and pushed it toward her. "Sit."

"I barge in here uninvited, and you're so nice to me. Why are you always so nice to me?" She slid against the barn wall until she reached the floor, then curled her bare legs to her chest.

I lowered myself beside her and hugged my legs, too. Glancing at our identical positions, she cracked a smile, as heavy as lead yet as fragile as glass. But when her eyes found mine, her smile shattered. She looked away, tears spilling down her flushed cheeks.

Unable to help myself, I wrapped an arm around her and pulled her close. "Is this okay?"

A small nod against my shoulder. Her body shook as she finally let out whatever she'd been holding inside.

Dewey was a dead man.

"You can talk to me," I murmured. "Whenever you're ready."

She swiped at her wet face. "I'm sorry, I just—I didn't know where else to go."

I resisted the urge to wipe away her tears. "Colette and Millie are working?"

"You can't tell them I was here. Or anyone."

She was trembling as if the barn wasn't sweltering. "Luxe, what happened?"

"Dewey traveled," she blurted. "He rewound time from the inauguration to tonight."

I froze. No wonder he'd disappeared so abruptly during the show. "The inauguration? But that's—"

"Seven weeks away. Which means he's aged *seven hundred weeks*."

"Christ. That's over thirteen years."

"I knew you'd do the math." A frail smile graced her lips, gone in an instant.

I sat up taller. If she'd come here to talk to me, I wasn't going to let her down. "Why did he travel? Did his family attack again?"

A small nod. "His brother, George, shot me, apparently, and was about to shoot Dewey. Dewey had a split second to travel, and he went too far." Her hands shook as she took another sip of water.

Luxe lying on the floor, lifeless. I shook away the horrible image. "Did he say why George did it?"

"Because Dewey won. And I helped him." She dragged her

hands over her face. "It never ends. The Chronoses are after me now. And Dewey—"

"He won't let anything happen to you." The admission tasted bitter on my tongue. No matter how I felt about the guy, I couldn't deny his power. "Clearly, he's willing to go to great lengths to protect you."

With a groan, she buried her head in her hands. "That may be an even bigger problem."

So she wasn't as enamored with Dewey as she seemed. Gently, I turned her chin so I could see her face. "Luxe, did he hurt you?"

She exhaled slowly, her expression unreadable. "No," she finally said. "I just got the impression that he's not the man I thought he was."

No kidding. "Is there a chance Dewey lied about what happened?"

She shook her head. "I spoke to Trevor Edwardes when I left. He said the memory had been replaying in Dewey's mind. George tried to kill Dewey, and Dewey traveled back too far."

Well, that certainly complicated things. "Maybe Dewey's wrong. Did he see you, ah, die?"

"He said I was lying backstage, on the ground, covered in blood. Trevor's going to listen closely to Dewey's thoughts in case he left something out." Her brows pinched together. This close, I could press my finger on the little crinkle they formed and smooth it out. If only taking away her pain was that easy.

"Maybe something else happened. Maybe you faked your own death. To get away."

That earned me a soft chuckle. "And why would I do that?"

"Maybe you wanted to see the world. Maybe you realized you

were working far too hard, and you needed a vacation. Maybe," I continued, emboldened by the twitch of those perfect lips, "you wanted him off your back so you could run off with a handsome stranger."

Her weak smile was all the reward I needed. "I told you, I stopped wanting to leave Charmant the moment I grew up."

"And I told you, I don't believe that."

She rested her head against the barn wall. "It's possible that I'm starting to feel trapped."

"See? Now we're getting somewhere."

"Dewey mentioned marriage." She looked away, her eyes beginning to well once more.

My newfound hope came crashing down. "Marriage?"

She nodded.

"Do you *want* to marry him?"

She didn't answer for a heartbeat. Then another. Finally, she shook her head.

Sweet, selfish relief. She needed to untangle herself from him as soon as possible—but he wasn't going to give up so easily. He'd already shaved *thirteen years* off his life. The more chips a guy like Dewey had on the table, the less likely he was to fold.

"Christ," I muttered, slouching against the wall. "This is bad."

"And now you see my predicament." She lifted her hands as if weighing her options. "Stay my current course and help a bad man become mayor, then marry him even though my time-traveling in-laws are already trying to kill me. Or . . ." Her right hand remained in the air. "Well, there is no other option, is there? I'm not going to quit on my family, so my only choice is to stay alive and miserable."

"You deserve to be happy. Like you were during the show."

Her face lit up for the briefest of seconds. "I knew you'd see that. But while I let my focus slip, Dewey became some future Dewey, and I didn't even notice I'd dropped his lightstring in the process."

"Lightstring?"

Alarm flashed in her golden eyes, though she flicked her wrist dismissively. "It's a magic thing. You wouldn't understand."

I ignored the way that stung. "Do you charm him all the time?"

"He's never given me a jewel." She kicked at the hay, her gaze cast downward.

"*I* didn't give you a jewel, either."

My words lingered between us. There was no denying the truth—that first night, she'd somehow charmed me into almost leaping over the balcony and giving up my mother's brooch. And in the Fun House, I'd been so smitten by her, I'd hardly been able to form a sentence.

I pressed the pad of my thumb to the corners of her eyes, then the corners of her mouth. Her skin was frigid despite the relentless heat of the night. "When you're charming him, you grimace. Using magic hurts you, doesn't it?"

"Revelle magic hurts the jewels, not us." She wouldn't look at me.

"But your magic is different," I said slowly. "Your magic hurts *you.*"

"Don't—even thinking such thoughts is dangerous."

Not an admission, but also not a denial. "How?"

"If an Edwardian heard your thoughts, he'd tell a Chronos. And if the Chronoses suspected there was a way around the usual cost of magic, they'd stop at nothing to find it out."

She was afraid. And she was right: the Chronoses possessed

powerful magic, and the only thing that held that power in check was the time it shaved off their lives. Trys constantly lamented how much she wished she could travel without turning old and gray. But if there were a way for the Chroneses to change the past as often as they wanted?

For that sort of power, they'd do terrible things.

She sat up straight. "This is bad, Jamison. Really, really bad."

"I didn't mean to pry——"

"You can't tell anyone. You understand that, don't you?"

I held my hands over my heart. "I promise."

She gripped the sides of her head, loosening her pinned curls. "I'm being so selfish."

"Selfish? If I'm not mistaken, you've been in pain for your family for a long time. Have you been doing this your whole life?"

Another dismissive wave. "Only a few years. I figured it out when I was eleven."

"How?"

"My mother had just died." Her body sagged, as if uttering the words was exhausting. "My cousins and I went to Main Street to beg. None of us had ever panhandled before, and we were bad at it. We wound up sitting on a curb across from an ice-cream parlor. Children waltzed inside with their mothers and returned with chocolate all over their faces. I was so jealous. So very jealous and hungry. When I spotted a wealthy-looking man entering alone, I focused on him, willing him to buy us something. I wished it so hard, the whole world went black. And to my shock, when he emerged, he had a box of chocolates for us to share."

"That's incredible." Her will was so strong, even magic bent to it. "Did you tell them?"

She shook her head. "Only Uncle Wolffe. I wanted to tell

Colette and Millie, but the more people who know, the more dangerous it is for us all."

She was retreating into herself again, folding up like a paper doll. "So you've carried this burden alone."

"Burden?" She laughed darkly. "*I'm* the lucky star. My magic is a gift."

"It doesn't sound like one."

"Does it matter?" Her eyes dimmed as she shook her head. "Without Dewey, all my family has left is a big, sober, leaking circus tent. Magic or not, we need him."

The bastard had her convinced she was trapped. "The Revelles have survived worse."

"We have, but we're in too deep now, thanks to me."

"What about making your own liquor?" I suggested.

"Tried it. Tastes like battery acid, and we can't keep up with the demand."

"Can the Effigens help you?"

"Their magic requires *more* of everything. If we want stronger drinks, or better-tasting ones, they need to combine several drinks in one. We'd waste our supply within days."

"And he's really the only bootlegger in Charmant?" I pressed. "That seems hard to believe."

"He's the only one left. All his competition disappeared."

Her ominous words hung in the air.

She was in more trouble than I'd realized. "Where does Dewey think you are now?"

"I put him to sleep."

"You can *do* that?"

Those sparkling eyes narrowed. "You think I'm a monster."

"No! Not at all! I mean, I knew your magic was powerful, and that its effect lingered for weeks—"

"What do you mean, lingered for weeks?"

Whoops. No need to make this about me and my ridiculous crush. "That's not the point. The point is: you're a Revelle, one with an incredible gift. If you can put Dewey to sleep, surely you can figure out a way to beat him. You still have nine days to sabotage the election."

"He'll just turn back the clocks over and over until he wins. I'm pretty sure he's already done it. And if he suspects that I'm onto him, he'll do it again." She rubbed her temples and winced. Even now, she was in pain. And she was frightened, though she wouldn't admit it.

"So you'll pretend to love him." The words turned to ash on my tongue. That she'd have to spend another second with him, after he'd rattled her—it was beyond repulsive. "Why not use your magic to give yourself a little space from him? At least until we have a better plan."

"One that doesn't end up with me dead?" Her smile was sad.

"We're not going to let that happen." *He* wasn't going to let that happen. I couldn't even successfully punch a Chronos, but Dewey would keep her safe.

"As long as I hold on to his lightstring at all times, I think I can control him." She nodded to herself, a bit of her usual strength returning. "I'll make him believe he and I are desperately in love, and I'll keep him from hurting anyone—or letting his family hurt mine. That buys me time to figure out what the hell to do next."

"Buys *us* time." I gave her my sternest look. "You're not alone in this. Not anymore."

She looked at me then, shadows lining her tired eyes. "I shouldn't have dragged you into this."

"I'm glad you did. Are you going to tell Wolffe?"

"Not yet. The fewer people who know, the safer for us all. Once enough time has passed that Dewey won't be able to travel back to erase what I've learned, I'll tell my uncle."

Silence settled over us.

"So technically," I mused, "we've already lived the next seven weeks, but Dewey erased them."

"Strange, isn't it?"

"It could have been the best summer of our lives." An eerie sensation trickled through my bones, not unlike déjà vu. What, exactly, had he stolen from us?

Luxe relaxed against the barn wall. "Maybe I fixed things with my cousins. Maybe we went to the midsummer fair by the harbor, just like we used to, and we stayed up until sunrise."

"Maybe I tracked down my parents." *Maybe I found them*, I silently added. "If you knew the rest of summer didn't count, and you could do anything you wanted, what would you do?"

She crinkled her brow. "No consequences? Hard to picture."

"Try."

She fiddled with a piece of hay. "I suppose I'd take a vacation."

I couldn't help but smile. "I knew it. Every time Roger or I mention our travels, your face lights up like a Christmas tree."

"But I'd come back!" she insisted. "Maybe just see what's out there a teeny-tiny bit, then come back home."

Home. She spoke it with such certainty, such quiet fervor.

"How about you?" she asked. "Besides find your parents, what would you do with seven weeks you knew didn't count?"

"Oh, you mean besides the one thing I've wanted to do my whole life."

She snorted, and my heart squeezed. "I mean it. What else would you do?"

"I've been living the last three years as if they didn't count."

"Just rub it in, why don't you?"

"It's not as nice as it sounds. Seriously!" I flicked hay at her as she rolled her eyes. "Once, a little after I left St. Douglas's, I took a wrong turn and nearly fell off a cliff. It hit me: not a soul would have mourned me if I died. No one would've noticed or reported me missing. I would have lain at the bottom of that ravine until my bones were picked clean by vultures." I'd meant it to be an amusing tale, but my throat tightened with each word. I'd never quite gotten over it, how nothing had tethered me to this world. Until Roger, of course, and eventually Trys.

"That's terrifying." Gone was her teasing tone.

"It's fine." I looked away. "But I don't need another summer where I float through life alone. I want to grow roots. I want to have people in my life who notice if I'm missing."

"Roger and Trys would notice," she said quietly.

"Two wonderful degenerates. A far cry from your ninety-six Revelles."

Luxe peered up at me. "Make that three."

My breath caught. Was she being a friend? Or was she still haunted by the memory of that incredible kiss, too? I couldn't help myself; my gaze slipped to her lips.

She leaned closer, candlelight painting her golden. "This very moment could be erased, too. Dewey or another Chronos could travel, and this would cease to exist."

My pulse quickened. "As if it never happened."

"As if it doesn't even count." Her gaze drifted to my mouth, her bare arm brushing mine.

What was wrong with me? I was thinking about kissing a girl who'd just run barefoot from an obsessed time traveler's bed. Tears still glistened like jewels on her lashes. She wanted support, not another lovesick admirer.

I folded my hands behind my back, where they couldn't complicate things any further.

She jumped to her feet. "How's the search going?"

My pulse still thudded through my ears. "I'm sorry?"

"The search for your parents." Her rushed words were punctuated by a too-bright smile. "How's that going?"

"The search? Yes, the search." I wiped the sweat from my brow. "It's a mess, actually. Everything here feels familiar, yet I have no idea why."

She knew I'd gotten the wrong idea, that I'd read too much into her kindness. Even now, pity lingered in her bright eyes. "Would you want to know," she began carefully, "what happened to your parents, even if it made you sad?"

"Of course," I said without hesitation. "Anything to move on."

"Then you should talk to my grandmother again. She's hiding something."

I stared at her as she kicked at fallen hay. "Did she tell you that?"

"Sort of." Her teeth scraped her bottom lip. "She didn't tell me what it was, but she recognized your parents. I could tell."

Damn. That didn't bode well for my parents still being alive.

"Talk to her tomorrow," she said. "Maybe try to butter her up first."

"I don't think I'm any good at that."

"I doubt that." Her gaze drifted toward the wall. "Roger and Trysta are coming."

"How can you tell?"

She only tapped her head. "Do you want me to go?"

I never wanted her to leave. But she looked so exhausted, a breeze could blow her over. "You should rest."

"From now on, I'm not sleeping. At least, not while Dewey's still awake." She stretched, suppressing a yawn. "What a night we've had."

We. Despite everything, I liked the sound of that.

Roger's boisterous singing drifted through the open windows, and Luxe paused by the door. There was so much more to say, wasn't there? Words of encouragement. Empty promises. An apology for nearly kissing her again.

"Good night, Jamison." She slipped into the night, as graceful as a dream.

As she passed the window, her telltale signs of pain emerged: her full lips wrestling with a grimace, the corners of her eyes crinkling with tension. She'd been charming Dewey from a distance the whole damn time.

EIGHTEEN

JAMISON

Roger insisted we couldn't visit Nana until at least noon, so I lay awake all morning, trying to conjure a plan to untangle the Revelles from the time traveler's clutches.

They could survive without the winter theater. And with moonshine, they might be able to stretch their supply to keep their doors open a little longer. Buying from other Night District businesses wasn't an option. Every day, another storefront shuttered its doors, unable to afford Dewey's high prices. And if the Revelles turned against Dewey, could they survive his wrath?

Hard to outsmart a time traveler when I couldn't even *punch* a time traveler.

A little before noon, Roger led Trys and me to the long, barracks-like building behind the Big Tent. The salt air and sun had stripped the wood of its color, leaving it gray and bare. The Fun House occupied the second floor, but the first floor was for the Revelles.

"Three to a bedroom, usually, and more if you complain," Roger said proudly. He led us down the narrow hallway lined with old playbills, family portraits, and the occasional declaration scribbled on the wall: *Caroline Revelle, 1876, brought the crowd to their feet with her operetta! Arthur Revelle, 1893, juggled seventeen fireballs!*

Trys flattened against a wall as a pack of small children rushed past. "In my house, I used to go an entire day without seeing anyone but Dewey and my tutor. Even on the weekends."

"We can't all live in mansions, Trysta dear."

"I didn't mean it like that." She ran her hand along a poster of a beautiful woman posing on a tightrope. "I would have killed for something like this."

"Me too." Part of me still would.

Roger pointed to the name on the tightrope walker's poster. *Ruth Revelle.* "See Nana?"

"Wow. Your grandmother was a looker." Trys smoothed the poster's folded edge.

"Don't let her hear you say that in the past tense." Roger knocked on the door. "Nana? Are you decent?"

"I'm never decent," Nana's muffled voice called. "But I'm always ready for company."

Roger opened the door—and took a step back as if he'd been struck.

An elderly white lady sat in the chair across from Nana, two horns barely visible in her pale hair. Flanking her on both sides were two young women. They were both beautiful, with iridescent ivory horns peeking out from sheets of dark, wavy hair, and eyes as green as summer grass. The one closest to us stared at Roger as if he were a hallucination.

Nana could not have looked more pleased. "Roger, you remember Margaret, of course."

My gaze snapped to Roger. So this was the elusive Margaret. After years of hearing about her, she'd become a myth to me, but the girl gaping at us was certainly human, though as pale as a ghost.

Never before had I seen Roger rendered speechless. He stared at Margaret desperately, as if she'd cease to exist if he looked away. Whenever he'd spoken of their relationship, he'd done it with his usual air of casualness, and I'd known it was an act. That she'd hurt him. But now I saw the truth of why he'd avoided coming back here.

He was still head over heels in love with her.

The longer Roger stared, the deeper the blush that crept up Margaret's cheeks. I stepped in front of him, giving his shoulder a hard squeeze as I passed. "I'm Jamison, Roger's friend."

She shook my hand gingerly, though her gaze still flitted to Roger's. "Nice to meet you. I'm, ah . . . This is my grandmother, Lucy, and my sister, Rose."

"I remember you from the party," Rose said, all the while keeping her eyes on her sister. She, too, was pallid, with dark circles under her eyes as though she hadn't slept in days.

"And I'm Trysta Chronos." Trys thrust an aggressive hand forward, forcing Margaret to take it. Trys never forgave anyone who hurt those she loved. "I've been *dying* to meet you."

The Effigen women blanched. Lucy pushed to her feet, and Margaret and Rose stood to help her. "We should be going. Thank you, Ruth."

"Of course," Nana replied evenly. "We Night District families look out for one another."

With another wary glance at Trys, they left.

Roger whirled on his grandmother. "What was that about?"

"Don't look at me like that. Lucy is an old friend, as you know. She came by because of some concerning developments that have the Effigens quite upset." Nana watched Trys from over the top of her teacup, her eyes wet and swollen. Whatever conversation we'd interrupted, it hadn't been a pleasant one.

"You can trust her." Roger placed a hand on Trys's shoulder.

Nana didn't look convinced, but she set the teacup down. "Did you know Rose has a son? A baby boy, about three years old."

"I remember. She was pregnant when I left."

"Well, the boy's gone missing."

Roger cursed under his breath. "That's terrible. Did they file a police report?"

"With the Edwardians? Of course. But the Chronoses' guard dogs don't seem to be investigating much. And to make matters worse, he's the second Effigen to have gone missing this month." She glanced at each of us. "Have you heard anything?"

"The Strattoris reported a few people missing," Trys offered. "Dewey mentioned it."

Dewey. I bit my tongue hard enough to bleed. As far as I knew, Trys hadn't seen him since he'd aged. And I hadn't told them about Luxe's night with him, not just because it wasn't my story to tell, but because I had no idea how to tell Trys that her brother was a greedy piece of—

"He said the Strattoris are refusing to leave their compound," Trys continued. "He's had to pay handsomely for their services, and even then they seem hesitant."

"That *is* something. Thank you, Trysta." Nana gave her hand a squeeze, too, and Trys beamed. "Now what can I do for you three?"

Roger gave me an encouraging nod. I cleared my throat. "Actually, I was wondering if I could ask you about my parents again."

Nana's smile slipped. "I already told you, I don't know anything."

"Luxe seemed to think you might."

"Did she, now?" With a sigh, she turned away, stacking the teacups left behind by Margaret and her family. "Well, I thought for a moment I might have recognized them, but I didn't. Now, if you don't mind, it's time for my nap."

Roger glanced at the clock on the wall. "It's only noon."

"When you're my age, you nap whenever you damn well please." She faked an exaggerated yawn, then hurried us out of her room.

After she shut the door, I wheeled on Roger. "Well? Was she telling the truth?"

"Who knows? My grandmother has been practicing her poker face for a long time."

I stared at the closed door. If Nana was hiding something, she had to tell me. She *had* to. Even if I had to knock on this door every day until she did.

"I'm sorry, Jame-o." Roger clapped my back as we made our way back down the narrow hallway. "Want to walk around the Night again? Maybe something else will jog your memory."

I shook my head. "I've walked this whole island a dozen times."

Trys stuck out her cane, halting me in place. "Not the whole island," she said carefully.

Of course. "The Day District."

Roger frowned. "Is that such a good idea? Jamison's had two black eyes in the last three weeks, courtesy of Chronoses."

"I'll go, too," Trys said. "It's a long shot, but we might as well have a look."

She wasn't only offering to keep me company; she was offering to keep me safe, with that magic of hers. "Thanks, Trys."

"Okay if I sit this one out?" Roger's jovial tone was a bit too forced as he held open the door for us. Seeing Margaret had truly rattled him.

Trys and I exchanged glances. "You okay?" she asked him.

"I'm fine! Better than fine, I'm the bee's knees. The cat's pajamas. The duck's quack." He clapped me on the back. "Go get beat up by some more time travelers, Jame-o, then tell me all about it."

As we watched him walk down the beach, Trys sighed. "Bet you two emeralds he's planning to sit on the barn roof and belt out sad ballads."

"We'll force it out of him later," I agreed. "How far is the Day?"

"Far." She twirled her cane. "I hate walking uphill."

"Are you sure you're up for it?"

"Not at all." She blew the air out through her teeth. "Let's go."

No sign was needed to mark the beginning of the Day District. The streets sloped upward, as if we were ascending into a different world, one with clean cobblestones and freshly painted black lantern poles. The farther we climbed, the more the Night District stretched out beneath us, the mismatched buildings quaint and minuscule—except the Big Tent, which still loomed large, a tantalizing purple-and-black bruise on the horizon. Surrounding the Night on all sides was the ocean, bluer than the sky but just as vast. The mainland hid somewhere beyond the hazy fog on the horizon, but it felt a million miles away.

Trys sat on a bench to rest. Behind her, row after row of colorful candies glistened in a shop window. Children in bonnets and ribbons slowed to gaze longingly at them.

"I never pictured children in the Day," I admitted. "Only conniving Chronoses and stone-faced Edwardians."

Despite her unease, Trys cracked a smile. "Plenty of families without magic live here, too. Some of the wealthier merchants settle down in the Day if they can afford it."

Could my parents have lived in the Day? With renewed interest, I glanced around the street. "This is starting to look familiar."

She quirked a brow. "You sure?"

"Not in the slightest." I sat beside her as she rubbed her ankle. "You were five when you broke your foot, right?"

"Got it crushed by my sweet horse during riding lessons. A few blocks from here, actually."

"You rode horses?"

"All rich girls ride horses."

I took off my fedora and wiped the sweat from my brow. "I've always wondered: Why didn't you travel?"

She sighed. "I'd never used my magic before. If I hadn't blacked out from the pain, I might have tried, but by the time I woke up, I was afraid I'd go too far and end up ancient."

Like Dewey.

She rotated her ankle and winced. "My father forbade my mother from finding a relative to travel for me. He fetched a

Strattori instead, and paid one of our housekeepers to take the injury. It was part of being a Chronos, he said. 'Learn to be comfortable at the top.' But I refused."

Of course she did. "Even at five, you had your principles."

"Even at five, I was stubborn." Her smile faded. "I was tempted, though. There are twenty-six bones in the human foot, and my horse crushed eighteen of mine. But I didn't want the housekeeper to hurt, either. She was on her feet all day long. And she always snuck me sweets, unlike my father, who I hardly knew. I couldn't do it to her."

"Good for you, beating Mayor Chronos at his own game."

"I wouldn't say that." She stopped stretching her ankle. "He had my horse put down."

Jesus Christ. How Trys had been raised with such cruelty yet still turned out so kind was beyond me.

"Let's go." Standing, she pulled me to my feet. "I want to see if you recognize anything."

"Trysta."

George Chronos stood in the doorway of a shop across the street, two police officers flanking him. Trys's grip on my arm tightened.

"Did Dewey send you?" His voice, like his cold stare, was void of any affection for her.

"What? No, I was just—"

He stormed across the street. "*Stop* following me. And tell Dewey to back off. Having his people watch my every move isn't going to win him the election."

Pain flickered across Trys's face, lightning quick, but when she spoke, her voice was perfectly nonchalant. "I don't know, Georgie, maybe Dewey's campaign is going a little too well. Maybe that's why you hired a hitman to try and kill him in a Night District alley."

"*Et tu*, dear sister? You really think me capable of fratricide?" George took a step closer. "If I wanted Dewey dead, he'd be dead. Now, I suggest you and your—friend"—George gave me a once-over—"scram. Unless you're planning on returning home, in which case, I'll bring you to Father myself."

"And waste my life traveling for a bunch of corrupt politicians?" She stepped away from the hand he offered. "No, thank you."

"For the *family*, Trysta." Disgusted, he shook his head. "Just go. Tell Dewey to call off his dogs, or things are about to get much worse for him and his Night District trash."

"Say that again," I growled, pushing him right in the chest, "and I'll—"

"You'll what, throw another punch?" George laughed outright. "Haven't you learned not to pick a fight with a Chronos? We *always* win."

Trys grabbed my wrist as George strolled away. "Let him go. He's not worth it."

I glared at the back of his fancy suit. From behind, he could have been Dewey. "Your brothers are assholes."

"Dewey, too?" She tilted her head. "I see your 'magical hangover' is alive and well."

I pushed down my urge to tell her what Luxe had told me—it wasn't my place, and Dewey would show his true colors soon enough. Monsters always did.

Turning away, my gaze caught the store from which George

had emerged. *Fortune-Teller*, the sign read. With the brick exterior painted black, and voluminous scarves blocking the window, it looked more like a Night District tourist trap.

I looked inside—and couldn't breathe.

The back of a maroon fainting couch was pushed against the window. I'd sat on that couch before. Traced the iron upholstery tacks holding the velvet in place.

"We have to go in there."

Trys followed my gaze. "That's Mag the Hag's shop. She gives me the creeps, but if George was just in there . . ." She groaned. "Let's go."

The door was locked. Trys pointed at a little box beside it. "She only accepts payment up front. Otherwise, customers could just barge in asking questions she'd have to answer."

"Edwardian?"

"A *very* old one. Less of a fortune-teller and more of a glorified gossip. She's amassed the island's secrets and sells them to the highest bidder. Hence why she's in the Day and not the Night: deeper pockets here." Trys reached into her purse and produced her last gems: two tiny rubies. She placed one inside the box. It tumbled down a dark chute in the door.

A window on the other side of the chute opened, and a wrinkled hand swiped the jewel.

"The other one, too," an old woman's voice cooed.

Trys groaned. "I could get Revelle magic for less."

"Don't be cheap with me, Trysta Chronos. If you want me to answer your questions about your brother, you need to pay my fee."

With a sigh, Trys placed her last gem inside. It clattered against the metal pipe as it slid down the chute.

I tried the handle again, but it was still locked.

"Hey!" Trys banged on the door. "I paid. Now open up!"

"But your *friend* didn't." Amusement punctuated each word.

"I don't have any gems." Jewels or not, I needed to see this room, to speak to this woman and see if she knew anything—

"You have many questions for me, Jamison Jones. About your parents."

The Day District disappeared. Trys disappeared. All that was left was the door in front of me and the roaring in my ears.

Jones.

Trys gave me a funny look. "Jones isn't even your last name. It's—"

"Port?" the woman interrupted. "No, Port is but a nickname, short for Sport, which your father liked to call you. But you couldn't pronounce *s* when you were little, so it sounded like 'port.' To keep you hidden, your parents made it your surname so only they could find you."

Stay here, my love. We'll find you when it's safe.

In a panic, I emptied my pants pockets, my coat pockets, but I had nothing. Trys checked her purse, too. "I'm all out."

My empty wallet held one familiar bulge.

"Jamison, don't!" But Trys was too late.

My mother's brooch slid down the chute and into the waiting hands of Mag the Hag.

The door opened.

I hardly noticed the dark room, the too-sweet incense burning, the familiar red couch. "What do you know about my parents?"

She was the oldest woman I'd ever seen, with eyes nearly eclipsed by loose, wrinkled skin. Scarves covered her hair, save a few white wisps. She smiled, revealing no teeth. "I know what happened to them."

I stepped closer. "Tell me. *Please.*"

Using the table for support, she lowered herself into a smoking chair and draped a scarf over her shoulders. "Let's start with the easy questions. Go ahead, Trysta Chronos."

I opened my mouth, but Trysta threw me a warning look. "Why did George come here?"

"He came here to ask me why Dewey is having him followed. You Chronos siblings are quite a mess, aren't you?"

Trys ignored the dig. "What did you tell him?"

"I told him what I've heard buzzing in the heads of the Edwardians this morning. That your brother Dewey had a little time-traveling mishap. Apparently, George attempted to take out Dewey and the Radiant Ruby, and Dewey jumped back in time to save them. Traveled too far, though. Tell me, have you seen your brother today?"

Trys paled. "How far did he travel?"

"Far enough to lock himself in that mansion of his all day, for fear of being seen." Mag's cutting gaze flicked to me. "Ask your friend here. He already knows."

Surprised, Trys turned to me. I nodded guiltily. This wasn't how I wanted her to find out.

"With the election only eight days away, all of Charmant will see soon enough." Mag cocked her head. "Any other questions?"

Trys braced herself, her fingers digging into the faded velvet couch. "Is George behind my uncle Frank's attack on Dewey?"

Mag sighed. "Ah, the million-carat question. If George convinced your uncle to go after Dewey, he hasn't done it yet—and he never will, now that your uncle is gone. And if George *shot* Dewey at his inauguration? Well, that also hasn't happened yet, so who can say if it will? Your family's magic is far too complicated, if you ask me."

Trys slumped against the couch.

"The only person who knew for sure why he attacked Dewey was your uncle, and he's dead." The old woman turned to me. "Your turn."

With trembling hands, I removed the photo from my wallet. "Tell me what you know about my parents."

Trys elbowed me. "You have to phrase it as a question, or—"

"I'll lie? If only." Mag snickered, a wheezy laugh that morphed into a dry cough. When she looked at me again, her humor faded. "You don't remember me, do you?"

My heartbeat slowed. "I remember this room."

"And I remember your eyes. It's hard to forget that startling blue, especially when you were little. They took up half your face, and long days on the beach had browned your skin, making the color even more startling."

I swallowed. "How old was I?"

"Three, maybe four. Your parents brought you here twice."

"Why? Why did they come to see you?"

"For answers. Like you."

She watched me carefully, her eyes clouded with sadness. I leaned forward, not blinking as I met her gaze. "Please."

Her hands folded on top of each other. "They came to see me the day after their daughter disappeared. Your sister. She was only a baby, just shy of her first birthday, and she vanished from her crib in the middle of the night. They paid handsomely for answers . . . but I found nothing. No witnesses. No clues. Not a whisper of the entire ordeal heard by anyone in my family, and trust me, boy, I hear everything. They feared the Chronoses were behind it because your parents were friendly with the Revelles. Mayor Chronos's police investigation was less than satisfactory, but of course, there was no proof that was on purpose."

Beside me, Trys didn't move an inch.

"What happened next?"

The old woman sighed. "Weeks passed. Two, maybe three. They came again and told me the kidnapper had returned with a ransom: he'd give them back their daughter, unharmed, if they did something terrible for him. Something neither of them wanted to do."

I hardly felt Trys's hand grip my arm.

"They asked me to find this man for them. He might have been a Chronos, given his ability to time his entrance perfectly to avoid detection, but he wore a Revelle theater mask. The face of a tiger, whiskers and all."

"What happened next?" I demanded.

"They offered me everything they had for a lead—their business, their savings, everything. But I couldn't find out anything about the man. It was as if he was a ghost, haunting only them. He showed up again, repeating his demands and giving a final warning. They were . . ." She paused, her matter-of-fact voice quieting. "In my line of work, I meet many desperate people, but that sort of desperation, that anguish . . . They watched you like a hawk. You tried to wander away to pet my cat, but your mother grabbed you and held you tight against her. Hearing her thoughts was like eavesdropping on Hell."

I tucked away each heavy word, not letting myself feel the weight of them. Not yet. "What happened to them?"

"They couldn't bring themselves to do what he asked. He provided no proof your sister was even alive, and his demands . . . well, they were steep. To protect you, they brought you to the Night District orphanage and arranged to have you transferred somewhere far away from Charmant. They isolated themselves from the other Night District families, especially the magical ones. They trusted no one. Without their children, they were absolutely heartbroken. It was years before they even came to see me again."

I swallowed. Hard. "When?"

"Seven years ago."

Seven years. My parents were still alive seven years ago. I was twelve, living in that damn orphanage, and they'd been here, on Charmant. Trying to bring me home.

Maybe they were still here.

"Your father didn't trust me, so he kept guard outside my shop. But your mother came inside. She asked about you and your sister. I hadn't heard a whisper about either of you. And she told me about the visits. Every now and then, the masked man returned and made the same offer: if they did what he said, they'd see their daughter again."

Mag paused to pat her brow with a handkerchief. Trys still gripped my arm. "What happened next?" I managed to ask.

"They'd suffered long enough. I read it in your mother's thoughts: she'd lost too many years with her children, and she was going to do whatever it took to get them back. So they did what he asked. They rented one of their boats to three Revelle women and drowned them."

Ice flooded my veins.

No.

"The man told them exactly what to do to make it seem like an accident, but it didn't matter. My kin heard their guilt, divers found the bodies half-eaten by fish, and even though the police searched for your sister's kidnapper, your parents were sentenced to the electric chair."

My heart stopped beating.

A fly buzzed nearby. Landed on the edge of Mag's teacup, already empty.

"It was a public execution. I didn't attend, but I saw the scene play over and over in people's minds for weeks. Terrible way to die." She shuddered. "Your mother was the first woman to go that way in Charmant. Evelyn Jones—I'm sure you can look it up somewhere."

The buzzing filled my ears, my bones, vibrating with enough ferocity to break me.

"Thank you," I heard Trys say. Felt her hands on my back, the cool of the knob, the sunlight blinding.

I gripped the black doorframe before Mag could shut it. "My father's name?"

"James." She offered me a small, wilted smile. "That's why they named you Jamison."

Son of James.

Relentless, burning sunlight, pounding pavement, that roar in my ears, drowning out Trys calling my name, her hurried steps keeping pace with mine, spinning, spinning—

My stomach emptied itself all over the pristine cobblestones. Onlookers clutched their pearls as I upchucked again, again, again.

My parents. Dead. My . . . sister. Gone. Stolen. Probably dead.

And my parents had killed Luxe's mother. Millie's mother. *Roger's* mother.

Trys gripped my shoulders as my stomach lurched again.

"I have to tell them," I heard myself saying. Over and over.

"You will." She pushed my sweaty hair off my forehead. "Just breathe, Jamison. Don't worry about that yet."

They were going to hate me. Luxe. Colette and Millie, and, oh God, *Roger* . . .

No Revelle would ever be able to look at me again.

NINETEEN

LUXE

I woke in a panic and checked my memories. Still there. Dewey hadn't traveled to before our awful conversation, or I wouldn't have even thought to check.

By sheer stubbornness, I fought the urge to drift back to dreamland. Colette and Millie still slept soundly beside me, but Dewey was an early riser, and I couldn't risk him waking before me.

It had been one week since our night in the Diamond Room. One week of charming him all day, of sleeping only when I felt myself on the brink of collapse. Without my magic lulling him into contentment, Dewey could hurt someone. He could realize I was only pretending to care about him and travel back to when I was still unaware of his true character. But one week meant it'd cost him another two years to redo that night in the Diamond Room. Was that too high a price to keep me in the dark?

I couldn't risk finding out.

Digging into my little inkwell, my mouth opened in a silent scream as the pain flooded me. Closing my eyes, I followed the long lightstring drifting above Dewey's mansion on the harbor.

His aging made him blisteringly insecure, and his family's attacks made him paranoid. More than once in the past week, he'd suggested I sleep at his mansion, breaking every uppity Chronos rule of propriety. *For your own safety, my sweet. The election is just days away, my sweet.* Though I used my magic to temper those possessive urges, I let some paranoia take root. If his family struck again— *when* they struck again, really—we needed our time traveler to be our guard dog.

The other negative feelings—the insecurity, the regrets, the swift jealousy each time I stepped away—simply wouldn't do. When it came to me, Dewey needed to be in a perpetual state of happiness. From the moment he woke until he finally drifted to sleep, my magic carved away all other worries, leaving him feeling beloved. Bold. Content with the sophisticated man whose reflection greeted him in the mirror. The more people who saw his aged face for the first time, the harder I had to work to temper his misery. It was the one mistake he couldn't undo.

But I never left him to his own devices. I couldn't risk it.

I'll have Colette fall in a much larger hole next time.

Before Dewey arrived to fetch me for yet another long day of canvassing together, I slipped into Uncle Wolffe's office to practice the techniques Trevor had showed me. Now more than ever, I needed to keep my thoughts private. But I hadn't even been there fifteen minutes before Aunt Caroline poked her head through the door.

"Dewey's here for Luxe." She winked at me.

I suppressed the urge to slump into the armchair. Each day, he arrived a little earlier, making small talk with my skeptical family while waiting for me. Every movement of his was so rehearsed, each smile careful and practiced, as if appearing kind was something he'd studied.

As I rose, covering my yawn, Aunt Caroline tousled my hair. "Not enough beauty sleep, ice princess? I didn't see you in the Fun House last night."

"The election's in two days," I whined, "and canvassing in high heels hurts my feet."

She caught my wrist as I slipped by, whirling me to face her. "Make sure you rest, Luxie girl. It's no fun teasing you while you run yourself ragged."

"Don't worry." I patted her hand. "I'll be nice and lazy again after the election."

"I mean it. Your mother may be gone, but we're still watching out for you. All of us."

For a long moment, I didn't trust myself to speak, not with the knot swelling in my throat. Uncle Wolffe rearranged the papers on his desk, his lightstring battling the grief he so expertly avoided.

"I'm taking a break tonight," I finally said, "and going to the midsummer fair with Colette and Millie." Jamison had given me the idea when we'd dreamed of a summer without consequences. Colette and Millie had been shocked when I'd asked but had agreed to come.

"Good." She let go of my hand. "No Dewey?"

"No Dewey." If he let me out of his sight, for once.

He waited for me in the hall, his lightstring glowing maroon as I appeared. That was the kicker: underneath the calculated, calm exterior, underneath the aggressive streak and the possessive urges, Dewey genuinely cared for me. "Ready, my sweet?"

I took the arm he offered. "Ready."

We spent the afternoon knocking on doors and shaking hands. If anything, his older face was working in his favor. People who didn't know him assumed he was in his thirties, and those who did, I charmed into being touched by his tale of saving my life. We were quickly becoming Charmant's favorite couple. And I played my part well. Because as much as I didn't trust Dewey, he was at least trying to win my family's favor.

Unlike George, who'd shot me, apparently.

Dewey sat in the front row during yet another rehearsal for the election night performance at the winter theater. Hours later, during my trapeze act, he lounged in the executive suite with Trevor, his lightstring brimming with a possessive fervor that made me want to crawl out of my skin.

I needed a break. I needed space. More than anything, I needed to speak with Trevor alone. If anyone knew what lurked underneath Dewey's mask, it was his dutiful mind reader.

But Dewey waited backstage for me after the show. "Excellent job, my sweet! Are you ready to call it a night?"

I endured his kiss, keeping my head high and my smile serene. "Actually, I told my cousins I'd stop by the fair with them, remember?"

"The election's the day after tomorrow. We should rest."

"*You* should rest." I squeezed his hands. *You wish to give me space tonight. You wish to see me rejuvenated by time with my cousins.* "I'll see you in the morning?"

He hesitated as my magic wrestled with his selfish instincts. "I don't think it's wise."

"Trevor can keep me safe. Isn't that right, Trevor?"

Flustered, the Edwardian tugged on his collar. "Yes, Miss Revelle."

"It's settled, then." I kissed Dewey on both cheeks. *You're feeling exhausted, and you wish to see me go.* "You take your guards, and I'll take Trevor."

"You're just stopping by the fair? Then you'll head home?"

I flashed him my sweetest smile. "Absolutely."

During the last week of July, tents and food carts lined the narrow grasslands between the harbor and the sea. Still safely in Night District territory, though not far from Dewey's estate and, behind it, the Day District. With every step I took toward the bed where he tossed and turned, his swirling lightstring shortened and my piercing headache subsided a smidge.

My magic was *not* a fan of the constant strain required of it these days.

"I did as you asked," Trevor said, "and I've paid close attention to Mr. Chronos's thoughts. You're right; he's been hiding a lot from me."

I knew it.

"But he's far from the first person on Charmant to pretend to be someone he isn't." He slowed his step to look at me. "Plenty of people think ugly thoughts, but Dewey *does* kind things. He has never denied me a day off. He's given me raises before I've even asked. Frankly, I couldn't ask for a better employer."

A week ago, I would have agreed with him. "He hurt Colette," I reminded him. "I can never forget that."

He looked pained. "I know. But who would you prefer as mayor: the man who twisted your cousin's ankle to be your hero, or the man who's willing to kill his own brother for power?"

"Neither." I made a beeline for the balloon arc at the entrance.

Trevor hurried to catch me. "You don't want to marry him. I

understand that. But he loves you. He'd do anything to win you over, including keep your family safe."

"Anything except give me a jewel." With a big enough rock on my finger, I could supplement my secondary magic for months, maybe even years. And if he did win the election, the Revelles' influence on the new mayor was guaranteed. All I needed was a big, fat diamond.

Millie waved us over to where she and Colette stood by the entrance. She took Trevor's arm. "How are you feeling this fine night, Mr. Edwardes?"

"I am feeling very happy to be here with you."

Millie beamed, her lightstring tingeing scarlet as she fell into step with him. Interesting.

"Dewey's fine with you spending a night with us?" Colette asked me, her voice hushed. "So close to the election?"

Wonderful. Even without seeing the painful string of light tethering me to him, Colette knew I was on a tight leash. "I don't need his permission."

"Did you help him take out his dentures before you left?"

I elbowed her, trying to hide my smile. "We shouldn't make fun of him for aging."

"Can you imagine waking up tomorrow and being thirty-four?" She shuddered.

"That's older than our mothers were." *When they died.*

Her graceful steps sputtered to a stop. We used to talk about our mothers all the time, but we were out of practice.

"That's right," she finally said, her voice soft. "And they were beautiful."

I tried to conjure my mother's face, but time had blurred the details. I was forgetting her.

As delicate whorls of grief floated through her lightstring, Colette looped her elbow through mine. "Well, Nana's an absolute fox, so I daresay we have decades of beauty still ahead of us."

"I wouldn't mind her boobs."

"Keep dreaming. Look, there they are." She pointed to Roger, Jamison, and Trysta.

A head above the crowd, Jamison was hard to miss. The sleeves of his navy button-down shirt were rolled to his forearms, and dark tendrils of unruly hair escaped his fedora. Instead of his earnest golden hue, his lightstring was an unusual blue, like the night sky just before the first stars appear. He was hurting, but he brightened at the sight of us. At the sight of *me*.

My foolish heart stuttered. He'd been avoiding me for days. Maybe he'd finally forgiven me for practically throwing myself at him.

Millie nudged me. "You should go for it, you know."

I smoothed the embroidered edge of my summer frock. "I told you, we're just friends."

"Ah yes, your first night out in *years* just happens to be when your new 'friend' is here. Hi, fellas!"

"Good evening, dolls! And Trevor, of course." Roger tipped his hat.

Trys gave me a nod. An improvement, at least. As she turned to Colette, her lightstring sparked like fireworks. That was new. I glanced around, but of course, no one else could see it.

"Well?" Roger threw his arms around his friends. "What's the plan?"

"Why don't we do all the touristy things? The Ferris wheel first, of course." It'd been the highlight of my summer when my mother used to take me. "Then we'll hit the food carts and make our way through the fair games . . . Why are you all looking at me like that?"

Millie blinked innocently. "Like what?"

"Like I'm slurring my words like Nana after too much wine." I hugged myself against the cool breeze. "This is how we always do the fair, right?"

"It's just, you haven't been out with us in a while," Colette said carefully, "and the way we do the fair now has sort of . . . matured."

Of course. I was describing a night on the town for eleven-year-olds. They hadn't stopped coming here just because *I'd* stopped going with them. "How do you usually do it?"

Roger lifted a shoulder. "Before I left, it was Russian roulette with Effigen drinks, then as many zeppole as we could stomach without throwing up."

"Effigen drinks will kill our budget, but . . ." Colette's smile grew as she glanced around the circle. "Why don't we make tonight a bit of a competition?"

"You? Turning something into a competition?" Roger feigned shock.

"Ooh!" Millie clapped excitedly. "Let's play Hats!"

Colette grinned. "You read my mind."

"Oh, this is my favorite! We still do all the things Luxe mentioned, but while we do them, try to get someone to give you their hat." Millie's gaze danced around the circle. "At the end of the night, the person with the best hat wins."

Trysta frowned. "You want us to just ask people to give us their hats?"

"You can ask. Or . . ." With an exaggerated flirty smile, Colette threw an arm around Trysta's shoulders, snagged her hat, and flicked it onto her own head. "You can do it like this."

Jamison hesitated. "I'm not sure that'll work for me."

"With that baby face, I think you'll do just fine." Millie winked at me conspiratorially. I stepped on her foot.

"Doesn't he have an innocent face?" Trys pinched his cheek. "I tell him that all the time."

"Winner gets to choose a dare for the rest of us. Sound good?" This time, it wasn't a challenge glittering in Colette's eyes as she looked at me. It was something more delicate.

Hope.

I took Trysta's hat from Colette's head and placed it on mine. "I sure hope you like losing, Col."

She laughed. "I never lose. You'll see."

Roger led the charge to find drinks. Jamison hung back, and I risked slowing down to keep pace with him.

"What's going on there?" I nodded toward Colette and Trys, whose heads were bent in whispered conversation.

The corners of his mouth tugged upward. "If it *has* happened, they're both being tight-lipped about it."

At least I wasn't the only one who didn't know. "Is this why Colette's been sneaking into bed at dawn?"

"I've caught Trys smiling—for no reason. Which may not sound like a big deal, but for her, that's practically shouting their love from the rooftops."

Colette whispered something in Trys's ear, and Trys laughed, smacking Colette's arm.

Glancing at Jamison, I buried the nagging pull of envy. "Are you okay?"

"Don't worry about me. Everything's Jake."

I gave him a look. He knew I could see how dim his lightstring was tonight.

Removing his hat, he played with the brim. "I found out what happened to my parents."

"From Nana?" I stopped walking.

"No, an Edwardian in the Day District. Mag."

"Mag the Hag." Of course; the old Edwardian collected shiny secrets like a magpie.

Shiny secrets like mine.

I grabbed his arm. "Did you talk about me?"

He flushed. "What? No—"

"Did you think of me at all? Even for a moment? Because if she knows about my . . . I'm screwed. We're all screwed. And—"

"Luxe, it's okay. I didn't think of you once. I swear it. Not even for a moment."

For some reason, his words were far from comforting. I withdrew my hand before he went running for the hills again.

"I didn't mean it like that." His hand raked through his hair. "I just . . . I was distracted."

"By your parents. Of course." Careful not to look at him, I kept walking, all the while willing my cheeks to stop blushing. "So what did you find out?"

His lightstring was so blue, it was almost black. Whatever he'd learned, no part of him wanted to speak of it. "Let's just have fun, and at the end of the night, I'll tell you everything."

"Whenever you're ready," I said softly. "Besides, tonight is all about fun. And hats, apparently." I scanned the crowd for one worthy of stealing.

He bent toward me and dropped his voice. "Can you have fun while you're charming him?"

Of course he could tell. No wonder he and Roger were close; their carefree exteriors hid big hearts, ones they kept attuned to everyone else's needs. A small nod was all I dared.

"But you're in pain."

"You'd be surprised how quickly one can adapt to pain."

"I wouldn't be, actually." His sapphire eyes cut right through me. "So your plan is to use your magic all the time now?"

"And a jewel, if I can get him to give me one." I checked on Dewey's lightstring. In the minutes I'd let my focus slip, brutal self-doubt had clawed its way back into his mood. If I let him fall asleep like that, he'd toss and turn all night, plagued by nightmares I couldn't see. Slowing my step, I dug deeper into my inkwell, ignoring the hot lash of pain across the base of my skull. *You're safe. You're happy. And you're sleepy. Very sleepy.*

My magic fought against the strain of the distance, pressure building behind my eyes, against my skull, as if the inkwell was going to burst—

Jamison steadied me, and I leaned into him, determined not to pass out. All I had to do was hold on during this little magical hissy fit, and it would pass.

It would pass.

"What happened?" Colette was so close, I breathed in her coconut shampoo.

Finally, Dewey fell asleep. "I'm okay," I managed to say. "I just . . . tripped."

She lifted her brows. Revelles didn't trip.

"It was me and my big feet," Jamison blurted. "I got in her way."

Colette's gaze fell to where Jamison still steadied my waist. He wisely let go.

Millie threw an arm around Colette. "You know what they say about big feet?"

Jamison's cheeks grew brighter by the second. "I, ah, don't—"

"Big socks." With a grin, Millie dragged Colette away.

"Thank you," I whispered to Jamison.

He handed me his handkerchief. Yet another bloody nose. "It's still dangerous for you, right? Even if you're not using your magic, if an Edwardian—"

"Only if we think about it. Which we won't, because we're burying our thoughts in hooch." I took his forearm, ignoring the heat of his skin as I pulled him toward the others.

"Love your horns." Roger winked as he took his change from the Effigen bartender, slipping an emerald into his revenge stash. He turned toward us, arms bursting with colorful drinks in souvenir glasses shaped like naked people. "These were cheaper than I expected."

"Dewey slashed the price of booze this week." It was part of his election strategy: making people so grateful, they'd forget he was the reason prices had been sky-high. After the election, there was nothing stopping him from raising them again.

Trys took the drinks from Roger and passed them around. "Silly Willy for Trevor. Sunshine Special for Millie. The Philosopher for Colette. Arbor Righty for Jamison. Cow Spots for Roger. And"—with a too-sweet smile, she handed me a glass of shimmering gold—"for the Radiant Ruby, a tall glass of Gold Digger."

"Ha ha." I took the glass without letting my smile break. Better to be a good sport than to give Trys the satisfaction of biting back.

Before I could take a sip, Jamison pried it from my fingers, replacing it with his green one. "Let's trade. We all know I could use a little more gold."

He clinked the golden drink to mine, but Roger nearly knocked us over. "The toast!"

Colette lifted her glass. "Cheers?"

"A *good* toast."

"Oh! What's that toast that Nana always says?" Millie wrinkled her brow.

"I remember it." Roger raised his glass.

"The Day District fools go to sleep with their jewels
in bedrooms as lonely as hell.
But when the Big Tent's your home, you're never alone,
so raise a glass to the family Revelle!"

Trys cracked her neck on both sides before draining her glass. Roger whistled at her, then did the same.

"We're chugging these?" I murmured to Millie.

"Usually, we just sip them, but when in Rome, right?" She tilted her head back and began to chug the cloudy yellow liquid.

Jamison still held his drink. "I'm following your lead here," he admitted.

It had been years since I'd had an Effigen cocktail. The enchanted booze would help protect me from mind readers, but there was no telling how strong it was. "Bottoms up, Mr. Port."

I hardly registered the flicker of emotion in Jamison's eyes before I swallowed. My drink was thicker than I expected, though nearly odorless, its only taste a lingering bitterness. Like I'd chewed on tree bark, but delicious tree bark.

Bark. Bark bark.

Roger slammed his empty glass on the bar cart. "Let's go find some hats."

The strings of lights glimmered overhead as we wove our way through the food carts. I paused to smell the savory spiced meats. Melted butter slathered on balls of half-baked dough. Swirls of cotton candy that stretched nearly as tall as Jamison. As tall as the trees themselves.

God, I loved trees.

Those beautiful, neon evergreens wagged their bark hips as skillfully as any Revelle dancer. Each time I blinked, they glowed brighter than the stars, brighter than lightstrings—

Millie squeezed my arm. "Remember when Roger used to get us fried doughnuts, and we'd eat them by the docks?"

As if I could forget the dusting of powdered sugar on my tongue, my hands, our laps. "How did he manage to afford all those?"

"Oh, he definitely stole them." Colette shook her head but couldn't hide her mirth. "Probably used his revenge stash to charm his way into enough for all of us, didn't you, Rog?"

But Roger was too busy flirting with the woman behind the fruit stand. Atop the inky, cloudlike hair framing her pretty brown face was a towering hat of bananas, pineapples, and apples.

Millie whistled. "Now *that's* a hat."

"She's never going to give it to him." Colette scowled as Roger rubbed one of the bananas, and the woman laughed. Magic or not, Roger had her in his clutches.

"You're just jealous you didn't see it first." Trys pulled Colette's arm. "C'mon, I want chocolate-covered pretzels."

"You okay?" Jamison asked me.

"You're like a tree, you know?" I called up to him. "A ridiculously tall tree."

"A tree?" His gorgeous face broke into the first genuine grin he'd cracked all night, golden light pouring from his mouth. I waved my hand in front of it, watching the beams break and reform over my fingers.

"Did your drink work?" I asked as he tore a pretzel in half, handing me the bigger piece.

"I think so. Unless you dyed your hair gold."

"Ahem!" Roger strutted in between us, an enormous pile of real fruit stacked like a pyramid atop his head. Jamison tried to whistle appreciatively, but he couldn't stop laughing.

No matter what else happened, that laugh made tonight a success.

We meandered through the magicians and their gimmicky tricks, my tree trunk never straying from my side. "How's your pretzel?" he asked.

"It's delicious," I gushed. "Like leaves."

"Leaves?"

"Leaves and sap and—oh! The Ferris wheel!" I pulled him toward the spinning lights. "Can't we ride now? Pretty please?"

"Of course." Jamison nodded to Roger, whose face was practically hidden by the enormous fruit hat. The seven of us made our way to the back of the line.

Millie sidled up beside me. "If you want to ride with Jamison, make sure you're standing next to him when it's time to get on."

"I'll ride with anyone," I insisted.

"Sure you will." She grinned knowingly as we joined them in line.

Glancing up at the Ferris wheel, Roger adjusted his heavy hat with both hands. "Remember the one in Chicago? Or was that California?"

Jamison shuddered. "You kept rocking the damn thing. I was sure you'd get us killed."

Chicago. California. They'd grown wings and seen the world. Meanwhile, I was a firefly circling a jar. Entertaining to watch, but slowly suffocating.

The line shifted again, and the Ferris wheel operator helped Trys and Colette climb inside their passenger car. Millie lingered beside me, letting the gap between her and Jamison yawn wider. *Last chance*, she mouthed.

I shouldn't. Dewey might ask Trevor to report everything we did back to him.

The Ferris wheel operator motioned for Jamison to climb into the next car. Roger stepped back, offering either of us the free seat. Millie dangled her leg in front of her, taking the final step in slow motion, her antics making Trevor wheeze with unbridled laughter. Effigen booze or not, he was smitten.

The trees themselves beckoned as I stepped forward and, to Millie's utter delight, sat beside Jamison.

TWENTY

JAMISON

The Ferris wheel operator fussed over Luxe's comfort far longer than mine. By some miracle, she didn't slap his too-eager hands. But I suppose Luxe was used to all sorts of attention.

Finally, he let her be, flipping his controls to lift us up a few yards so Millie, Trevor, and Roger could climb into the next bucket. Alone with Luxe, I tried to shift so I didn't encroach on her space, but the cart was too small, and my knees kept bumping hers.

She turned to me, her eyes glowing with excitement. And even though my Effigen drink had been a bit of a dud, even though the weight of what I needed to tell her was heavy enough to break the Ferris wheel, that smile was my own personal elixir.

"You're having fun," she declared, looking pleased with herself.

"So are you." The wheel turned, lifting us farther over the operator's head. "For once."

"I have fun all the time."

"Liar." Beautiful, beautiful liar.

The breeze was cooler up here. Luxe pulled at her sweater, and I helped her adjust it, fighting the urge to wrap my arm around her.

"I haven't seen much of you this week." She kept her gaze trained on the treetops.

I was a terrible friend. First, I had nearly kissed her, and then, after she confided in me, I'd disappeared.

And, of course, my parents had murdered her mother.

I'd tell her later. Coming here, with her cousins, was on her list of things she'd do with the summer do-over Dewey had inadvertently given us, and I wasn't going to ruin it for her. Not yet.

"I'm sorry," I said. "I'll explain everything soon, but it's been a strange week."

"You can say that again." She peered down at Millie and Trevor entering the next cart. "How's Roger? I heard Nana had Margaret in her office."

"Hard to tell. He hasn't breathed a word about it since. But the way he looked at her?" I shook my head. "I've never seen him look at anyone that way."

Luxe's smile was sad. "They were so perfect together. She got Roger to start taking himself seriously, and he always had her laughing. Because she grew up in the Night, she wasn't fazed by his Fun House work. Not until the same customer started asking for him every night, crafting twisted fantasies for Roger to bring to life. She was worried, and probably a little jealous. They bickered about it until . . . well, you know."

My hands curled into fists. "Until the jealous bastard cornered Roger and threw a lit gasoline rag in his face."

He'd spent an entire month in the hospital recovering and left with a bill large enough to bankrupt his family for the season. Afterward, he could no longer stomach the Fun House, not when some of the customers wanted to incorporate his scars, his *pain*, into their fantasies.

The night's merriment winked out of her whiskey eyes. "Is that what he told you?"

"Roger said the customer wanted to ruin him. To make him undesirable to Margaret or anyone else. That backfired, of course. I've seen girls in bars stroking those scars."

All the color drained from Luxe's face. "That's not what happened."

"But the scars . . ." Those were burns; I knew that from St. Douglas's. Punishment by fire was rare, even for the friars, but once, a boy five days into his first fast had reached into a scalding pot in search of food. His scars weren't so different from Roger's.

Unless . . . Strattori magic.

My hand flew to my mouth. "The bastard went after Margaret."

Luxe nodded grimly.

"Jesus Christ." The pain Roger must have felt, first in seeing Margaret suffer, and then having that suffering transferred to him. "Strattori magic can be a curse, can't it?"

She scoffed. "Strattori magic didn't drive Roger's customer so mad with jealousy that he waited outside the bakery, lit a gasoline rag on fire, and threw it in Margaret's face. And Strattori magic didn't curse Margaret with a lifetime of regret for letting Roger unburden her of unfathomable pain. She can't even stand to look at any of us anymore."

Christ. With that sort of guilt, no wonder their relationship hadn't survived.

"Love is the curse," Luxe said. "Not magic."

I gave her a funny look. "You can't blame love."

"Why not?" She arched a single brow. "Love is useless."

"Useless! You don't mean that."

"Love poisons the minds of otherwise sane people. It's the worst kind of drug."

"You love your family," I pointed out.

She flicked her wrist. "That's different. *Romantic* love is the lie. Trust me. I sell it every night."

She was being purposefully obtuse. "That's not love; that's lust."

"Yet the customers *love* it."

I gaped at her, which only made her smile grow. And even though she was goading me, I couldn't let it go, couldn't allow Luxe Revelle to resign herself to a loveless life.

With the bravery only an Effigen drink could provide, I scooted toward her, the cart rocking as I leaned so close I could taste her minty breath on each inhale. "So you mean to tell me, right now, while you're alone on a Ferris wheel with a not-so-bad-looking guy, you feel *nothing*?"

Her breath caught, the tiniest sound. "Absolutely nothing."

She didn't move away. Emboldened, I wrapped two fingers around her slight wrist, pressing them against her racing pulse. "Liar."

The Ferris wheel turned higher, carrying us to the apex, the glittering lights of Charmant stretching over the island. To our right, the ocean faded into the black mist of night.

"Even if I felt . . . something"—her husky voice caught on the last word, sending a thrill to my core as she leaned closer—"Dewey wouldn't approve."

My teeth ground together. "He doesn't own you."

"I know. I just don't think he likes to share."

"And what do *you* want?"

There it was: the only variable in this equation that mattered. But could she truly answer it before knowing what my family had done to hers?

Her teeth pulled her bottom lip as she bit back her words. I shouldn't have wanted to kiss her. Not with Effigen drinks surging through both of us, the heady rush of the night sky twinkling around us, those perfect lips having just uttered *his* name. Not when she was only being kind because she was trying to cheer me up.

Who was I kidding? She didn't just pity me, and I didn't just fancy her. Something was happening between us, something that could no longer be ignored.

Something my past could ruin before it had a chance to bloom.

I tucked a windblown curl beneath her jeweled hair comb. Her pulse thrashed between my fingers, wild and unbound. "What do you want?" I repeated, this time more softly.

"To take him down." The fire in her eyes could have burned the entire island. "To charm him into a docile mayor who won't hurt me or anyone I love. To stop his family from targeting mine, stop George from tormenting us, stop the entire Chronos family from ruining my family's chance at prosperity, for once. I want to take them all down."

"Then let's do it."

Her fingers tangled with mine, sending a thrill right to my core. That first kiss had been so mind-blowing, and back then, I didn't even know how fiercely she loved, how hard she worked to keep her family safe.

Kissing Luxe with Trevor nearby would be careless. Reckless. But neither of us looked away, the pull of gravity between us growing, growing still.

The Ferris wheel surged forward, dropping us so abruptly that I yelped like a puppy as I grabbed the bar. Laughter burst from Luxe, guffaws so deep, she struggled to catch her breath.

I was so, so suave.

"You didn't tell me you're afraid of heights!"

"It, ah, didn't come up." I slowly relaxed into the seat, that almost-kiss so potent I hardly noticed the distance to the ground.

The sun teased beneath where the horizon met the ocean. Not quite day, but no longer night. The weak light silhouetted the four Revelles as they did cartwheels in the surf, booze and egos egging them on as their gymnastics grew more absurd.

Trys and I huddled together by the dunes, watching them splash about the surf. Trevor snored loudly at our feet, his baby's bonnet tied awkwardly around his chin.

"Here." She handed me the nearly empty bottle of wine, her sailor cap crooked on her head. She'd wooed a US Navy skipper for it, which had earned her fifth place. Luxe and her Ferris wheel operator cap placed fourth, while Colette and her bejeweled cowboy hat took third, which she'd aggressively protested. When Trevor reappeared with a lace baby's bonnet, I thought Millie might break a rib from laughing. She had scored a very tall white top hat, while I'd managed to convince a mainlander to trade my fedora for her floral bonnet, but none of us could beat Roger and that outlandish fruit tower.

His dare had been simple: sunrise on the beach.

I shivered as the wind whipped off the waves, carrying their laughter. Luxe's skirt was soaked to her knees, and Roger had fallen on his ass so often he was drenched. "Maybe I should grab some blankets from the barn."

"You and I both know you're not going anywhere." Trys nodded toward where Luxe ran along the surf, kicking seawater at Roger. I'd never seen this smile of hers. Not only free of her pain, but just . . . free. "It's worse than Betty, isn't it?"

How little I'd known of the world when I'd met Betty. Her qualifications were woefully simple: she paid attention to me. But Luxe? She was extraordinary—and utterly unavailable. "Betty who?"

"Oh, Jame-o." Trys leaned against me. "What am I going to do with you?"

"I know you don't care for her—"

"That's not true." She played with the sand, letting it slip between her fingers. "I like that she's scrappy. And she's loyal to her family, which I respect. I just wish she weren't perfectly poised to break your heart."

They shrieked with laughter as Colette walked on her hands, managing to stay upright as a wave lapped against her face. Beside me, Trys's shoulders shook with her silent amusement.

"As if you're any better," I pointed out. "I see the way you look at Colette."

She masked her smile. "No comment. So Luxe and my brother—that's not real, right?"

Dangerous territory, though it was no secret that Dewey had bartered liquor in exchange for Luxe's support in the election.

"She'd do anything for her family. And they really need booze."

"After everything Dewey's sacrificed for this election, and for Luxe, I daresay he's committed." With her head bent, Trys traced a circle in the sand. This was the first she'd spoken of her brother's aging.

He was committed, all right. Committed enough to propose.

"I'm sorry for not telling you sooner," I said. "It didn't feel like my information to share, but I'm still sorry."

She shrugged. "When are you going to tell them about your parents?"

I had been planning on telling Luxe tonight, but watching her laugh with her cousins, I couldn't bring myself to ruin it. Not when they were just finding their way back to each other. "Tomorrow. I should tell Roger first."

Trys rested her head against my shoulder. "No matter what happens, we can always hop on the ferry earlier than planned. On to the next adventure, okay?"

I heard the words she didn't utter: *This can't end well.* As if I didn't know.

"Here." She reached into her pocket. "Hold out your hand."

I did as Trys asked, and she dropped something cool into it.

My mother's brooch.

"Where did you . . . ? *How* did you—"

"I went back and made a trade with Mag." She avoided my imploring stare.

"But how? What did you give her?"

Trys lifted a shoulder. "Nothing important."

"Trys." I waited until she faced me. "Tell me."

She exhaled through her teeth. "Okay, fine. I stopped by my parents' and sat through an entire lecture. But I didn't take a single gem from them," she added quickly. "I snuck into my old jewelry box and found something the old lady couldn't resist."

Stunned, I sat there, staring at the brooch. "I can't believe you did that for me."

But I could. She'd traveled for me. Faced her past for me. Before she could resist, I scooped her into a big hug. "Thank you."

She groaned but didn't swat me away.

Millie sang a raunchy tune in falsetto, using an empty wine bottle as a microphone.

"Did they drink more than us?" I asked.

"They must have."

Colette returned first, seawater dripping from her hair, her clothes. "Jesus, it's cold! Aren't you going to hug me?"

"No way." Trys scooted away from her. "You fools chose to get wet, not us."

Ignoring her protests, Colette wrapped her dripping arms around Trys's neck. "Afraid of a little water?"

"I didn't say I was afraid." Trys remained perfectly still as Colette leaned closer. "See?"

"Are you sure? Because it feels like you're shaking."

"Only because it's freezing out here." Trys met Colette's fierce gaze.

Lightning quick, Colette kissed her. A peck on the lips, a dare and a test.

I turned to Roger, whose grin already stretched from ear to ear.

Trys wrapped her arms around Colette's neck and kissed her deeply. Millie and Roger whistled and cheered. Luxe's eyes found mine, her tired smile a mirror of my own. Even if she felt the same, I'd never be able to kiss her like this, in front of our friends. Not with Dewey in the picture.

Breaking the kiss, Colette wrapped her arms around Trys. "See? It's not so cold."

"Not for us. We Revelles were practically raised by the ocean." Roger threw himself onto the ground and waved his arms to make a sand angel. The wet sand clung to him like breading on a chicken cutlet.

Millie flopped beside him. "Remember when our mothers used to bring a bar of soap and wash us right here?"

I didn't move. Didn't take one goddamned breath.

"A bar of soap and a bottle of wine." Untangling herself from Trys, Colette lowered herself next to Millie, scooting close. "I don't think I had a proper shower until I was ten."

A smile played on Millie's lips. "They sure knew how to have fun."

The three of them lay there, Luxe lingering by their feet as if she still wasn't sure if she should join them. Her eyes found mine, and my chest squeezed. *Go*, I mouthed to her.

Carefully, she sank into the sand beside them.

Millie stared at the stars. "Those summer nights were the best."

"*They* were the best." For once, Roger didn't filter the longing from his voice.

The beach grew silent, save Trevor's soft snores and the waves lapping the shore. In the faint glow of dawn, their solemn faces seemed younger.

"I miss them." Colette's voice was heartbreakingly quiet.

Roger sighed. "Me too."

"Me too," Millie whispered.

Luxe's eyes squeezed shut as she wrestled with her own grief.

I'm in love with her.

The realization hit me like Cupid's arrow, right through my chest. Damnit, it was true—completely hopeless, but true. I loved her when she was brave onstage, even more when she was brave offstage. But most of all, I loved her now, with her family. Truly *with* them, and not wielding her secrets like a shield.

I loved her, and I'd never be able to tell her. Not when she couldn't let herself feel anything for me. Soon she wouldn't even be able to *look* at me without thinking of her mother's murderers.

Luxe stared at the stars above, unmoving, save the pinkie she hooked around Colette's.

Twenty-One

Luxe

"Luxe?"

Someone dared to pull the sheet off my bed. With a groan, I wrestled it over me once again.

"Get up, my sweet. Rise and shine."

The last thing I wanted to do was rise *or* shine, no matter how irritated Dewey sounded.

Seven hells. *Dewey.*

I threw the sheet off to find my very rich, very peeved benefactor standing in my very messy bedroom. His scowl made him look even older. Would I ever get used to this face of his?

"Late night, I see." His forced smile strained at the corners.

I blinked at him innocently. "My cousins and I might have had a *little* too much fun."

"Just you and your cousins?"

Damnit. I'd overslept, and he'd turned into a jealous mess yet again. If I tapped into my little inkwell, he'd see the onset of my pain. He might even grow suspicious.

"Just us. And Trevor, of course." I smiled shyly, pulling the sheet to my chin. "Might I have a moment to freshen up?"

He kicked a stray piece of clothing off his shoe. "Was Jamison there?"

"Oh, that's right. He's with Roger so much, I counted him as a cousin."

His frown only deepened.

I rose, my hair a mess, my nightgown unwashed. It would have to do. Swallowing the caustic taste of my own breath, I cracked a smile. "I missed you. Give me a moment to freshen up, and we'll have breakfast."

"Breakfast was hours ago. You slept right through it, along with three interviews I'd scheduled for us. Your afternoon dress rehearsal begins in thirty minutes. You do remember the election is tomorrow, don't you?" He glanced at his watch, his mouth tightening to a thin line. "I'll wait outside."

As soon as the door clicked shut, I gripped the bedpost and tapped into my inkwell.

The swift pain, plus the hangover—I lowered myself to the bed, squeezing my head as I fought the urge to let go of the swelling, churning magic, the pressure cresting, bursting . . .

Finally, I opened my eyes, my mind adjusting to the barbed thing flailing against it. Dewey's lightstring was easy to find: a dark, jealous blight just outside my door. Damnit. I should have monitored him more closely, should never have slept in.

Last night had been incredible, but *this* was the cost.

I leaned against the bedpost, my head spinning as I coaxed away each of his negative feelings. *You trust me. You're happy with me, and I'm happy with you.*

Lies, lies, and more lies. I was going to whisper lies down his lightstring for eternity.

Step one, get Dewey to give me a damn jewel. Step two, figure out the rest.

Once Dewey's lightstring was calm, I slipped on my rehearsal attire and pulled my hair into a big, bushy bun. The leotard must have stretched in the wash, because it hung loose on my hips. *You find me attractive*, I whispered down Dewey's lightstring. Judging how he'd looked at me when I'd awoken, that was a lie, too.

I checked myself in the full-length mirror hanging on the back of the door. Beneath my nose was slick with blood. I hadn't even felt it. As soon as I got that jewel, I'd let my body rest.

Once I cleaned my face and brushed my teeth, I swung open the door and greeted Dewey with a big smile. "Shall we?"

His lightstring calmed as I infused it with contentment. The halls were crowded with Revelles getting ready, but he hardly noticed them glaring at us. He never should have entered our personal chambers. My bedroom. He was growing bolder.

"Are you staying for rehearsals?" I asked lightly.

His lightstring surged with frustration. "I have the boat cruise, remember?"

Whoops. For Dewey's second-to-last day of campaigning, he'd found a way to advertise his new fleet of heated ferries. During a round-trip cruise to Manhattan, he'd rub elbows with his most generous campaign contributors: business moguls from New York with summer homes in Charmant and a vested interest in being on the bootlegger's good side. The press was invited, too, of course, along with one hundred lucky constituents.

"Of course." I squeezed his arm. "We'll meet for the event on the promenade after?"

Our schedule is a priority for me. You are a priority for me.

"I'm already looking forward to it." He leaned closer. "Have you given more thought to my proposal?"

Amorous maroon tinged his lightstring, but mostly, it was a steely, determined gray. I sharpened my smile. "Have you given more thought to filling that setting with a diamond?"

"If people think you have control over me, they'll lose faith in my ability to govern fairly." He checked his watch. "I have to go. I'm meeting Roger by the ferry."

"Roger's going with you?" I couldn't hide my surprise.

"I asked him to represent the Revelles, since you're busy rehearsing."

He wouldn't hurt Roger, would he? I wouldn't be able to charm him all the way in New York. "How thoughtful."

He patted my arm. "If we're going to marry, I need to get to know more of your family. Especially since Roger's leaving in a few days."

I tripped over the top stair. "He's leaving?"

"He and Jamison have some orchard job they do every fall. Trysta, too, though field work is unsuitable for a Chronos." Dewey studied me, his brow creasing.

They were leaving. All three of them. And soon.

I'm unbothered by their departure. You are my focus.

"I have to go, my sweet. I'll see you after tonight's show." He brushed his lips to mine as if he'd done it thousands of times. A familiar kiss from a stranger's mouth.

In the mess hall, Millie's forehead was pressed against the kitchen table. I perched beside her, my palms scraping the worn wood. "That smells delicious."

She startled, spilling her coffee. I grabbed a rag to soak it up.

"Good, you slept later than me for once." She rubbed her eyes. "I can't believe we have to perform trapeze like this."

"I can't believe we let Roger convince us to stay out all night."

"The *night* isn't the problem; it's your boyfriend Dewey's insistence on daytime rehearsals that's killing me."

"He's *not* my boyfriend," I said, a little too sharply.

An easy smile settled on her lips. "I know. Just making sure you do."

My entire body ached as I took the seat beside her. Dewey's lightstring rumbled with displeasure as he stepped farther away from the Big Tent, and I sent a dash of happiness down it.

"Are you wearing my leotard? You're swimming in it."

I pulled at the loose fabric. "It's just old, I think."

Millie stifled a yawn. "Last night was fun."

"It looked like you and Trevor had a good time," I said casually.

Her smile softened. "He asked if he could 'call on' me. How sweet is that?"

"Mildred Revelle, are you blushing?" I pressed the back of my hand to her cheek. "I believe you are!"

"Would it be insane of me to go out with an Edwardian?"

"Far saner than what I'm doing. Or Colette, for that matter."

Millie sipped her coffee. "She keeps pretending it's just for fun, with Trys leaving soon, but I know better."

Apparently, I was the last to know of their plans to go. "When exactly are they leaving?"

"Why don't you ask Jamison yourself?"

"He's here?" I scanned the empty mess hall, as if I had somehow missed his tall self.

"Who else do you think brought *good* coffee from Sweet

Buns?" She nodded toward the hall. "Last I saw, he was visiting Nana."

To talk about his parents again, I'd bet. I gave her arm a gentle squeeze. "I'll see you in the rafters."

With a groan, she rested her forehead on the table again. "Don't remind me."

Sure enough, Jamison stood at the end of the hall with Nana, both of their lightstrings as purple as the Big Tent's stripes. Grief.

As I approached, Nana swiped at her eyes. "Morning, my sleepy girl. Rehearsal starts in twenty."

"Are you all right?"

"Perfectly fine. Where's Dewey?" With her back turned, Nana couldn't have seen Jamison's smile falter. And he couldn't have seen the glisten in her eye.

As if I needed her to stir up trouble for me. "Uncle Wolffe's looking for you," I lied.

She gave me a knowing look, but her smile was sincere when she turned back to Jamison. "You come visit me whenever you like, you hear?"

"Thank you, Mrs. Revelle. That means the world to me."

"Please, call me Nana." She opened her arms for a hug, and he slipped into them, crouching slightly so he didn't tower over her. He was so thoughtful, even in how he hugged. So kind, even though his lightstring tinged the tiniest bit green with envy around my enormous family. For a fleeting moment, I let myself picture how gently he'd hug Nana as she grew older. I pictured him being a permanent part of all this. The Big Tent. Our life.

Nana winked as she sashayed past me. Once she rounded the

corner, I turned back to Jamison. "What were you two talking about?"

"My parents." He ran a hand over his hair, ruining whatever he'd used to tame it this morning. "I didn't want her to feel bad for not telling me about them herself."

"Nana hasn't felt bad about anything in decades."

He didn't crack a smile. "Can we go somewhere to talk?"

I had rehearsal, but I wouldn't make him wait, not when he was finally ready to tell me. Not when he was hurting. "Follow me."

Jamison had to duck under the doorframe of the next hall to avoid smacking the top of his head. "Are you staying to watch the dress rehearsal?" I asked, keeping my tone light. Foolishly, I didn't want his visit to be a quick one, especially during a rare, Dewey-free day.

"Your grandmother invited me. Last one, right?"

"Last one here. Then one final run-through tomorrow in the new theater. And then it's showtime." I stole a glance up at him. "I hear you're leaving."

His step faltered. "Trys wants to stay for the election, but we'll leave right afterward. That's the plan, at least."

He didn't want to leave. Worse, I didn't want him to go. "So two more days."

He stopped walking, those bright eyes searching. "That's right."

Don't go. It took everything I had to suppress the selfish thought as we stared at each other in the empty hall, the humid air in the Big Tent heating by the second.

I pasted on a bright smile. "You've got a job lined up, and I've got a winter theater with my name on the marquee. We'll both be swimming in gems! Or dollars, I presume."

Before he could utter another word, I pushed open my bedroom door.

Colette sat on the bed, her tight curls freed from her usual elaborate updo, her skirt hiked up to her waist. Two lipstick-stained mugs sat on the night table.

"What is it?" Jamison asked behind me.

"Shh!" I tiptoed backward.

Colette's graceful footsteps creaked the floorboards. "Trys?"

I pulled Jamison's arm and yanked him through the next door, a small linen closet. He opened his mouth, but I pressed my palm over it.

Colette's feet padded just outside, and we both froze.

Jamison exhaled against my palm, his breath warm. Heat radiated from each point where our bodies pressed against each other in the narrow closet. His knees leaning on my thighs. His lips beneath my hand.

In a few days, he'd be gone.

I removed my hand from his mouth, letting it trail down his cheek. He watched its path with haunted eyes.

Neither of us dared move.

Gone was the darkness in his lightstring, replaced by something brighter. Something smoldering. His hands found my waist, and my heart quickened.

That first kiss, we'd been strangers. Now I *knew* him. I knew how he nagged Roger about taking sips of water when they'd been drinking, how his first instinct was to throw a punch when someone insulted his friends, no matter how futile the fight. How he turned lemons into cleaning solution and panicked each time we let go of the trapeze.

I couldn't help myself—I let my hand graze his hair. Soft and thick, just as I remembered.

His gaze drifted to my lips, then back to my eyes. He wasn't jumping away this time. Neither of us was any good at self-preservation.

A force as natural as gravity pulled me closer, and I wrapped my arms around his neck, lifting onto my tippy-toes. A torturous inch remained between my mouth and his. I hovered there, fighting the selfish urge to close that gap.

Trevor would know. And if Dewey asked, Trevor would be forced to tell him. Dewey's jealousy would shatter his fragile ego, unleashing the cruel streak he kept hidden beneath his polished exterior. Dewey had made all his bootlegging competition disappear. What would he do if he viewed Jamison as competition for *me*?

And even if we managed to keep it a secret, Jamison would have to watch me dote on Dewey. Touch Dewey. Look at Dewey like Jamison looked at me right now: like I was the sun and the moon and all the stars. Anything to get Dewey to give me a jewel.

"I'm glad you have a job lined up." I almost sounded like I meant it.

His heart beat rapidly against my chest. "There are always other jobs. Here, on Charmant."

Stay, I longed to say. It took everything I had not to pull him closer. "What about Roger and Trys?"

"I don't think either of them is ready to leave, though they won't admit it."

Stay.

But . . . Dewey. The election.

Summoning all the strength I could muster, I forced myself to step into the mercifully empty hallway. As Jamison emerged, I turned away, not wanting to see the hurt seeping into his light-string. He deserved better.

"This is Trys's watch." He bent to pick it up off the floor, then held out the crushed glass face. A folded note dangled from the platinum cuff.

I snatched it. Thick, creamy paper, sealed with a black wax symbol: a clock.

My blood turned to ice.

We always win.

"Fire! Fire!" a child's voice yelled.

Jamison shouted something, but he might as well have been speaking a different language.

The Chronoses had struck again.

TWENTY-TWO

LUXE

The Chronoses were here, in my home, coming after my family—

"Luxe." Jamison shook my shoulders. "We have to go."

He pulled me down the hall, ducking his head into each room along the way and shouting, "Fire!"

This couldn't be happening. Roger had to be pulling some elaborate prank. Or my uncles, up to their antics again.

But the bells were ringing, and a noxious, smoky scent poisoned the air.

Colette ran into the hallway, struggling with the skirt of her dress. Jamison grabbed her arm. "Where's Trys?"

"She went to the kitchen, but she didn't come back." She searched the hallway. "Maybe she got out already?"

Jamison's face fell. He tried to turn around, but the crush of Revelles swept us farther from the kitchen. He took my hand, not letting the crowd separate us. "C'mon!"

The three of us rushed toward the beachside exit at the end of the hall, but my family started to trickle back. "Door's jammed!" someone yelled.

Over their heads, flames crawled along the ceiling.

Flames, in our home. Our very flammable, canvas home.

We barreled down the hall, slowed by the crowd. Everyone was here for the last rehearsal—too many people, moving too slowly . . .

The smoke thickened as we neared the theater. Glass shattered and screams erupted, the soundtrack of a nightmare. As we shuffled into the pit, the surge of my family behind us nearly knocked me off my feet. I risked a look up—

Fire crept toward the ceiling's pinnacle, raining ash and debris down on us.

"What's the holdup?" Jamison pushed toward the front doors. The customers' entrance.

"We need to leave *now!*" Uncle Wolffe shouted.

"The doors are sealed shut!" Millie yelled back. Nana was beside her. At her feet was little Clara, a protective arm over her brother's shoulder. Her tear-filled eyes found mine, and I couldn't muster a brave face.

Every single person I loved was in this tent.

"It doesn't shut!" Colette barked. How many times had we tried to keep the tourists out, or the wind out, or the sand and the rain and the damn drunks out, to no avail?

"Let me through." Aunt Caroline pushed her way toward the door. She fisted the fabric beside it and attempted to pull it apart.

It didn't give.

"What the hell?" She tried to punch through the door, but her fist didn't even make a sound.

Flames devoured the wooden stage, crackling and roaring as they slid into the pit, driving us closer to the unyielding doors.

Jamison pulled me to my knees and tore off a piece of his under-shirt. "Smoke rises, so you need to stay down. Put this over your nose and mouth. If it gets hot, find a way to wet it, okay?"

"Try it again!" Nana cried.

Aunt Caroline hurled herself into the door. It still didn't budge.

I'd singed the tent with enough candles to know that you could burn a hole in the canvas fairly quickly. But the walls of flames were unrelenting, as if the fire itself had been charmed to burn slowly but spread quickly, leaving us trapped at the hollow center of a ten-story bonfire.

Only an Effigen could combine the properties of several flames into a single potent fire, but they were our allies—they wouldn't.

"We're trapped!" Sweat dripped from Colette's forehead, her brow. We were going to boil alive before we even burned.

I closed my eyes and dug into my little inkwell, searching for Dewey's lightstring. His ferry might not have left yet, and if I could find the right combination of emotions to get him to hurry back . . .

His lightstring was nowhere to be found. He was out of range.

We were all going to die. To burn alive—

No. Dewey would undo it as soon as he heard.

But if he were going to travel to help us, *he'd already be here.*

Jamison and my uncles tried to yank the doors wide open, tried to hurl themselves against the dark wood, but the doors didn't even shake.

"Something's blocking them!"

It might be an Effigen fire—but a Chronos would have the foresight to block the exits.

They sealed the doors.

They fanned the flames.

They meant to kill us all.

Coughing filled the cavernous space. Coughing—and those encroaching flames, spreading across the pit now, trapping us against the hot canvas, the crush of people tightening.

Uncle Wolffe cracked a wooden chair over his knee and tried to jam the leg through the side of the tent. My eldest cousins searched the canvas walls, punching and kicking the many patches we'd added over the years. Nothing worked.

A baby wailed. His mother cradled him close and sang to him, her voice breaking.

Beside me, Colette tore off the bottom of her dress and wrapped it around her mouth. "I'm going to find something sharp."

"Wait!" My coughing fit stole the word before she could hear it.

"Luxe?"

The smoke was too thick; it was going to kill us before the flames—

"Luxe," Jamison repeated. His button-down shirt was gone, and sweat stained the neck of his torn undershirt. "Luxe, Trys isn't here."

"No one's coming to help," I whispered.

"I need to find Trys. She would have traveled already. Something's wrong."

"They *always* win." My mother. My aunts. Had they felt like this as they sank to the bottom? Knowing they had to watch each other die? They'd choked and gasped and filled their lungs with salt water as they witnessed the light blink from their beloved sisters' eyes, knowing they couldn't help them, couldn't save them, couldn't stay alive for *us*.

"Focus, Luxe." Jamison gripped my shoulders. "You're not powerless. Not even close."

I blinked at him, at the urgency in his voice.

I was the advantage my mother didn't have, the quirk in our magic to balance the scales.

Slowly, I nodded.

He kissed my forehead hard before he disappeared in the smoke.

Digging into my inkwell, I hardly felt the rush of pain, the pressure slamming against my skull. No time to cry out, to do anything but steady my breathing. The infamous Big Tent of Charmant was aflame. There were people outside. Bystanders. Tourists poised to watch with detached horror, or Charmantians who didn't wish to risk meddling in Chronos business.

I grabbed their lightstrings.

Many were frozen in fear. A few were already taking action, though I couldn't see them or hear them. I doused them all with an overdose of empathy, determination, and grit.

You want to help us. You want to find something sharp and rip a hole in the tent.

I gripped their lightstrings, carving away each misgiving, each wavering feeling of hopelessness. Only compassion. Only action.

My mind went black as I extended my reach, embracing the Effigens blocks away, dousing them with the need to act on behalf of my family. To bring some antidote to whatever substance the Chronoses had used.

I gripped every damn lightstring in the Night District, stripping them of all feelings except the urge to save us. *There are children inside!*

My head slammed against the too-warm wooden floor, the magic threatening to crack open my skull. Still, I clung to those lightstrings with everything I had, even as the darkness closed in around me, even as sunlight ripped into the tent, blue sky and—

TWENTY-THREE

JAMISON

The Revelle tent was a maze of smoke and flames.

I couldn't find the kitchen, or even my own feet. I had no idea where I was going, let alone where I was.

Kitchens had ovens. And ovens needed vents. So the kitchen had to be along the outside wall. The canvas one.

On all fours, I crawled through the darkness.

"Trys!" I yelled. Screams sounded in the distance. Panicked screams, not end-of-life screams. The Revelles were still trapped.

Another dead end. I tried the next. And the next.

The hallways weren't straight, and my mental map was precarious at best. If I'd had Luxe's magic, I could have found Trys's lightstring. If I were an Edwardian, I could have heard her thoughts. And if I could fucking time travel, I would have gone right back to sunrise, when we were all safe on the beach. Together.

But I had no magic, no tricks.

"Trys!" Still no response.

Finally, my hands found the tough fabric of the outer tent. Feverish but ungiving.

The kitchen had to be somewhere along here.

Minutes passed like hours. The screams quieted. A good sign. Unless it wasn't.

I could have died right then, searching for a friend who wasn't even there. Caught up in the same ancient rivalry that had ensnared my parents. My . . . sister. But Trys was my family now, and her watch had been left beside that damn threat. They couldn't take her, too.

"Trys!" Turning slowly on my hands and knees, I wound through another narrow hallway, away from the canvas wall—

More flames. I skittered back from the heat licking my face.

"Help!"

I froze. A female voice. Not Trys's.

"Where are you?" I fumbled on my hands and knees down what seemed to be a hall.

"Over here!"

I crawled toward the voice as quickly as I dared, crushed glass and fractured wood piercing my palms. The smoke was so thick, so low, I could hardly see two feet in front of me.

"Hurry!"

So close to that voice. My free hand pressed against the wall until part of it gave way, like a door swinging open.

Kitchen doors.

"Hello?" The smoke was thinner here, though it rushed through the swinging doors. I rose to my feet. Pots and pans jangled over my head. Several fridges. Cupboards full of hard-earned food.

And two figures curled atop the island at the center, unmoving. Trys and—

Dewey.

I lunged for Trys. Despite the relentless heat of the fire, her skin was cool. Clammy.

"Trys?" I shook her, but she didn't respond.

She was pale. Dewey, too, his strangely older face lifeless.

Glass crunched behind me. I swiveled to see a woman pointing a gun at me.

She squeezed the trigger.

My shoulder erupted in searing pain. Before she could shoot again, I dove to the floor, crying out as I hurled myself to the other side of the island.

Leaving Trys and Dewey on the counter between us.

"What are you doing?" I exclaimed. "We're all going to die if we don't get out of here!"

Tears streamed down the woman's face. "I'm sorry."

Her hands trembled as she cocked the gun again.

I ducked, and the bullet ricocheted off a pot hanging from the ceiling.

The fire roared outside the kitchen. Glass shattered, and in the distance, sirens wailed.

Her sobs gave away her position. I risked a peek over the counter. Her iridescent ivory horns caught the light from the flames.

"Stop," I pleaded, pressing myself against the kitchen island. "We can both survive this if you just stop!"

She stepped closer, glass breaking beneath her feet. "He said I have to kill whoever tries to save them. It's the only way to get my son back."

Her son. Now I recognized those horns. "Wait a second. You're Margaret's sister."

The sound of crunching glass ceased.

"We met in Nana Revelle's room. I'm Roger's friend, Jamison. Remember?" I risked a peek over the counter. White streaks snaked through her black hair. She was aging, and fast.

Impossible. She was an Effigen, not a Chronos.

"Your son's missing." That was why they'd been there that day, searching for clues about his disappearance. "A Chronos took him?"

Glass shattered in the distance, the smoke thickening as it slipped beneath the kitchen door. Soon we'd all be dead.

Tears streamed down Rose's face. "If I do this, he'll bring him back."

"Was it George?" The bastard had threatened Trys and Dewey a week ago.

Gun still cocked, she shook her head slightly. "He wore a mask. A Revelle theater mask, like a tiger. He was just here a moment ago."

Every hair on my arms rose. Slowly, I stood, lifting my palms as I glanced around. "A Chronos did the same thing to my parents: he told them if they wanted my baby sister back, they needed to do something terrible to the Revelles. But he used them, and they died without ever seeing her again. I don't want the same to happen to you. Let's get out of here, and we'll find a way to get your son back."

The gun wobbled in her unsteady hands. Every second, more wrinkles crept across her tearstained face.

"Rose? That's your name, right?"

A curt nod, and a sniffle. Smoke thickened just over her head.

"Roger said you make the best doughnuts. He's been bragging about them nonstop since the moment I met him."

A sob escaped her. She covered her mouth with her hand, the heavy pistol trembling in her other hand.

"Can you put the gun down, Rose? We need to get you to a Strattori."

Finally, she lowered the pistol, turning her arms to examine the wrinkles deepening by the second. "What's happening to me?"

I could have cried from relief, had I not had two unconscious bodies and a rapidly aging woman to get out of the fire. "We need to leave."

"I started it," she whimpered. "I used my magic to make the fire spread twice as quickly with half the fuel."

"Okay. What does that mean?"

"It means it's going to burn for hours." She ran a shaky hand over her withering face. Older than her grandmother now. "We have to use the antidote. I'm supposed to get the two Chronoses out, too."

"How?" At this rate, the smoke was going to kill us before we had a chance to escape.

She fumbled in her pockets, pulling out a small vial. Christ, she was startlingly old now, her snow-white hair thinning. A cough overtook her, and I pulled her to the ground, away from the thickest smoke. My hands shook terribly as I removed my undershirt and ripped it into strips.

"Here." I wrapped the fabric around her nose and mouth, her skin shriveling like a raisin. "Give me the antidote. Hurry!"

She lifted a trembling, withering hand, the vial slipping between her fingers.

The little glass shattered.

"No!" I cried, trying to gather it between my fingers, but it was useless. "Do you have another?"

No response.

"Rose?"

She fell to her side, her frightened eyes wide and glassy and utterly still. Gray skin flaked like ash as her body continued to age, even though she was gone.

Gone, without her son.

I swallowed the awfulness of it. Time to find a way out. Fast.

The kitchen's back door was nothing more than a zippered flap in the tent. It didn't budge when I kicked it.

I yanked at the zipper. It wouldn't even wiggle.

Broken glass cut my knees as I crawled back to Dewey and Trys. I picked her up and tried to rouse Dewey, but no response. "C'mon, you bastard, wake up."

He'd have to wait. Trys didn't stir as I cradled her against me and rushed toward the door from which I'd entered—

Flames roared as soon as I kicked it open, so hot on my face, I yelled out. Craving the oxygen, they rushed into the room after us, spreading across the canvas, the ceiling—

We were trapped.

Lowering us to the ground, I leaned against the cupboards farthest from the door, the flames creeping closer.

"Wake up, Trys." I shook my friend, but she didn't respond.

"Trys? Please, wake up."

She could get us out of here. Magic or not, she'd know what to do.

But Trys didn't move. Nor did Dewey when I shook him.

I was on my own.

I could do this. I just needed to think for a moment.

If Roger lost Trys and me at the same time . . .

No. I could do this. I had to get us out.

Laying Trys on the ground against the thick fabric wall, I crawled back to Rose. As I removed my undershirt rag from her face, I tried not to look at the glint of exposed cheekbone between patches of drooping skin. I dragged the rag over the broken glass where the antidote had spilled, soaking up whatever I could. Ceramic shattered as the flames overtook the shelves, sending them crashing to the ground.

I darted back to the tent's outer exit, rubbing the rag over the seam between the flaps, then took a knife from the counter and stabbed at it. The knife bounced back, clanging uselessly to the floor.

The Big Tent trembled, a great beast about to collapse.

TWENTY-FOUR

LUXE

The sunlight blinded me, the smoke stinging my eyes.

"Luxe, answer me! Are you all right?" Millie shook me roughly. "She's bleeding. We need a Strattori."

I lifted my head. Chaos, all around me. Thick black smoke streaming from the Big Tent, blotting out the sky like spilled ink on blue satin. My dazed family in the street, crying, as the tourists watched from a distance. Another spectacle for their entertainment.

"Is everyone okay?" My throat burned as though I hadn't had a drop of water my entire life, and my chest ached something awful, from the smoke, or my magic, or both.

Tears streamed down Millie's soot-covered cheeks, leaving clean trails in their wakes. "I don't know. Uncle Wolffe's trying to do a head count." She shook her head. "You passed out. The smoke—"

I pushed onto my elbows. "Where's Colette?"

"Safe, but . . ." She swiped at her tears. "Trys is still missing."

I need to find Trys, Jamison had said. My heart stopped. "And Jamison?"

"I haven't seen him."

I jumped to my feet, the world spinning, my steps faltering.

"Where are you going?" Millie steadied me, but I slipped from her grasp, my sights set on the front entrance, the firefighters gathered there.

He went back for her. I hadn't tried to stop him, hadn't offered any parting words as he ran back into a wall of flames.

Colette's arms flailed wildly as she argued with her father. With the fire's roar, and the firemen shouting orders, I only picked up bits of what she was saying. *Trys. Die. Useless pricks.*

I grabbed her. "What's going on?"

"Trys is still inside. And these assholes," she practically spat at the firefighters, "are refusing to get her."

"Like we told you, miss, this thing's about to collapse." The fireman tugged at the collar of his heavy gear. "I can't send my men on a suicide mission for one person."

"Two people!" I exclaimed.

Uncle Wolffe's stern face froze. "Who?"

"Jamison." I squeezed Colette's arm as horror washed over her. "He went back for Trys."

"Even if there were a dozen people trapped inside, we're outta time." The fireman winced. "I'm sorry. The most we can do is soak it from the outside so it doesn't take out the whole block, but this thing's gonna fall any minute now."

I could hardly hear myself think, couldn't breathe. "*No.*"

Colette surged toward the flames, but Uncle Wolffe grabbed her. "I can't allow you to kill yourself for—"

"For a Chronos? If they were Revelles, you'd never let them die."

"They're already gone." Uncle Wolffe's grip tightened around his daughter. "I'm sorry."

Gone.

The fireman caught me as the world spun, darkness blotting the edges of my vision.

Jamison couldn't be dead. There was so much we hadn't said, so much we hadn't done.

You're not powerless. Not even close.

I couldn't hear my family as they pulled Colette and me away, as they screamed for Dr. Strattori. Couldn't see my home burning as I dug deeper into my empty inkwell, reaching for any wisp of power, my chest burning, my head shattering . . .

Lightstrings blinked into existence. Pain, so much anguish, the sad blues of the Revelle auras as dark as the noxious smoke. I tried to block out their suffering, looking past an ashen Dr. Strattori as she screamed noiselessly in my face. I kept my focus on the furiously burning Big Tent, searching for the two lightstrings that had to be inside.

I only found one. An earnest one I knew too well, its golden hue stained with anguish.

He was giving up.

"Lie down!" Nana barked. "You're bleeding! Why is she bleeding?"

Dr. Strattori gaped at me as she tried to examine my chest, but I pushed away her cold hands. "He's alive," I rasped.

"What?" Colette gripped my arm. "How can you tell?"

"He's in the kitchen. We have to help him; we can't just—"

"I know. *I know.*" Ignoring Dr. Strattori's protests, she helped me to my feet. "What about Trys?"

297

"I don't know. I can't see her."

"But how can you—" She shook her head. "Never mind."

Millie grabbed our hands. "What are we waiting for?"

"Where are you three going?" Nana called after us.

I didn't have enough magic to charm her into letting us go. Instead, I bowed my head, doing my best to look downtrodden. "I just need a moment alone."

"Me too," Colette mumbled.

Millie dipped her head. "Me three."

Nana shook a fist at us. "If you take one step closer to that tent, I swear on your grandfather's grave, none of you will see the light of day again."

"Yes, Nana," we said together.

Her suspicious eyes bore into our backs as we walked down the street. Slowly, too slowly, with that tent about to collapse . . .

At the corner, I broke into a sprint.

Twenty-Five

Flames licked my feet as I stabbed at the thick fabric to the right of the door. To the left of the door. Above the door. As close to the flames as I dared.

Grabbing the antidote-soaked rag again, I rubbed furiously at the fabric, then stabbed with the knife. Rub. Stab. Finally, *finally*, the knife cut through the black swath of canvas.

I had no time; the flames were closing in and the smoke was unbearable—

I slashed at the tent, widening the hole. Emboldened by the fresh oxygen, the flames leaped off the walls.

"Help!" The destruction around me drowned out my hopeless pleas as I stabbed and stabbed, forming a big X in the tent canvas. A few more inches in either direction, and I'd be able to push Trys through—

Something fell on my back. I cried out, my voice drowned by the devouring flames. We were out of time.

Lifting Trys around the waist, I shoved her feetfirst toward the hole. The angle was all wrong, her body too limp. She needed to be pulled out; she needed—

Trys's legs disappeared, her narrow hips catching against the fabric as the hole ripped wider.

Someone was helping from the other side.

As soon as Trys's feet disappeared, I turned and dragged Dewey off the counter, then dropped him in front of the hole. If I died because I saved this bastard . . .

Feetfirst, his body stretched the hole even wider. Flames licked my arms as I dove through after him, making it as far as my shoulders before getting stuck. That bullet wound screamed like hell as debris rained on my legs. The ceiling groaned something awful, the cupboards opening, dishes spilling to the floor—

Hands slid into mine. Soft palms with calluses from gripping the trapeze swing.

Luxe's strong arms tugged me. Hard.

More people grabbed my arms, helping me as I tried to push my way out of the hole. My legs were burning, my shoulder screaming, my body much too big—

I landed on the soft dirt.

"Hurry! It's going to fall!"

The Big Tent groaned loud enough to wake the dead.

Colette and Millie ran back toward the street, Trys hanging precariously between them. Luxe yanked me into the reeds behind the swaying tent. We half ran, half crawled, until the dirt was more mud than grass. I didn't stop until the sea lapped against my ankles.

The salty air was the sweetest I'd ever tasted, and I gulped it greedily. It soothed my scorched throat, my ashy lungs. As I caught my breath, Luxe barreled into me. She was alive. Her hair was a wreck, and her skin was feverish, but she was alive.

I hugged her tightly against my chest, ignoring the shooting pain in my shoulder as the Big Tent groaned again. "Don't look," I murmured into her hair.

She squirmed to face the destruction of her home.

Swirling plum and ebony stripes folded inward, the enormous poles smacking together with a thunderous *crack*. Like a house of cards in a breeze, it just . . . folded. The Big Tent of Charmant, the Revelles' home, their theater, their everything.

Gone.

Screams filled the air. Mournful, wailing cries. I covered Luxe's ears, turning us away as the plume of dirt and sand pelted our skin, but there was no protecting her from this.

When it was done, seagulls cawed over our heads.

In a daze, we stared at the naked sky where the Big Tent was supposed to stand.

As if remembering herself, Luxe pushed my bare chest with both of her hands, hard enough for me to stumble back. "You're a damn fool!"

"Me? Why?"

She threw her mess of soot-covered curls out of her face. "You went back *into* the fire!"

"For Trys!"

"You could have died! Both of you!"

She was shaking something awful. I reached for her, to hold her against me like we'd done in the closet, when, for a fleeting moment, I thought she'd felt the same. "I couldn't leave her."

"Of course not, I just . . . I thought you were *dead*."

She hugged herself, struggling to regain composure. Blood peppered her arms, her hands, the front of her dress.

"Luxe," I said softly.

Her eyes were squeezed shut, but no tears. Not yet.

"Luxe," I repeated, even softer. Helpless, I stood there, fighting the urge to go to her.

She launched herself at me, burying her head against my injured shoulder, her arms tight around my neck. I held her close, relishing every inhale and exhale against me as she gasped for air, for control.

The pain she had to be feeling. The fear, the loss—I could hardly stand to see her so destroyed. No wonder Roger had convinced Margaret to let him take away her suffering.

Acrid smoke obscured her sweet shampoo as I buried my nose in her disheveled bun. "You stink."

Her shoulders shook with a humorless laugh. "So do you."

"Thank you for looking for me." With Roger in New York and Trys unconscious, no one would have realized I was missing until it was too late.

"Like I said," she murmured against me, "there are three people looking out for you now."

I gripped her tighter, and her trembling arms did the same to me. "You're a good friend."

"You know it's more than that." She pulled back, soot-stained arms still around my neck. "That's the problem. I always look for you. In every crowd, at every show, I always know exactly where you are. No matter how hard I try not to."

"Really?" My heart swelled with each impossible word.

Her eyes searched mine, as if there were any doubt about how I felt. "Really."

I lowered my head, gently pressing my forehead to hers. "I

haven't stopped thinking about you, either. Not since that first night."

She lifted onto her tippy-toes, swaying. "It's a bad idea, getting involved with me."

"It's an *excellent* idea." I wiped the soot from her cheeks. Exhaustion weighed down her smile as she leaned against me, not feigning invincibility. Not feigning indifference.

Her nose caressed mine, heating me from head to toe. "I really shouldn't."

My hands tangled in her mess of curls. "If you want me to walk away," I whispered, my mouth millimeters from hers, "I will."

Her grip on my arms tightened, rooting me in place.

I lifted her chin, closing the distance between us.

"Ahem."

Our heads whipped toward the voice.

Dewey stood between the beach and the blaze, his black suit no longer recognizable beneath the dirt and soot. His legs wobbled something awful, and dark bruises marred the skin beneath his narrowed eyes.

His gaze swept over where I held Luxe against my bare chest. "I see."

Luxe went rigid. "Dewey, I—"

Coughing seized him. Luxe stepped toward him, but he raised a hand. A silent command. "How long?"

"It's not what it looks like—"

"How. Long."

"Nothing has happened, I swear—"

He shook his head, his hands tightening to fists. "I need to see a Strattori."

"Dewey, wait!" Luxe trailed after him, glancing over her shoulder one last time, regret written all over her face.

And pain. The tightness in the corners of her mouth. Her perpetual sacrifice.

TWENTY-SIX

LUXE

My magic sputtered as I reached inward, dragging my nails along the walls of my empty inkwell, pain crackling through my chest like cursed lightning. But nothing happened.

"Dewey!" I ran after him, not daring to look back again and see the hurt written all over Jamison's face. How selfish I'd been, telling him how I felt, no matter the consequences.

There were always consequences.

"Wait!" I stumbled over the curb, acrid smoke assaulting me. We'd lost *everything*. Our home. Our business. Everything we owned.

We couldn't lose Dewey, too.

With my hands on my knees, I tore into myself, searching deeper, deeper, for my magic. Pain oozed from my head, my spine, as hot as those flames, spreading through my chest—

There. Mere drops. I had to make them count.

My rib cage felt ready to burst open under the strain. Night gathered around me, threatening to pull me under, but the light-strings blinked into existence. Dewey's was a tempest, but I didn't have time to sort through his feelings, instead homing in on his jealousy.

Jamison is nothing to me.

"Please!" My voice broke from pain, from exhaustion, from the kiss that almost was. Dewey turned on his heels, his expression as hard as stone.

"I know what that looked like—"

"Do you?" He stalked toward me. "The last thing I remember is being drugged by an Effigen. I wake up to the Big Tent nearly falling on top of me. When I finally have the strength to move, I take off in search of *you*, to ensure your safety. And where were you? In *his* arms. He isn't even wearing a shirt!"

"He got you out of the tent—"

"I've given you thousands of dollars' worth of liquor. I've given you the nicest theater in Charmant. I've given you *my heart*." His voice broke on the last words. "What has *he* given you?"

"Nothing. I just—"

"Exactly: nothing." An insidious darkness poisoned his lightstring. "Has he told you who his parents are?"

"His . . . parents?"

"James and Evelyn Jones. Those names ring a bell, don't they?"

I blinked, those hateful names surprisingly painful, even after seven years.

"I see he failed to mention them." He coughed again, a deep rattling that wouldn't cease.

Jamison's parents were the Joneses? The ones who'd drowned my mother and aunts?

Another one of Dewey's tricks—it had to be.

"Pocket," Dewey wheezed, patting his coat. I slipped my hand into the pocket, removing a wad of newspaper clippings.

CHARMANT COUPLE CHARGED IN TRIPLE HOMICIDE

EDWARDIANS CONFIRM CHARMANT COUPLE DROWNED REVELLE DARLINGS

JAMES AND EVELYN JONES, 30 AND 28, FIRST CHARMANT EXECUTIONS BY ELECTRIC CHAIR

I shoved the clippings into his hand. "I don't need to see these."

He shoved them back. "Look closer."

My throat burned with a sickening taste as I unfolded the smallest article—and stopped.

In the center was a photo of a couple standing on the beach. Identical to Jamison's photo, from the carved dock to the brooch the woman wore. Jamison's brooch.

Jamison's *parents*.

The Joneses with their infant daughter in 1905, the caption read, *weeks before they reported her missing. Not pictured is their son, Jamison, whom neighbors say hasn't been seen in years.*

"He lied to you, Luxe. You see that now, don't you?"

The article shook in my soot-stained hands. Jamison was a *Jones*? The magic-haters who'd killed my mother, my aunts?

The photos matched. There was no other explanation.

"He's trouble. I won't have him get between us." Dewey stepped closer. "Do you understand me?"

He was telling me this while my home still burned, right behind us. Even if it was true, it was unfathomably cruel.

A person showed their true colors under duress, Nana liked to say. Dewey was a goddamn Chronos, through and through, trying to manipulate me when he thought me weak. If it were just me, I'd spit on his fancy suit and curse the day I ever agreed to our arrangement.

But the Big Tent was gone. The Fun House, too. No shows. No customers. No *home*.

Dewey was my family's only hope, especially if *his* family wasn't done with us.

I dug deeper into my inkwell, that strange pressure in my chest threatening to snap my spine like a wishbone. Now, more than ever, I needed a jewel to supplement my magic. And if it had to be an engagement ring, so be it.

You trust me. You don't want to lose me. You feel how much I love you, and you love me.

I let him see my desperation as I took his hands. "I feel *bad* for him. He has no money, no family, no prospects in life. I was kind to him, and he latched on to me. When the Big Tent collapsed, he comforted me, but it meant nothing, I swear."

The dimmest spark of relief blossomed in Dewey's lightstring, and I clung to it. "So the two of you never . . . ?"

"Of course not." *You trust me. I'm completely in love with you.* "I'll swear in front of Trevor, if it'd help you feel better. I just pity him, that's all."

The hateful words slid off my tongue like spoiled milk, and Dewey lapped them up. He tugged on his lapels. "I have friends, you know. They'll make him disappear, if I say the word."

Disappear, like the other bootleggers. "He's Trys and Roger's best friend. Let me find a way to let him down gently."

Dewey's lightstring darkened, the allure of violence too tempting. I tried to temper it with whatever drops of magic I had left, the taste of iron sharp on my tongue.

"He needs to be gone," he finally said. "And if he refuses, we're doing it my way."

I wouldn't let it come to that; *couldn't* let it come to that. "Thank you, Dewey." *You feel loved by me. You're happy with me.*

He raised my hands to his mouth, kissing my knuckles. "Move in with me."

"What?"

"Your home is gone. Forget about propriety. I can pay a priest to wed us now, if you'd like. But I need you safe."

I racked my mind for any alternative, anything that prevented me from spending the night there. Not just tonight, but always. There was no going back.

What choice did I have?

You want me to be with my family tonight. But his lightstring hardly moved in my grasp.

Blades sliced through my chest as I dug deeper for any wisps of power remaining. There had to be more in there somewhere, but the pressure in my head swelled as I dug deeper, my empty inkwell ready to burst.

"You're bleeding." He leaned closer, pressing his handkerchief to my nose. "Let's get you to a Strattori."

I eased my grip on his lightstring. My magic needed time. *I* needed time.

More than that, I needed a big, fat jewel.

"I'm okay." I took his handkerchief and dabbed at my nose. "Too much smoke."

"Come home. I'll have a Strattori meet us there."

"What about my family?" Even if we could afford the hotels, they were full for tomorrow's election festivities. My family had nowhere to go.

"I'll have blankets brought to the winter theater. They can stay there for the time being. My queen, however, deserves a castle." He laid a soft hand on my cheek.

I glanced around. Flames still ravaged the heaping pile of destruction that was the Big Tent. Revelles still wept in the street, and Jamison—well, Jamison deserved an explanation. "I don't even know if everyone made it out. Let me check on my family first."

Pitch-black anger burst from his lightstring. As I soothed it, the world tilted.

"Two hours." He gripped my shoulders and pressed his mouth to mine. Hard. "Send the boy packing, check on your family, and return home. Trevor won't leave your side until then. Understood?"

Jamison. Gone.

I lifted my chin. "Understood."

TWENTY-SEVEN

JAMISON

We laid Trys on the cot and waited.

Her dark blouse rose and fell as her lungs struggled to fill with air. The soft whistling that accompanied each exhale was nothing like her thunderous snores. Too quiet.

According to Dr. Strattori, the next twenty-four hours were critical. If she didn't wake by tomorrow night—election night— she might not wake at all.

"I know this isn't the time," Millie whispered to Colette, "but her pantsuit is *fantastic*."

As Colette stroked Trys's hand, she cracked a wilted smile, but her eyes didn't leave Trys.

"It must be the pinstripes," Millie continued. "I can't pull off pinstripes. They make me look too—"

"Curvy?" Roger croaked, his voice like sandpaper. He'd been boarding one of Dewey's new ferries when he heard about the fire and all the Revelles trapped inside. By the time he found us, his shirt was drenched with sweat, and his vocal cords ruined from yelling.

"Huh. I was going to say 'fabulous.'"

My stitched-up shoulder hurt something awful as I sank into the hay. Dr. Strattori said the wound was clean, that I was lucky the bullet had only grazed me. She'd said it reluctantly, as if a dead mainlander wouldn't be the worst outcome.

"Lucky" was not how I'd describe today's events.

Millie filled a tin cup of water and handed it to Colette, who drank it absentmindedly. "Her cane burned in the fire."

"I'll steal one from the lost and found." Roger rubbed his head, no sign of his usual efforts to protect his carefully styled hair.

"What lost and found?" Colette asked. "It's gone. Every inch of the Big Tent is gone."

Her words hung heavy over all of us.

"Do you think she'll travel?" Millie asked softly.

If Trys did, today would cease to exist. For everyone but her, there'd be no memory of that sinister smoke cloud licking our heads, no heart-pounding fear. No Luxe on the beach. *I always look for you. In every crowd, at every show, I always know exactly where you are.*

"She won't travel," I said. "She won't want to erase what her family did today. We need to remember it. All of us."

"Well, I, for one, wouldn't mind *not* losing everything in a fire and just taking Trys's word on the whole ordeal." With a sigh, Millie leaned against the barn wall.

Colette pushed Trys's dark hair from her face. "The fire started four hours ago. Even if she woke and traveled right now, that'd be four hundred hours off her life, which is . . ."

"Sixteen days." I winced. "Each hour is another four days."

Millie blanched. "When you put it like that, I quite prefer our magic."

"That's the part I don't understand." Roger leaned forward, resting his long arms on his knees. "Why did Rose *Effigen* age rapidly? You're sure that's what you saw?"

As if I could forget her lying there, hair silvering, gray skin flaking away. "She looked just like Frank Chronos did in the alley."

Millie shivered. "How positively awful."

"How positively *strange*," Colette said. "I'm sorry, Rog. I know you knew Rose."

"She and Margaret are close. *Were* close." With a groan, Roger pushed himself to his feet. "I'm going to see if the Effigens need anything. Or if anyone's found George."

He couldn't sit still, not when he knew Margaret was suffering. Even after three years, it was so hard for him to stay away. "Do you want company?"

He shook his head. "Stay with Trys. If she wakes, find me."

A cold wind rattled the barn as Roger left. I shook off the blankets we kept over the hay and laid one over Trys, offering the other to Millie and Colette.

Millie pulled the scratchy wool over her and Colette's shoulders. "Luxe got another one of her nosebleeds during the fire. And she was doing that weird crumpled-up face, like before she goes onstage. I swear to God, she was using her magic—but how?"

Colette scrunched her forehead. "And she closed her eyes and literally located Jamison. What the hell was that about?"

Two sets of sparkling eyes turned my way. I busied myself rotating my arm to test my injured shoulder, trying my best to appear casual.

Colette's eyes narrowed. "You know something, don't you?"

"Me?"

"Oh my God, he does know something!" Millie jumped to her

feet, cornering me against the wall. "She has a secret, doesn't she? Something with her magic."

"I don't know what you're—"

"You know we could just charm you into the truth," Colette interrupted.

"Wouldn't I have to give you a jewel?"

Colette held out her palm, beckoning with her fingers. "If you're telling the truth, you have nothing to hide. Just hand one over."

Part of me longed to tell them the truth. Luxe needed help. She couldn't continue to carry the burden of her family alone.

But it wasn't my decision. "This isn't a conversation you should be having with me."

Colette groaned. "She'll never tell us. She'll just hide in my father's office until we stop asking."

"Please, Jamison," Millie pleaded. "We just want to know if she's okay. She hardly ever sleeps. And she's losing weight. None of her costumes fit right anymore."

"If she's in danger, you would tell us, right?"

Was Luxe in danger?

She was lonely. Of that, I was certain. She missed her cousins and the relationship they used to have, but her secret had formed a wedge between them.

"Your silence is far from comforting," Colette said drily.

"C'mon, Jamison." Millie kept her gaze trained on mine. "Let us help her."

They loved each other as relentlessly as siblings, as fiercely as best friends. Cousinhood was magic in its own right.

"I'm sorry," I finally said. "You'll have to talk to her."

A weighted look passed between them, another silent conversation.

Millie flicked the tip of my nose. "Be good to her, Jamison Port. If you break her heart, we'll break your handsome face."

"Me? Break *her* heart?"

"She was beside herself when she thought you were a goner." Colette rubbed Trys's hand. "Absolutely heartbroken."

"And she talks to you," Millie added. "A hell of a lot more than she does any of us."

"I don't think that's it. I just—I just never know when to shut up, that's all."

"It's a good thing," Colette said. "You should tell her how you feel. Maybe you can thaw the last bit of ice that's keeping her from us."

"Dewey can provide for her." My body sank under the weight of the truth. Dewey was probably snuggled under cashmere blankets with her right now, his smoke-filled lungs someone else's problem. "He can provide for all of you. Meanwhile, I don't have enough gems in my pocket to buy the morning paper."

Colette waved a hand. "We Revelles don't need much. Besides, Dewey's not her sweetheart. He's her . . . customer, I suppose."

"More like her employer," Millie said.

"Employer. Exactly."

It was worse than that. With the Big Tent obliterated, all their survival hinged on Dewey's generosity—and on his being elected mayor tomorrow. "Does it matter?"

"Of course it matters!" Colette's chin jutted forward. "If everyone who paid for our company laid claim to us, we'd be empty shells with nothing left."

The doors flew open, wind rushing in.

Luxe. How much of that had she heard?

She entered stiffly, her mouth creased in quiet pain. Her hair was still a wreck, her leotard torn, and her long legs streaked with the same lethal soot in Trys's lungs. A faint sheen made her face shine in the candlelight.

"There you are!" Millie threw her arms around her. Over her cousin's shoulder, Luxe's mask of poise fractured, revealing her bone-deep exhaustion. She'd been through so much today.

And she was *still* charming him.

"How's Trysta?" Luxe asked, avoiding my eyes.

"Keeping us on our toes." Colette's hand didn't stray from Trys's, not even when she twisted to examine her cousin. "You look like you're going to pass out again. Sit."

"I'll rest soon enough."

"Where are you sleeping tonight? You're always welcome here in the barn, isn't that right, Jamison?" Millie elbowed me, her tired smile tinged with mischief.

Luxe couldn't see me blushing, not while she so expertly avoided looking my way. "Uncle Wolffe's fitting as many people as he can in the orphanage. And Dewey's letting the rest sleep in the winter theater."

"How generous," Colette said flatly. "Sleeping on the floor."

"Better than the streets."

Colette arched her brow. "I can't imagine him letting his *star* sleep there."

"Actually, I'll be staying with him." Luxe studied a crack on the floor as scarlet crept over her ashen cheeks.

Silence. Even the wind ceased whistling through the barn.

Of course he'd found a way to use the fire to further ensnare her. That was the natural order of things in Charmant: the Effigens and Revelles despaired, the Edwardians observed, the Strattoris stayed out of it, and the Chronoses prospered.

Colette's eyes narrowed. "You can't do that."

"This isn't the mainland, Col. No one cares about propriety."

"It's not about propriety, it's about being here for your family."

"You need to rest!" Millie exclaimed. "You collapsed during the fire, and you haven't even seen a healer. You need to be with *us*."

Luxe shifted on her feet. "Dewey's had a rough day, too."

Colette folded her arms over her chest. "Oh, poor Dewey! Did the creepy old guy have *his* home burn to the ground? Was *his* girlfriend almost killed by her own family?"

"His family tried to kill him, too." Luxe pinched the bridge of her nose. "He inhaled quite a bit of smoke."

"And I'm sure that's someone else's problem now. Someone desperate enough to get paid to ruin their lungs."

They stared at each other: two stubborn Revelles, each trying to protect the other.

Finally, Luxe looked away. "Trevor's outside. He wanted to make sure you were comfortable having him come in."

To give them much-needed privacy. Even though he worked for Dewey, Trevor was all right in my book.

"Of course." Millie checked her hair in the mirror.

Trevor entered uncertainly, glancing around the barn. When his gaze landed on Millie, his face fell. "Miss Revelle, I'm so glad you're okay. I was so worried when I heard the news."

"You really mean that." Tears glistened in her eyes.

"Of course I do."

Before the first tear fell, Trevor cut across the barn and knelt beside her.

As Millie buried her head in the crook of his neck, Luxe finally looked my way and nodded toward the door.

Grabbing my jacket and a blanket, I slipped into the night after her.

The wind whipped off the ocean, but Luxe avoided the shelter of the dunes, instead turning farther down the beach. She moved slowly, each step labored. I offered her my arm, but she shook her head.

"Are you okay?" I asked. "What happened with Dewey?"

"Not here," she murmured. "It was hard enough to shake Trevor."

With each step, the giddy music of Main Street faded, replaced by the rustling reeds and the hush of the ocean. Luxe was so lost in her thoughts, she didn't even notice me studying her as she marched us farther away from civilization. The full moon painted her in strokes of silver, highlighting the faint bruises under her eyes, the gauntness in her cheeks. She'd been running herself ragged all day—all summer—and she showed no signs of stopping.

Even now, she was still charming Dewey.

A pier rose from the water in the distance. Luxe slowed. "If we sit under there, it might not be so cold."

"The blanket should help."

She picked a spot close to where the weathered wood met the dunes. Despite the shelter from the wind, the cold crept in through the wet sand beneath the flannel blanket. Luxe shivered, and I covered her shoulders with my jacket, her skin icy under my fingertips. Her eyes finally lifted to mine, a protest forming on her lips.

"You're turning blue." And there was something thrilling about seeing her wear it.

She stared at the dark ocean. "My mother used to say this was the quietest place in Charmant. With seven brothers and sisters, she needed hiding spots."

Without the cacophony of the Night, or the Big Tent's music lilting over the beach, it felt like a different world entirely. "It's peaceful."

"Jamison . . ."

I could practically see the wheels turning behind those guarded eyes. Whatever she was about to say didn't bode well for me.

"Dewey told me about your parents. What they did."

My heart sank. There it was.

"You should have told me."

"I know." I couldn't even look at her. "I was planning on it, but—"

"You've been acting strange all week. That's how long you've known, isn't it?"

Of course she'd noticed. There wasn't an emotion on Charmant that Luxe didn't see. "I was going to tell you last night, but you were having so much fun. And the thought of you looking at me the way you are now . . ."

"How am I looking at you?"

"Like I'm the son of the people who took your mother from you." Bile burned the back of my throat, but I forced myself to face her.

She winced. And she didn't deny it. "I think it's time for you to leave."

"Leave the beach?" I stared at her. "Or leave Charmant?"

Her silence was all the answer I needed.

"Luxe, look at me." I turned her chin toward me, unable to hide the desperation in my voice. "I'm sorry, okay? When I found out, I should have told you right away, it's just . . . My parents caused so much pain. Not just for you, but Millie, Colette. *Roger.*"

Between the fire and Margaret's family, Roger's grief was already overflowing. There couldn't be a worse possible time to lay this on him.

"You should have told me. *Me.*" She jabbed her finger against my chest. "I've told you all my secrets."

"You're right. I have no excuse. I just—when I walk into the Big Tent, your family greets me like I'm one of them. They tease me and put me to work, just like they do Roger." The truth of my words struck me like an ax. I loved the Revelles. All summer, they'd let me pretend I was one of them, and I didn't want to ruin the ruse.

I forced myself to stare right at the hurt shining in her eyes. "The selfish truth is that I wasn't ready to give that up. Once everyone knows, I won't be Roger's orphan best friend anymore. I'll be the son of the people who murdered their loved ones, and they'll never look at me without thinking about that." And neither would she.

The ocean threw itself onto the sand and the tide dragged it back. Over and over.

"I blame you for keeping this from me," she finally said, "but not for what your parents did. I've always believed the Chroneses were involved somehow."

"Dewey didn't tell you that part?" Of course he hadn't.

She frowned. "What part?"

I explained what I'd learned from Mag about my sister and the Chronos who kidnapped her. How my parents sent me away for my protection. The years that passed—seven whole years, they were alive and missing me desperately, while I was stuck in that blasted orphanage, missing *them* desperately—before they relented to the Chronoses' demands.

"That's terrible," she whispered.

"My parents still made a choice."

"Hardly a choice at all." She slipped her cold hands in mine, and my heart swelled like a balloon. "So that's how the Chronoses avoid getting caught. They force desperate people to do their dirty work."

Like Rose Effigen, who only wanted to see her little boy again. It wasn't right that she was gone. That her son was still missing.

It wasn't right at all. "Do we know where George Chronos was during the fire?"

"Wolffe's already on it. But I meant what I said, Jamison. You should still leave."

Her hands continued to grip mine. For someone who wanted me gone, she didn't seem eager to put any space between us.

"Because of Dewey?"

"Does it matter?"

"Of course it matters." Because it had to be Dewey. The thought that she'd want me gone for other reasons, that she regretted what she said on the beach—*that* was intolerable.

"You were going to leave in a few days. Leave tonight and get to your orchard job early."

"I'm *not* leaving Trys." *Or you.*

I couldn't walk away from Luxe, not when she was more trapped than ever. As if magic-less me could help her. No wonder she was resigning herself to Dewey.

I stood and faced her. "So what's your plan? Charming him every second of every day?"

A defiant shrug. "If that's what it takes."

"You're going to collapse like you did that first night. Or he'll ask Trevor the right questions and discover what you're doing. And then what?"

"I'm not going to use my secondary magic forever. Just long enough to get him to give me a jewel, and then I'll make sure he does everything in his power to keep my family safe."

She had an answer for everything. And *she* was always the answer. "So he's just going to hand over a big, fat ruby if you say please?"

"More like a diamond ring."

I gaped at her, at the pink blossoming on her pale cheeks. "You'll *marry* him?"

"I prefer to think of it as a very long engagement." She let sand fall between her fingers.

Christ, she was playing with fire. I crouched in front of her. "He'll never let you go."

She still wouldn't look at me. "I'll use the jewel to replenish my magic when I need to, and I'll charm him into keeping his promises to my family. Once enough time has passed that his family can't undo our progress, I'll slowly charm him into growing bored with me."

She had it all planned out. As much as I hated to admit it, her plan could work—as long as he gave her a jewel. A goddamn ring.

"So that's why you want me gone. So you can have a happy engagement with the potential mayor, without any trouble from me."

"*He* wants you gone." Her voice caught, the only hint of emotion as she looked away. "And it's probably for the best."

I took her hand and she closed her eyes, those long lashes resting against her cheeks. "Tell me you want me to leave, and I'll go. Just tell me what *you* want. Not what Dewey wants, or what your family needs. What do you want, Luxe?"

It was the only thing that mattered.

Her whiskey eyes pleaded with mine. She didn't want to say it.

"What do you want?" I repeated, this time softer.

"It doesn't matter," she whispered, "because I can't have it."

My pulse thundered through my veins. "It matters to me."

Fear flickered across her face. Leaping ten stories above a crowd was no problem, but *this* frightened her.

"I want a different life, one where I don't have to pretend to care for someone to keep my family safe. I want to be free of Dewey, free of the Chronoses. And I want to be good enough for you."

I stared at her, not daring to move. "You don't think you're good enough for *me*?"

"I've never met anyone like you. You're kind, Jamison. All the time. You're brilliant. And humble. And I haven't been able to stop thinking about you since that first night in the Fun House. But I'm not like you," she added, her voice breaking. "And I *have* to be with Dewey. I don't want to hurt you, but—"

"You can't hurt me."

"I'm a Revelle." Sadness glistened in her moonlit eyes. "There's no way for this to end without you getting hurt. Which is why you have to leave. My life is too messy. *I'm* too messy."

"You feel the same?" I was breathless. Floating.

She wore no masks as she softly replied, "Of course I do. Ever since that damn kiss."

I pressed my free hand to her cheek. Our foreheads met.

"That one didn't count," I murmured. She hadn't even known who I was, and I hadn't realized everything she had at stake that night. "We deserve a do-over."

The words had barely rolled off my tongue before we kissed.

Her mouth met mine with a gentleness that sparked fire through my veins. Still, I kissed her slowly, savoring the thrill of her lips brushing mine. She'd had my heart in her hands all summer, but there was still so much we couldn't say, so much she wouldn't let herself feel. Yet each tender kiss was laced with confessions, whispered promises we didn't dare utter aloud. It was a dance of possibilities—a life without Dewey, without our parents' intertwined fates.

I pulled her closer, and she wrapped her night-chilled arms around my neck, deepening the kiss. My hands got lost in the tangles of her hair, my breath stolen by her soft lips. They grew bold against mine, no sign of her perpetual pain as our mouths found each other, over and over. I held her as if she might disappear, but she melted against me, erasing every millimeter of space between us. Her hands ravaged my hair, every pass of her lips leaving me desperate for another. The damp sand underneath us was a chill I hardly felt as I ran my hands down the firm muscles of her back, her soft gasp setting me aflame. I was utterly hers.

There was no turning back.

Her mouth grazed my jaw, and I buried my groan in the nape of her neck, kissing away soot and ash and sweat and sand. Her legs tangled with mine as my heart beat so rapidly she had to feel it. She tore at the buttons of my shirt, her hands cold against my chest. I captured them in mine and broke the kiss, pressing my forehead to hers.

"You're freezing." I ran my hands up and down her bare arms, covered in goose bumps. "Maybe we should—"

"No. No more waiting." Her swollen lips formed a line of resolve. "My home is gone. Time travelers are gunning for us. Who knows what tomorrow will bring?"

Ash from the Big Tent still clung to us. Far from the perfect time, or the perfect place, but she was the perfect girl. Magic or not, I'd been right that first night: Luxe Revelle was my destiny.

Lowering myself over her, I ran a hand through her tangled curls. "I'm yours," I whispered. "Always."

TWENTY-EIGHT

LUXE

We lay entwined under the pier. Sweaty, shivering, unable to move.

It had been perfect. *Jamison* had been perfect. The things he could do with those strong hands, that clever mouth. My toes curled at the memory.

"You're shaking." He pulled me closer, and I let myself melt in his arms. Lying here with him was almost enough to forget the Big Tent was in ruins. And that the Chronoses were still out there, somewhere, disappointed they hadn't killed us all. And Dewey's threats. And the election—the polls opened in a matter of hours.

The Big Tent was gone. Soon Jamison would be, too.

Reality wedged itself between us, sharp and uninvited. Dewey's mood grew more restless by the minute. Anger had tangled him in its dark web, and detangling him required more magic than I had left. I needed to save some for tomorrow night. I needed a damn jewel. I needed *rest*.

And yet I couldn't bring myself to disturb this enchanted moment.

Jamison thumbed the loose strap of my leotard. "Magic or not, I think I fell for you the moment I laid eyes on you."

I snorted. "Definitely magic."

"I almost jumped off the balcony for you, you know."

The memory of him clambering over the railing made me smile. "I noticed."

He settled against the blanket. "The Fun House was even worse. I think I've replayed every word you uttered a thousand times since. At least *before* you made me jump out the window."

My heart squeezed. "I wasn't using magic after the show."

"Really?"

I traced the line of his jaw. "My inkwell was empty."

He rolled onto his side and tucked one of my frizzy curls behind my ear. "I wonder if we ever met before," he said softly. "Maybe we played together on the beach when we were little."

Jamison was from Charmant—from the Night District. His parents had owned that boat rental business a few blocks from the Big Tent. "Do you think," I began, "if the Chronoses hadn't interfered, and you'd grown up in the Night, we would have still ended up here, on this beach?"

"I know it." No hesitation, no trace of doubt in his voice. "I would have had a ridiculous crush on you long before you noticed me."

"I wouldn't have been the star," I pointed out. "My aunt Adeline would have handed over the reins to Colette."

His warm hands cupped my face. "Luxe, I couldn't care less that you're the star. Hell, it'd be much easier if you were a backup performer."

We both heard the words he didn't say: *So Dewey was someone else's problem.*

"Even if my parents were still alive, we would have ended up here." He planted a soft, slow kiss on my lips. "You're beautiful, you know that?"

I fought back the urge to point out that I still smelled like that terrible smoke, felt sand in unspeakable places, and would not have noticed if a seagull had nested in my hair.

"And this"—I combed the unruly tendrils falling over his forehead—"has been driving me crazy all summer."

"I know, I know. I need a haircut."

"Don't you dare." After tonight, I'd never even know if his hair was long or short.

Dewey's lightstring slipped from my grasp yet again. Time to face reality.

My exhaustion clung to me like a lead blanket I couldn't lift. It was an effort to stand, and even harder to keep upright. Jamison helped me fix my disheveled leotard, then wrapped his jacket around my shoulders. I'd hold on to it forever, a token to remember his scent, his touch.

But where would I keep it? I had no bedroom anymore. No home.

He rubbed my arms for warmth. "Do you want to come back to the barn?"

I groaned, leaning into him. "I want to board the next ferry and never return."

"Then let's do it."

I gave him a look.

"I mean it," he said, those bright eyes alight. "Let's find some desolate place where no one cares about the Chronoses or the Revelles. I'll teach at the only schoolhouse for miles, and you'll start a dance studio. Or you can sing. Or you can do absolutely nothing, if you'd like."

I laughed, and his smile was so sweet, I wanted to bottle it up and keep it forever. "Living together unwed on the mainland? What a scandal!"

"Well, if you're concerned about propriety, Miss Revelle, the boat captain could perform the ceremony. As soon as we leave Charmant."

"And do we have children in this fantasy of yours?"

"Lots, of course."

My eyes widened.

"I mean, very few! Only one or two."

I couldn't sustain my smile, not when Dewey's faint lightstring still wavered just over Jamison's shoulder. A leash, tethering me to him.

Jamison frowned. "What is it?"

I stared at the sky, the smoke from the Big Tent veiling the stars. "When I was little, I drove my mother crazy with all my talk of the world outside Charmant. She worried I'd disappear forever, like my father. She didn't understand that Charmant is my home, that I'd always return. But in this fantasy of yours, we'd never be able to set foot here again. I'd never see my family again."

Like embers in the wind, our dreams vanished.

"If you want to stay in Charmant forever, then I'll stay forever, too." He pressed a kiss to my forehead. "You're not alone in this mess anymore. We'll find a way out together."

"I wish you could stay," I said honestly. "I wish this weren't goodbye."

"What do you mean, goodbye?"

"Because you're leaving," I reminded him, hating every word. He kissed each cheek gently. "I'm not going anywhere."

"We talked about this." I tried to keep my voice steady, tried not to betray how much I wished he could stay. "You need to leave. Right away."

"Yes, but that was before I knew you feel the same as me. I can't leave you now."

He was so stubborn, so optimistic, even now. "I'm glad we had tonight, Jamison. I truly am. But it doesn't change anything. My family still needs me to keep Dewey happy."

His brow furrowed. "You can't mean to tell me that you're actually going to marry him."

"If that's what it takes to get a jewel and keep my family safe, then yes." I let go of him and turned away. "I'm late, in fact."

His silence grew heavier with each crash of the waves. I shook the sand from my hair and straightened my leotard, gathering the strength to walk away for good.

"You can't." His voice was hardly a whisper over the crashing ocean. I couldn't look at him, couldn't bear to see his lightstring.

"I told you," I whispered. "I told you this was goodbye."

"There has to be a better way. You can't—you can't become his *wife*." His voice tripped on the last word. "I can talk to Wolffe. Or even Dewey—"

"No." I couldn't even think of Jamison hurt, Jamison *dead*. "I'm really glad we had tonight, but my situation hasn't changed."

"But that was before I knew how you felt. Before we kissed." He pressed a hand to my cheek. "Luxe, I think I'm falling in—"

I covered my ears, backing away from him. "Don't say it."

"Love? But Luxe, I—"

"*Don't* say it." I'd been selfish enough. I didn't deserve those three words from him.

He nodded, his face brave, but hurt flashed through his lightstring.

"It's not you," I said quietly. "I told you. I can't love anyone." Even now, a small, selfish voice inside urged me to turn my back on my family, on the dangers we still faced, and to leave Charmant with Jamison right now.

As if Dewey wouldn't time travel and make sure I never left.

Jamison caught my wrist as I turned away. "Don't give up. We have to keep fighting."

Anger flashed in Dewey's lightstring, as dark as the smoke that still rose from my home. Bracing myself, I gripped it tighter. "*This* is how I fight. Get the jewel, tame the beast." The beast who, by tomorrow evening, could be mayor.

He watched me as I shrugged off the warmth of his jacket. "I may not be able to see emotions like you, but I know a dog with a bone when I see one. He'll never let you go. Not until there's nothing left of you for him to take."

Every muscle in my body tensed as I grabbed Dewey's lightstring once again. It was becoming too much—the pain, the Big Tent, the long night ahead of me. "Goodbye, Jamison. I really hope Trysta is okay, but either way, you need to leave."

It'd be safer for them all off Charmant, Trys included. And she wouldn't let anything happen to Jamison. She'd traveled for him once already. She'd do it again.

"Don't walk away," he called after me. "Please, Luxe, don't make yourself live bait."

With every heavy step away from him, wind whipped off the

water, drowning out the rest of his protests. Dewey's lightstring grew red-hot, and I nearly cried out in pain as my pitiful drops of magic snuffed it out.

Dewey's lightstring fell from my grasp a dozen times before I reached the wrought iron gates outside his mansion. My magic had all but blinked out, leaving me with a splitting headache and bone-deep exhaustion. Even if opening night weren't tomorrow, I'd have to use it sparingly.

A long bath, a little sleep, and I'd pull myself together.

Trevor waited at the bottom of the long driveway. He nearly collapsed with relief when I stepped underneath the streetlamp. "Oh, thank goodness! He was ready to have my head."

"I'm sorry. I wanted to—"

"Better if you don't tell me." He offered me his arm. "I can't read his thoughts well from here, but he's in a mood."

We began the ascent up the driveway. "How mad?"

"Livid. At us both."

"I truly am sorry." Every decision I made had consequences far beyond me. I needed to remember that. "From now on, I won't put you in that position."

He squeezed my arm. "After the election, I'll organize a fundraiser at my church. Maybe a clothing drive, or we'll collect household supplies. Whatever the Revelles need."

"You'd do that for us?" Tears threatened as I regarded Trevor. My friend.

"Of course. It's about time our families worked together. Besides, we both work for Dewey now."

"I don't work for him." But my protest rang hollow.

No Big Tent. No Fun House. Like it or not, Dewey's winter theater was our only hope of ever being able to rebuild.

Dewey waited against the tall columns framing the entrance, his arms folded tightly across his chest. My magic was too weak to wash away the anger written all over his face.

With lips still swollen from Jamison's kisses, I grazed his cheek. "You didn't have to wait up."

He glanced at his watch. "You were supposed to be here nearly two hours ago. I've been worried sick."

"It was hard to leave my family." I cast my gaze to the polished marble floor. "There was so much to look after."

"And who looks after you, my sweet?" He pressed a hand to my back, guiding me into his cavernous foyer. "I have a Strattori waiting for you in my study. Go upstairs and get washed up first."

The warm glow of the Strattori's candles were visible through the glass panes of the study's French doors. "I thought the Strattoris were holed up in the cliffs." Helen was the only one I'd seen in weeks.

"For the right price, I can get anyone to do anything." He halted his step, turning me to face him. "You inhaled quite a bit of smoke. And you fainted. Again. I need to make sure my star is ready to help me win an election tomorrow."

I hardly felt sturdy enough to traverse his grand staircase, let alone follow him around all day *and* perform trapeze at his party tomorrow night. But I fixed my smile, squeezed his hands, and gripped the railing as I followed two pretty maids upstairs.

The bath, at least, was exquisite, the water hot enough to leave my skin pink and tender. The warmth soothed my pounding head and sore muscles. More than once, I had to pinch my eyelids open to keep from falling asleep. By the time I emerged from the claw-foot tub, the water was black with the sooty remains of my home.

Numbly, I watched them swirl down the drain.

The closets were full of dresses tailored to my size. Day District gowns with heavy skirts and muted petticoats, the sort of frills my cousins and I liked to mock. Far too many for Dewey to have acquired them all tonight. And the vanity drawers contained a hairbrush just like the one I'd had at home, only newer. My hair serum, too, the one Colette used to tame my curls. I combed it through my wet hair, watching in the oval mirror as ringlets began to form.

He hadn't traveled to buy me such trivial things, had he? That would be unhinged.

With my damp curls pinned away from my face, I padded down the stairs in a white ruffled nightgown. I hadn't worn anything this innocent since I was a little girl.

Dewey's and the Strattori's hushed voices drifted from the patio as I followed his maid to the study. She closed the French doors behind me. I half expected her to lock them.

The ivory candles of a traditional healing ceremony cast long shadows along the walls. Those candles were more disconcerting than the echoing halls, the deafening quiet, even the creepy closets full of frumpy dresses tailored to my size.

This Strattori wasn't my family's perpetually drunk, custom-flouting physician. And this wasn't my home.

Yet it was everything I'd once wanted, wasn't it? Charmant's bootlegger dedicated to my family. An elegant winter theater, entirely ours, if he won tomorrow.

My family protected. Alive.

I walked the circumference of the room, running my finger along leather-bound books with their binding still intact. All for show.

His pedestal desk had but one drawer. My Revelle blood hummed to life as I touched the handle. There was a jewel in there. A massive one.

I tried the drawer. Locked.

With a glance over my shoulder, I removed a hairpin. The lock was the simplest kind, a dead bolt that twisted out of the way when I pressed the pin against the right spot. Every Revelle child who wanted candy from Nana's stash knew how to pick locks.

The drawer slid open without a sound.

A black velvet box sat atop a folder. With trembling hands, I cracked it open and gasped.

The ring was absurdly beautiful. That same radiant Art Deco setting, with a series of sparkling diamonds embedded in the platinum band. The delicate whorls of diamonds thickened to frame the massive emerald-cut diamond centerpiece. As clear as air. As wide as my thumbnail. Too many carats to count.

With this ring, I could charm him for months, maybe even years, before he noticed the stones disintegrating.

But it wouldn't work unless he gave it to me.

As quickly as I could, I combed through the rest of the contents of the drawer. It was organized: a folder of receipts, a ledger I couldn't decipher, and, tucked so far back I almost missed it, a leather notebook. A journal.

With a furtive glance toward the door, I opened it.

Diagrams. Numbers. A list of dates, some crossed out, others circled. Was this how Dewey kept track of how much his body had aged? The times he'd traveled?

I turned the page—and gasped. My mother's name. Over and over.

1. ~~Catherine Revelle alive, Jamison Jones dead.~~ Colette is the star, but Luxe's magic is weak and Catherine keeps her from me. George wins.
2. ~~Catherine dead, Jamison dead.~~ Luxe is the star but her magic's weak. Luxe despises me.
3. ~~Catherine dead, Jamison alive.~~ Luxe is the star, magic strong, but still chooses Jamison. Act like Jamison?
4. ~~Catherine dead, Jamison alive but off Charmant.~~ Luxe is the star, magic strong, but Jamison returns, turns her against me. Make the Revelles need me?

The words blurred together, the list going on and on. Jamison, my mother, Colette, my magic—it made no sense.

Footsteps padded just outside the door. I flung the journal back in the drawer, placed the jewelry box on top, then closed it without locking—

The Strattori entered alone, her simple white garb at odds with the decadent mansion. Circling the room, she checked her candles, hardly looking at me or the desk on which I leaned.

"Lie down on the couch, Miss Revelle." Her voice was cool but not suspicious.

Grateful she wasn't an Edwardian, I obeyed. "I'm fine, just tired. We won't be transferring any injuries tonight."

"Let's see what I find first." She lifted her hands over me, mumbling the long incantation the traditional Strattori preferred. So many unnecessary rules to their magic. I'd seen Dr. Strattori transfer broken bones with a bottle of bourbon in one hand.

How much did I truly know about other families' magic?

Trevor would know what Dewey's notes meant. I'd ask him as soon as I could slip away.

Once she ceased her prayer-like chants, the examination carried on for several minutes. Perhaps, like Revelles, some Strattoris were more powerful than others. Or perhaps all the candles and prayers were props, much like the gaudy fake gems that decorated the Fun House.

But the Fun House was gone.

The Strattori's eyes shot open. She sucked in her breath.

I lifted my head. "What is it?"

"*Shhh.*" The urgency in her voice pinned me in place as she closed the study door. When she returned, she kept her eyes open as her hands continued to hover above me.

They hovered above my chest. My heart.

She couldn't *see* my strange magic, could she?

"Impossible," she hissed.

I rolled away from her. "I think this examination is over."

"What have you done, girl?"

Every inch of me stilled. "What? Nothing."

All the color drained from her face. "Shadow magic. You—You've found a way to use shadow magic."

"That's ridiculous. Shadow magic isn't real." Helen Strattori might have been a mean drunk, but at least *she* had common sense.

"Your lifeline is nearly empty." Seeing my blank stare, she spread her hands wide. "Long, shiny bits of light? The source of our magic. Our life."

I gaped at her. "You mean lightstrings? Emotions?"

"You odious child." She backed away. "If you've seen the lights, you've tampered with the darkness. Do you know what will happen if this gets out? Not only to your family, but to *all* of us?"

"Shadow magic isn't real," I repeated more sternly. "Even if it were, I'd never hurt anyone."

"Not someone else." She lifted a trembling finger. "*You.* Somehow, you've drained your own lifeline. It's all looped and twisted—and dark. I don't even know how you're still alive."

Her words slowed as I blinked once. Again.

Impossible.

I must have spoken aloud, because her anger softened. "I'm sorry, but you're on borrowed time. You have a day or two. A week, at most."

I forced a laugh. My magic caused pain, yes, but it wasn't shadow magic. It couldn't be.

I wasn't *dying.*

"You're mistaken." I rose to my feet, ignoring the way the world swayed, the way pain blossomed from my head, my chest, even without my magic. "I don't see lifelines; I see people's emotions. It's harmless."

The nosebleeds. The weight loss. The fainting.

The pain.

My mind was as thick and slow as mud as she blew out her candles, hastily throwing them in her medical bag without waiting for the wax to cool. "You can't tell a soul," she hissed, reaching for the door. "If a Chronos finds out—"

She gasped.

A knife rammed through her center, a red stain blooming across her crisp white tunic.

My own heart stopped beating.

Dewey pulled out the knife he'd stuck in her back, the silver tip receding like quicksand. She curled onto the floor, her mouth opening and closing, eyes imploring, so full of fear—

Run, she mouthed. Her legs kicked out helplessly, twitching once, twice.

She stilled.

I backed away from Dewey, digging into my little inkwell too late, much too late . . .

He wiped the blade with his index finger and winced. "A waste of magical blood. Wouldn't you agree?"

The backs of my thighs struck his desk hard enough to bruise. "What have you done?"

"Don't worry, my sweet." His smile was as warm as the blood pooling across the floorboards. "We can't have anyone discovering our secret, now, can we?"

TWENTY-NINE

JAMISON

By the time I returned to the barn, Roger was back by Trys's side. She still lay on the cot unmoving, save those labored breaths. Colette still stroked her hand, and Millie looked as if she wanted every detail of what had happened between Luxe and me.

I slammed the doors closed behind me.

Millie's smile faltered. "Where is she?"

"At Dewey's." I motioned for Roger's flask. He appraised me for a long moment before wisely handing it over.

"What?" Millie jumped to her feet. "Didn't you tell her how you feel?"

"I did." I drained the flask, then took our liquor crate off the shelf, holding each empty bottle up to the candlelight. Of course tonight was the night we ran out of booze.

And the only way to get more was Dewey. Fucking Dewey.

"Well, what did she say?" Roger asked.

We still had moonshine. I uncorked the jug with my teeth. "She said what they always say. 'Thanks, but no thanks. You're a good guy, Jamison. If only you had something to offer.'"

Colette's face fell. "She didn't say that, did she?"

"Of course not. But she did say she's going to marry Dewey."

"What?!"

Millie jumped to her feet. "Marry Dewey? You can't be serious."

"I wish I weren't."

The worst part was, she was trying to protect us all. That's all Luxe ever did: protect those she cared about.

But she wouldn't let me do the same for her. And why would she? I had no magic, no money, nothing to get her out of this mess. She needed Dewey. She was going to let him hold her. Kiss her. Stand before a priest and *marry* her.

The acrid moonshine sent me into a coughing fit. Roger lifted a brow but said nothing.

Millie crouched beside me. "But she cares for you! I know she does."

"Does it matter?"

"You're upset—"

"I'm fine." I took another swig and smiled through my teeth. "This isn't the first time a girl has realized there's no future with a broke orphan, isn't that right, Roger?"

"Luxe isn't Betty," Roger said carefully. "She's at the end of her rope. We all are."

"What a lousy day." Colette held out her hand for the moonshine. Reluctantly, I passed it to her.

"They killed Rose Effigen. Took her son." Roger looked down at Trys, his face long. "They can't keep getting away with this."

Just like they did to my parents. My sister.

"George tried to kill Trys, too." Millie shook her head. "*And* Dewey. His own siblings."

"They're the only time travelers on our side," Roger pointed out. "If Jamison hadn't found them, they'd be dead, and we'd be defenseless."

"If George wanted them dead, they'd be dead," I muttered.

Colette arched her brow. "He knocked them unconscious, then lit the Big Tent on fire. I don't think that's Chronos for 'I love you.'"

And yet they were alive. "George Chronos could have had Rose shoot them, but he specifically told her to save them instead. He was sending a message. That's why he left his little calling card with Trys's watch."

We always win. The exact same words he'd used after he sucker punched me.

"Why are they doing this to us?" Millie's voice was flat. Defeated. "It's not like *we're* running for mayor."

"It doesn't matter." Colette kept her eyes on Trys, her free hand trying—and failing—to brush away the tight curls falling over her face. "Publicly supporting Dewey is like staging a coup. Now they're teaching us a lesson."

"Will they ever let us be?" Millie asked quietly. "Haven't they taken enough?"

Roger jiggled his little sack of gems. "Why don't we ask our spunky little friend? I think it's time to wake her up."

I spun around to face him. "You can do that?"

He pretended to look affronted. "Jamison, don't tell me you believe all that *Oh, Luxe is the most powerful Revelle* nonsense. All I have to do is find the jewel our dear Trysta gave me, and I'll charm her into feeling very, very awake."

Colette sat up straight. "What if she's not ready to wake up?"

"Want me to wait for you to fix your hair first?" he teased.

"My hot comb's buried in the ashes," Colette mumbled, rubbing Trys's hand. "What if you make her worse?"

"Then we'll fetch old man Dewey to undo my error."

Dewey could literally bring back the dead. Luxe couldn't overlook that sort of power, not after everyone she'd lost.

Marriage couldn't be the only answer. There *had* to be another way to keep the Revelles safe.

"Now to find the jewel." Roger poked around in his worn leather pouch.

Millie peered over his shoulder. "I can't believe you still have your little revenge stash."

"It's not a revenge stash, it's a *just-in-case* stash, and of course I do."

"Trysta willingly gave you a gem?" Colette asked.

Roger's smile was nothing short of smug. "I see she hasn't given *you* one yet."

"*I* haven't asked for one."

Millie pulled Roger's arm for a closer look at the gems. "Do you have a jewel from me?"

"I have one from each of you. Here's Trys's. Just needed a little magic to call to it." With a sideways glance toward me, Roger's smile tightened. "Here goes nothing."

Clutching the black opal, he closed his eyes.

Nothing happened, save the glittery silt drizzling between his fingers as his magic extracted its cost.

"It's not working." Panic laced its way into Colette's steely voice. "Why isn't it working?"

The shimmering black dust gathered on the floor. Still, Roger kept his eyes closed.

Trys had to be okay. It had taken the first two years of us traveling together for her to actually trust us. I wouldn't let myself imagine life without Trys, *couldn't* let myself.

The sparkling pile of black sand grew taller.

"Damnit." Roger's brow creased as he dug deeper into his magic, the opal crumbling.

Trys shot upward, clutching her chest as she struggled to breathe.

I grabbed her by the shoulders, easing her against the pillows. Her cough was so dry, so unrelenting, Colette jumped to her feet to fetch water. Maybe Roger had made a mistake, bringing her back so soon.

"Jamison!" Trys rasped, her voice sandpaper.

I gripped her frigid hand. "I'm here, Trys. We're both here."

Roger took her other hand. "Right beside ya."

Her frantic eyes searched my face. She tried to talk again, but the coughing overtook her. Colette pressed a glass of water into her hands, and Trys drank it greedily.

"Rose Effigen," she managed to say. "The fire . . ."

"We know." Grief flickered across Roger's face, but he kept his voice low and soothing. "Dr. Strattori said you're too tough to kill. Your family's going to have to try harder next time."

The coughing overtook her again, and we held her upright as she gasped for air. The water seemed to help, but even as she drank it, her eyes were glued to mine.

"Should we fetch Dr. Strattori?" I asked.

She shook her head, her eyes wide. Panicky.

I leaned closer so she wouldn't have to strain her voice. "What is it?"

"I wasn't the target," she rasped.

"I know. Dewey—"

"Not Dewey," she wheezed. "Not the Revelles." She gripped my shoulder, her panicky eyes burning into mine. "*You* were."

THIRTY

LUXE

"Is the tea to your liking?" Dewey asked.

As if a warm beverage would be enough for me to forget that he'd just sliced through another human being.

"Smells lovely," I replied evenly.

Shadow magic. That was how I charmed without jewels. So if Dewey could use shadow magic, too . . . did that mean Dewey could travel without aging?

But he *had* aged. His premature wrinkles were proof.

He watched me as if I were a cornered animal, ready to run. But he wanted to trust me. In all those crossed-out timelines, he wanted me to choose him.

He wanted a queen.

Taking a careful sip of my lukewarm tea, I studied Dewey over the rim. After what the Strattori had said, I couldn't risk peeking at his lightstring, but he seemed thrown by my reaction to his abrupt violence. He expected me to understand why he'd done it.

Think, Luxe. My family had taught me plenty of ways to ease someone's mood. To loosen lips.

I rose from the table, giving my chaste nightgown a small tug to lower the neckline. Without looking up from his untouched tea, Dewey stilled. I lowered myself to his lap, rested my arms over his shoulders, and kissed him. *Wrong mouth, wrong mouth, wrong mouth,* a wicked voice inside me sang. I pushed it down. "Talk to me, Dewey."

His eyes were still guarded as they scrutinized me. "Trevor, is Luxe using her magic?"

He *knew*. He knew my magic didn't require jewels.

Trevor's voice trembled as he replied, "No, sir."

"And did she use it during that kiss?"

"No, sir."

"Interesting." Dewey's arm slid around my back. "You know, we've had this conversation many times, yet you've never done that."

Every part of me wanted to leap from his lap. How many times had he rewound the clock? Two? Ten? More? And what had happened all those times I couldn't remember?

I schooled my face to a mask of calm. "I'm glad I can still surprise you."

"You must have questions." His thumb traced circles on my lower back.

"I do."

"Ask away."

I leaned into his touch as if he didn't repulse me. "So you can do what I do?"

"We are the same, my sweet." His arms tightened around me.

"How?"

He hesitated. Without my magic negating his insecurities, he didn't trust me.

I shifted in his lap so that I straddled him. His eyes widened, his lips parting as I rested my hands on his chest. "Tell me."

"You are laying it on *thick*." His hands trailed over my shoulders. "You can transfer the cost of your magic. I can do the same."

Panic flooded me, the rush of blood to my head dizzying, deafening. If he could travel without aging, he was unstoppable. He had endless do-overs, endless opportunities . . .

"But you've aged!" I blurted.

He flinched, and I nearly reached for my magic to smooth away his disgust. "Not that I don't like this more sophisticated you," I added, running my hands through his hair.

"A mistake I plan on correcting once I see if I've gotten this timeline right. Like I told you, my brother tried to kill us both." His face pinched. "I didn't have time to use shadow magic. I wasn't prepared, but next time, I'll travel back even further, and I'll stop him long before he pulls the trigger. This wrinkled timeline will cease to exist."

It was an effort not to panic, not to run away screaming. But there was no escape.

Magic always has a cost. Pain was too transient, too cheap a price for what it allowed me to do. But if the pain was truly shadow magic . . .

No. There *had* to be a limit, a weakness for us both. One I could exploit.

"How does it work for you?"

He hesitated. "I have questions of my own, you know."

"A question for a question?"

He appraised me, his hands still caressing. "Trevor, if either of us tells a lie, please interrupt. Understood?"

348

Trevor blanched. "Yes, sir."

"I'll answer your question first," Dewey said. "Like you, I have my familial magic, and my *other* magic, as you call it. To access my other magic, I need the assistance of someone with magical blood. Once I draw blood the right way, a string of light appears."

The right way? Did he perform some sort of ritual? Did his victims suffer?

I swallowed. Hard.

"I imagine it works differently for you, as a Revelle, but the lightstring leads me through their past. It weaves through whatever door they've entered, and keeps going, back and back until the moment they were born. With their lightstring, I can travel backward through time, and I can stay in the past until their lightstring dims entirely and the connection . . . expires, then I'm back in the present."

I turned over every word, searching for a weakness. "And you're free to do as you please in the past?"

"As long as I stay near their lightstring, I'm free to do as I please. Time is shaved off my blood donor's life, not mine."

Blood donor. Lightstrings. My head swirled. "So when you use your family's magic, you take over your past self, because there can only be one. But what happens to the, ah, past you when you follow a lightstring?"

"I love how inquisitive you are. Every single time." He took a sip of his tea, watching me over the rim. "There can never be two of the same person at once, whether I use regular Chronos magic or shadow magic. With Chronos magic, my 'past self' ceases to exist because a new timeline begins. But with shadow magic, whenever I land in my donor's past, my own past self is rendered unconscious. I faint, like you. I've even seen myself lying there, which is strange, to say the least. Once I return to the present, the past continues, only altered."

Dewey unconscious on the alley floor. Frank Chronos rapidly aging. Dewey unconscious in the fire. Rose Effigen growing old like a Chronos.

He was using shadow magic *the whole time.*

His eyes glowed like embers as he leaned closer. "My whole life, my family treated my fainting spells like a weakness—but really, it was a sign of power beyond their wildest imaginations."

Dewey had made Rose set that fire. Somehow, Dewey had made his uncle attack Jamison in the alley. "Why—"

He pressed a cool hand over my mouth. "I gave you three questions. My turn."

I swallowed my growing nausea, not letting myself think about his fingers pressed to my lips, his thighs beneath my buttocks. "I'm all ears."

"Your magic makes you faint, too."

Not a question, but I nodded.

"Why?"

I hesitated. For years, my magic had been a private, unspeakable thing, and Dewey was the last person I wished to know anything of it. But I needed him to trust me. "My magic isn't limitless. If I push myself too hard and use it up, I pass out."

He considered that. "How long have you been able to charm without jewels?"

"Since I was eleven years old. After my mother died." An easy truth, at least.

"Eleven?" Dewey looked to Trevor, who nodded. "Interesting. Your grief probably helped. I believe shadow magic is born out of a certain desperation. But how did you draw blood?"

The Strattori's words echoed in my mind. *You've drained your own lifeline. . . . I don't even know how you're still alive.*

I flicked his nose playfully. "Question for a question, remember?"

His fingers grazed the bare skin of my neck. "Ask away."

"Who taught *you* shadow magic?"

"You did, my sweet." He laughed at my surprise. "Well, not the particulars, but you inspired me. That timeline no longer exists, of course, so you don't remember. You passed out during a dress rehearsal, and I realized that when you were awake, I was in bliss. When you were unconscious, I was a wreck. Eventually, I persuaded you to admit to charming me, even though I'd gone to great lengths to never give you a jewel. You'd found another way. And after some trial and error, I did, too."

His calm, teasing tone sent a chill down my spine. Persuaded? There was no way I had willingly told him anything. "I had to," I said quickly. "I needed to make sure—"

"You were wise to use every advantage you had." He pushed back a wisp of hair from my forehead, the gentle motion so like Jamison's that I held my breath to keep the flood of emotions in check. "Have you drawn *my* blood?"

I shook my head. Dewey turned to Trevor, who nodded in confirmation.

"I can't figure out how you get away with it. No one seems to disappear, except my donors."

The missing Effigen children. The Strattori boys. "I've been really careful to make sure they don't, ah, expire. I'm still figuring it out myself."

His brows lifted. "Perhaps you can teach me."

"I'd like that." I buried my panic, forcing myself to smile at him.

"You and I are unparalleled," he murmured, trapping my hands in his. "Think of how unstoppable we'll be in the mayor's office. I can rewind time for any do-overs, and you can control the people's hearts. Everyone will love us. Even your family. Even *my* family."

Charming the Chronoses. Further ensnaring ourselves in this battle with his family.

"And imagine what our children will accomplish," he continued. "Enchanting time travelers, not limited by aging or gems. They will bend life to their every whim."

Children. With him.

Catherine dead, Jamison alive. Luxe is the star, magic strong, but still chooses Jamison. Act like Jamison?

Those scribblings were timelines. Ones that no longer existed.

Dewey was searching for the proper combination to have the life he wanted. He'd traveled over and over again—*killed* over and over again—so he could have power. Money.

Me.

His thumb traced circles on my hand, and I fought the urge to pull away, not letting myself think about the fact that this vile man had been tampering with my life—my pain and grief and loss—to get me exactly where he wanted me.

"I have one more question."

The walls of the cavernous dining room crept closer, his words echoing.

With gentle hands, Dewey pushed me from his lap, rose from the chair—and dropped to one knee.

Even though I wanted—no, *needed*—this to happen, I still felt traces of Jamison's touch all over me. Still pictured his too-long hair, his messy silk tie loose around his neck, his black eye from trying to box a time traveler. Willing to fight, even when his back was against the wall.

Something inside me fractured.

"Trevor? The ring?"

My Revelle blood began to sing before I spotted the crushed-velvet box Trevor carried. Jewel magic, the answer to my prayers.

Dewey opened the box.

There it was, the largest diamond I'd ever seen, sparkling beneath the chandelier.

"Marry me, Luxe Revelle. You are my only equal. My queen."

It wasn't a question. Deep down, perhaps he knew it was a command.

We both did.

Marriage would protect my family from being on the wrong side of Dewey's wrath. And it would break Jamison.

But with Dewey under my spell, they would all be safe.

Ignoring the sharp glass shards where my heart once beat, I said, "Yes."

Dewey's eyes widened. "Really?"

"I'll marry you. I'll marry you right now, if you'd like." The steadiness in my voice surprised even me.

"Trevor, did Miss Revelle mean that?"

"Yes, sir."

Dewey pulled me closer, his face full of awe. "Is Miss Revelle using her magic?"

"No, sir."

"So this is real?"

I rested a gentle hand against his cheek. "This is real."

His wide grin was so childlike, it was almost endearing. Almost. "Pardon my surprise, it's just that you've never said yes before."

"Well, I'm saying it now."

"You'll marry me," he repeated. "Tomorrow night, at my victory party, in front of all my loyal supporters from Charmant and New York."

From its crushed-velvet bed, the diamond called to me. So close. "Tomorrow night sounds perfect."

Dewey wrapped his arms around me. I imagined he was Jamison and threw my whole heart into the kiss. I crushed him with my lips, giving him the goodbye we should have had at the beach: our mouths desperate, hearts breaking, knowing it was for the best. I kissed him like I might have done in countless erased timelines in Dewey's journals. A murderous time traveler had kept us apart, over and over, and Jamison would never know.

I kissed him as if it were the last time I'd ever see him. As if I needed to let him go.

Once it was done, Dewey pressed his forehead to mine. That enormous diamond still beckoned, inches away. Any moment, it would be on my finger, and he wouldn't be able to hurt another soul.

"Trevor," he breathed, "during that kiss, did Miss Revelle use her magic?"

"No, sir."

Relief flooded his face. "And was she thinking of me?"

My blood went cold in my veins.

Trevor looked distraught. His lips twisted as he tried to hold the words back, but his magic showed no mercy. "No."

Rage flickered in those cold brown eyes as Dewey shrugged me off him. Damn the risks, I *needed* my magic, needed to calm his anger until Jamison's ferry was long gone.

"*Who* was she thinking about?"

I was too slow, too late—

"She was thinking of him, sir. Jamison."

"Because I feel bad for him!" I blurted, those pathetic tears finally spilling down my cheeks. "The reporters will be at the show, and they'll write about our wedding in every New York paper. And it'll break his heart."

"She's telling the truth, sir," Trevor interrupted. He failed to mention the many other reasons I thought of Jamison—

No. I wouldn't think of him now. Or ever again, if I wanted him alive.

Dewey studied me carefully. "I won't be made a fool. If you're double-crossing me—"

"He's leaving. As soon as Trys is well enough to travel, he'll be gone."

"Trys won't wake up for days." He oozed certainty.

Horror froze me in place. He'd done this before—hurt his own sister so she couldn't stop the fire. If he rewound the clocks to do it again, next time he'd make sure Jamison didn't make it out alive.

"I know how to get rid of him. For good." I took his hands and leaned as close as I dared, my nose brushing his. "Now can we please get back to the part where we're ruling Charmant together?"

For a long moment, only the rhythmic ticking of the hall clock broke the silence. I didn't look away, didn't even blink as he weighed my words.

"If I ever see him again," he finally said, "he's dead."

"That won't be an issue."

He looked to Trevor, who nodded. "She has a plan, sir."

A plan to charm you into a docile little puppy.

"Good." Dewey removed the ring from the box, stealing my breath. Power radiated from the exquisite diamond, and my Revelle magic hummed in anticipation.

The bastard handed it to Trevor.

Oh no.

"Trevor, will you put this on Miss Revelle for me?"

No!

The wrong man slid the engagement ring onto my finger.

THIRTY-ONE

JAMISON

"I still maintain that this is a terrible idea," Roger announced.

Sweat dripped from my forehead as I tossed another charred wooden beam in the pile. "Your family just lost everything. The least we can do is stick around to help."

"*I* should stick around to help; *you* should be halfway to New York by now."

With a grunt, I picked up one side of a heavy beam and waited. "Why, because this isn't my family?"

"No, you dope, because a family of time-traveling psychopaths wants you dead."

Trys had recounted the moments before the fire: a crying Rose Effigen, surrounded by candles. The fire spreading within seconds. Rose pleading for Trys to yell for me. Sobbing. Begging her to do it. Trys, seeing the gun, refusing. Rose had covered her face with a sickeningly sweet rag, and the next thing Trys knew, she was in the barn, struggling to breathe.

We heaved the beam onto the pile to be carted away, then paused to rest.

"Jamison." Roger waited for me to look at him.

"I know. George Chronos, who I've known for all of two seconds, wants me dead."

"You did punch him."

"Must have been quite the punch." I wiped my face on the bottom of my shirt. "Or I'm going to be a very big deal in Charmant someday. Maybe I'll open a show of my own and wow tourists with my ability to recite Bible verses under duress."

He didn't crack a smile. "The Chronoses want you dead. It's time for us to go."

I didn't need Luxe's magic to see how much leaving his family pained him. The Revelles were in a bad way. Earlier, Nana had broken down while walking past the Big Tent's ruins, and they'd had to carry her back to the orphanage. Colette and Millie hadn't slept a wink—and tonight, they were performing dangerous acrobatic feats at Dewey's election party.

The show must go on, Colette had said bitterly this morning. They needed money, needed to prove to their skittish customers that they were here for their entertainment. The Fun House business would continue after the curtains closed tonight. Dewey had rooms reserved for the purpose. For a cut, of course.

Dewey: the answer to all the Revelles' prayers.

"I can't leave her," I told him. "He's bad news, Roger. He's never going to let her go."

Roger exhaled slowly. "I know."

"Every time I try to picture getting on that ferry, I see him down on one knee. And she's just wearing that fake smile of hers as he touches her, kisses her, does whatever he pleases . . ." I raked my hands down my face, as if I could wipe the damn scene from my mind. "I can't do it, Rog."

He gripped my shoulder. "I get it. Trust me, I do. But I can't let you throw away your life for her. If she's staying with Dewey, you need to move on."

But he didn't know *why* she was resigning herself to a miserable life. He didn't know about her strange magic, how she couldn't even let herself sleep for fear of dropping Dewey's lightstring. He didn't know how much she suffered every single day.

I wiped my dirty hands on my pants. "I do have my pride, you know."

"Good." He winced. "Because they just got here."

I whipped my head around. Last I'd heard, they'd been making their rounds at the polling sites, a jazz parade trailing behind them. The upbeat music had wafted over the ruins of the Big Tent like salt in our festering wounds. *My* wounds—the rest of the Revelles had taken turns leaving to cast their votes for him.

It wasn't hard to spot him, his chest puffed like a proud boxer and his arm wrapped around Luxe, his shiny trophy.

Roger squinted. "What the hell is she wearing?"

A frilly powder-blue gown better suited for a doll. "I guess Dewey got her a new wardrobe."

"She looks like a pastel marshmallow."

A ridiculous pastel marshmallow. The dress wasn't *her*; it was part of whatever role she was playing, the one she was determined to play for the rest of her life.

Her eyes drifted to mine and widened. Dewey's, too. "She does *not* look happy to see me."

"She did tell you to piss off," Roger reminded me, rather unnecessarily. "Maybe you should take off your shirt again. That seemed to work for you yesterday."

Dewey made a beeline toward us, his head bent like a bull ready to charge.

Let him. Let all five feet, nine inches of him charge.

Her ridiculous dress snagged on the debris as he pulled her arm, his face purpling. She spoke quickly to him, trying to slow him down, but he wouldn't be deterred.

And then his anger just . . . disappeared. As if it had evaporated.

Pain flooded her face as her magic exacted its cost. I took one step, two steps, ready to catch her, but she straightened, her haughty mask snapping back into place. She pressed her hands to Dewey's and whispered something in his ear, her lips brushing against his cheek. Eyes on me, making sure I saw the intimacy of the kiss. As if dragging my heart over the splintered remains of the Big Tent would be enough to make me leave. Still, I couldn't look away. Not as she grazed her mouth over his, lingering there long enough to garner looks.

My teeth gnashed together, pain radiating down my jaw.

With Dewey on her arm, Luxe floated across the wreckage to where Wolffe and the rest of her uncles hauled debris. Her sweet mouth moved as she spoke to them at length.

Her head hung low. Their jaws dropped at whatever she said.

Wolffe's head jerked to where we stood. To me.

"Uh-oh." Roger shifted so his back was to his father, who was storming toward us at an alarming rate, Roger's uncles in tow. "This isn't good."

"What could she have said?" I tried to catch Luxe's eye as she trailed behind them, but she cast her gaze on the rubble.

"He's not slowing down." Roger took a step backward, nearly tripping over the debris. "Maybe we should—"

Wolffe's enormous fist slammed into my stomach.

The air whooshed from my lungs as I was thrown onto my back, charred wood splintering underneath me. I couldn't breathe, couldn't muster a single—

"We let you into our home!" Wolffe's kick landed just above my ribs.

"Our lives!" Another kick. I couldn't even suck in the air to cry out.

"Our *family*." He wound his foot for the next kick—

Roger threw himself in front of me, hands raised. "What the hell are you doing?"

Wolffe glared at him. "Don't turn your back on your family again, son. Stay out of this."

"Not until you leave him alone!"

Wolffe pointed at me. A single finger, trembling with rage. "He started the fire."

"What?" I wheezed. One of Roger's uncles pushed me back down as I tried to stand. "I did no such thing. I swear it!"

"Luxe saw him sneaking around our private rooms right beforehand. She saw him in the kitchen with Rose Effigen."

Christ. She wasn't afraid to play dirty.

Luxe stood a few feet behind them, her head buried in Dewey's shoulder. He held her as if comforting her, all the while leering at me with a victorious grin that I wanted to claw off his face.

Roger barked a laugh. "This is ridiculous. He was with me the whole time."

"*You* weren't there," Wolffe snapped.

"But Jamison risked his life to *save* people! He saved—"

"Trysta and Dewey Chronos," one of his uncles spat. "A little suspicious, now that I think about it."

Behind them, Dewey's eyes narrowed, but when Luxe laid a hand on his arm, he ceased his protest.

Her hand. An enormous diamond ring.

The air rushed from my lungs once again. "He proposed?"

A hush passed through the crowd. Apparently, I wasn't the only one who didn't know.

"Last night." Luxe leaned against Dewey, pausing to admire her ring. "We're to marry tonight, after Dewey is declared the winner."

She couldn't marry him *ever*, let alone tonight. She was supposed to charm him into a long engagement. Once she was his wife, there was no turning back.

She'd gotten a jewel from him—and she was still sending me away.

"Can we all just take a moment and calm down?" Roger still stood in front of me, hands raised as if ready to strike. Slowly, I pulled myself to my feet.

"You brought a traitor into our fold," Wolffe growled.

"Jamison's the furthest thing from a traitor. I trust him with my life."

Colette stepped forward. "I'll vouch for him, too, Father."

"Me too. He's one of the good guys." Millie stared imploringly at Luxe, who looked anywhere but at her cousins. Or me.

Look at me, I pleaded. *Just look at me.*

Luxe hesitated. "I didn't want to have to do this . . ."

"It's for the best, my sweet." Dewey patted her arm. "Go ahead. Show them."

"Since Jamison arrived on Charmant, he's been using a fake name." Luxe handed her uncle a wad of newspaper clippings. "Look at the picture. It's identical to the one Jamison has in his pocket. His real surname is Jones."

My heart slowed to a stop, all my adrenaline gone.

"That's ridiculous!" Roger didn't take the article Luxe thrust toward him, didn't even consider the possibility that she was right. "Tell them, Jamison."

I couldn't look at him. Couldn't utter a single word.

"His parents are James and Evelyn Jones." Genuine pain flashed across her delicate features as her eyes finally met mine. "His parents killed my mother. *Our* mothers."

Colette grabbed her arm. "What the hell, Luxe? Why would you say that?"

Shouting erupted, the Revelles surging forward. Roger pushed them away. "She's lying!"

"Ask him." Unshed tears made Luxe's eyes a deeper amber. "Better yet, ask an Edwardian to confirm it."

Colette and Millie turned to me. Roger, too, rolling his eyes as if this were the most ridiculous thing he'd ever heard. My best friend. My brother.

I couldn't keep my head high, couldn't meet his eyes as I uttered, "It's true."

Roger stumbled back, the look of betrayal on his face worse than any of Wolffe's blows.

The crowd surged forward again. Someone grabbed me, but I shook them off. "But I didn't set the fire!" I exclaimed, trying to be heard over the shouting.

"Impossible." Roger stared at me as if I was a stranger.

"Arrest him!" someone shouted.

"Call the Edwardians!"

"No, let's take care of this ourselves!"

The mob grew around us. Beautiful Revelles, young and old. Aunt Caroline, who, just the other day, had taught me how to knot a tie properly. Uncle Thomas, who had greeted me with a clap on the back all summer. Even Colette and Millie stared at me like I'd drowned their mothers myself.

The Revelles were the closest I'd ever come to a family. And now they wanted to tear me to pieces.

"I had to tell them." Tears streamed down Luxe's face as she finally, finally looked at me. "I had no choice."

She meant that. For her family, she'd break both our hearts. Completely. Irrevocably. And her mask was so carefully crafted, no one saw how much she was sacrificing.

Aunt Caroline glared at me as she embraced her niece. "You did the right thing."

Still, Luxe's eyes bore into mine as if she wanted this moment tattooed on my brain. "Just leave us alone, Jamison. Dewey's my equal in power. My equal in magic. My equal in life."

And then she was gone, eclipsed by the crowd as I staggered from the blow her cruel words delivered. Someone pushed me from behind. Another person grabbed my ankle. And then I lost my balance, falling on the debris, my injured shoulder screaming in protest.

"She's lying!" I cried out to no one, to anyone. "She's just pretending because she's trying to protect me. To protect you all!"

No one heard. And even if they did, they wouldn't have believed me. She was their star. He was their savior. I was an outsider.

"She doesn't want to marry him—*listen* to me!"

Roger pulled me to my feet. Hurt still lingered in his eyes, but he didn't let go of me as he turned to face the mob of Revelles. "If you want to get to him, you'll have to get through me first."

They paused, knuckles cracking.

"Roger, I—"

"Not now." He glanced behind me. "Now, we run."

THIRTY-TWO

LUXE

Jamison was a fool. A big-hearted, bright-eyed fool who'd ignored every warning I'd given him. Who'd stayed, despite the eleven ferries he could have taken by now.

A fool who needed to run faster.

The crowd surged after him and Roger. They were fast, but Jamison kept turning back, searching for me.

The Revelles hate you. They never want to see you again. I never want to see you again.

His lightstring dimmed and dimmed, its golden hue obfuscated by deep rejection. Still, I dug into my magic, fighting the bone-deep exhaustion that threatened to pull me under. I grabbed more Revelle lightstrings to erase their doubts about his role in the fire. I focused on their pain. Their anger. Their need for someone to blame.

No matter how much time passed, no matter if I had days or weeks or decades left to live, I would never, ever forgive myself for hurting him like this.

But he'd live. And so would my family.

Dewey chuckled beside me. "They're going to kill him."

"Trys won't let them."

His nose scrunched with distaste. "That does make him rather hard to dispose of."

Catherine Revelle alive, Jamison Jones dead, his journal had said. *Colette is the star, but Luxe's magic is weak and Catherine keeps her from me. George wins.*

Those scribblings had kept me up all night. Dewey had been playing God, trying to find the right combination of life and death to seize power. And with my help, he was on his way to the mayor's office. All morning, he'd dragged me from one polling center to the next, ordering me to use my magic to charm everyone into voting for him. Each time, he asked Trevor to confirm I was doing as he said.

So I did.

You're on borrowed time, the Strattori had said. But I was still here.

"Well done, my sweet." Dewey patted my cheek. "You took a play right out of my playbook."

"What do you mean?"

"He loves you." He scoffed, and I fixed my ruthless smile to match his. "Love is the greatest weakness. Once you find out who someone loves, you can make them do anything."

Like Rose Effigen and her son. Or Frank Chronos and the son he'd left behind.

If only I could carve Dewey's smirk off with my bare hands.

"Look." Dewey chuckled as he pointed down the block. "They have them trapped."

The crowd surged forward, pinning Jamison and Roger against a wall. A fight broke out, someone's fist connecting with

Jamison's handsome face for the third time this summer. He wasn't even trying to fight back.

Seven hells. They were supposed to scare him away, not actually hurt him.

Pushing through my fatigue, I grabbed more of their lightstrings, the Strattori's warning blaring through my mind. But I'd whipped the crowd into a frenzy. I needed more magic.

Jamison had to get out of here, no matter the cost.

Diving into my magic was like diving headfirst into a frozen lake. There was nothing left but hard ice and terrible pain. The pressure surged in my head, my chest. I stumbled, white lights blocking my vision as I gripped my head. I thought I heard Dewey call my name, but I couldn't stop, not until I found the last drops of magic, somewhere—

My little inkwell shattered.

I cried out, my chest flooding with sharp pain, filling my lungs, drowning me—

"Luxe?"

Ice encased my lungs, and I coughed, the fluid surprisingly warm as it oozed down my chin, into my hands.

"Luxe, what's happening? Are you all right?"

The mob's lightstrings were still clutched in my mind's fist. *You don't wish to hurt him. You wish to let him go.*

"Luxe, damnit, talk to me!"

Dewey's lightstring was dark and slick as oil as I gripped it. *You're not worried. You're not violent. You're happy and content and preoccupied.*

His panic and his anger subsided.

"I'm okay." Each inhale unleashed a flurry of fresh glass in my chest. But the mob was receding. Jamison was limping away, Roger beside him.

A dry, rasping cough seized me. Dewey rubbed my back, and I fought the urge to squirm.

"Should we fetch a Strattori? Can't have you coughing like that tonight."

"It's the smell of all this ash. I can't stand it." *You wish to leave me be.*

He checked his watch. "I'm going to have the press get some photos of Wolffe and me on top of the ruins. I can see the headlines now: *Dewey Chronos Vows to Rebuild the Night.*"

Rebuild? My head whipped toward him so quickly, the world spun. "Do you mean that?"

"What does it matter?" He touched my cheek. "You don't need the Big Tent anymore."

I swallowed my rage. There'd be a time to strike back. Not yet.

"Clean up, will you?" He tossed me his handkerchief. "In a little while, we'll go back to the polls so you can charm a few more votes my way. Not too many, of course. Don't want my family suspecting what you can do."

As if it could get any worse.

Once he left, coughs seized me yet again, and I covered my mouth with his handkerchief, his expensive cologne invading my nostrils.

When my coughing finally relented, I removed the handkerchief.

It was red.

Red like garnets. Like rubies.

You're on borrowed time.

Trevor rushed to me, his brow creased with worry. "You need to stop using your magic."

"I can't." I let him help me to my feet, every muscle in my legs screaming in protest. "Have you been reading Dewey's thoughts?"

"Yes, but he's much better at hiding them than I realized. Right now, he's obsessed with the election. And with Jamison." He leaned closer, his face pained. "I had no idea, Luxe, I swear. I really believed he was good."

Trevor was truly shaken. How often was a mind reader wrong about someone's character? "He fooled us both," I whispered.

"The missing Strattori boys, Rose Effigen's son . . ." He paled. "That was him."

He'd gone after the magical families with the fewest allies, with members most likely to leave Charmant. "We need a plan."

Trevor glanced toward where Dewey shook Uncle Wolffe's hand, posing for pictures on the ashes of my family's home. "What do you need from me?"

I hesitated. If Dewey asked him what we discussed, it'd ruin my ruse. But the Edwardians were the Chronoses' closest allies. If anyone knew, it would be one of them. "How do you kill a time traveler?"

Trevor's lip wobbled. He had cared for Dewey. Betraying him wasn't easy—but I'd phrased it as a question.

"In their sleep. Using something painless and lethal, so they don't wake up, not even for a split second. If they have a chance to travel, you're as good as dead."

I was already as good as dead.

No. I refused to believe that. As long as my heart continued to beat, I still had a chance to take down Dewey. Then I'd figure out the rest.

The Effigens likely had a poison that would do the trick, but what Effigen would help me now, after Rose was lost in the fire? All it would take was one overheard thought, and they'd be complicit in assassinating the future mayor.

But there was one Effigen who used to know me well. Who might take a chance on me.

That unrelenting cough seized me again, as if I'd swallowed mouthfuls of ash. I took Trevor's hand and held on for dear life, all the while willing my legs to remain upright.

"Stop charming him," he begged. "Take care of yourself."

I squared my shoulders, steeling myself. "I will."

Once everyone else was safe.

By showtime, Jamison was long gone. His lightstring had faded into oblivion as the ferry carried him from Charmant. It was the deepest, darkest blue.

Better for him to live with a broken heart than die with a whole one.

Trysta had been with him. Roger, too. When they were nearly out of reach, I'd sent one final charm down their lightstrings: *You feel protective of him.*

They were gone.

I should have felt something. Relief that he was safe. Shame for what I'd done to force his hand. Something, other than the unbearable pressure radiating from my chest. With my inkwell shattered, I couldn't seem to turn my magic off. Lightstrings danced all around me, a taunting reminder of what I'd done.

You're on borrowed time.

Uncle Wolffe knocked and poked his head into my dressing room. "You good?"

"Just peachy." Each breath felt like shrapnel in my lungs, and I'd gotten winded just from fixing my hair, but I managed a smile. "Have they finished tallying the votes?"

"Almost. But my sources say Dewey's lead can't be beat. By midnight, he'll be declared the winner."

A Chronos with shadow magic was now the most powerful person on the island. And it was my fault.

"Dewey wants the audience in a good mood before I announce the winner. The plan is for you to perform, then join him onstage right after."

Join him onstage . . . to marry him.

Uncle Wolffe's brow wrinkled, the thick white powder creasing. "You don't look good."

"I'm fine. Just bracing myself." I swallowed my nausea.

After a furtive glance into the hall, he lowered his voice. "You don't have to marry him. You know that, right?"

Tears burned behind my eyes. I held my breath to keep them there. "I know."

"Charm him into wanting to wait. There's no rush."

If only that were still true. But Dewey had all the time in the world, and according to that poor Strattori, I didn't. "I want to do this, Uncle Wolffe. Trust me."

"I keep thinking about your mother. What she'd say." He exhaled slowly, his frown at odds with his bright, clownish makeup. "Showtime's in ten, but you have all night to change your mind."

His footsteps thundered down the hall, drowned out by my family's abrupt laughter. Tonight was a celebration for them, a reprieve from the awfulness of the fire. The Big Tent was gone, but we were still performing. We were still alive.

Another knock on my door, this time so quiet I nearly missed it.

Margaret quickly shut the door behind her and tugged off the scarf she'd tied over her dark hair and ivory horns. Her eyes were red and bloodshot, her pretty face pallid but smooth. I'd only seen Margaret briefly in the immediate aftermath of her attack, but the memory of her festering wounds and bubbling skin was hard to shake.

"You came," I breathed. "Thank you."

"It's the first time you've written in three years," she said. "I figured it's important."

Important enough to interrupt her grieving. To put her life at risk, too.

She was a shadow of the sixteen-year-old girl who'd been a regular fixture backstage at our shows. No twinkling eyes, no easy smile. But she'd still answered the note, still come when my family needed her. "Are you okay, Luxe?" she asked.

I nearly laughed. I was the furthest thing from okay. "It's better if you don't know."

"You're right. Here." She handed me a clear vial, no bigger than my pinkie finger.

My heart quickened. The poison.

After glancing around the empty dressing room, she dropped her voice. "A few drops under the tongue is all it takes. It's very potent and should work nearly instantly. But you have to be careful not to get any on yourself. And if you get caught—"

"I'd never rat you out." I gripped the little vial in my fist. "I swear it."

"I know. Lack of loyalty has never been a Revelle flaw."

Margaret didn't quite smile, though her eyes softened. "Reckless-ness, on the other hand . . ."

"I'll be careful. I promise."

She glanced around the dressing room as she retied her scarf. "I should get out of here before anyone sees me. I wouldn't want to upset Roger."

I opened the door. The hall was empty, though Revelle voices still sounded from backstage. "It's Dewey's guards you need to worry about. Roger left this morning."

I'd meant the words to be comforting, but Margaret's face fell. "Oh. I didn't know."

I made him, I longed to tell her. Roger was as stubborn as his father and sister, but being home and not seeing Margaret had been torture for him. He would have eventually gone to her. But I'd ruined that.

"Thank you." I squeezed her arm as she turned to leave. "And I'm so sorry about Rose."

Margaret paused in the door, her eyes bright with unshed tears. "Make them pay," she whispered. "And you be careful, Luxie girl. Whatever you're up to, we're all rooting for you."

She hugged me with surprising strength, and then she was gone.

As the backstage lights flashed, I tucked the vial of poison in my vanity drawer, a little wedding-night present for my soon-to-be husband. I'd marry him. Celebrate his victory with him. Be nothing but the perfect wife all night. And then I'd take him to bed and use my magic to make him fall asleep. Once he was out cold, I'd slip him the poison and end this nightmare.

Till death do us part.

Alone, I walked to my starting position.

This was the moment I'd been dreaming of all summer. A brand-new theater. Expensive costumes and walls that wouldn't leak on rainy nights. A rich benefactor sitting front and center, two dozen long-stemmed calla lilies in his lap. Yet, like a candle melted by the relentless sun, my dream was warped. The theater wasn't ours, the Big Tent was gone, and whenever I looked at those purple blooms, all I saw was the Big Tent's burning canvas.

Gossip was an elixir to my family's woes, and hushed murmurs followed me to the trapeze ladder. All afternoon they'd whispered about how I was marrying a Chronos, how I'd been mistaken about Roger's poor friend. Let them talk about me. Let them focus on anything except the harsh reality of our precarious existence.

We had no home, no backup plan, no second chances.

Nana kissed both my cheeks and held my face between her hands, searching. "We can insist on a long engagement and find another way."

But there was no other way. Nana knew it, even if she wasn't ready to admit that we needed Dewey. I smiled bright enough for our entire eavesdropping family to see. "I *want* to marry him."

She leaned closer, those warm hands not leaving my face. "Don't hide behind your pretty smiles with me, child. I know you don't love the man. And I know Jamison didn't set the fire."

I climbed onto the first rung of the ladder and winked over my shoulder. "Who needs love? I'm going to be the mayor's wife."

The ladder to the trapeze platform was a cold, inflammable steel. At the top, Colette and Millie sat with their legs swinging over the ledge, taking in the crowd.

Colette's eyes narrowed as she scrutinized me. "They washed you out."

My whole life, Colette had done my makeup for every performance, onstage or off. Having outside help was an insult to her work. To us.

"Day District fools," I replied coolly. "They didn't know what they were doing."

She watched me from beneath her mink lashes. One blink. Then another. "Here," she finally said, reaching for a small case she'd hidden behind a wooden beam. Grabbing her rouge, she went to work on my cheeks. "I can't let our esteemed *star* go out there looking like a ghost."

Millie grabbed my hand to examine my heavy ring. "Wow. How much did this cost?"

My cheeks burned. "I, ah, didn't ask."

"I'm not talking about money."

Colette's brush paused on my cheek. Waiting.

If the Strattori was right, would I spend my last days alone with my secrets, like I'd spent these past years?

"Jamison didn't set the fire," Millie said firmly. "You know that as much as we do."

Sadness eclipsed Colette's lightstring. Because of me, Trysta had left before she'd had time to heal, before they'd had a chance to say goodbye. It would be a long time before Colette forgave me.

"I'm sorry." My voice was so small, I didn't think they could hear me over the music. "I'm sorry Trys left. I'm sorry I said those terrible things about Jamison. And most of all, I'm sorry we grew apart."

"Hey." Colette reached for me. "We're still here, okay? You're our family, even when you act like an ass. Just tell us why you're doing this."

"Tell us the truth," Millie urged me. "That's all we ever wanted."

With careful fingers, I wiped an escaped tear. I was so tired of lying. After everything they'd lost because of Dewey, after everything I'd put them through, they deserved the truth.

"Dewey's time traveled. A lot. He's reset time, over and over, to make sure he wins the election. And to make sure I end up with him and *not* Jamison. He wanted him either dead or gone, so I chose gone."

Millie's hands flew to her mouth. "What? How has he traveled so much?"

The urge to protect was firm and swift, but I'd lied so many times, and I'd still ended up here. Alone.

"Shadow magic," I finally said. They deserved to know. And if something happened to me, better to arm my family with the truth.

Their eyes were as wide as opals. "Impossible."

"It's real. I don't know exactly how he does it, but Dewey hurts people with magical blood—this allows him to travel, and *they* age instead."

The color drained from Millie's face. "But he *has* aged!"

"I know. But not nearly as much as he's traveled."

Colette covered her mouth. "Frank Chronos in the alley. That's why he aged so quickly."

"And Jamison said Rose turned old and gray in a matter of minutes."

Jamison. The knife in my heart twisted deeper.

"Aw, Luxie, don't cry!" Millie pulled me against her for a tight hug. "You did a very selfless thing, sending Jamison away. And this whole Dewey business . . . we'll figure it out together. Trevor will help us."

"We need to take Dewey down." Already scheming, Colette glared at where he sat in the front row.

"He gave you that enormous diamond," Millie pointed out. "That should buy you time."

If only it were that easy. "He had Trevor put it on me."

"Oh." She crinkled her nose. "How romantic."

I managed a smile. "It's fine."

"No, it's not," Colette said firmly.

"Okay, maybe it's not," I admitted, "but Dewey is our landlord now. We sleep on his floors, perform in his theater, and charm customers in his hotels."

Not a coincidence. Every misfortune pushed us right into his waiting hands.

I lifted my chin, just as my mother had taught me to do before a particularly daunting leap. *There's strength in pretending, Luxie girl.* "If Dewey turns on us, we have nothing. Truly nothing. But I have a plan. You understand why I can't tell you more. Not yet."

Colette studied me, her lightstring eclipsed with worry. "What do you need from us?"

My heart squeezed. How quickly they forgave me; how eager they were to help. "Dewey can't suspect I don't want to marry him. So you two need to be by my side the whole ceremony because I don't think I can stomach it alone. Okay?"

"Don't tell me you hid ugly bridesmaid dresses backstage." Millie shuddered. "I look terrible in pink."

My lips quirked. "Wear whatever you want."

"Good. I'll make sure to ask Trevor how beautiful I look."

"Well, I'm going to 'accidentally' spill my champagne on Dewey during the reception." Anger seeped in Colette's light-string like smoke. And I hadn't yet told her about Dewey's role in our mothers' deaths.

Catherine Revelle alive, Jamison Jones dead. Colette is the star, but Luxe's magic is weak and Catherine keeps her from me. George wins.

"He'll just travel before you have the chance."

"That makes him hard to kill, doesn't it?"

Very hard indeed. One wrong move, and he'd rewind the clock and leave me clueless about my failed plan. Maybe he'd even erase the last twenty-four hours, so I'd once again be in the dark about his shadow magic. Even if I managed to succeed, the Day District was full of time travelers looking for a reason to punish the Revelles. A dead Chronos, even one who'd turned on them, might be reason enough to retaliate.

Killing a time traveler was the hard part. Marrying him was far easier.

The saxophones' brassy notes climbed higher and higher, whipping the audience into a frenzy. Showtime.

Colette helped me to my feet. "Are you ready?"

I'd gotten dizzy just from climbing the ladder. But I was a Revelle. I'd bury my pain, bury whatever sinister magic was ravaging my lungs, bury whatever scraps of my tattered heart remained, and I'd do it with a pristine smile.

One more night. Once Dewey was asleep, I'd end this, once and for all. And if fate granted me a little more time, I'd spend it with my cousins. And maybe, if by some miracle he forgave me . . . Jamison.

Millie threw her arms around me before she dove for her

trapeze swing and leaped from the rafters. Colette followed on her heels. The awestruck crowd craned their necks as my beautiful cousins twisted and flitted, graceful birds diving in sync.

"Ladies and gentlemen, the moment you've been waiting for," boomed Uncle Wolffe.

The crowd roared for me. For Luxe Revelle, the Radiant Ruby of the Night. Colette signaled me from the opposite rafter. From far below, Dewey grinned with predatory pride.

The drums went *rat-a-tat-tat*. Faster, faster, as the music reached its crescendo. Gripping the swing, I leaped from the edge.

Time to go out with a bang.

THIRTY-THREE

JAMISON

Curtains of mist closed over the bright lights of Charmant. The mystical island blinked from existence as if I'd imagined it.

I was fond of imagining things.

Roger pressed his flask into my hand. I shook my head.

"You sure? It's going to be a lot harder to find booze on the mainland."

"I don't want to drink another drop of his alcohol." Bad enough that we were on his ferry.

Dewey was her hooch man. Her landlord. Her *fiancé*. And I was the guy whose parents killed her mother.

Roger held the flask upside down, letting the last meager droplets fall to the ocean. "Well, that was a whirlwind of a trip."

That was an understatement.

Trys rubbed her temples. Dark shadows marred her ivory skin as she stared into the night. We'd found her waiting by the ferry, pale and dazed, but ready to go.

Once we reached New York, we'd have to splurge for a hotel so she could rest.

"We shouldn't have left," I said for the millionth time.

"It's over." Roger perched on the railing, the moonlight illuminating the boat's wake behind him. "If you try to jump overboard one more time, I just might let you."

We were much too far now to swim back, especially with those swirling tides.

Roger studied me as I backed away from the railing. The ordeal with his family chasing us away had rattled him.

"I should have told you about my parents," I finally said.

"So tell me now."

I did. I told him everything, from the déjà vu I'd experienced the moment I spotted Charmant, to the Night District orphanage and its tire swing, to Mag the Hag and the story she told that would haunt me forever.

By the time I finished, Charmant was long gone.

"Wow." Roger shook his head. "I'm sorry, Jame-o. I really am."

"No, *I'm* sorry. For what my parents did and for not telling you right away."

"You're no more responsible for their actions than Trysta is for the Chronoses'. Besides, it doesn't sound as if they had much of a choice."

"There's always a choice." I gripped the side of the bench, staring at the moonlit waves. It'd been easy to idealize my parents, especially while I was still at St. Douglas's. But they'd given in to the Chronoses' demands. They'd killed three innocent, beloved women. For me.

"Do you blame Rose Effigen for trying to take your life in order to save her son's?" His forehead crinkled. "Eerily similar method, now that I think of it: kidnap a child to make the parents do your dirty work. Is that your family's preferred strategy, Trysta dear?"

Trys shot him a look. "We're not monsters."

"But George is."

"And Dewey." My blood boiled as I pictured his joyful smirk when the Revelles had turned on me. The possessive way he'd held Luxe close.

"Leave Dewey out of this," Trys warned. "Luxe turned on you for her own reasons."

"She *didn't* turn on me. Dewey threatened me, and she thinks sending me away will keep me safe." I was a fool for leaving, for letting her chase me off the island. "We have to go back."

"Did you forget the angry mob? Or the fact that she's marrying him?" Trys stared at me pointedly. "He gave her a diamond engagement ring. A huge one. If this was really about keeping you safe, she'd just charm him into leaving you alone."

Her words cut like a knife, but she was right.

Jewel magic would be easy for Luxe. It wouldn't even hurt her. We could have kept seeing each other, and Dewey would never have been the wiser.

But she'd sent me away.

Dewey's my equal in power, Luxe had said. *My equal in magic. My equal in life.* In the end, had that mattered more than whatever there was between us?

Trys ran her palms along the wooden cane Roger had found to replace the sleek black one that had burned. "I don't mean to kick you when you're down, I just—I shouldn't have left."

"How did you know to meet us on the dock?" Roger asked.

"I don't know. I felt like I needed to find you guys and make sure you were okay. As much as I don't want to blame my family, someone blackmailed Rose to kill Jamison. And it couldn't have been Dewey. He was knocked out, too."

I slumped on the bench beside her. Not only couldn't I protect Luxe, but I needed my magical friends to take care of me.

Gone were the whimsical tides surrounding Charmant. Instead, the waves lapped against the hull in straight, lazy lines, carrying us back to New York, where booze was illegal and magic was hidden and weak. Three hours and a world away.

Roger slid off the railing and sat on Trys's other side. "You and Colette really hit it off?"

"Do you know how she got me out during the Swap Trot?" A heavy smile fought its way to her lips. "Somehow, she unhooked one of my suspenders. I almost lost my pants."

"So you like my sister because she tried to *undress* you?"

"I like her because she puts her heart into everything she does, even winning a ridiculous competition. But I didn't even say goodbye." Trys's voice was flat, her eyes expressionless. "It doesn't make any sense. I had every intention of staying longer and then catching up with you in a few weeks, but I just . . . left."

Neither of them had been ready to go. They'd been lying to themselves about leaving since the moment we'd set foot in Charmant.

I jumped to my feet. "Let's go back. Trys, you and Colette deserve a happy ending. And you, too, Roger. You didn't end up speaking to Margaret, did you?"

Roger's face fell. He'd finally been ready to see Margaret, to tell her family what we'd learned about Rose's fate. "We left before I had the chance."

"Then it's settled. We stay on the ferry in New York and go right back to Charmant."

But we'd be too late. By morning, Luxe would already be Mrs.

Dewey Chronos. Soon they'd be standing on the stage of the new theater, hands clasped, declaring their love for all to see. And if watching them together didn't kill me, the Revelles certainly would.

Another Wolffe punch to the gut would hurt less.

Roger arched a brow. "Might I remind you of the angry mob again?"

I waved a hand. "That was Luxe's doing. She made a scene to keep Dewey from coming after me." It was the only explanation—to accept that she didn't care for me, that she truly preferred him . . . I couldn't bear it.

Trys gave me a hard look. "If a time traveler wanted you dead, you'd be dead."

"You did die," Roger mused. Seeing my blank look, he shrugged. "That crate on the promenade. Technically, it killed you, and Trys saved your life."

My heart slowed to a stop.

"Charmant wasn't kind to you, Jame-o."

The roar in my ears drowned out his teasing tone, the crash of the waves against the ferry, everything. "How many times have I almost died since we arrived?"

Roger frowned. "Quite a few, actually."

I ticked them off on my fingers. "The shipping crate on the promenade, which fell off Dewey's ship. A Chronos tried to pummel me to death in that alley, but he turned into a corpse before he could finish the job. And then the fire . . ."

". . . when a Chronos blackmailed Rose to shoot you." Roger held his fist to his mouth. "A time traveler really has been after you all summer."

"*Dewey's* been after me all summer. No other Chronos has any reason to want me dead."

"As convenient as it is to blame my brother for everything, he's not a murderer." Trys glared at us both. "Maybe he's a little corrupt, like all politicians, but he's not morally bankrupt."

"He threatened me," I reminded her. "He told Luxe he wanted me gone."

"Look at you! You're obsessed with his fiancée. You're turning her into this innocent girl who's marrying him against her will. But the truth is, she's had *him* wrapped around her finger all summer, and she likes it that way."

Another dry cough seized her, shoulders trembling as she struggled to regain control. She waved away the water Roger offered. "It can't be Dewey," she rasped. "If he'd been time traveling all summer, he'd be ancient."

"He *is* ancient!" I exclaimed.

She rolled her eyes. "He looks like he's in his thirties, not dead."

That snake had spent the summer trying to convince everyone he was the benevolent benefactor. Like he'd just happened to catch Luxe when she fell that first night. Happened to have a new theater ready to go when the Revelles' burned to the ground. When *he* burned it to the ground, making them even more reliant on him.

He was dangerous—and Luxe was about to tie herself to him irrevocably.

"It is rather suspicious," Roger conceded, "but Trevor Edwardes confirmed that Dewey aged because he traveled back seven weeks. I asked Trevor myself."

"You see? He couldn't have done all those things," Trys said. "Magic has strict, unbendable rules."

"Magic doesn't always follow the rules," I pointed out. "How do you explain Rose Effigen turning into an old lady before she died?"

"Maybe you inhaled too much smoke and hallucinated. Or maybe her mother slept with a Chronos. It's strange, but it doesn't make my brother a murderer."

Roger leaned against the railing. "Trys is right; the laws of magic don't bend. Trust me. I've tried."

"We've *all* tried," Trys said. "Every single magic wielder in Charmant. It's impossible."

And yet Luxe *had* bent the laws of magic. I stared at my friends, the words lodging in my throat. It was her secret. But if Dewey had discovered it, she was in trouble. They all were.

"Luxe's-magic-doesn't-follow-the-rules." The words rushed out of my mouth in an incoherent jumble. "She can charm without jewels or gems."

Roger stilled. "Say what now?"

"She can charm without jewels." They needed to believe me, needed to understand.

"How?"

"All I know is that it hurts. She experiences intense pain, then she can charm at will."

"Impossible." Trys waved a dismissive hand. "Magic requires checks and balances. Pain is too temporary."

"That's how she charmed Dewey all summer. He didn't give her a jewel until today."

Trys knew her brother well enough to believe that, at least.

Dewey's my equal, Luxe had said, her eyes boring into me as though she wanted her words carved into my broken heart for eternity. *My equal in power. My equal in magic. My equal in life.*

I leaned closer, my mind spinning. "What if his magic bends the rules, too? What if he could transfer the cost to someone else? Like Frank Chronos. Or Rose Effigen."

Roger paled.

Trys jumped to her feet. "You yourself just mentioned that he's aged a decade!"

"I know how it sounds—"

"It sounds insane." She shook her head. "You know I love you, Jamison, but it's time to face the facts: You fell for a girl who likes pretty, expensive things. She fancied you for a bit but is marrying someone who can give her pretty, expensive things. You did the same thing with Betty. After so many years alone, when someone shows you a little love, you get stuck on them."

The truth of her words hit like a punch.

But that wasn't Luxe, was it? That was one of her masks.

My equal in power. My equal in magic. Those whiskey eyes burning with meaning. But her power was unparalleled. Her magic, unique.

Unless she was trying to tell me that *Dewey's magic was just like hers.*

Her worst fear was a Chronos discovering her secret. If Dewey had realized what she could do, if he'd figured out a way to avoid the cost of his own magic, the Revelles were in deep trouble. We all were.

Dewey wasn't just jealous; he was unfathomably dangerous. That's why she was tying herself to him. Why she had me chased out of Charmant.

My body thrummed with the need to get back to her before she married the bastard. "We have to go back. We have to turn this ferry around *now.*"

"What? No!" Roger shook his head emphatically. "If it's true, and Dewey has found a way to make other people age instead of him, that's even more reason to keep you out of it."

"But Luxe—"

"Jamison." He gripped both my shoulders, forcing me to stop pacing. "When a time traveler is trying to pop you and you scram, you stay scrammed. You don't go back."

"She's going to *marry* him." I'd let her chase me away so easily, even though I knew this was what she did, over and over: self-sacrifice.

"By the time we get off this ferry and onto a new one, the ceremony will be done."

"We have to do something!"

I hardly felt Roger let go of my shoulders, hardly heard Trys as she groaned, "You can't be serious."

"Look at him, Trys. A thousand time travelers couldn't hold him back." Roger glanced toward the captain's room. "Maybe I'll see if I can . . . convince the captain."

"What are you waiting for?" I practically pushed him toward the staircase.

Roger took the stairs two at a time.

Trys glared at me. "I want no part in this."

"I know you think I'm being ridiculous—"

"I *do* think you're being ridiculous, but I want to go back. Not because my brother's a murderous arsonist, but because I shouldn't have left in the first place."

"That could have been Luxe's magic," I said carefully, "charming you into wanting to leave." To protect me. Everything Luxe did was to take care of the people who mattered to her.

I mattered to her. And I'd fallen for her act, just like everyone else.

Roger slid down the railing, out of breath. "So the bad news is I've definitely met this captain before and he definitely holds a grudge. No way he's giving me a jewel."

My heart sank. "What's the good news?"

"There is no good news. There's literally no way for us to get back to Charmant in time." He winced. "I'm sorry, Jame-o."

I scrubbed my fingers through my hair, ignoring the heavy sense of defeat. If only *I* could travel back in time. Or charm people into doing as I pleased. But I had nothing of value, except my mother's brooch. And my words.

And, as Trys was fond of reminding me, my innocent face.

I stormed the stairs to the captain's deck, calling to Roger over my shoulder, "Stay close behind, but don't let him see you."

The captain grimaced as I entered uninvited. His skippers jumped to their feet.

I raised my hands. "Sir, I'm sorry to disturb you, but you need to turn this boat around immediately."

"Two in one night? Get 'im out of here."

The skippers lunged for me, but I sidestepped them. "The girl I love is in danger and I know you have no reason to care, but I need you to turn this boat around so I can help her."

His stern expression didn't change, though he adjusted the gold band around his ring finger. "Dewey Chronos will have my head if I mess with the timetables. We're due in New York in two hours. You can stay aboard and turn around then, if you'd like."

"I don't have two hours; I need to be back in Charmant in an hour, tops. Please, sir." I reached into my pocket, and the skippers stiffened again, but I produced my mother's brooch. "This is the most valuable thing I own. I'd like you to keep it. For your troubles."

I lobbed the brooch at him. Frowning, he let go of the wheel to turn it over in his hands.

"I'm no Revelle," I added hastily.

"If you were, you would ask for this back."

"Keep it, sir. Please, help me get back before I lose her forever. I can't breathe, thinking about what she's going through. She's the sweetest girl on the planet, sir. The most selfless, stubborn girl I've ever met. So help me keep her safe. Turn the boat around." I backed toward the door again, moving slowly.

He sighed. "What's her name?"

I blanched. "Excuse me?"

"Her name. The girl you love."

I kept my gaze steady as I replied, "Luxe Revelle."

Laughter bubbled from deep in his rounded belly. He turned to the skippers, their faces dripping with mirth. "Did you hear that? The Radiant Ruby herself. Even if we turned around right now, there's no way you'd be back in time for the wedding. And no offense, but your pockets aren't deep enough to compete with our new mayor."

With my head hanging low, I continued my retreat.

"A piece of advice, fella. Save your money for a nice mainland girl. A Revelle will bring you nothin' but trouble."

I was halfway out the door when he tossed me back the brooch. I sidestepped the jewelry just in time.

Roger's waiting hand reached out and grabbed it.

THIRTY-FOUR

LUXE

When I was learning to hone my magic, my vision blackened if I held a single lightstring for more than a few seconds. With practice, I built a tolerance to the pain. Fainting hardly felt voluntary, but it was also a relief. Evidence that I, too, was making sacrifices.

Tonight my pain would not stop me. My health would not stop me. This performance wasn't just about propping up Dewey, it was our chance to prove to the world that they could burn our homes and our tent, but the Revelles would not be crushed. Our show went on. Always.

I'd broken Jamison's heart. I'd conjured shadow magic. I was going to marry a vicious man, from a long line of vicious men, so my family could have a fighting chance at a future. And then I was going to poison him.

Tonight would be extraordinary. I'd make sure of it.

Swing, flip, dance. Grab more lightstrings. Dance some more, then return to the trapeze bar. Head high, back straight, toes together.

When my vision clouded as the pain reached its crescendo, I

had a choice: Give in to the darkness or refuse to collapse. Fight through the pain and override my instinct for self-preservation.

As long as I was still breathing, I was going to earn every jewel for my family. We'd need them to face whatever tomorrow brought.

The audience was on their feet, their applause roaring in my ears as the curtains closed for intermission. The fancy electric lights backstage were as blinding as the lightstrings floating away from my grasp. I could still see them, but I didn't dare reach for them, not with that stabbing in my chest during every inhale. My inkwell was long gone, but in the hollowness where my magic once lived, a different sort of power lingered.

I could hardly hear my family's excitement as I stumbled backstage, dark clouds gathering in my periphery. Loving hands patted my back, offering comfort and praise. Years of practice allowed me to keep smiling until I reached the privacy of my dressing room.

As soon as the door closed behind me, I collapsed on the sofa. Never before had my hands shaken so badly.

Breathe.

My magic was a problem for the second act. For the next ten minutes, it was okay if I let go of Dewey's lightstring. The audience was ecstatic, and he was, too. Within the hour, Wolffe would declare him Charmant's new mayor. He didn't need me to fix his mood.

Air wouldn't come, my windpipe shrinking to a straw, rasping, breaking . . .

Breathe.

If Jamison were here, he'd tell me to drink water. With

trembling hands, I poured myself a glass, then pushed him out of my mind. I certainly couldn't think of Jamison now, when I needed to keep my wits about me. Intermission was so short, and I didn't have much time, and the audience was expecting me, and my family needed me—

The door burst open.

"There she is!" Millie flung herself onto the couch, her cheeks shiny and flushed. "You were amazing. Wow, Luxe, I've never seen anything like that."

Something cool dripped from my nose. I wiped the blood with my towel before they could notice.

Ever the hawk, Colette leaned closer. "You don't look right."

"Leave her alone. Wasn't she great?"

Colette poured more water into my glass and pressed it into my hand. "You were a little late on that third jump."

"Col—" Millie warned.

"Other than that, you were incredible. I've never seen you so focused."

"And sexy, too." Millie's eyes glittered. "I bet you'll star in quite a few fantasies tonight."

I nearly choked on my water, setting off a coughing fit. They giggled.

The cough continued to hold me in its iron fist, not letting me breathe.

This wasn't another fainting episode—this was slow and heavy, like concrete poured over my chest, hardening. Even if that poor Strattori hadn't said a thing, I would have known something was terribly wrong.

I needed air, needed it desperately.

Colette pried my fingers off my mouth as I continued to

394

cough. Pressing the glass to my lips, she forced me to take small sips of water. The cool liquid slid down my scorching throat.

"Thank you," I rasped, placing the glass back on my changing table.

My cousins ignored me. They stared at the glass.

Scarlet clouds trailed through the water, rising and twisting in strands much like lightstrings. It would have been pretty, had it been anything other than blood.

"Luxe?" Millie's voice was robbed of all its gusto.

I opened my mouth—to explain, to lie, I wasn't even sure anymore—but the coughing seized me again, and a cool numbness started in my hands, my feet.

Not yet. Not when I still had another act. Not when the audience was packed, their pockets full of jewels to throw to us during our final song.

Not when Dewey still lived.

Colette pressed her handkerchief against my mouth. It smelled like coconut, just like her. The coughing slowed as I tried to breathe in my sweet cousin.

When I removed her handkerchief from my lips again, it was stained with blood.

Colette jumped to her feet. "I'll fetch Dr. Strattori."

"Don't."

Millie frowned. "Luxe, this is serious. This isn't something you can ignore."

"I know!" I squeaked. Deep breath. "I know. Just don't bother, okay? She can't help me."

Colette took her bloodied handkerchief from my hands and spread it. "What the hell?"

The familiar urge to lie bubbled to the surface. I didn't want them to worry, or to be complicit in Dewey's death.

But I was so tired of pretending. Of lying.

I was so, so tired.

"Turns out, my magic is different, too. And not a good different, though for a long time I thought it was."

"*Magic* is doing this to you?" Millie asked.

Time slowed as I blinked. Our mothers pregnant together. Three little girls with ribbons in their hair hiding backstage. The meals we shared after they drowned. The way we'd linked pinkies in silent support when one of us cried through the night. How long I'd pined for their affection, watched them laugh without me, *live* without me. Their hurt when I pulled away. Their willingness to let me back in so easily.

"Shadow magic," I managed to say. "I've accidentally been using shadow magic for years. But unlike Dewey, I haven't been hurting anyone else. Just myself, somehow."

They stared, waiting for me to crack a smile, to tell them it was all a joke. But the coughing seized me again. Colette held the glass to my lips, her gentle hand on my back.

Once the coughing slowed, Millie crouched in front of me. "Stop it, Luxe. Stop whatever it is you're doing to yourself."

"I'm trying." If only it were that simple. Even now, when I wasn't calling to my magic, fear-tinged lightstrings danced over my cousins' heads.

Still holding the bloodied glass, Colette studied me. "This is how you found Jamison during the fire."

I nodded. I had no fight left.

"What? How?" Millie demanded.

"The fainting," Colette said.

Another nod.

"The weight loss."

And another.

"This is why my father named you the star." She looked away, her throat bobbing. Years of being my backup had made her doubt herself. Her talent.

"It should have been you." Somehow, those words were harder to utter than anything else I'd shared. "He knows I can charm the audience without jewels. I make them believe they're having the time of their lives."

"Without wasting any gems." She covered her mouth, shaking her head. "All these years, I couldn't figure out what I was doing wrong. If I didn't smile enough, or didn't look enough like my mother, or looked *too* much like my mother. But it was never about me, was it?"

Tears shone in her eyes. That I'd made her doubt herself, her talent, her beauty—that was unforgivable. "I'm so sorry, Col. It should have been you."

The lights dimmed. Millie glanced toward the shut door. "Damnit. Intermission's over."

"Let's go." I forced myself to stand.

Colette blocked the door. "You can't be serious! A breeze could knock you over."

I squared my shoulders, my limbs growing heavier with every moment I remained upright. "Dewey can't know anything's wrong. The show must go on."

The lights blinked again. Still, Colette held the knob. "After the show, you're telling us everything, okay? And don't you dare use your magic, not if it's making you sick. Deal?"

"Except she's getting married after the show," Millie said under her breath.

In silence, we walked back toward the rafters. For our final act, Millie would start at stage right. Colette would swing in from stage left, and they'd do a brief routine before my grand entrance.

Colette insisted I climb the ladder first. We settled into our usual rhythm in uncomfortable silence: hands dipped in powder, jewels pressed against us for strength.

As we waited for Wolffe's signal, Colette studied me. "You have a plan, don't you? Other than just marrying the guy."

Marrying was the easy part. Killing him would be much harder. "I've got some ideas."

She arched a brow. "Nothing reckless, I hope."

"Nothing you wouldn't do." I straightened my shaky legs and stretched.

She glared at the front row, where Dewey sat tall, those flowers in his lap. "I'd kill him."

I nearly laughed. The Revelle drums quickened, readying for her entrance.

Her head whipped to mine. "Jesus Christ, you're going to try to kill him, aren't you?"

Always too smart for her own good. "If something happens to me tonight, there's a small vial in my dressing room."

"You can't kill a time traveler!"

"It's next to my lipstick. All it takes is a few drops."

"*Luxe*." She grabbed my shoulders, her determined face the only thing in my field of view. "We're going to figure this out together. Okay?"

The same thing Jamison had said. I managed a nod.

A moment later, she was on her feet, gripping the swing, her shoulders squared and her back arched. Every muscle in her lean body was honed for this, like a bird with hollow bones.

The crowd's excitement hit new highs as she swung off the platform.

Their lightstrings were exactly where I'd left them: elated and excited and thoroughly enraptured. From the front row, Dewey's smoky one brimmed with pride. The votes were nearly all counted. He was about to have everything he wanted, and he'd gathered an enormous, adoring crowd to witness his victory.

I couldn't turn the lightstrings off, but I didn't dare grab any, not when that thick metallic taste still lingered in my mouth. I was no good to my family dead.

A few auras glowed backstage. Two tourists and a Revelle, climbing through a window. I leaned over the edge to signal to Dewey's guards to help the lone Revelle take care of the overzealous fans—

Wait.

I knew that lightstring, even if it was heavy with worry. Even if the gold tinge was nearly gone.

Impossible.

I scurried down the ladder. At the bottom, Nana grabbed my arm. "Where are you going?"

"Give me a moment."

"You have to be onstage at the end of this song. Wolffe's going to announce the winner!"

"I know." I shook myself from her grasp as gently as I could.

If Dewey or any of his guards saw, Jamison would be shot

without hesitation. He'd declared him persona non grata before the show. *A wanted man in our theater, dead or alive.*

And even if Trys traveled to save him, Dewey had all the time in the world to hurt him again and again and again . . .

Trys's jet-black bob slunk behind a wardrobe. I grabbed her. "What are you doing here? You need to get him out before—"

"Before what?" Trys narrowed her eyes. "Before you stomp all over his heart again?"

The crowd gasped at a particularly complex maneuver of Colette's. I was running out of time. "Before your brother kills him."

"My brother's *not* a murderer."

"Luxe?"

Jamison's voice knocked the air from my lungs, as if I'd fallen off the trapeze and landed square on my back. Frozen, I stared at his unruly hair, his crumpled shirt, and the dark shadows framing his dimmed eyes.

"What are you doing here?" I pulled him between two wooden props. It was hard to be mad when every inch of me relished his proximity. He stared at where my hand lingered on his arm, and his face softened.

I retreated. He was supposed to be far away. Safe. "You need to leave."

There was no time. I needed to be on that platform. If I was even a second late, Dewey would wonder why I'd missed my cue.

Those bright eyes held my gaze. "I won't let you sacrifice yourself for me."

"You have to go," I pleaded. "Dewey has his guards crawling all over the place. They'll kill you without thinking twice."

He took in my blood-peppered costume, my pallid skin, before settling on my engagement ring. "You can't marry him. *He's* the one behind the fire. He's the one behind the attack in the alley that day. All summer long, he's been trying to keep us apart."

Much longer than that, I desperately wanted to say.

The crowd gasped at something Colette and Millie did. It was time for my leap.

My head weighed a hundred tons as I turned away from him. "I don't need saving, Jamison. I *want* this."

"I don't believe you."

His lightstring was liquid in my grasp. All it would take was a tiny bit of magic. A smidge to exaggerate his lingering doubt. The insecurities he'd managed to beat back long enough to return to Charmant, despite how I'd decimated his hopes.

Crushing him was the right thing to do. But in what universe was it right to break the heart of a good person over and over again?

"I marry him, and you're safe, and my family's safe . . ." My voice broke on the words, and he wrapped his arms around me. I hadn't the strength to push him away again.

"No one's safe, Luxe." His voice was quiet, his heart beating steadily against me. "That's the hard truth: no matter what you do, no one is ever a hundred percent safe."

Tears burned behind my eyes. If Dewey realized I wanted him dead, he'd have no one to blame but me, as long as I acted alone. But if he thought Jamison helped me . . .

The band played the note signaling my entrance.

"Just let me try," I whispered, pressing my hands to Jamison's face. He had come back for me. Of course he had come back for me. "Let me try to fix this."

He kissed my palms. "I can't let you trade your life for mine."

I'm dying, I longed to tell him.

The band repeated my entrance riff.

"I'm sorry." I let go, the world spinning—

The shiny wood floors slammed into me.

His lightstring flashed with worry as he knelt beside me. I took his hands as if I could pull myself to my feet.

But I couldn't.

"I need to do this," I pleaded. "Go, Jamison. Just leave."

He pressed my hands to his heart, its beating somehow slowing my own pulse. My body always responded to his, even that first night.

"I couldn't live with myself if I let you do this. So I'm staying. Even if you don't feel for me what I feel for you."

Hope dripped from every word. Part of him still expected me to reject him, still didn't believe I could love him.

"I already told you what I want," I forced myself to say. "Now leave."

"Liar." He hovered over me, dark hair falling into his eyes as he held my gaze.

He wouldn't believe me, not without my magic. And I was so tired of lying.

I wrapped my arms around his neck and pulled him to me. It was a brief, gentle kiss, but it soothed the burning in my chest. "Go to the slide you recognized. Find somewhere to hide nearby. Once Dewey's asleep, I'll find you, okay?"

He kissed me once, twice, his smile growing. "I love you," he whispered.

"I—"

"You have *got* to be kidding me," Dewey spat.

Every inch of me plunged into ice.

Dewey stood in front of the curtain, his lightstring a storm of rage. Even without seeing it, Jamison angled himself between us.

The protective movement didn't go unnoticed by Dewey. "Get onstage, Luxe."

I shook my head.

"Your audience is waiting. Get on the stage."

"*No.*"

Dewey blinked once. Twice. "Guess we're going to do this the hard way."

Everything happened quickly.

Dewey lunged toward Jamison, his elbow cocked and ready to jab.

Jamison turned toward me, his back taking the brunt of the blow.

Dewey reached into his topcoat, the one with the diamond-shaped clock, and pulled out something dark silver. A gun.

He has a gun!

I couldn't get the words out soon enough.

He cocked it at Jamison, who was trying to shield me, his back still to Dewey. I tried to scream, but I was too slow, and Dewey was too close—

"Stop!" Trys leaped between them, spreading her arms to block as much of Jamison as she could.

My body sagged with relief. Trys was here. Dewey wouldn't hurt Jamison with Trys here.

Her cane clattered against the floor as she gaped at her brother, at the gun in his hands.

Dewey kept it aimed at us. "Get out of the way."

"How could you?" Her eyes welled as she stared at him, her hands still spread in front of her.

"Get out of the way, Trysta. *Now.*"

Her outstretched arms trembled. "If you shoot him again, I'm just going to travel again."

Again?

My knees threatened to buckle. Jamison stepped closer, his back pressed against me.

Dewey looked pained. "There's no way for you to stop this. You'll be the only one aging."

"This isn't you. You're not a killer."

Dewey's finger twitched over the trigger. "I have given *everything* for her! He is the only thing standing in our way."

"It's not that simple," Trys pleaded. "You know that."

"If you'd only seen what I've seen, you'd understand. The things we will achieve together. Our children will move mountains!" His wild eyes flitted to me, pleading.

He meant every sickening word.

We were at a standoff. Trys shielded Jamison. Jamison shielded me.

And still the band circled back to the same chord, waiting for my dazzling entrance.

"Stop!" Trys begged. "He's my best friend."

"I'm your brother. You'd protect him over me?"

"I'm protecting you both. Please, just put the gun down."

"I didn't want it to be like this." Regret flooded his lightstring. There was still a human heart in him, and it was hurting.

Trysta's face softened. "I know, Dewey. You're a good—"

The gunshot roared in my skull.

I grabbed for Jamison, pulling him down to the floor with me.

A second shot exploded. Blood rained onto my bare arms, and Jamison cried out—

Trys crumpled to the floor, red pouring from her chest.

A sound of pure anguish tore from Jamison's throat. He lunged for Trys, but Dewey swung the gun to him.

"Do what I say, and I'll bring her back."

All the color drained from Jamison's face. Trys remained motionless, save the blood seeping from her chest.

So much blood.

Footsteps thundered all around us as people came to investigate. Roger skidded to a halt and threw out his arms, keeping the rest of the family back. Tears spilled from Jamison's devastated eyes as he yelled to him—to protect him from Dewey or the sight of Trys—but he was too late.

Roger's jaw slackened, his lightstring dimming to blue-black. "Trys?"

"Stay away from her!" Dewey spat, but Roger lowered himself to Trys. His hands—hands that were strong enough to perform trapeze for hours without so much as a tremble—shook violently as he searched for the wound. As if he could stop the bleeding.

As if it weren't already too late.

"What did you do?" Roger's voice was a raw, broken thing. Trys's blood ran through his fingers like crimson paint. Jamison tried to reach them, but Dewey swung his gun wildly. At Jamison. At the backstage crew fanning out around us, all Revelles.

"Stay back! Come one step closer, and I'll shoot."

He was going to kill us all.

Pain barreled through my skull as I tried to access my power. It radiated down my chest, my stomach, to each of my limbs.

But no magic answered my call.

The band played my entrance melody more insistently.

"Please, Dewey," I pleaded. "Let's just go talk somewhere."

"So you can charm me and lie to me again? Absolutely not."

"My sweet—"

"Trevor!" Dewey barked.

Trevor poked his head out from behind a curtain. Our eyes met. *Go!* I shouted in my mind. *Get help.*

But what would help do? Dewey would just restart the clock and none of us would even remember what he'd done.

No, there was no escaping Dewey.

As Trevor approached, Dewey swung the gun around in a sweeping arc. "If you stay calm, everyone will be fine. *Everyone.*"

"It'd be a lot easier to believe that if you'd just put the damn gun down!" I cried.

His jaw set in resolve. "This is for your own good."

Roger's lips moved in quiet prayer as he pressed his hands to Trys's wound. I'd never seen him so broken, not even after Margaret. "Let me get Dr. Strattori. Please!"

Dewey didn't even acknowledge him. His eyes were trained on Jamison, who shook beside me, his lightstring a dark and tortured purple.

Still the band played on.

"Just tell us what you want us to do." My voice was steady now.

"I need Jamison to answer one simple question for me."

From where he cradled Trys, Roger's face snapped toward Jamison. "Don't say a damn thing."

Dewey's lightstring calmed by the second. He knew he had us. "He doesn't need to answer. All he has to do is *think* of the answer, and Trevor will fill in the blanks for me."

My limbs went cold.

If he were to shoot Jamison again, without Trys, Jamison wouldn't survive. There were no more second chances.

"Where did the three of you meet?"

Jamison's gaze tore from Trys's body. "What?"

"You, Trysta, and Roger. Where did you meet?"

I imagine it works differently for you, as a Revelle, but the lightstring leads me through their past. It weaves through whatever door they've entered, and keeps going, back and back until the moment they were born.

He could *end* Jamison before we even met. "Don't tell him anything!"

"Trevor, is Jamison thinking of where they met?"

Trevor's mouth twisted as if trying to separate from his own body. "Yes, sir," he said through gritted teeth.

"No!" Roger cried.

I dug deeper into my magic, despite the burning in my lungs. I scraped every corner of myself in search of lingering power. Shadow magic drained lifelines. I was still alive. Somewhere in me, I still had life to give.

"Tell me where," Dewey commanded him.

Trevor stilled. Dewey was so accustomed to Trevor's obedience, he hadn't even phrased it as a question.

I searched even deeper, hardly registering the claw of pain down my lungs, scraping the very core of me.

"*Now*, Trevor."

The Edwardian's voice was small as he replied, "This isn't right, sir."

"Really? After everything we've been through together, you're going to make me force it out of you?"

"Yes, sir, I am." Trevor took a step back, readying himself to run—

Dewey swung the gun around to his assistant, pressing it against his forehead. Trevor paled.

This was hopeless. Even if I could muster the magic to knock Dewey out, as soon as he woke, he'd come right back at us. He would never quit, not unless I somehow managed to stop his heart from beating before he had a chance to jump back in time. And if Dewey died, Trys was gone forever, because there would be no one here to travel and bring her back.

With the barrel of his gun still pressed against Trevor's head, Dewey still managed to look wounded. "You're really going to make me ask?"

"Yes," Trevor whispered. "You don't have to do this."

The heavy diamond on my finger warmed. The ring *Trevor* gave to me. Could I charm him into lying, into avoiding the cost of his own magic?

"You won't even remember that I've done this," Dewey said. "But *I'll* remember where you stood when it mattered. Now tell me: Where did the three of them meet?"

The jewel's magic was silk between my fingers, easy and cool. *You wish to stall, to give a detailed description of the wrong place . . .*

Trevor's mouth wrangled itself open, the involuntary need to respond fighting the magic from my diamond. His wide eyes snapped to mine, understanding dawning in them. *Just trust me,* I whisper-shouted in my mind. *Name any other place.* If I could keep him calm and keep the truth from his lips, Dewey would travel to the wrong place, and Jamison would live.

Roger shouted and stomped on the floor, trying to drown out any answer, and I dug deeper into that sweet jewel magic, diamond dust raining from my hand—

"Tell me *now*," Dewey ordered. "You have one last chance."

You long to name Florida. California. Anything but the truth. I looked at him in horror as his lips twisted, my magic colliding with his. Any answer, and Dewey would leave him alone.

Trevor's lips ceased struggling, and his eyes found mine. "Tell Millie I'm sorry."

The gun went off, and Trevor hit the floor.

A deafening ringing exploded through my mind, drowning out the music, the screams as I stared at a gaping pink hole in Trevor's head where his face used to be.

I tried to yell for him, tried to reach him, but Jamison held me back as I crawled, hands slipping on the bloodstained floor, oh God, the blood . . .

"He did it to himself!" The gun shook in Dewey's hands.

There was nothing recognizable left of my friend. No sign of the eyes that had struggled against my magic, the horror in them as he realized I was charming him.

What had I done? If only I'd left him alone. Or if I'd charmed him into running away, or falling asleep, or literally anything else.

I doomed him.

More Revelles now, skidding to a halt. Dewey swung the gun wildly at all of them, and they disappeared, taking cover behind the crates, the wardrobes. If they yelled for me, I couldn't hear them, not over the roar of the audience, the ringing in my ears.

Jamison pulled me against him. Little pink chunks clung to my fishnets. Trevor.

The muzzle of the pistol dug into the back of my skull. The ringing sound ceased, replaced by the band's upbeat melody.

"Tell me where you met." Dewey's voice broke. "*Now.*"

Jamison went still.

My magic didn't answer my call, only pain. "He won't hurt me," I rasped. "Don't answer."

Dewey simpered at us. "Is that a risk you're willing to take?"

"He'll travel and kill you before you even know who he is. Don't say a word."

Jamison gripped me against his chest, his lightstring tortured. He'd just lost Trys. Trevor still bled on the floor. Jamison was so afraid of me being next.

"He won't," I repeated, this time quieter.

Dewey made a disapproving noise. "Fine. But I will shoot *him*." He swung the gun to Roger. "I can kill him right now. Or I can travel back to right before the three of you met and prevent your paths from crossing. No pain for Trysta and Roger. They won't even miss you."

"Don't you dare!" Roger roared. Trys's graceful frame hung limp in his arms.

Jamison stared at them, his eyes wild.

"Your friendship or their lives," Dewey said calmly. "You have three seconds to choose."

"Don't do it," I begged him. "He'll kill you!"

"Two."

"What do I do here?" Jamison pleaded.

I grabbed onto Dewey's lightstring, but it hardly flickered.

Dewey yanked Roger by the shirt. "One."

"In Washington, DC!" Jamison cried out. "At the train station in Washington, DC."

Dewey lowered his gun, beaming at me the same way he had after he'd wiped the Strattori's blood off his knife. As if everything he did was for my benefit. I wanted to claw that smile right off his face, but any sudden movements and he'd travel.

It was over.

No amount of magic could make Dewey forget an actual memory. I had no idea how shadow magic worked for him—if he could use the blood he'd spilled tonight, or if there was more ceremony involved—but he was going to kill Jamison, and he wouldn't age a drop in the process.

The band played, their tune wild and upbeat. But I was back here.

It didn't matter. Any moment now, this would all be erased.

Utterly wrecked, Jamison's knees buckled. Roger buried his head in his hands. Trysta remained motionless. And Trevor, sweet Trevor, my friend despite everything . . .

Dewey couldn't have looked more pleased with himself. He ran a hand over his suit jacket, brushing away bits of the carnage he'd caused as he circled Jamison. A victory lap.

"You're not as wonderful as everyone believes you to be. Your parents, on the other hand . . ." He chuckled to himself. "It took years before they cracked."

All the blood drained from Jamison's face.

Dewey cocked his head, a predator relishing his kill. "You

have no recollection of all the different versions of yourself I've seen. Loving, doting parents made you an arrogant little boy. The orphanage made you soft. But in every version, you're a rat, sneaking right back in to take what is *mine*."

My limbs went cold.

Jamison staggered back. "You—You killed my parents?"

"Technically, the electric chair fried them."

"Impossible," Roger growled. He was baiting Dewey, buying time. But for what? "No one can travel back that far. Not even you."

"I'm still getting used to my newfound talents, but I assure you, it can be done."

I closed my eyes and searched within for any part of me that felt alive. Anything I had left to give.

"Bullshit," Roger sneered. "You tripped and fell into the past. You think that makes you powerful?"

"Not just one time. Many times." Dewey grinned as if he expected them to be impressed. So desperate for adoration, even now.

Jamison stepped toward Dewey, thrumming with anger. "*You* took my sister?"

Pain choked every syllable, his devastation filling the spaces between words. I dug deeper into my magic, searching.

"I've killed you, you know. Drowned you on that beach you're so fond of, your chubby little arms splashing as if you could stop me. But for some reason, in that timeline, Luxe's magic never developed." His face scrunched with distaste.

Catherine Revelle alive, Jamison Jones dead. Colette is the star, but Luxe's magic is weak and Catherine keeps her from me. George wins.

Catherine dead, Jamison dead. Luxe is the star but her magic's weak.
Luxe despises me.

"Time is a fickle thing. If you have a terrible accident far from Charmant, before you've met your friends, life here will be unaffected. I just need someone with magical blood to lead the way." He grinned at Roger.

Shadow magic. Using Roger. To kill Jamison before any of us met him.

Dewey glanced around at the Revelles inching closer, then at Trys's body, and his smile faded. "Well, as enlightening as this has been, it's time."

He'd kill them both, undo this summer, undo *everything*—

I emptied myself, letting the claws of my magic scrape against everything I had left to give. The pain burned my flesh, the pressure so great in my head that blood vessels burst in my eyes. Fighting the urge to collapse, I dug deeper into it, into all the things that made me alive. The Strattori said I was emptying my own lifeline. As long as I was still alive, magic was still within my reach.

Memories flashed behind my eyes as the darkness closed in. My mother fixing my curls in pigtails, humming the Revelle theme song. Nana sneaking me candy backstage, my mother pretending to be mad. My aunts teaching me trapeze with Colette and Millie. The thrill of growing up under the same roof as my best friends, of chasing them through the winding halls of the Big Tent. Performing together, closing my eyes as I threw myself into the air, knowing they'd catch me. Lying on the beach with them, Colette's pinkie linked with mine. Jamison's thumb pressed to my pulse on the Ferris wheel. Our stolen kisses in the sand.

I dug into every moment I'd felt loved. Every moment I'd lived.

Dewey's face slackened, and he turned to me, slowly, realization dawning too late.

You love me, and I love you, and you're tired, so very tired . . .

The gun clattered to the ground. Dewey's eyes fluttered, his knees buckling.

"Catch him!" If the fall woke him, all it'd take was a split second, and he'd travel.

Roger leaped forward, gripping Dewey with his bloodstained hands and easing him onto the floor. He looked up at me, jaw slack.

"I charmed him," I tried to say, all the while gripping Dewey's lightstring so hard, my chest felt like it was about to explode. Finally, his eyes began to close. "I think I— *No!*"

Jamison pressed the gun to Dewey's temple and squeezed the trigger.

THIRTY-FIVE

JAMISON

"No!" Roger shouted, grabbing the gun from my hand.

Dewey's eyes remained shut. The red hole in his temple was a neat, symmetrical wound, so different from Trevor's.

But he was dead.

I'd shot him. I'd never even gone hunting for a bunny, or deer, or whatever it was men hunted for, but I had just killed a *human*.

A wild, ravenous applause drowned out the music.

"I'm sorry." A strange giggle bubbled deep in my throat. Apologizing yet again.

Roger stared at me like I was the devil himself. "*Trys!* You forgot about Trys!"

Trys.

On the floor beside Trevor. Lifeless. And I'd just killed the time traveler who could have saved both of them.

I fell to my knees, taking her limp wrist in my hand, searching for a pulse.

No, no, no.

Wordlessly, Luxe slumped to the ground beside me.

"Take the bodies. Fast!" someone thundered. Wolffe. He must have heard the gunshots.

More Revelles streamed out from where they'd been hiding. Luxe's aunts grabbed Trevor, and I forced myself to look away. Two of Luxe's uncles picked up Dewey, carrying him deeper into the backstage maze. Nana followed, wiping away the trail of blood with a bar towel.

They reached for Trys, but I held her tighter.

Roger glared at them from her other side. "Not until she sees Dr. Strattori."

"She's gone." Wolffe laid a gentle hand on his son's shoulder.

"Are you a doctor?" Roger snapped. "No one touches her! Not until every Strattori on Charmant tells me she's gone. Not until they swear it in front of the Edwardians. Not until God himself descends from the heavens and declares it so." He pushed back her hair and set his jaw in a firm line. "Not even then."

Wolffe studied the devastation written all over Roger's face before crouching beside him. "You heard my son. You, get Dr. Strattori. You, stand guard over there. No one else moves! If anyone so much as *thinks* about this too loudly, we're as good as dead."

All it would take was one Edwardian to read one of our thoughts, and the Chronoses would know. Two of their kin, shot backstage at the Revelle show.

If I turned myself in and begged for them to bring her back, maybe she'd live.

Roger leaned against his father, looking younger than I'd ever seen him as he fought back tears. All around us, the Revelles sprang to action, casting wary glances my way. Because they thought I set the fire—or because I'd killed a man?

As Aunt Caroline furiously scrubbed the stained floor, Colette skipped backstage, her brow shining with sweat. "They need you out there, Pops. Time to announce the results."

Wolffe moved to stop her, but it was too late.

There was blood everywhere. Mostly Dewey's, but also Trys's. Luxe had even managed to get blood on her face.

"Luxe!" Colette shrieked. "Are you okay?"

"It's not mine," Luxe replied quietly. I felt her gaze on me, but I couldn't bear to see her look at me like Roger did. Like I'd shot Trys and Trevor myself.

When Colette saw Trys, she let out a raw, broken cry.

I squeezed my eyes shut. This couldn't be happening.

A small, cold hand slid into mine. "I understand why you did it," Luxe whispered to me, but her face was pale.

"You yelled no," I rasped.

She gave my hand a weak squeeze. Dark shadows framed her eyes. She was so tired, so drained from it all.

Dewey was gone. She'd never have to charm him again.

But Trys . . .

Roger's hands pressed the wound in her chest. *Please, God, not her heart.* If there was any chance God worked on some sort of points system, I needed to cash in on my twelve years in a religious orphanage. I'd killed a man, and if God took Trys as punishment . . .

"What happened?" Colette cried, searching Trys's dark, bloodied clothes for the wound.

"Not now," Luxe murmured. I squeezed her hand again, but she didn't squeeze back.

Helen Strattori rushed to us, pushing me out of the way. Trys's hand fell from mine, and Dr. Strattori let out a disapproving noise as she took in the bullet wound. As if it were Trys's fault that she'd been shot.

By her brother.

Who I'd killed.

Wolffe squeezed Roger's shoulder. "The audience is expecting me to announce the winner. I need to get back out there."

"But he's dead!" someone shouted.

"You think I don't know that?" Wolffe snapped. "Everyone go take a nice, long bow to give me a minute to figure out how the hell to buy us some time. Maybe give 'em an encore."

Colette held out her bloodstained hands. "You *can't* be serious."

"If the audience realizes anything is amiss, we're as good as dead. Go, sweetheart. You can't help her now."

Colette didn't budge. Helen Strattori ripped open Trys's shirt and held her hands above the wound.

Roger held Trys close. "Transfer it to me."

"You know I can't," Dr. Strattori replied calmly, not looking up from Trys. Her magic could sense the damage, but without Trys's consent, she could only treat her using regular medicine. "Go, Colette. I've got it from here."

Colette's face twisted. She wiped her hands on a towel, then lifted it to Luxe's red lips. "You coming?"

"Soon." Luxe's voice was barely audible. I'd never seen her so exhausted.

I pushed her hair off her face. Her skin was as cold as ice. Shock, perhaps. "Do you want me to get you some water?"

A groan sounded from beneath the Strattori's hands.

"Trys!" Roger yelped.

Sweet, sweet relief flooded me. I grabbed Trys's hand, and Colette squeezed her eyes shut, tears of relief streaming down her cheeks.

Trys blinked open her eyes, taking in Roger, Colette, and me. She groaned again. "What happened?"

Roger shook his head slightly. Not in front of the Strattori.

"The bullet missed your heart, but it's close to your lung," Dr. Strattori said. "I need to bring you to my surgery."

I squeezed Trys's hand, tears blurring my view of her as she squeezed it back.

"So she's going to be okay?" Colette asked.

Dr. Strattori took a long sip from her flask. "Whoever shot her either had terrible aim or very, very good aim."

Trys's face crumpled, her hands burying her face as Roger and his aunts helped Dr. Strattori load her onto a stretcher.

"She's going to be okay," I repeated to myself. To Luxe. "Did you hear that?"

Trys was going to make it. Luxe was free of Dewey. We all were.

The nightmare was finally over.

Wolffe reappeared and shooed Colette away. His scowl deepened when he saw Luxe's and my intertwined hands. "We could use you out there, Luxe."

She remained silent, her eyes closed.

I pulled her damp curls from her eyes. "Can't you do it without her?"

"The audience is expecting their new mayor and his bride. We need her to buy us time." He crouched beside us. "Are you drained, Luxe?"

He was speaking in code. He didn't know how much she'd told me.

Luxe's legs shifted, but she couldn't stand. Her whole body trembled.

I pulled her closer to me, blanketing her in my warmth. "She's been through a lot, sir."

Wolffe folded his arms but left without her. Anyone with eyes could see she was on the verge of passing out.

"I've got you," I murmured against her hair. "It's all over, and you're all right, okay?"

"I'm sorry," she breathed.

"You don't have to apologize for anything." Despite the blood that still marred her hands, her face, despite all the blood that had been shed, I found it in me to smile. "You're free now."

"He turned back time." Her eyes fluttered closed, her expression distant and dreamy. "Over and over."

"I know, love. And no matter what he did, we still found each other."

Her voice was so small, her face so peaceful. "I'll always find you."

As I caressed her cheek, her lips relaxed into a soft smile. No more pain, no masks of bravery or indifference. Her job was done.

And now her life could begin.

Beyond the curtain, Wolffe's voice boomed, "How about one more song for our candidate?"

The crowd roared to life.

"Luxe?" Nana appeared in the wings, her voice uncertain. "Can you get out there?"

I gave her an encouraging squeeze. Whatever she wanted to do, I'd make Nana accept it.

Luxe didn't move.

"Luxe?" I pushed her relentless curls away from her face. But the Radiant Ruby of Revelle was gray.

Gray like ash. Like *death*.

I gave her shoulders a gentle shake. "Luxe?"

She didn't stir.

"Get Dr. Strattori back here!" I yelled.

Nana took one look at her and stumbled backward.

"Go!"

Finally, she hurried away.

The impatient crowd began chanting Dewey's name. "Dew-ey! Dew-ey!"

"Someone help!" We were alone. In the center of the most decadent party of the summer, we were utterly alone. "Something's wrong with Luxe!"

The applause for the Revelles reached its crescendo, the chant louder and louder. Dust motes floated in the bands of light peeking through the curtains. Little flecks swirled through the air over us, coming to rest upon Luxe's lips. Her rush of breath should have sent them spinning away.

Seconds passed. The dust settled, embedding itself in her cherry lipstick.

"She's not breathing." Panic eroded the strength from my voice. When had she stopped breathing? "Where is the fucking doctor?"

Millie and Colette emerged from the curtain together. They froze when they saw Luxe.

"Help her!" I pleaded. Why wasn't anyone doing anything?

They were beside us a moment later. Millie pressed her head to Luxe's chest, listening for a pulse.

Her panicky eyes found mine. She shook her head.

Impossible. She wasn't doing it right.

I wrapped my fingers around Luxe's wrist and waited for life to thrum through her veins.

"What's going on?" Roger was here, too, hands stained red from Trys's blood. "Did she faint again?"

I squeezed her limp wrist harder.

Millie laid a hand on Luxe's cheek. Once she felt the iciness of Luxe's skin, her eyes slid to mine again, tears overflowing.

"No," I found myself saying.

Millie turned to Colette, her cheeks shining under the too-bright lights. "She's gone," she rasped.

"Gone?" Roger repeated. "As in she overexerted herself again?"

A sob escaped Colette, echoing backstage as she folded inward.

No. This couldn't be happening. We'd only *just* gotten free, only just begun . . .

I cradled Luxe to my chest. If only I could make her warm, then she'd be okay. And we could leave. Or we could stay. Dewey was gone, and she could finally live . . .

"Jamison? Do you hear what I'm saying?"

"You're wrong." I could hardly hear my own voice over the crowd screaming for Dewey. Wolffe reappeared, barking orders to the dancers. He skidded to a halt when he saw Luxe.

Finally, *finally*, Dr. Strattori returned with Nana.

"She collapsed," I explained. "I think she's just exhausted from the show. There was a bit of excitement back here, and—"

Silencing me with a stern look, Dr. Strattori pressed a gentle hand to Luxe's face.

Revelles filed in around us. I couldn't escape their questions, their soft cries. They filled my head, distracting me from what needed to be done, which was finding a way to help Luxe.

Dr. Strattori let out a small gasp. "What a strange, magical wound. I've never felt anything like it."

"Can you help her?" Wolffe asked quietly.

A single shake of her head. "I'm sorry."

"She's just tired." We needed to stay calm. Luxe wasn't going to appreciate the fuss when she awakened.

With a gentle finger, I wiped the dust from her lips. Dr. Strattori looked at me, her stern face full of pity.

"No," I announced, and for the briefest of seconds I felt relief. Dr. Strattori was wrong, and that was that.

The fainting, the weight loss, the nosebleeds . . .

"*No*," I repeated, this time more forcefully.

God might have spared Trys, but I'd killed a man. One who couldn't fight back.

There was always a cost.

Dr. Strattori pressed her head to Luxe's chest and listened. Sitting up, she sighed. "I'm sorry, I really am. The most you can do now is be here for her, so she can pass on surrounded by those who love her."

Colette clung to Luxe's limp hand and shook her head furiously.

Millie placed her hand over Colette's, her words swallowed by her efforts to hold back her sobs. Tears streamed down her face. Nana's face, too, as she did the sign of the cross on Luxe's forehead. "My sweet, sweet girl," she whispered, her voice breaking. "Your mother's waiting for you."

This was her home. Charmant. Her family. Her cousins. She had so much to live for, so much life left in her . . .

I grabbed Dr. Strattori's arm. "Transfer it to me."

"I can't," she snapped, pulling her arm away. "And even if I could, it's a fatal wound, rife with dark magic."

"Try it."

She watched me suspiciously. "It would kill you."

"But would she live?"

She hesitated.

That was all I needed. "Transfer it to me."

"Jamison, you can't." Roger pulled at my shoulder.

"I have to! She can't die!"

His rough hands gripped me. "I know, Jame-o. But you literally *can't*."

"He's right," Dr. Strattori said. "Without Luxe's explicit permission, I can't access my magic. Even if I wanted to."

It was the most kindness I'd ever received from the stern doctor, but still, I wanted to wring her neck.

Luxe needed to wake up. Needed someone to wake her up.

I grabbed Roger's arm. "Use your revenge stash."

"And let you sacrifice yourself?"

"It'll give her a chance, even a small one, to fight back!"

"Jamison, please, she won't let you do that—"

"I don't care!" My voice echoed backstage, and Wolffe's warning died in his throat. We were supposed to be acting normal, but there was no normal without her. There was *nothing* without her.

Roger grimaced. I'd put him in an impossible situation, but I had to help her, no matter the cost.

"What about me?" Millie pressed a hand on Luxe's arm.

"Dr. Strattori, if we wake her up, could you transfer it to me instead?"

Nana's face blanched. "What? No!"

"It would kill you, too," Dr. Strattori said. "Even with magic in your blood, it's too much for someone to bear."

Luxe bore it. She bore it for months without ever complaining. Alone.

Alone. I grabbed Millie's arm. "What if we both did it?"

Dr. Strattori looked at me as though I'd grown two more heads.

"What if we did it together?" I couldn't get the words out fast enough. We had no time; she could slip away at any moment. "If we split the wound between us—does that increase the odds of survival?"

Her brows pressed together at the center of her forehead. "I've never done anything like that before."

"But is it possible?"

"Any other Strattori would tell you no," she said carefully, "and that you could both die in the process. But . . . maybe."

Millie's eyes met mine. "Let's do it."

I whipped toward Roger again. "Wake her up. Use your revenge stash."

His jaw clenched and unclenched as he considered our options. Finally, he fished the velvet sack from his pocket. Jewels spilled over the floor.

"Hurry!"

Luxe was too cold, too gray, and her chest no longer rose and fell . . .

He held a ruby in the palm of his hand. "Found it."

Millie and I laced our fingers together. She gave me a firm nod.

"Wake up, cousin," he murmured. "You're very awake right now. You're feeling completely alert."

Red dust rained off the ruby, like dried flecks of blood.

"Come on, Luxie girl. You're feeling loved by your family—and you want to open your eyes to see us."

She was still cold, so cold—

"You want to kiss Jamison," he tried. Millie cracked a brief smile.

And Luxe's lashes fluttered.

My heart leaped into my throat as I squeezed her hand.

The Strattori bent over to her. "Luxe Revelle, with your permission, I will transfer your fatal wound to Mildred Revelle and . . . this young man right here."

I glared at Dr. Strattori. "Fatal" was not helping our cause.

Luxe didn't respond, but her face pinched ever so slightly.

"And me," Roger announced. "If we go down, we go down together."

Gratitude flooded me as he rested his hand on top of mine and Millie's.

Still Luxe didn't move.

"It's okay, Luxe." I let my free hand rest on her cheek. "Let us help, okay?"

"No." The word was faint but clear. "No more . . . *suffering*."

"We can all survive this if you share the burden."

Roger leaned over Luxe. "Don't be a martyr. Isn't that what you used to tell me?"

Luxe tried to lift her head, but a coughing fit seized her, rattling her entire body. The coughs kept going and going, not even letting her inhale between spasms.

I shot Roger a look, but he shook his head. There was nothing more he could do.

Her brow was ice-cold as I pressed my lips to it. "I told you we'd find a solution together. This is it. Just let us help."

A tear slid down her cheek as she shook her head.

That Revelle stubborn streak wouldn't budge.

"For once, just say yes," I pleaded. "*Please.* If not for you, then for me."

Her eyes squeezed shut.

"Damnit, Luxe!" Colette grabbed her face. "You promised we'd share everything now. So don't you die on me. We're in this together. You hear me?"

Her eyes fluttered open once more. They found me. They found Colette.

And she finally nodded.

"Do it," I urged Dr. Strattori, pressing my palm more firmly against Luxe.

Dr. Strattori hesitated. "Still, with you not having magic, there may be consequences—"

"*Do it!*" Millie hollered.

The pain was immediate, like icicles wedged into my head, my chest, all my vital organs. I had to bite my tongue to keep from yelling out—

No. I *was* yelling out. I opened my eyes, despite the blinding pain, to see if Luxe was okay—

My God. This was what she had dealt with for all those months. *Years.*

I squeezed her hand tighter and tighter. If she blamed herself for this, if it killed me but spared her . . .

"Let me help, too!" Colette sounded far away.

"She won't give me permission." Helen Strattori's voice was still cold and clinical. "You only have it for these three."

"Luxe, don't be stubborn! Let me help!"

"Transfer it to me!" Aunt Caroline called.

"And me!"

Her aunts rushed forward in their cancan dresses. Wolffe, too, and the rest of her uncles. Nana. Cousins. Second cousins. Every Revelle backstage placed their hands on Millie, on me, on Roger, on Luxe herself.

For their star, they would hurt. For their niece, their grand-daughter, their cousin and friend. For all she'd given for them, they'd endure this for her.

"No!" Luxe cried, but pink bloomed on her cheeks like spring washing out the dullness of winter.

I pressed my palm against her warm face. "Let them help you."

A tear slid down her cheek. "No more sacrifices for me."

"They're your family, and they love you." I lowered my mouth to her ear. "Let them."

"I can't!"

"Let them in," I whispered. More and more hands touched us. Ninety-six Revelles. "No more carrying this alone."

I felt, rather than saw, the moment she gave her consent. The pain diminished like water down the drain. My vision cleared; my lungs sucked in the cool air greedily.

A coughing fit took Luxe again, but her cough was dry now. And when she removed her hand, no blood stained her fingers.

She was alive.

With surprisingly steady hands, I pulled her to her feet.

Her face was wet with tears, but as she wiped them, she smiled. Not her kaleidoscope smile, but an authentic, relieved, million-carat Luxe Revelle grin. She was alive. Golden flecks sparkled in her brown eyes, her skin tan enough to showcase a smattering of freckles. It was as if she'd been a faded version of herself all summer, and now she stood before me with resplendent beauty.

Luxe smiled as her family closed in around us, squeezing us. She let them in, let herself be surrounded by their love.

The pain was a pinch in my chest, fading by the second. When it was divided among so many people, it wasn't any worse than heartburn.

"I can never thank you enough," she tried to say.

"Don't thank us." Nana took Luxe's face between her palms. "You need to leave, child."

Luxe blinked at her. "Leave?"

"Not just leave." Wolffe's smile faded. "*Run.*"

Luxe whirled toward me, her eyes wide. "If anyone finds out . . ."

That I killed the new mayor. A Chronos. "I know."

Wolffe pressed a hand on each of our shoulders. "Leave Charmant, both of you. And don't let anyone see you. We'll send word once it's safe."

"But if they find out—" I protested.

"*When* they find out," Wolffe replied evenly, "we'll deal with it. The longer it takes for them to realize he's dead or missing, the more it'll cost them to bring him back."

"Dew-ey! Dew-ey!" the crowd chanted. They were growing restless, eager for confirmation that their candidate had won.

"We'll go together?" Luxe searched my face. As if I'd ever say no to her.

"Of course." I pulled her close and kissed her forehead. Over the top of her head, I found Roger. "What about Trys?"

Trys had been shot protecting me. Trys needed surgery because I'd killed her brother.

"I'll take care of her," Roger promised. "Go."

Luxe was hugging her cousins now. This was really happening.

I turned back to Roger. "As soon as Trys is back on her feet, you'll find us, right?"

His face was unusually solemn. "I, ah, think I'm going to stay to help. Maybe I'll take Luxe's part in the show."

"*I'll* take Luxe's part," Colette corrected him.

Roger smiled at his sister. "Still, I should stay."

No, I longed to say, but his mind was made up. His family needed him.

He gripped my shoulders. "When it's safe, I'll send a letter to a place special to us both, okay?"

He was speaking in code, in case an Edwardian one day heard some memory of this conversation and tracked us down.

"We'll come back," I promised. "Once it's safe."

"This isn't goodbye. Two months is sixteen years for the Chronoses. Four months is well over thirty. Just . . . be hard to find for a while."

Even now Roger was thinking ahead. He was always looking out for everyone else. For me. "And then you'll find us?"

"Of course." He hugged me tightly. "Don't waste a drop," he

whispered in my ear. "I expect *lots* of stories when we meet again, okay?"

I couldn't wrap my head around saying goodbye to him. "And tell Trys—"

Roger released me. "I'll tell her. Now go."

Luxe reluctantly untangled herself from her family's embrace. Her face was wet, but when Colette whispered something in her ear, she smiled her real smile. No more hiding.

"Cancan dancers, get back out there!" Wolffe barked. "Buy us some time."

"Where's Trevor?" Millie asked, glancing around.

Luxe's smile shattered.

"I've got this," Roger murmured. "Go."

"But—"

"Dewey's guards are heading backstage," Wolffe interrupted. "You're out of time."

As she watched Millie, her face torn, I touched her arm. "It's now or never."

She slipped her hand into mine.

Hand in hand, we fled the theater.

THIRTY-SIX

LUXE

We ran toward the back exit, but one of Dewey's guards stood in front of it. His eyes widened at our abrupt appearance. "Where's Mr. Chronos?"

"In the restroom." I dropped Jamison's hand. "Excuse us. I could use some fresh air."

The guard's brow furrowed as he looked me over. Was there still blood on my face? Or on my leotard, Trevor's blood—

Oh God. *Trevor.*

"What's going on here?" the guard demanded.

Seven hells. I reached for my magic—no, no more magic.

The guard's gaze snapped to Jamison. He lunged for him, but Jamison darted back, grabbing my hand.

I pulled Jamison through the maze of offices and dressing rooms, the guard's heavy boots thundering right behind us. Somewhere backstage, mournful cries wafted over the crowd's relentless chants for Dewey. Millie? Because Trevor was dead. I'd tried to stop him from speaking, but I'd only made it worse for him, and now—

Jamison pulled me into a dark room and locked the door. I nearly tripped on the pillows and blankets strewn all over the floor, from where my family had slept. Jamison hoisted himself onto the desk, opened the window, and stuck his head out. "Clear."

I hopped onto the desk next to him. "You first."

Banging erupted against the door. "Open this immediately!" a deep voice roared.

Jamison moved between the window and the rattling door. "Go. I'll be right behind you."

Sliding out the window was easy, and the drop was only six feet. I moved aside for him.

Jamison threw a blanket out. "Wrap this around you."

Always thinking. I hid in the shadows as he hoisted himself out the window, his long legs tangling. Once he got to his feet again, he brushed off his pants. "Not bad for a non-acrobat."

I risked the briefest kiss. "Let's go."

The cancan dancers' song wafted over us as we hurried down the alley. Jamison kept his hand in mine, squeezing as if he feared he'd lose me. Again.

We rounded the corner—

Dewey's guards. Two of them. They whirled to face us.

Please don't recognize me, please don't recognize me. But my silent pleas were useless without a jewel. Or shadow magic.

"You're not supposed to be here." He glared at Jamison and reached for his holster.

No! No more guns.

I knocked it out of his hand and sprinted past him.

"Stop those two!"

All these guards—at least a dozen for election night—had

never been for my protection or even Dewey's protection. They were another layer in Dewey's plan, a barrier meant to keep Jamison from me.

Dropping the blanket, I sprinted even faster, my lungs lighter than they'd ever been, despite the dizziness from the Strattori magic. For years, my magic had eroded my strength. When was the last time I'd moved so fast, so freely?

No, not free. Not yet.

Jamison's long legs kept pace with mine, but footsteps thundered in our wakes. More guards. "We need to hide."

"We need to *leave*." Grabbing Jamison's hand, I darted down the next street. The bright lights of Main Street blurred ahead, the street music blaring as we raced through the crowd. Citizens of the Night milled about, drinking and eagerly awaiting the results of the election. Tourists, drunk and jolly, crowded the sidewalks. We slowed down, ducking our heads as we tried to blend in, but Jamison was too tall, and I wore nothing but a blood-speckled leotard. But this was the Night District. No one so much as blinked at us.

This was my home. Not Dewey's, not his Day District guards'—mine. Even with the Big Tent's glaring absence, I could have navigated these streets with my eyes shut.

Staying with the crowd, I zigzagged toward the promenade. The ferries were three blocks away. Two.

The crowed grew thinner, but there was no sign of the guards. Jamison shook off his jacket and put it over me. To hide my bloody leotard. Trevor's blood. Because of me . . .

"Not yet." Jamison squeezed my hand. "We'll fall apart later, but not yet."

Regret still shone in his fierce blue eyes. He'd taken a life today, and even though I loved him for it, Dewey's loss had almost cost us Trys.

One block now. The neat row of Dewey's long, elegant white ferries glinted in the moonlight, but in front of the entrance to the long dock, two police officers stood on the corner, talking.

Their gaze cut to us. Edwardians.

If they'd heard either of our thoughts, knew about Trevor—

"Sing a song," I whispered to Jamison.

He shot me a confused look.

"In your head. Quick!"

The taller officer frowned at us. I had to think about something else, anything else.

The Day District fools go to sleep with their jewels
in bedrooms as lonely as hell.
But when the Big Tent's your home, you're never alone,
so raise a glass to the family Revelle!

I leaned into Jamison, letting my legs sway as though I couldn't handle my liquor, and I kept repeating Nana's drinking song in my head, like Trevor had taught me. Jamison played the part of my concerned beau well, mumbling a church hymn while propping me up. As we passed, he tipped his hat at the officers.

"Aren't you Luxe Revelle?"

My heart stopped beating.

"Excuse me! You're Miss Revelle, aren't you?" The officer walked toward us.

We slowed to a stop. Wide-eyed, Jamison searched my face.

Back straight. Head high, just as my mother taught me. I turned to face them, flashing my stage smile. "Hello, gentlemen."

The younger officer blinked rapidly. "You *are* her."

"In the flesh." I winked. "Are we acquainted?"

"No, but . . ." The officer shook his head as if to clear his thoughts. His thoughts. He could read minds.

The Day District fools go to sleep with their jewels
in bedrooms as lonely as hell.

"Where's Mr. Chronos?" the second officer asked.

Jamison tensed beside me.

"How should I know?" I replied evenly.

"But the election. They should be announcing the results any moment."

"He lost." I wrapped my arm around Jamison's. "He's probably off sulking somewhere."

They let us take one step. Two steps.

Jamison rested his hand on mine, squeezing as we stepped onto the dock.

"Stop them!"

Dewey's guards—too many to count.

"Halt!" the Edwardian shouted. "Stop right there."

The dock was narrow, with nothing but boats and water on either side. We kept running toward the end, but there was nowhere to hide.

We were trapped.

The guards slowed as they reached the dock, fanning out to block our exit. They knew they had us. The officers, too, their faces tense with concentration as they eavesdropped on our minds.

They'd drag Jamison to jail. Or worse.

But when the Big Tent's your home, you're never alone,
so raise a glass to the family Revelle.

Hand in hand, we jumped off the end of the dock.

The water was freezing, the quiet disconcerting as we plunged beneath the surface. Gone were the officers, the music. The salt burned my eyes as I squinted for Jamison, but I couldn't see anything in the blackness. This was how my mother had died—in this very water, sinking to the bottom, that damn cinder block tied to her ankle . . .

Frantic hands bumped my arms. Jamison grabbed me, pulling me through the water, not yet surfacing, though my lungs burned. Deeper into the darkness, we waded. How he had any notion of where to go was beyond me.

I needed air. I couldn't take it anymore.

We surfaced together, greedily pulling the cold night into our lungs.

"There they are!"

We'd only made it ten yards from the dock, where a dozen uniformed men stood, their flashlights in the water. Two jumped in.

"Hold your breath!" Jamison pulled me down, down, so deep, seaweed tickled my arm. The bottom, where my mother had been found. My throat squeezed tight, but I tried to ignore it, focusing instead on Jamison's hand. Finally, mooring poles appeared. A dock.

Hidden underneath, we came up for air. There were guards right above us, flashlights forming spotlights in the dark water.

Even if we could manage to escape from beneath their noses, how could we possibly leave Charmant? Dewey owned all the ferries; for all I knew, he'd given them orders not to let us through. And even if, by some miracle, they didn't recognize us, we had no money. No time.

Jamison pressed his forehead to mine. "I can turn myself in," he whispered. "Or we can try to sneak onto a ferry and take our chances."

I gripped his neck, our skin slick with salt water. "You told me there's a whole world out there. I want to see it."

He grinned, then sank into the water again. I followed him, diving so deep, my ears popped beneath the suffocating pressure. Still, we swam silently beneath the surface. Our only way out.

Darkness loomed over us as we passed underneath a large boat. A ferry. We surfaced again, slowly. The shouting was more distant now. I motioned to the ferry, but Jamison shook his head and pointed to the next.

We went under again, their shouting blurred by the rush of water over my ears.

Jamison pulled me toward the third ferry. The lights were on, illuminating the massive engine in front of us. If it turned on while we were in the water, it'd pull us into it and tear us to shreds.

"This one," he whispered.

They all looked the same to me. None had ladders or stairs or any way to board. Still, Jamison lunged for the lower deck. When he missed—by a lot—he cursed under his breath.

"Should we try another?" I whispered. But there was no time. Even now, the guards' yells drew closer, panning out to search each dock, each ferry.

"It has to be this one."

"Then get me on your shoulders."

He looked at me like I had three heads, but there was no time to protest. He sank under the water, and I climbed atop him awkwardly, kicking him in the head. A six-foot-something man treading water was ridiculously unstable, but I'd balanced on less.

With my feet planted squarely on his shoulders, I leaped for the platform—and missed, my body smacking the side of the ferry. But I managed to grab the railing.

"I heard something! This way!"

My sides screaming, I pulled myself up and scrambled onto my belly. Hooking my legs around a pole on the lower deck, I lowered my arms in the water. Damnit, he was heavy; we both began sliding in, but he grabbed the bottom of the railing and hoisted himself over me.

"Check that one!"

We scrambled across the deck. Passengers laughed from inside Dewey's new luxury ferry, but on the cool August night, no one else was outside. At least not down here.

"Stop right there!" someone yelled from the upper deck.

We scrambled to our feet, but the captain thundered down the stairs. There was no place to hide on the deck. Nowhere to go but back in the water.

We were caught.

The captain's deep belly laugh froze me in place. "You did it. You really did it."

"I told you, sir." Jamison wrapped a hand around my waist. "Will you help us?"

Jamison and the captain *knew* each other?

"Dewey Chronos will have my neck."

Jamison winced. "I can guarantee he won't be a problem, sir."

"Is that so?" The captain studied us, his fingers twisting the golden band on his finger.

If only I could dip into my magic. Just one more time, and we'd be okay.

"Please, sir," I begged. "My family can pay you."

"I've had enough Revelle jewels for a night." He unlocked a door behind him. "If you get caught, tell them you found this storage room unlocked. I was never here."

The storage room was more like a closet, but we gladly scrambled inside.

Before we could thank him, he shut the door, cloaking us in darkness, save the sliver of moonlight sneaking underneath the door. Jamison wrapped his wet arms around me. Water dripped from his shirt each time he shifted. From my hair, too.

We shivered against each other. Freezing, but so, so alive.

And almost free.

Feet pounded on the deck, and we tensed. The captain's voice boomed, his deep laugh unmistakable. I held my breath. If they opened this closet, we were dead. They'd put Jamison in jail. Maybe even me, too, because if it wasn't for me, Trevor would still be alive.

After an eternity, the deck quieted. No more footsteps. No more captain.

I leaned into Jamison and checked my memories. Dewey was gone; he couldn't erase this timeline anymore. Only another Chronos could, and with every passing moment, the cost to them grew a hundredfold. Without Dewey, George could be mayor. Knowing my uncle, he'd declare him the winner and let the audience think Dewey was off sulking somewhere, just as I'd claimed to the officers. With enough charms and bribes, the election officials could report the same, and no one would be any wiser for it. The rest of the Chronoses might not even look for him.

The floor rumbled as the engines roared to life.

Hope made my heart race faster than the Revelle drums. We were really leaving Charmant. We could go anywhere. Together.

In the pitch black, I tilted my head toward Jamison, my mouth grazing his chin, his cool cheek, before finding his lips. His heart beat wildly beneath his drenched shirt, and I laid a hand over it.

For the first time in a long time, I let myself picture those magazine photos I used to hang on my wall. Mainland cities. Mountains. Pyramids.

The ferry surged into motion, and we nearly tumbled apart. Laughing, Jamison pulled me back into his lap. "Where do you want to go first?" he murmured in my ear.

I nestled against him, smiling into the darkness. "Everywhere."

EPILOGUE

LUXE

The soft notes of the clarinet faded as we entered the decadent hotel lobby. I whirled toward Jamison. "Can we afford this?"

He beamed. "I may know nothing about gemstones, but I know dollar bills."

Dirty mainland money. The coins, I liked, but in four months, I still hadn't gotten used to the crinkled bills.

"We can only stay for a night," he admitted, tucking my hand into the crook of his arm.

We made our way to the front desk, slowing to admire the enormous chandeliers. Gold accents frosted every surface, from the ceiling panels to the marble floor. The hotel was like a gilded cake. My Revelle blood hummed as guests floated through the lobby, jewels whispering from beneath their long fur coats.

"This is *too* nice," I murmured, though I couldn't look away from the gorgeous décor. My fingers itched for my precious camera, the used one Jamison had bartered for in Philadelphia. I'd take a picture later. Nana absolutely had to see this lobby.

"They paid me well at the docks," he said quietly. "Besides, we said we'd celebrate."

Four months. It'd been four months since we left Charmant, which meant that if a Chronos wanted to turn back time to investigate Dewey's death, they'd have to shave thirty-three years off their life. Would they be willing to sacrifice so much for their estranged kin?

After four months, we'd celebrate. We'd promised each other that.

The young woman behind the desk motioned for us to approach. Her cheeks flushed ever so slightly as she ogled Jamison, but once she took in our plain clothes, sullied after so much travel, her smile thinned. "We don't allow non-guests to use our facilities."

Irritation hummed from Jamison, but I pressed a hand to his chest. "Actually, we're checking in."

"One room or two?" She kept her eyes trained on Jamison as if I hadn't spoken. Such a ridiculous mainland custom, ignoring women.

"One." I waved Dewey's heavy engagement ring. "Do you have a honeymoon suite?"

Her eyes widened at the enormous rock on my finger. Even in a place as decadent as this hotel, the diamond was unparalleled. We'd debated keeping it hidden in our belongings, but the desolate campgrounds we frequented never felt sufficiently safe to leave it behind. So I dyed my hair golden, cut it in a bob like Trys's, and prayed no one would recognize me—or question the origins of the extravagant ring I wore.

"That's positively beautiful," she admitted rather reluctantly. With a slight shake of her head, she returned her attention to Jamison. "We have a honeymoon suite, sir, for six dollars per night. I presume that's out of your budget."

Jamison winced. Six dollars was more than we had, and even if we could afford it, the price was absurd. We could stay a week at a decent hotel for less.

Before he could reply, I tugged off my ring and held it out to her. "Want to see?"

Surprised, she plucked it from my hand.

I smiled sweetly. "Heavy, isn't it?"

"It is." With a soft sigh, she placed it in my waiting palm.

My Revelle blood surged to life. *You're feeling exceptionally generous. You wish to give us the honeymoon suite for free.*

"You know what? The honeymoon suite shouldn't go to waste. Why don't you take it? On the house, of course."

Feigning surprise, I rested my head on Jamison. "That's too kind, isn't it, darling?"

Amusement danced in his sapphire eyes. "Shockingly generous. Thank you."

"I'll have the bellhop bring up your bags. Anything else you require?"

He took the key from her outstretched hand and tucked it in his pocket. "If it wouldn't be too much trouble to have the *Times* sent to our room in the morning, that'd be great."

I squeezed his arm. Jamison scoured the New York papers for news from Charmant. We'd seen articles about George's electoral win and Dewey's disappearance from the public eye. Sulking in Italy, according to anonymous sources. Uncle Wolffe had done well. We'd also found plenty of write-ups about the Revelles' winter extravaganza. It was, of course, the must-see show of the year. Tales of the new star's acrobatic feats were spreading far and wide, attracting tourists from all over. By now, Colette's ego had to be insufferable.

In one of her interviews last month, she'd been photographed with Trys, who looked healthier than ever. Jamison had practically keeled over with relief. His guilt had abated since then, though some days, it hung heavy over both of us. He still blamed himself for losing control. For almost losing his friend.

I knew that feeling all too well. Trevor's shy smile visited me whenever I closed my eyes. Sometimes we were backstage again, and I was foolishly trying to stop his magic. Sometimes it was me squeezing the trigger.

One day at a time.

"Jewel magic?" Jamison murmured as we walked toward the grand staircase.

"Of course." I waited until he looked at me. "I promise."

The shadow magic still called to me sometimes, like a pretty little gem nestled in a dark corner of my mind, begging to be released. I never touched it, not even when we ran out of money and were in desperate need of a break. Without magic, making ends meet on the mainland was a bit of an adventure. We hitchhiked. Meandered off the beaten path. Made friends and listened to their stories, marking our map with new places. Like that enormous waterfall on the Canadian border, the roar of the rushing water so much louder than I'd imagined. Or that speakeasy in Chicago, the jazz so mesmerizing, we never touched our drinks.

Once we'd changed, we meandered down Royal Street, arm in arm. Walking in New Orleans was like strolling through a vibrant painting, one that dripped with color and music and *life*. In the last four months, I'd learned, to Jamison's teasing dismay, that camping was not my favorite activity. So we'd settled into a pattern: a week off the beaten path to save money, and then a real mattress and shower to reset and find work. Jamison, as always, was happy to oblige.

I paused to snap a photo of a trio of flappers dancing outside a jazz club, laughing. If only pictures could capture music, too. Colette and Millie would love this song.

Jamison relaxed his arm over me. "Told you the musicians here rival the Revelles."

I scoffed. "Don't let Nana hear you say that."

"I won't dare say it in her presence."

I leaned against him in gratitude. He always spoke of our eventual return to Charmant with certainty. As much as I loved traveling together, I missed my family, especially after everything they'd done to heal me. And to keep us hidden.

As if reading my mind, Jamison paused in the middle of the cobblestone street and lifted my face to his. "Hey. We'll get back there soon."

"I know. Roger will find a way to send word any day now." I lifted onto the tips of my shoes to plant a lazy kiss on his lips. I was never, ever going to grow tired of kissing him whenever I pleased, no matter who watched.

We parted reluctantly, and for a moment I stared into those bright eyes. Not a day passed when he didn't mention Trys and Roger, regaling me with some tale of their adventures together before he'd fall silent, his smile fading. Charmant was his home now, too. We'd return together.

I leaned against him as we began to walk again. "Take me everywhere you three went."

A smile tugged at his lips. "Did you bring your dancing shoes?"

"I'm a Revelle. I could dance circles around you in heels so high, you'd have to press onto your tippy-toes to kiss *me*."

He laughed, the sadness evaporating from his smile as if I'd charmed it right out of him. Love, I'd learned, is its own sort of magic, an elixir powerful enough to soothe even the deepest of wounds. Or perhaps it was this enchanting city. Of all the places we'd visited, only New Orleans tickled the back of my mind, as if my Revelle blood sensed the presence of magic here that wasn't mine. The mainland kept secrets of its own.

Jamison tightened his arm around me, and I held the camera out, snapping a picture of him. Together, we'd explore this city, and the next, and the next, until it was safe to return home. And even though we missed those we'd left behind terribly, we had each other. We'd chosen each other, time and time again, no matter the knots Dewey had tied in our timelines. No matter the cost.

And we wouldn't waste a drop of our precious time together.

ACKNOWLEDGMENTS

Before I began writing, books were magical things that appeared on shelves, shiny and whole. Now that my debut novel has been published, I have glimpsed behind the curtain and am awestruck by the scores of hardworking people who make book dreams come true.

First, thank you, dear reader, for picking up *Revelle* and reading it all the way to the acknowledgments. Though this is my first published novel, I have challenged myself to make each book better than the last, and I hope you'll hold me to that promise.

I am eternally grateful to Kristin Daly Rens, my kind and patient editor extraordinaire. From our first call, I was blown away by how much you "got" this story and its characters. Thank you for challenging me to tighten it and make it sparkle, as well as for sniffing out every loose end I'd snuck past critique partners. I am in awe of your eye for story.

Thank you to Lauren Spieller, my brilliant agent, for championing this book and for having my best interests at heart as I navigated this path for the first time. Your keen editorial eye helped me tighten this story in ways I never thought possible. Celebrating the book deal with you, in person, was a true highlight of this journey.

To the Balzer + Bray, Epic Reads, and HarperCollins teams: I am truly blown away by the level of attention each word of this story received. Thank you to editorial assistant Christian Vega, Annabelle Sinoff and Nicole Moulaison for production, Sabrina Abballe for marketing, and Patty Rosati for getting *Revelle* into schools and libraries across the country. Thank you to Caitlin Lonning and Alexandra Rakaczki for daring to copyedit a book with time travel in it. Your attention to detail is aspirational. Thank you to Sarah Nichole Kaufman, Chris Kwon, and Alison Donalty for dreaming up such a lush and whimsical cover (and the swoony interior pages), and to cover artist Zoë van Dijk for bringing it to life. Extra thanks to Nina Hunter for gorgeously hand-lettering the title. And my forever gratitude to *Revelle*'s authenticity readers, who played an integral role in the representation present in this story.

To Brenda Drake, Kellye Garrett, Gail D. Villanueva, Ayana Gray, Sonia Hartl, Irene Reed, and the rest of the Pitch Wars community, thank you for pouring your hearts and souls into such a life-changing program. To the Pitch Wars classes of 2018 and 2020, I am forever changed by your friendship and support over the years. And to Emily Thiede, who mentored this book through countless Zoom chats and voice memos, I simply don't have the words for how grateful I am that you picked *Revelle*—and me. Your friendship and continued guidance mean the world to me.

Alexa Martin, thank you, you wonderful human being, for boldly predicting in your acknowledgments for six consecutive books that I'd be published one day. Your friendship and support over the years have gotten me here.

Meg Long, everyone needs a friend and CP with your perfect

blend of honesty and compassion. Thank you for keeping my head straight, for reading twice, and for helping me think through my stuck points. Ruby Barrett, thank you for pushing me to deepen the romance and for crying with me when I finally got The Call. Rosie Danan, thank you for challenging me to take this story further and for believing that I could. Susan Lee, I'm so grateful I convinced you to beta read a fantasy novel, and for your honest feedback. Rachel Morris and Elvin Bala, your notes on *Revelle* and your company in the querying trenches kept me going more than you'll ever know. That your words aren't yet published is a crime.

My eternal love and gratitude to the other beloved Slackers who have supported me: Alexis Ames, Eagan Daniels, Leslie Gail, Rochelle Hassan, Jessica Lewis, Chad Lucas, LL Montez, Mary Roach, Nanci Schwartz, and Marisa Urgo. This book was born in our late-night sprints, fueled by our reward gifs, and persevered because of your unyielding belief in me. Everyone needs a Slack full of impatient friends anxiously awaiting their good news.

Ashley Winstead, you beautiful soul: thank you for your poignant notes on an early draft, as well as your speed-read of a later draft during a time crunch. I'm so grateful to have you in my life. Tauri Cox, thank you for feedback that equally challenges and supports, and for celebrating every win as if it were your own. Corey Planer, thank you for believing in this book with your whole heart at a time I truly needed someone in my corner. Ayida Shonibar, thank you for trading words with me again after all these years.

Hoda Agharazi, my first mentor, thank you for showing me the ropes of writing and for always being willing to provide your expertise. If it weren't for you, I wouldn't be writing these acknowledgments.

Michelle Hazen and Jamie Howard, thank you both for the gift of your detailed feedback and faith in me.

Thank you to friends who offered to read when I needed a boost: Sarah Underwood, Lauren Blackwood, Anna Mercier, Maggie North, Jessica Lepe, Falon Ballard, Jessica Parra, and Rebekah McDowell.

Heather DeFlorio, thank you for a lifetime of deep conversations, for reading everything I write, and for encouraging me to take my dreams seriously. Amy Hanna and Jason Redash, thank you for giving me the praise I needed to keep going. Jessica Watson, my book soul mate who was gracious enough to read this, too: you're stuck with me forever. I'm so glad that enormous stork on your lawn brought us together. Danielle Roth Luo, I'd be lost without you right next door, always willing to help or to listen. Kristyn Hovanec, thank you for cheering me on with champagne and charcuterie, and for supplying the word "gangway" that one time at Starbucks.

They say "write what you know," so in this book, I wrote the only sort of family I know: an enormous, loud, infinitely loving one. To my grandfather, the first writer in our family, thank you for teaching me the art of perseverance. Mom and Dad, thank you for instilling in me the belief that I can do anything, for making sure I fell in love with books, and for believing that my words were magical, even when I was young. I'm eternally grateful to you, and to Lori and Gary Smith, for supporting my family while I'm on deadline. Thank you to my brother-in-law, David Smith, for quickly reading a late draft when I needed fresh eyes, and to my brother, Bro, for harassing me to let him read it for two long years. Thanks to my sister, Noreen, for being the patient sibling. I suppose you can read it now.

To Alex: thank you for a romance so steadfast and unwavering, I need to write books in order to insert a little drama in my life. You have believed in me from the very first word, and have gone above and beyond to make writing a necessary part of my life. If Chronos magic were real, I'd find you in a million timelines. And no, you are still not Jamison.

Luca and Bodhi, my darling blue-eyed boys, thank you for sharing Mommy with the stories always bouncing around my head, and for being woefully unimpressed with my publishing journey. You are the lights of my life.

And lastly, to my sweet and feisty Nana: I love you. Thank you for the poolside heart-to-hearts about love, friendship, and family. I will carry your words with me, always and forever.